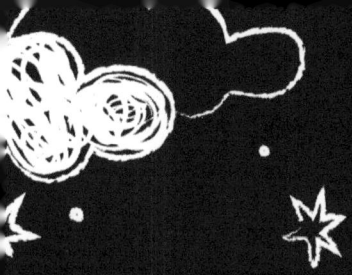

SPEARCREST PRINCE

Audentes
Fortuna
Iuvat

Copyright © 2023 by Aurora Reed

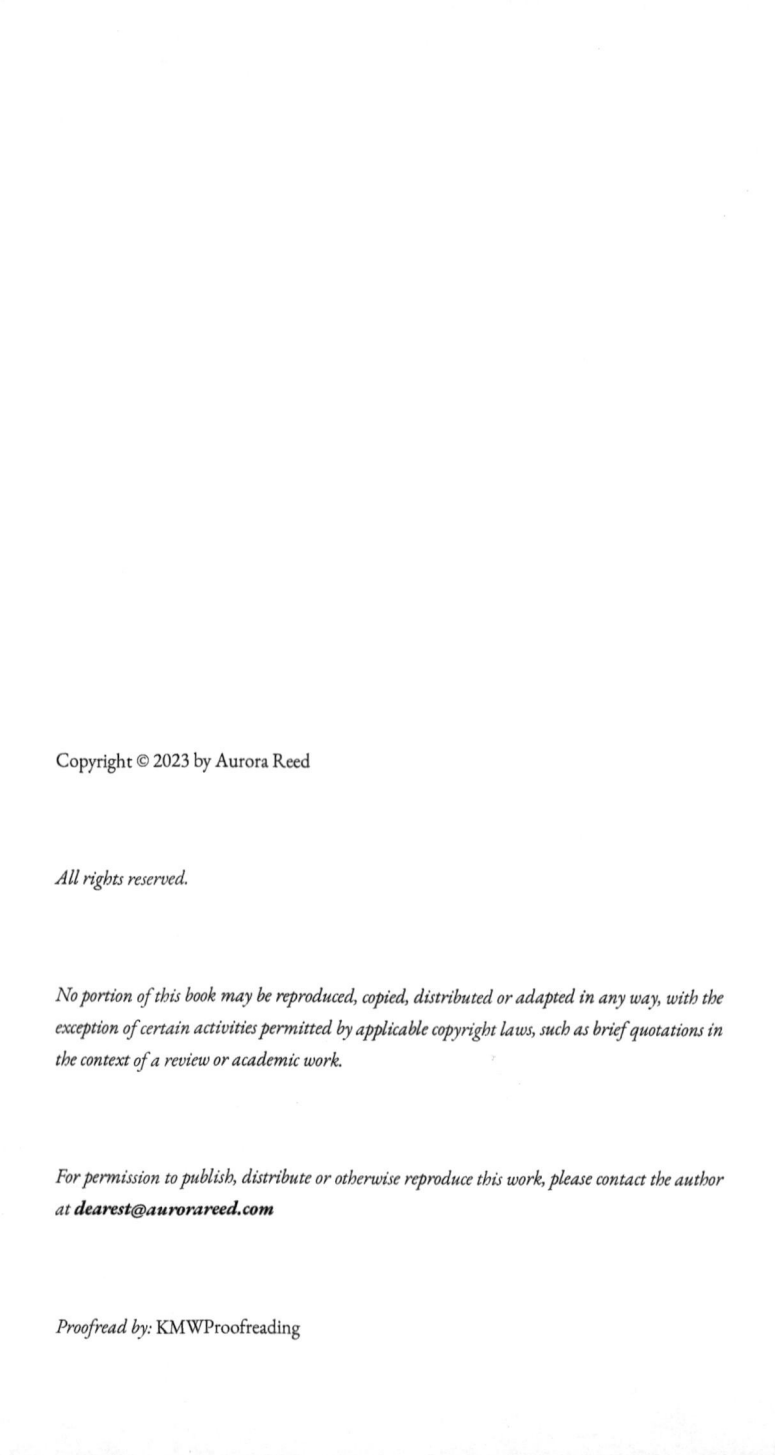

All rights reserved.

No portion of this book may be reproduced, copied, distributed or adapted in any way, with the exception of certain activities permitted by applicable copyright laws, such as brief quotations in the context of a review or academic work.

*For permission to publish, distribute or otherwise reproduce this work, please contact the author at **dearest@aurorareed.com***

Proofread by: KMWProofreading

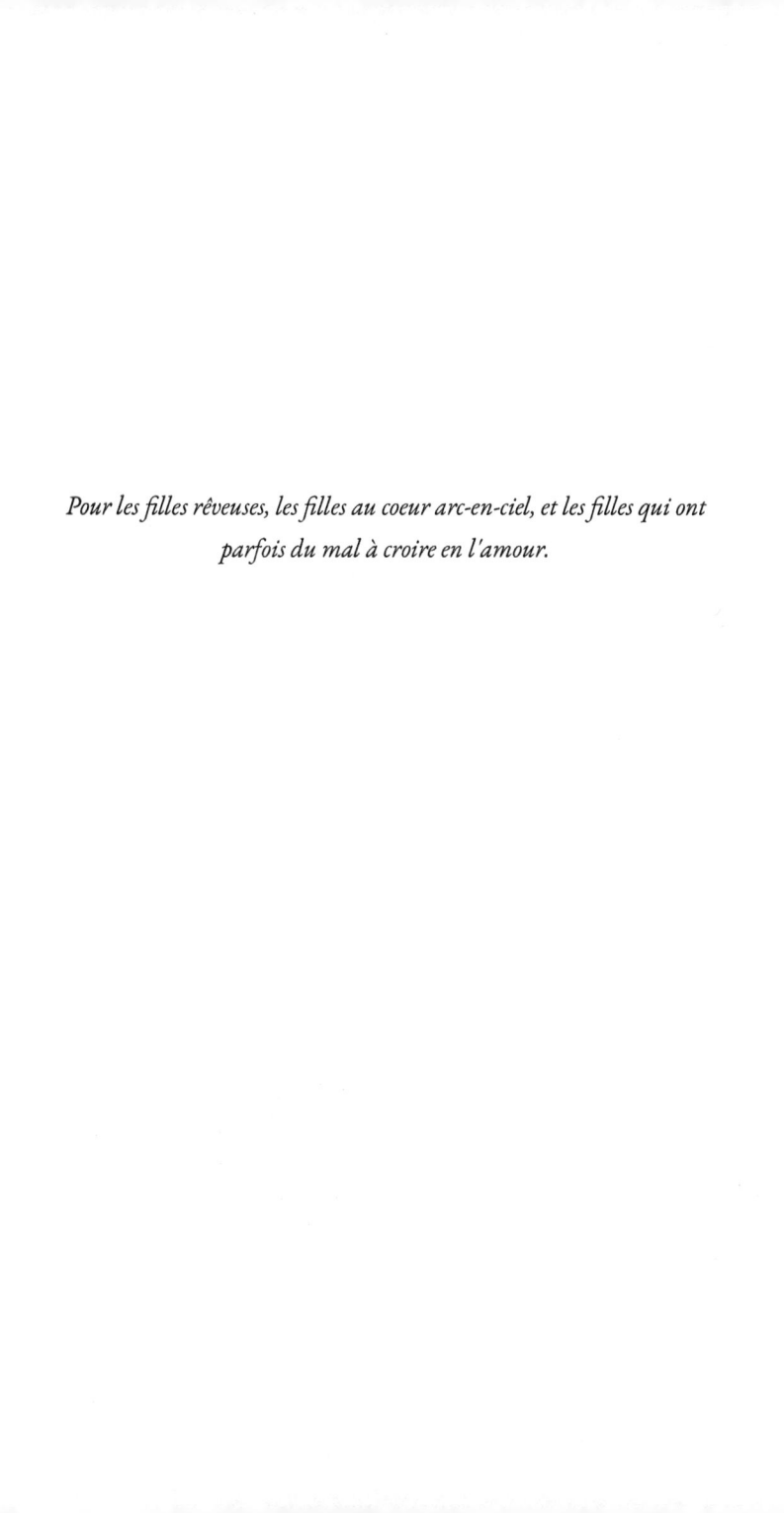

Pour les filles rêveuses, les filles au coeur arc-en-ciel, et les filles qui ont parfois du mal à croire en l'amour.

CONTENTS

Playlist	X
Author Note	XII
AUTOMNE	1
1. L'Amour	2
2. Le Plan	11
3. Le Toutou	17
4. Le Pari	22
5. Les Yeux Verts	28
6. Le Doigt d'Honneur	36
7. Le Roi Soleil	45
8. Le Baronnet	54
9. Le Prince	62
10. L'Invitation	69
11. Le Trésor	78
12. Le Bisou	86
13. La Bouteille	94
14. La Chapelle	102
15. La Chasse	109

16.	La Pomme	115
17.	La Vengeance	122
18.	L'Orgueil	129
19.	La Pièce de Résistance	140
20.	La Cigarette	148
21.	Le Portrait	153
HIVER		161
22.	Le Crapaud	162
23.	Le Poison	170
24.	La Pratique	178
25.	La Limousine	186
26.	La Bague	193
27.	Le Choix	203
28.	L'Ordre	211
29.	Le Poing	219
30.	Putain d'Idiot	228
31.	La Menteuse	236
32.	La Méprise	243
PRINTEMPS		251
33.	La Peinture	252
34.	La Clémence	258
35.	La Confession	264
36.	La Daurade	272
37.	La Sanction	280

38.	Le Joli Garçon	288
39.	Le Portrait	296
40.	Le Lit	303
41.	La Vérité	311
42.	L'Exhibition	320
43.	La Fiancée	329
FIN		339
Dear Reader		340
Annotation & Study Guide		341
Acknowledgements		344
About Aurora		345

PLAYLIST

La Vie est Belle – La Belle Vie
Roi – Videoclub
Cent fois – Alice et Moi
Baise-Moi – Terrenoire
Garçon manqué – Iliona
Ce qu l'on veut – Synapson + Tim Dup
Amoureuse – Clio
Naïve – Therapie TAXI
Risumi – Polkadot Stingray
Everything Matters – AURORA + Pomme
Elle ne t'aime pas – La Femme
Do Well – SIRUP
Mai – Videoclub

Hanoï café – Bleu Toucan
Ceux qui rêvent – Pomme
Lemon – Kenshi Yonezu
Crush – Requin Chagrin + Anaïs Demoustier
J'attends – Ben Mazué + Pomme
A la Folie – Juliette Armanet
Vérité – Claire Laffut
Un peu plus souvent – Alexia Gredy
▫▫ (color) – hama
Les mots qui te font rêver – Alice et Moi
Shinunoga E-Wa – Fujii Kaze

Author Note

Dear reader,

This book takes place at the fictional private boarding school **Spearcrest Academy** and is set in the **United Kingdom**.

Speacrest Academy is a **High School and Sixth Form**, so students are aged **12** to **18**. If you are a US reader, I've included a little comparison guide of US and UK school years for reference.

UK High School (also known as Lower School) Years
Year 7 = 6th Grade
Year 8 = 7th Grade
Year 9 = 8th Grade
Year 10 = 9th Grade (Freshman Year)
Year 11 = 10th Grade (Sophomore Year)

UK Sixth Form/College (also known as Upper School) Years
Year 12 (Lower Sixth) = 11th Grade (Junior Year)
Year 13 (Upper Sixth) = 12th Grade (Senior Year)

The main characters in Spearcrest Knight are all in <u>UK Year 13 (US Senior Year)</u> and <u>18 years of age</u>.

I hope this guide makes sense and helps you during your time within the hallowed halls of Spearcrest Academy.

AUTOMNE

"L'Amour dont je subis l'abominable loi
M'attire vers ce que je crains le plus, vers Toi !"

Renée Vivien

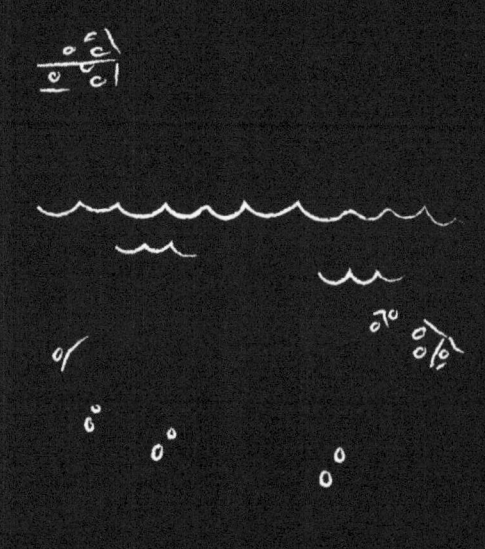

Chapter 1

L'Amour

Séverin

I LOVE EASILY—I ALWAYS have.

I loved easily as a child, trusting those around me with wide-eyed innocence. Like my first day of primary school, when everyone was very nice to me, so I brought roses for everyone in the class the following day. Or when I was six and loved my mother so much that I asked her to marry me when I was older, and when she told me she was already married, I burst into tears.

I loved easily as a teenager as well, even when I was told it wasn't the thing for boys to do. At first, I threw my heart at any girl who captured my attention. Then I threw my heart at the perfect girl—or rather, the girl I thought was perfect for me. Kayana. The girl I thought I would live with happily ever after, like the prince and princess in a fairy tale.

In hindsight, proposing at sixteen could never have ever been anything more than a mistake, but I didn't realise that back then.

No—it took my heart being torn to shreds to learn from my mistakes. Like any lovesick idiot, I had to be hurt before I learned better.

Before I learned how vile love is, how predatory. The way it attaches itself to a host and infects it from the inside, leeching all life and emotions from it until the host is nothing more than a husk. The way it's addictive even as it destroys.

And if love is the drug—the poison—then sex is the cure, the crimson antidote.

I'm smarter now than I used to be. I surround myself with girls I can only fuck but never love. Girls who are pretty and polished, the type of girl you see on a magazine cover—almost too perfect to feel real.

The problem with always going for girls your type is that they all start to look the same after a while.

They dress well. They have long, curled hair, manicured nails, ethereally beautiful faces. Not just beautiful but impeccably curated, well put together. I don't date, but I do take girls out, and if I have a girl on my arm for a party, she has to look the part. The same way I carefully select every item of clothing that goes on my body, every piece of jewellery that complements my outfit—the girl I choose must be the perfect accessory.

But I'm a gentleman. If a girl enters a party on my arm, she will end the night more than satisfied. Just because I'll never fall in love with them doesn't mean I can't treat them like goddesses while they're in my bed. I love pleasure, and nothing pleases me more than pleasuring women.

After all, there's a reason I can get any girl I want; my reputation precedes me.

But this is my last year at Spearcrest, and it's getting increasingly more difficult to keep track of names and faces.

I sit on the steps outside the Old Manor with my friends and a girl at my side. My arm is draped around her shoulders, keeping her warm against the autumnal wind.

Later, I plan to take her somewhere private—one of the many secret hook-up spots around Spearcrest—and sweeten the bitterness of the new academic term with some mutual orgasms.

She's petite, with long blonde hair in glossy curls. Her eyelashes are long as a doll's, and her make-up is immaculate. Her nails are perfect, gleaming ovals, the colour of corals. Her skirt is rolled up, a cardigan of fuzzy pink wool replacing her blazer, and a pair of glossy Prada pumps are on her feet.

Her look perfectly complements mine, but for all the croissants in Paris, I can't remember her name.

Polly? Poppy? She's British and a Spearcrest student, so I can only assume she's part of the English upper class or the daughter of a nouveau riche family trying to elevate themselves—a phenomenon I'm far too familiar with as of late. I can only assume she must be named something old-fashioned yet feminine. Elsie, or Harriet, or Maisie.

Does it matter?

I draw her to me and run my hand down one of the delicate golden coils of her hair. Maisie—or whatever her name is—doesn't care if I remember her name or not. All she cares about is how I'm going to make her feel at some point today and the prestige of being able to tell everyone she fucked a Young King.

Talking of which.

Zachary Blackwood ascends the path up to the Old Manor, his vintage leather satchel slung across his chest, books under his arm. Zachary is the smartest student in the school and the heir to one of the most powerful families in England—and he looks the part. His brown skin is free of flaws, his tight black curls are perfectly coiffed, his shoes polished to a high shine. A whole garden of badges adorns the lapel of his impeccably pressed blazer.

He's courteous, cultured and quick-witted—

"Well, Sev!" he calls, climbing the flat marble steps in long strides. "What's this rumour everyone's talking about? Did you get engaged in the summer and somehow forget to tell us? I wanted to be the first to personally congratulate you on your matrimonial endeavours!"

—and he's the most arrogant know-it-all I've ever met.

The girl next to me, Maybe-Maisie, stiffens under my arm. For fuck's sake. I have no intention of marrying the girl—but I don't want to make a fool out of her in public either. A few steps away from me, Evan Knight, the golden boy of Spearcrest, raises his head from where it was lying propped against his backpack, his blond hair catching the sunlight.

"What?" he asks in a tone of consternation. "You got *engaged*? Does that mean you're going to get married?"

Evan, athlete extraordinaire and all-American dreamboat, has never been the brightest bulb in the pack, no matter how golden his reputation is.

I roll my eyes at him. "No, people generally get engaged for shits and giggles."

Evan frowns. "Who pissed in your cornflakes, man?"

"Nobody pissed in my cereal, asshole."

"Then why are you in such a bad mood?" Zach asks, leaning against one of the marble pillars supporting the elegant arch that keeps the Old Manor stairs shielded from the rain.

"I'm not in a bad mood."

Well, I *wasn't*. But that was before my engagement was unceremoniously brought up. In front of my closest friends and the first girl I was intending to fuck this year.

"Right," Zachary says, his lip curling ever so slightly. "Sure. You're perfectly calm and in excellent health and so on and so forth. Glad to hear you're doing so well. So who's your fiancée?"

"I don't want to talk about her," I snap, glaring at him. "She's little more than some insignificant gold digger as far as I'm concerned."

At my side, Maybe-Maisie is looking more concerned by the minute. I have nothing to prove to her—but I do have a reputation to uphold. A reputation as a carefree, fun-loving playboy—not an angry, emotional, *engaged* man.

From her gaze, I can tell she's not happy with this, and when she opens her mouth to say something, I hurry to clarify things.

"As for the engagement," I add quickly, "it means nothing at all. It's not going to last. *I* didn't even choose her."

"Your parents pulling your strings again?" Iakov asks.

Iakov "Knuckles" Kavinski, the enigmatic son of an obscure oligarch, sits the furthest away from us, near the bottom of the steps, smoking a cigarette. Although his buzz cut and bruises scream at you to keep away from him, Iakov is the most principled person I know, with a strict honour code only he seems to know but still follows stringently. Although he's a man of few words, the empathy in his voice is clear.

Out of all of my friends, Iakov can relate the most to having to deal with controlling parents.

I sigh. "They arranged this whole thing and sprung the news at the end of the holidays. I'm engaged, it's going to be a four-year engagement, and then we're getting married after university—according to them."

Maybe-Maisie finally cracks and pulls away. "You're *actually* engaged?"

Her eyes are big and shiny. Although most girls I sleep with tend to understand and accept the unspoken arrangement between us, there are always exceptions. Girls who think they'll be the one to capture my attention, to keep it. To make me a one-woman man, to make me commit to them.

But that's never going to happen.

Especially not to Maybe-Maisie.

I give her shoulder a squeeze. "I'm sorry you found out this way, chérie, but this engagement isn't my decision or my choice. But I do think you should probably be on your way now. I don't want you to get hurt." She opens her mouth, but I smile. "Be a good girl, now. Run along."

With a tragic sigh, she stands and leaves, descending the steps while my friends watch her silently. I watch her stride away from the Old Manor with a twinge of guilt in my chest but say nothing.

"Why's your family forcing you to marry this girl, then?" Evan asks, looking truly aghast at my situation. "That shit sounds mediaeval as fuck!"

I suppress the urge to make a tart reply. Evan, of all people, shouldn't be judging anybody for their decisions. Not Evan: the guy who could have it all—so decided he wanted the one person he couldn't have.

"The Montcroix house hasn't finally run out of money, has it?" Zachary asks in a fake scandalised tone. "*Mon dieux!*"

Sometimes, I have the irresistible urge to slap the smug look off his face. But Zachary's family are close-knit and powerful—they look after their own. If I touched so much as a hair on Zachary's head, I'm pretty confident his parents would have me vanish off the face of the earth without a trace.

So I contain my annoyance as best I can, leaning back against the flat marble steps with a sigh. "No—far from. I'm an only child, so my parents think they can use me to make alliances, which is how I've ended up engaged to the daughter of the Nishiharas—"

"The Nishiharas?" Luca finally pipes up.

Luca Fletcher-Lowe is sitting with his back against a pillar and has been watching the conversation unfold without commentary. Luca is simultaneously at the centre of the Young Kings—he's the one our group built around—and yet he's the most aloof one in our group.

He's also the scariest person I know. His father owns Novus, the biggest chem tech company in the world. Where I'm full of burning emotion, Luca is a cold void. He might look unearthly with his pale hair and grey eyes, but if you look into those eyes, you'll see exactly what's inside him: nothing at all.

"You know them?" I ask, surprised that he's actually paying attention.

Luca is generally uninterested in anything we discuss unless it's to do with sex or violence. More than any of us, his tastes are... peculiar.

He shrugs. "They've worked with Novus before. They're not just crazy rich—they're building an empire."

This doesn't surprise me. When my father told me about the engagement, he mentioned the Nishiharas were acquiring some of our biggest businesses. The engagement is really my father's way of keeping some power and control since he doesn't have the wealth to compete with them.

He called it a "mutually beneficial" engagement, but he should really have called it a "damage control" engagement.

Not that I'd ever admit that to my friends.

I look up to find Zach's clever eyes fixed on mine. He gives me an arch smile.

"Oh, so *you're* marrying into the Nishihara family, then?" he asks.

"No." I throw him a dirty look. "The Nishihara girl is marrying into the Montcroix family."

The Nishiharas might have all the money they could ever need and be rich for generations to come, but climbing the top ranks of France's entrenched, centuries-old social hierarchy isn't pay to play.

"The Nishihara name means fuck all in France," I explain. "It's the Montcroix name they're after. *We* could marry into any family for money, but there are only so many six hundred-year-old names *they* can marry into."

"Wow," Zachary says, nodding slowly. "The wonders of the French class system. So, an arranged marriage, huh? To be fair, I would have been more shocked if you'd proposed to this girl out of love."

Well, he's not wrong about that.

I scoff. "I didn't even propose."

"That's so shit," Evan says, shaking his head. "Imagine getting married to someone you haven't even proposed to. I actually can't get my head around how mediaeval this is. You guys need to start living in the twenty-first century like the rest of us."

"Ah, yes, of course, advice from an American." I raise my eyebrows at him. "Because Americans are so renowned for their sophistication of thought and progressive ideals."

Evan frowns at me. "Hey, come on, now. You're starting to sound just like Zach."

"What are you going to do, then?" Iakov interrupts. He doesn't raise his voice, but when he speaks, everybody always stops to listen. "Marry the stranger?"

I sigh. "What choice do I have? I don't have any other siblings my parents can offer up, and they would disown me if I broke this engagement. They think we have too much to lose. They even had her shipped over to Spearcrest just so I could get to know her." I pull out a tiny velvet pouch shoved in my pocket. "Look what they made me bring with me."

I throw the pouch at Iakov, who catches it one-handed. He tosses what's left of his cigarette at the floor and stomps on it, then turns the satchel upside down over his open palm. An object falls out with a glint.

Iakov looks up. "A ring?"

"It's a family heirloom. Opals and diamonds from before Napoleon was even born."

Iakov nods and tosses the ring at Zachary, who looks at it with an appreciative frown.

"It's a nice piece," he says. "What on earth do they want you to do with it?"

"Give it to her—to the Nishihara girl. Like we're going to meet and fall in love or some shit."

"Fall in love?" Zachary gives a dry laugh, tossing me the ring back. "I think they know better than to expect you to do that. You don't love anybody but yourself."

His tone might be mocking, but Zach is telling the truth.

I loved too easily in the past. I made my mistakes and paid for them. Loving Kayana blew up in my face—proposing to her was the most humiliating mistake of my life. It was a painful lesson—but I learned.

Now, I know that loving myself is the only safe bet. Because ultimately, I'm the only person I can depend on, the only person I can trust. The only person who can never betray me or reject me.

As for everybody else in the world... they are either an ally, an adversary or a pawn.

I just need to work out which of these Anaïs Nishihara is going to be.

Chapter 2

Le Plan

Anaïs

I spread my acrylics out in front of me. I pick out my favourites: monestial blue, sap green and cadmium yellow. Bright, vivid colours, full of life and emotion. Then I place them back inside their tin box with a sigh.

The little alcove I sit in is cold and grey. Outside the window, Spearcrest Academy stretches below: ancient façades of red brick, spiky turrets, grass and trees.

Even though it's still early autumn, the sky is grey, the sun little more than a ghostly blur behind the wall of clouds. The wan daylight saps the colours out of the trees, the grass, the buildings.

Before I left home, I was given a whole collection of warnings about England. How cold it can get, how much it can rain. I was told how different people were going to be and food was going to taste. I was even warned that the air would smell damp and that the water would taste strange.

But nobody warned me about how grey everything would be.

Picking up my canvas, I prop it on my lap and start sketching. My pencil moves with ease, tracing the outlines of the trees, the plumes of clouds, the spiky skyline.

It's easy with a pencil, the grey graphite echoing the greyness of the world.

I've been here for almost a week now. It took me several days to find this little nook, a broad windowsill by an isolated third-floor staircase in a corner of the oldest building. I've come every day to paint the view out of this window.

Every time, I outline, I sketch, and then I look through my paints, and nothing makes it to my palette.

My colours are made for my old life. For Aurigny. For the white villa on the cliffs, the sun on the terracotta tiles of the garden, the green of the old sycamores, the fields of lilac and mustard, and beyond those, the brilliant blue of the Mediterranean.

But I don't have the colours for this new life. I don't have the colours for the brick façades of Spearcrest, for its twisted oak trees, its marble fountains and manicured lawns. I don't have the colours for the students in their dark uniforms, all looking exactly the same. I don't have the colours for the curious looks and arrogant sneers of everyone I pass.

A raven bursts out from a tangled thicket outside the window, startling me. I look up, following its lurching flight across the campus until it disappears beyond the looming shadow of the clock tower.

"Take me with you," I whisper.

"Who are you talking to?"

I turn with a start. A girl is standing in the staircase, leaning slightly to peer at my canvas over my shoulder.

She is strikingly beautiful. Dark skin, long dark braids down to her waist. The Spearcrest uniform looks different on her than it does on me: she wears thigh-high stockings with her school skirt and high-heeled shoes. Small gold rings adorn the shells of her ears, and her lips are glossy as the glaze on strawberry tarts.

Two girls stand behind her, waiting patiently. It's not hard to tell this girl is in charge. She smiles at me, waiting for me to answer her question.

"A crow that was flying by," I answer.

"Oh, really?" She tilts her head, her smile widening. "How odd. What's your name?"

"Anaïs."

"Ah-nah-ees," she repeats with perfect pronunciation. I nod, and she sticks out her hand. "I'm Kay."

"Nice to meet you."

I take her hand. Her fingers are long, her fingernails shaped into perfect points and painted to imitate the iridescence of pearls.

"It's lovely to meet you," she says sweetly. "We don't get many new students in the upper school." She lets go of my hands and gestures to her friends. "This is Matilda, and this is Aine. Say hi, girls."

Both girls give me a little wave, and I wave back. So far, this is a friendly encounter. If beautiful, queenly Kay is hiding a secret tyrannical side to her, she's doing a great job of keeping it concealed.

"Are you an artist?" she asks, pointing at my canvas.

I smile. "I try. It's not earning me a living yet."

"Earn a living!" She laughs airily, waving her hand at me. "You're so funny!"

I wasn't trying to be funny, but I keep smiling anyway. My time in Spearcrest doesn't need to be unpleasant if I play my cards right. All I need to do is get the qualifications I need. Aside from that, my plan is to make my life as easy as possible.

"So," Kay says, clapping her hands together and startling me once more. "Are the rumours true, then?"

"What rumours?" I ask with a frown.

"The rumours about you"—she lowers her voice conspiratorially—"and Séverin Montcroix."

When I moved here, it was with every intention of keeping my distance from Séverin. Just like me, he's been thrown into this engagement against his will, and I assumed he would wish to keep as far away from me as possible. A wish I was ready to honour. If I'm honest, I didn't even expect him to tell anyone he was engaged at all.

I certainly did no such thing.

But he must be chattier than I imagined, and I suppose that makes sense. If there's anything I've learned over the years of being forced to rub elbows with the French bourgeoisie, it's that they love to gossip.

So what to do now?

I don't want to confirm whatever rumours the beautiful Kay seems so eager to discuss, but I don't want to lie either. Mostly, I want to find out where that crow made his nest and crawl into that little bed of twigs until it's time to leave this cold and rainy country.

"Well?" Kay asks, leaning closer and lowering her voice. "Are you and him really... engaged?"

I give a noncommittal shrug and cringe against the corner of my little windowsill. If I close my eyes and dream of the stars, what are the chances that I'll manifest myself away from here and spin into the cosmos?

"Okay, look," Kay says warmly, waving a jewelled hand at me, "you don't have to tell me anything for now. Why don't we have a natter over a few drinks? A few of us are going off-campus next week to party in London. Do you fancy it?"

I peer up into Kay's golden-brown eyes, weighing my options. If I say no, I might risk offending Kay, my potential first friend in Spearcrest. A friend is something I would like, but not something I need. Back in France, I only had a handful of close friends—they were all I needed. As for Spearcrest, I'm only here for a year. I'll be fine alone.

After all, I came here with a clear plan:

Give Séverin ample space.

Make things as easy for myself as possible.

Get my qualifications.

Get through the year unscathed and ready for my escape.

There's nothing in my plan about not taking the hand of friendship if it's presented to me, especially when that hand is attached to such a warm and beautiful person.

I nod, smiling up at Kay. "That sounds lovely, actually. Thank you."

She claps her hands together. "Oh, gorge! I can't wait. You know, I'll be skiing in Megève this winter. I'll practise my French on you so I can hit on all the cute French boys—*oui*?"

"*Oui*, why not."

Reaching into her tiny Chanel bag, she pulls out her phone and flicks it open with a fingertip. "Here, put your number into my phone. I'll text you the details."

Since it's a brand-new UK number, I don't know it, and for a second, the feral animal part of my subconscious squawks at me to enter a random number. Giving my phone number to strangers isn't something I particularly like. I barely even like giving my number to people I *do* know.

Mostly, I only like using my phone to swap pictures and texts with Noël.

But Kay's been nothing but kind and friendly. Giving her a fake phone number would feel... ungracious.

I pull my phone out of my pocket to check the number and then enter it into Kay's phone before handing it back to her. She takes it with a wide, sunny grin.

"*Super!*" she says in a perfect French accent. "*Alors, à bientôt!*"

With a coquettish wave, she bounces elegantly away down the staircase and disappears from sight, leaving the rich scent of her perfume floating in her wake. I turn back to my canvas, letting out a deep breath.

So far, so good—right?

Now all I have left to do is prepare myself mentally for my first time going partying with the Spearcrest elite. My first time partying in London.

My first time partying away from the tiny safety net of my friends and my life in the south of France.

Later that afternoon, after I've given up painting and made my way back to my bedroom, a text pops up on my phone. It's from Noël.

Noël: *Tout va bien?*

Anaïs: *Oui.* I'm partying this weekend.

Noël: You're so cool!

Anaïs: Ha ha

Noël: Have fun, *petite étoile*. Stay out of trouble.

Anaïs: I always do.

Noël: Yeah, but it's a different sky you're shining in right now.

Anaïs: I'll be careful.

Noël: "Okay. *J't'aime fort. À bientôt.* x

I stare at the last words. *À bientôt.* See you soon.

It's the one thought holding me together. The thought I've been holding onto ever since I found out about the engagement, ever since I was forced to leave my home and friends behind and come here. It's the thought that's going to keep me going until the end of the year.

If everything goes according to plan.

Chapter 3

Le Toutou

Séverin

London is grimy, crowded and wildly overrated, but that's why it's a great place for losing yourself.

Around once a month, the elite of Spearcrest descend upon The Cyprian, one of London's most exclusive clubs. We come in separate groups: me, Evan, Zachary, Iakov and Luca in one limousine, and our female counterparts in another: Seraphina Rosenthal, Kayana Kilburn, Giselle Frossard, Camille Alawi and the ice queen herself, Theodora Dorokhova.

We meet at the club at midnight. From there, there's only one rule left: nobody can fuck someone else from Spearcrest. If someone breaks the rule, they pick up the tab for everybody else.

It's a fun rule not only because it forces everyone to play games, but because we also have to play the field.

It's not a rule everybody enjoys, though. That's why Evan and Zachary sit next to each other in a private booth, pulling faces like slapped asses.

The girl Evan wants isn't here. She's also as Spearcrest as it's possible to get: the ball-busting prefect Sophie Sutton—but pigs will fly before she ever steps foot in a club. Or sleeps with Evan.

And as for Zachary, the person he wants is definitely here, but he's not allowed to sleep with her.

Theodora Dorokhova isn't called the ice queen for nothing. Rumour has it her father has a bounty on the head of anyone who lays a finger on her before she marries.

I guess all aristocratic families are as fucked up as mine. Arguably, mine isn't so bad after all. At least I get to fuck who I want.

That thought cheers me up, but there's no cheering up the heartsick duo. Even if I try, Evan will just look for an excuse to talk about Sophie—as if we can't tell that every time he makes fun of her, he's really saying he wants her—and Zachary will end the night as he usually does... drunk and locked in some raging debate with Theodora about whatever philosophical or academic question they are using to scratch away the itch of tension between them.

I can't be bothered with any of it.

Iakov, on the other hand, is always good company on a night out. Iakov does everything hard. He drinks like a fish, dances like a madman, has the highest pain tolerance of anyone I've ever met, and will probably end up in some seedy club in Croydon, glassing someone or getting glassed. Probably both.

It's just how he is. More animal than man.

Iakov heads straight for the bar and orders hard liquor from the top shelf. Luca is at his side, leaning back with both elbows resting on the bar. His cold, dead eyes sweep the club, no doubt looking for tonight's victim.

Because *victim* is the only word I would use to describe Luca's sexual partners.

"How's things with the fiancée?" Iakov asks when I stand next to him to order my drink.

"Not even met her yet." I shrug.

Luca turns to look at me, an enigmatic smirk curling his lips.

"It's been two weeks," Iakov says, raising an eyebrow—the most emotion I'm going to get out of him.

"And?"

"And," Luca says suddenly, "we want to know whether you're going to fuck her or not."

I throw him a look. "Why? Are you waiting to get in line?"

His smirk widens, but he says nothing. It wouldn't surprise me if Luca tried to sleep with the little Nishihara heir just because she's engaged to me. He stole Giselle right out of Evan's bed before, and he even plucked Seraphina Rosenthal off my arm before I could even get into her pants.

Something inside Luca is dead and broken, and the only way he feels anything is if he thinks he's inflicting pain on someone. We're lucky enough that with us, it's indirect. Girls—not so much. But after he slept with her, Seraphina Rosenthal had a red mark around her neck for so long she was wearing Chanel scarves for a month straight.

"Who's getting in line for what?" Evan's American accent reaches me from over my shoulder.

He and Zachary approach the bar. Evan's already glassy-eyed—he's a total lightweight compared to the rest of us—but Zachary's gaze is sharp and amused.

"Fucking Sev's fiancée," Luca says.

"Nobody is fucking her." I give him a dirty look.

"*Fuck* her?" Zach raises an eyebrow, ignoring me. "But does she meet the standard for such a thing? What was your rule again, Sev?" He starts counting on his fingers. "Pretty face, pouty lips, perky ti—"

"Not pretty face," Evan corrects. "It's perfect face and pretty pu—"

"No it's not," I snap. "Don't be such a dick."

"And the personality, of course—we wouldn't want a robot, right?" Zach smiles sardonically. "What was the personality again? Powerless and pitiful?"

Iakov lets out a single low bark of laughter.

I glare at Zach. "It's polite and placid, actually."

He and Evan laugh out loud, but I don't care. It might be a shallow list, but I'm not ashamed of having standards. And this particular list of rules has kept my encounters with women short, pleasant and plentiful.

They can laugh all they want. At least I'm getting laid, which is more than the two of them are capable of achieving these days.

"Well, how many of these does the fiancée tick off, then?" Evan asks.

Zach nods. "Yes, Sev, how does she live up to your standards? Is she polite with perky tits or placid with a perfect face?"

I roll my eyes, resisting the urge to throw my drink into both of their faces. Why are they so interested anyway? This situation is so entertaining to them, but to me, it's just a source of endless irritation.

"I don't know, alright?" I snarl. "The little shit hasn't even bothered introducing herself to me yet."

Evan leans against the bar, frowning. "You two haven't even met yet? Hasn't she been here since, like, the first day of term?"

"She has." Now I'm finally talking about it, the frustration that's been building up inside of me unfurls fast. "From what I hear, she's settled into her dorms, going to classes. Just going about her daily fucking life without a care in the world. Not once has she tried to seek me out." I pause to take a drink, hoping it'll calm me down. But it doesn't, so I continue. "She hasn't even tried to text me, and I know for a *fact* she has my number because my parents gave it to her parents so that I could 'help her settle into Spearcrest'. Can you believe this shit?"

Zachary shrugs. "Maybe she's waiting for *you* to introduce yourself to *her*."

"What for?" I ask, incensed. "Am I the one marrying her for a grab at an aristocratic name? No. Am I the one who moved countries just to follow me around like a goddamn *toutou*?"

"A goddamn what?" Iakov asks in a grunt.

"A goddamn *toutou*—you know—*doggy*! The answer is no. I'm not the one clawing, I'm not the one following, I'm not the *toutou*. She is. So why she thinks I should make the first move is absolutely blowing my mind. She probably wants me to go crawling to her to make herself feel better about her pathetic social-climbing parents."

Luca's been observing me in silence. He tilts his head, and a slow, chilling smirk spreads on his lips. "Maybe she's not making the first move because she doesn't want to meet you at all."

I stare at him. "What the fuck are you talking about?"

He shrugs, but his smirk is full of cruel satisfaction. "Maybe *she's* the one trying to get rid of *you*."

I shake my head and wave my hand at him. "No. No, not a chance."

Luca laughs. He and Iakov exchange a glance. Iakov shrugs and finally moves on. "What's the plan tonight, then?"

"I'm getting drunk," Evan says.

"I'm getting laid," Luca says.

"I'll get drunk with you," Zach says, nodding at Evan.

"Me too," Iakov says.

"Fuck it." I turn, slamming my palm on the bar. "I'm getting drunk *and* getting laid. Let's do shots."

Chapter 4

Le Pari

Séverin

I GET SO DRUNK so fast after that.

By the time the girls arrive, I've left the bar far behind. I'm on the dancefloor, a girl in front of me, a girl behind me. One of them wraps her arms around my shoulders, the other grinds her ass all over me. They are a little older than me, but that's fine. I don't discriminate based on age. They are both gorgeous, their lips painted the same shade of fuck-me red. I'd sleep with them both at the same time just for the ego boost, but that's not how I roll. In threesomes, one person always gets left behind in the cold. Or they feel like they do, even if they don't.

But if I take a girl to bed, she's going to be made to feel like a goddess. She's going to come so hard she'll see stars, and I'll fuck her while she's still shaking from her first orgasm. I'll fuck her so good she won't be able to string a sentence together. And I'll leave knowing for a fact she'll never forget the night she spent with me—knowing no other guy will ever compare.

Being a great lover is my blessing and my burden in this world.

I do my best to use it well.

The red-mouthed girls are suddenly shoved aside, replaced by the imposing figure of Iakov and the chilling elegance of Luca. Taking my arms, they drag me to a corner.

"Right!" Luca shouts over the music. "Who are you leaving with?"

"Whoever I want!" I shout back, throwing my arms up and spinning around. I bite my lip and give Luca and Iakov my cockiest smirk. "Have you seen me? Every girl in here wants me!"

The music goes from a frantic synthetic beat to a soft, pounding bass. The ebb and tide of dancers shifts. Movements become slow and sinuous. The lights dim, bright blue and poppy red mingling into a deep under-sea purple. Girls glide and writhe in the music, an ocean full of sparkling, beautiful fish.

"How about that one?" Luca says, pointing into the crowd.

There's a mocking expression on his face, and I turn, expecting him to be pointing at the ugliest girl in the club. My eyes fall on a girl, and I can see why he's so amused, although it's not for the reason I expected.

Right on the edge of the dancefloor, there's a girl dancing all alone.

And she looks... Well, she looks ridiculous.

Unlike the tiny slinky dresses and silky curls of the girls filling the club, she's wearing a white T-shirt tucked into a short skirt made of huge blue sequins. Her feet are bare on the black dancefloor, and her shoulder-length black hair sticks at her temples with sweat.

She's dancing with her arms in the air, moving a little out of time, a glass in her hand, her drink splashing on her arm as she moves.

"You think I couldn't get *her*?" I ask, turning to speak to Luca and Iakov but keeping my eyes on the girl. "What, just because she's a little weird?"

"I don't think she looks weird," Iakov says, taking a sip of his drink.

I glance from him to the girl. "She's not wearing shoes, Iakov!"

"So?" Iakov shrugs.

"So, this is The Cyprian, not some stoner festival. Come on. She's not even dancing in time to the music."

"Let's make a bet," Luca says, a dangerous glint in his eyes.

"I'm not making a bet with you," I say, rolling my eyes.

"I bet you this girl won't fuck you," Luca continues, ignoring me.

"What do I get if she does?"

"My new Aston Martin," Luca says without hesitation.

"You don't even care about your cars," I point out.

"Fine, what do you want?"

"Novus stocks."

Iakov bursts out laughing. "Fuck, Luca, your dad will kill you."

"He will if Sev wins the bet, which he won't."

"You're on!" I give him my hand. He smirks and takes it.

We shake, and as soon as I let go, he adds, "You don't mind if I also have a go, do y—"

I'm shoving him out of the way and plunging into the crowd before he can even finish the question. Luca might be a total nutcase, but he never seems to struggle to get girls into bed. I suppose it's the upside to looking like a literal cartoon villain with his piercing eyes and silver-blond hair.

Moving quickly through the edges of the crowd, I draw closer to the weird girl, watching her long, awkward body move to the music. She can't dance for shit, truly. It's almost endearing. She has long, slim limbs, narrow hips and small breasts. She's graceless and a little awkward.

But her face is something else. Her eyes are closed, glitter sparkling on her eyelids and temples. Her mouth is open on a beatific smile. She's giving in fully to the music, letting her body do what it wants.

She looks insane. But she looks... free.

For a second, I find myself wishing I'd brought my camera with me. Sometimes, when a sight is particularly interesting, I have the urge to capture it, to immortalise it. Not on my phone, not with pixels, but on actual film. I like to develop it myself in the Spearcrest darkroom and watch the picture manifest like a ghost on the shiny white square.

But since bringing a camera into a club would be creepier than anything I've ever known Luca to do, I'm going to have to burn this image into my retinas and hope I remember it tomorrow.

The way my head is spinning and alcohol is singing through my veins, I probably won't.

Weaving through the crowd, I carve a path all the way to the girl. She's not at all my type, but there's something pretty and unearthly about her I rather like. Maybe it's how little of a shit she seems to give about how bad she looks. Or maybe it's the pretty shape of her eyes, her gracelessness. It makes her seem innocent. Almost celestial.

Like an angel who's been cast out of heaven and forced to live amongst mortals.

I dance to the music, drawing so close to her I can feel the heat from her skin. She smells clean and fresh and sweet, like lilacs and sea salt and cotton. The song shifts, carried by a high, ululating female voice, and a new beat kicks in. The girl opens her eyes and looks up to meet my gaze.

I lean down and speak in her ear.

"You're the worst dancer I've seen in my life!"

She laughs and pulls away from me. She turns on the dancefloor, waving her arms above her head, splashing us both with whatever she's drinking. She shouts her reply through the music.

"I don't care at all!"

She has a slight accent which I can barely make out through the deafening music.

I pull her closer, dancing into her. "You're going to make me look bad if we dance together!"

She wraps one hand around my neck, pulling my head down to hers so she can speak in my ear. "Then I'll dance alone."

I'm so drunk I can't do anything but smile. "That's even more embarrassing!"

"You don't need to save me from myself," she says with a roll of her eyes, moving away.

"No, I don't." I catch her by her waist and pull her closer once more. "It's everybody else I'm trying to save from you."

She laughs and throws her arms around my neck. Her wild, delighted laughter sends shivers across my skin like the shimmer of sunlight on the rippling surface of a lake. I pull her into me—she's a good height. Not too tall, but not short either.

The perfect kissing height.

She dances so awkwardly it throws me off my own rhythm. I laugh and spin her around in my arms, grabbing her waist. It's narrow, like the rest of her, but when I guide her hips with mine, she moves obediently. She leans her head back against my chest, and her hair brushes against my chin.

My cock stiffens, pushing against her ass. I want to pin her hips and grind into her, but I don't want to freak her out. This girl isn't from Spearcrest, so I'm okay to fuck her as far as the rules of the night go, but she isn't my usual type of girl. She doesn't feel worldly and clued-up.

Fucking someone who doesn't understand the arrangement is dangerous business. I don't date girls, but I don't want to hurt them either. This girl seems too unrefined, too innocent. And a stupid bet with Luca isn't a good enough reason to risk—

Then I feel a hand at my waist. I look down. The girl slips her fingers under my waistband, grabbing me by my belt. And then she's pulling me through the crowd.

And every rational thought flies straight out of my head.

Chapter 5

Les Yeux Verts

Anaïs

I PULL THE BOY with me all the way out of the dancing crowd, and after that, he takes things firmly in hand. Wrapping his arm around my waist, he leads me through the labyrinth of flashing lights and confusing shadows of the club.

My thoughts are just as confusing and labyrinthine. Really, I shouldn't have agreed to go partying with girls I don't know. I shouldn't have drifted off on my own, alone in a club in a country I'm brand new to. I should not have indulged in so many free drinks.

And I definitely shouldn't be doing this.

This guy isn't even my type: too pretty, too polished. His all-black outfit screams luxury and wealth, and his gold jewellery, green eyes and floppy black hair make him look like he's right off the front cover of a fashion magazine. He even looks a little bit familiar. His face gives me that feeling like seeing a stranger in a dream: familiar and unknown all at once.

But right now, I don't care. I miss home. I miss the sea, I miss my friends, I miss parties on the beach and the warmth of a body pressed against mine. I was never one for relationships, but I miss drunken kisses and careless nights.

I miss freedom and intimacy.

My mysterious partner slaps some money into an attendant's hand and pulls me through a doorway into a dimly lit coat room upholstered in red velvet. He slams the door shut and pins me to it; then his mouth is on mine.

And then everything falls into place. The moment becomes something new and beautiful, like the colours in an abstract painting forming a shapeless moment, an intangible emotion.

I open my mouth under his.

His kiss is searching and heated. He angles his head against mine, deepening the kiss. He tastes of expensive alcohol and spearmint. I wrap my arms around his neck and arch against him, anchoring my shoulders to the door as I roll my hips into his. He groans in response, grinding against me. He's hard—shamelessly, gloriously hard.

And then he breaks the kiss. Our mouths part with a wet sound and a rasping sigh.

He turns me around. I move easily in his hands, placing my palms and cheek against the dark polished wood of the door. I try to catch my breath, bracing myself for the clinking of a belt. This is faster than what I'm used to, but we're in a public place, and we're both here for one reason only. I suppose I can't blame him for being in a rush.

But instead of shoving my skirt up over my ass and thrusting himself inside me, Green-Eyes does something quite different.

He touches me.

He slips his warm palm up over my bare thigh, skimming my skin, sending a rush of pleasure through me. I press myself back against him. My breathing becomes short and raspy.

He stops, his hand resting on my waist, the warmth of his touch radiating through the thick fabric of my T-shirt.

"If you don't like this, tell me now," he murmurs in my ear.

I shake my head, cheek still pressed to the door. He kisses my neck, his lips brushing over my skin in soft, hot kisses.

A shudder skitters through me. He glides his hands up and down my arms in a gentle caress, then traces my sides, my waist. His hips grind against my ass, but it's through all the layers of clothing separating us. He pulls on the hem of my T-shirt, untucking it from my waist, and his hands slide underneath. His fingers brush, paper-light, over the ridges of my ribcage. They tickle the underside of my small breasts, and a tiny whimper escapes my lips.

It's not loud, but it's loud enough to hear over the music pulsing through the door.

Green-Eyes lets out a low chuckle. "Ah. You like that?"

He traces the underside of my breasts with his fingertips and then wraps his hands over them, squeezing. They are barely enough to fill his palms, but judging by the way his cock stiffens against me, he doesn't seem to mind. He rolls my nipples between his fingers and then pinches, drawing a gasp of surprise from me.

"Answer me," he says, low and rough in my ear. "Do you like that?"

I nod again, my cheek still pressed to the door. My body is alive with sensation, like there are flames trapped between my bones and my skin. I swallow and wriggle against him. I'm turned on, more turned on than I expected—more turned on than I've ever been.

"I like it too," he murmurs against my ear. "I like how your tits feel in my hands, your cute little nipples. I like that you're not wearing a bra."

I lick my lips, which are suddenly dry. He speaks with a slight accent—I didn't expect that. It's so faint I barely recognise it. But his voice is so hoarse it's already taking most of my concentration to make out his sultry words.

"What else do you like?" he breathes against my ear. "What would you like me to do to you?"

Keeping one hand on my chest, he slides the other out from under my shirt and lets it drop to my leg. He rakes his fingernails up my thigh, gathering my skirt. His hand stops right at the top of my leg.

"Do you want me to touch you there, too?"

I can barely trust my voice, so I nod instead. "Mm-hm."

"Say it," he breathes. "Tell me what you want me to do to you."

Asking for consent is the bare minimum I would expect from a guy, but Green-Eyes's style is something else altogether. Liquid heat trickles down between my legs, and I squeeze my legs together, desperate for some pressure, some friction—anything.

"I want to feel you inside me," I whimper.

He groans against my ear, and his fingers stop. "Are you sure about this?"

I nod, licking my lips. "Yes."

His body moves against mine. I hear him unbuckling his belt, and my heart skips a beat. He wraps his arm around my waist and pulls me against him. His cock is thick against me. He grinds against my ass, his cock pushing into the small of my back, then his hands are at my waist, pressing lightly.

"Lift up your skirt for me."

My hands tremble as I reach for my skirt, bunching it around my hips, exposing my soaking wet panties. I'm so hungry for his touch I ache. I spread my legs, arching against him.

"Please," I whisper. "Please touch me."

I've never begged before—I'll never beg again. But in this moment, begging feels like the right thing to do. In this moment, I'd get on my knees and do anything he asked.

His response is immediate and more satisfying than anything I could have expected. He lets out a sharp sigh like a growl, his mouth finds my neck, and he kisses a wet line up to my jaw.

And then he does. Exactly. What. I. Asked.

His touch is confident yet tender. He strokes me first over the fabric of my panties, featherlight friction to drive me insane. I grind into his touch, craving more. It's been a while, and Spearcrest has been so lonely. And this guy, in spite of his pretty boy looks and his rich kid outfit, knows exactly what he's doing. He's not the first person I've hooked up with at a party, but he's the first to get me this close to climax this fast.

When he pushes the fabric of my panties aside, I let out a keening whimper. His fingers slide between the wet folds of my pussy, and my hips buck against him, pushing back against his hard cock. A breathy laugh slips from his mouth, the wind of it sending strands of my hair flying against my cheek.

"Ah, so you really do like this," he whispers.

His tone is cocky, and I'd find it obnoxious if his arrogance wasn't so justified. I press my hips back against him, pushing impatiently.

"Are you sure?" he asks. The cockiness disappears from his voice, replaced by an earnestness that makes me shiver.

I nod. He reaches into his pocket and pulls out a condom. Biting down on one corner, he pulls, ripping open the packet. His weight lifts from me, and I wait, my heart a deafening beat echoing through my body. I hope it's loud enough to drown out the logical, sensible part of my brain, which is insisting I'm making a mistake.

"Hurry," I mutter against the wall, squeezing my eyes shut.

"So eager." Green-Eyes chuckles. Though his voice still drips with confidence, there's excitement in it, too. And impatience that matches mine. He lowers his head to mine, kissing my cheek. "What's your name, pretty thing?"

"Anaïs." My real name slips from my lips before I can even think of a fake name to give him.

He jerks back so fast it makes me jump. "*T'es française?*"

His question is a bucket of cold water to the face. I fix my panties and push my skirt down, turning sharply around.

"*Oui. Toi?*"

"*Bien sur.*" His entire body language has changed. His shoulders are tight, his jaw clenched. He steps back, closing his trousers and buckling his belt. "How long have you been here?"

He frowns at me, his expression full of mistrust. Now that his expression has changed so radically, he looks even more familiar than before. The uncomfortable thought that I've definitely seen him somewhere before settles heavily on my mind. I straighten my clothes and tuck my hair behind my ears. I'm still embarrassingly, torturously wet.

"I just moved," I answer truthfully.

He nods. His eyes are really a very beautiful shade of green. But there's a hint of cruelty in the shape of his lips. "To London?"

"No."

"*Fuck.*" He groans, wiping his hand across his face. "You know who I am?"

I roll my eyes. Assuming his earlier cockiness was just because he's a good lover and knows it was a mistake. He's just arrogant—arrogant and overly emotional. Typical rich French guy behaviour.

I suppose it's easy to ignore red flags when you're seeing through a crimson mist of lust.

"No," I reply. "Should I?"

"Why did you move here?" he asks, his eyes narrowing.

Arrogant, moody and *suspicious*. This guy is French and probably a Scorpio. I might have to return home sexually frustrated, but at least I dodged a bullet. A volatile and pompous bullet.

Still. I've not done anything wrong. Why should I lie? "For school."

"What school?"

"Some private school not far from here."

"Fuck!" he exclaims in a raspy roar, startling me. He rakes his hand through his black hair, an expression of anguish on his face. He paces up and down the tiny room as if in the throes of some great struggle.

I start edging towards the door, eager to be rid of this guy's overly intense presence, when he suddenly stops mid-step. Whipping around to face me, he points an accusatory finger at me.

"This," he says balefully through gritted teeth, "is *not* happening. Do you understand?"

Finally something we can agree on.

"I understand."

He nods angrily, but when I try to grab the door to leave, he stands in the way, stopping my exit. I look up at him questioningly. He doesn't seem to want my company any more than I want his, so why won't he let me leave?

"Right," he says, his tone suddenly austere. "And—don't just... you can't—you're in a club in London, for fuck's sake! You can't just follow random guys into dark, quiet places!"

Now it's my turn to frown. "You can't tell me what to do."

"Actually, I can." He narrows his eyes and leans into me. "*Le nom Séverin Montcroix te dis quelque chose?*"

Does the name Séverin Montcroix means anything to you?

My heart clenches like a fist and drops through my stomach. The mixture of alcohol, shock and embarrassment sends a wave of nausea through me. I clap my hand on my mouth, half out of surprise, half because I'm scared I'm going to throw up.

This time, when I yank on the doorknob, the green-eyed stranger—my fiancé—moves aside. I run out of the room as if the devil himself is after me, and I don't stop running until I reach the women's bathroom. I lock myself in, my back against the door, my heart beating madly, my nausea slowly receding. I squeeze my legs together, still wet from earlier, and sink to the marble floor, burying my head in my arms.

"*Merde.*"

Chapter 6

Le Doigt d'Honneur

Séverin

Outside the club, London stretches, dark and gleaming underneath a steady drizzle. Distant street lamps line the edges of the Thames, which undulates like an enormous black snake through the city. A ribbon of smoke draws me into the darkness of an alleyway, and I turn the corner to find Iakov, a cigarette dangling from his lips, frowning at his phone.

He looks up when he hears my footsteps, and slides his phone into his pocket, pulling out a pack of cigarettes to offer me one. It's a habit I'm always trying to quit but can never kick. Especially not with Iakov's way of silently offering me a cigarette whenever I look stressed.

"Things didn't work out with your new girl?" he asks drily.

I throw him a glare. "She's not my new girl."

He lifts his eyebrow almost imperceptibly. "That bad, huh?"

"She's not my type," I snap, taking a deep drag.

Smoking is thoroughly unpleasant, but just like drinking liquor, it's the discomfort that's really the point. I fill my lungs with acrid smoke and blow out a toxic wreath into the dank, dark air.

"Didn't seem to be a problem when you were eye-fucking her in the club," Iakov says.

That's hardly what I was doing, but if I deny it, then Iakov will just think I'm embarrassed—and I'm not embarrassed. *Anaïs* should be embarrassed—for being dressed like that in one of London's most exclusive clubs, for dragging some random guy off the dancefloor without even checking his name first, for trying to fuck a stranger when she knows full well she's *engaged*.

"She's got..." I try to think of an excuse. "Shit attitude."

"So?" Iakov says, his tone clearly implying that he thinks I have shit attitude too.

I glare at him. "So—I have standards, okay?"

Iakov scrapes a tattooed hand over his head, scratching his skull through his buzz cut. His knuckles are caked with bruised and crusted cuts. Iakov had a hard time at Spearcrest when he started, but it's been a long time since anybody in school has dared to lay hands on him. And yet he never seems to be without injuries these days.

I would ask what's happening, but we all know better by now. Iakov's life is like the Château d'If: impenetrable, impregnable, unfathomable.

"So she rejected you, then?" he asks flatly.

"Don't be a dick." I sigh. "Of course she didn't fucking reject me."

"Mm." Iakov gives a noncommittal grunt. "No Novus stocks for you, huh?"

"No."

We finish our cigarettes without speaking. Iakov's tone might be rough and biting at times, but he also knows the value of silence. Unlike Zachary, who would be giving me his opinions in the most slicing and harsh terms possible, or Evan, who would get drunk and commiserate with me, Iakov is perfectly happy to leave me to my thoughts.

Which is a blessing and a curse right now.

Because my thoughts are a complete mess, a chaotic storm. I'm thinking about Anaïs's stupid sequined skirt glittering in the club, the way she grabbed me by my belt to pull me off the dancefloor, the way she arched against me and shamelessly asked for what she wanted.

It was hot while it was happening—a great quality to find in some random girl at a London club—but in a fiancée, completely inappropriate.

Because no matter how I think about it, there are only two possibilities: either Anaïs knew who I was and was just trying to play mind games with me with her shitty attempt at seduction, or she genuinely didn't realise who I was and was perfectly willing to cheat on *me*, her fiancé, with *me*, some random guy she pulled at a club.

Either way, I'm furious.

There's absolutely no way Anaïs couldn't know who I am or wouldn't have recognised me. We might not have met in person yet, but my face is plastered all over social media, gossip blogs and tabloids. Besides, I can't imagine her parents wouldn't have used my appearance as a selling point when talking her into this stupid engagement.

My parents certainly tried—I just refused to let them manipulate me so easily.

What if she's not even who I think she is? Anaïs is a pretty common French name. What are the odds that a random girl named Anaïs would have just started at Spearcrest at the same time as my fiancée with the same name? That's my favourite theory, the most calming of them all.

Unfortunately, I don't get to hold on to it for very long.

Iakov and I finish our cigarettes, throwing the butts into a puddle gathered between the cobblestones of the alley, then head back into the club.

We're crossing a dim corridor when one of the bathroom doors opens, and a girl slips out. Her shoulder-length hair is tucked behind her ears, and her sequined skirt glitters even in the low light. She's quite tall, a little gangly—the figure of a volleyball player without any of the athleticism or grace.

Her steps falter when she sees us, and Iakov's head tilts ever so slightly in interest. Is he looking at her because he realises she's the girl from the bet—my *new girl*, as he put it—or because he's checking her out? It's hard to tell with Iakov. A sudden impulse makes me raise my hand and give the girl the middle finger.

Her dark eyes widen in surprise, and then she scrunches her face and returns the gesture, hurrying past us.

"Your outfit is garbage!" I call after her because I'd rather die than let her have the last word—or last middle finger, in this case.

She turns her head and replies in a deceptively sweet voice. "So was your kissing technique."

I give her my iciest smirk. "Still got you wet, though."

"*Pas vraiment*," she says airily, turning her back on me.

Not really. As if.

"*Sale menteuse!*" I call after her.

Dirty liar.

"*Gros bourgeois*," she calls back, and technically speaking, she's right. I *am* aristocracy after all.

"*Michto!*" I respond.

Gold digger.

"*Crapule!*"

Scum.

She disappears through the double doors in a burst of light and music. In her wake, silence reigns in the corridor. My chest is heaving, annoyance coursing through me. I can't believe she got the last word. I have half a mind to follow her into the club and drag her back out just so we can carry on exchanging insults.

But Iakov's gaze rests on me like the suspended blade of a guillotine.

"So you've met the fiancée, then," he says.

It's hard to miss the amusement in his voice, if only by virtue of the fact that Iakov is normally about as full of expression as a slab of marble. I whip my head around to pierce him with a venomous glare.

"You knew?"

He shrugs. "Why else would Luca convince you to fuck her?"

"He didn't—" I stop. "For fuck's sake!"

Iakov gives me half a smile. "At least you got your meeting over and done with."

"I can't stand her," I say honestly. "I can already tell she's going to be nothing but a massive pain in my ass. I want nothing to do with her."

"I doubt it," Iakov says. "You two seem made for each other."

I give him an incredulous look. "Are you insane? Have you seen her? Can you imagine taking her anywhere? She's wearing a T-shirt in a club, no shoes, no make-up—what kind of look is that?"

Iakov shrugs. "A look that got your attention."

"For being so ridiculous."

"Who cares what a girl wears anyway?" Iakov asks. "What's underneath is what matters."

My mind flashes back to the coat room, sliding my hands up that narrow body, those small breasts with their pointed nipples. My cock stirs, but I ignore it. There's a reason we were created with our brain so far from our crotch. The two aren't so much mismatched allies as mortal foes.

"Not in her case," I tell Iakov. "Trust me. Girls my type dress well *and* look good underneath their clothes."

"Girls your type don't even interest you," Iakov says, sounding unimpressed. "At least this one's interesting."

"This one's been picked for me by my parents, and I'm not about to let them control who I fuck or spend my time with. I don't give a shit about her body, her personality, or anything else. She could be Aphrodite, the goddess of love herself, and I still wouldn't give a shit."

I glare at Iakov as if he's the living embodiment of the Montcroix and Nishihara parents and their schemes. But as usual, Iakov is unruffled. He shrugs, and with his bleak, Russian nonchalance, he says, "I like her."

"You fucking have her, then," I say with a dismissive gesture, resuming our walk towards the dancefloor.

A rare grin appears on Iakov's face. Not his usual little crooked half-grin, but a full-blown one, wolfish and a little feral.

"You sure?"

I give him the middle finger just like I did with Anaïs. "Fuck off."

I'M SITTING IN A private booth, drowning my concerns in Iakov's top-shelf liquor, when the door slams open. I look up, half-expecting Evan, who always bursts into places like he's in the middle of a rugby game. Instead of a tall, broad American, though, I'm confronted with a beautiful girl in a slinky golden dress, her hair in braids so long they fall past her hips.

My heart sinks.

Kayana Kilburn, the party princess of Spearcrest, storms into the private booth, looking as stunning as ever. Her brown skin gleams in the light, and gold bracelets glitter on her wrists and upper arms. She looks as beautiful as always.

She looks as beautiful as she did the day she broke my heart.

She sweeps right past where Luca is slumped into the couch and stands in front of me, glaring down at me.

"What did you say to Anaïs?"

"Nothing that would be of concern to you."

Kayana might be the girl who broke my heart, but that doesn't mean she can talk to me like that.

"Well," she says, "Anaïs decided to leave, and I'm guessing it's all your fault."

"Did I ask you to bring her here, Kay?"

My tone is cold, but inside, pain and anger sear through me. Why is Kay so interested in being friends with Anaïs? If she hadn't played with my heart and snapped it like a careless child with a toy, then I might have been engaged to her by now, not some random stranger.

Although Kay hurt me more than any girl ever did, I've never wished her harm, and I never thought she wished me harm. But I don't trust her intentions for bringing Anaïs here.

At least she's gone now. That gives me some relief. Because if Anaïs left, then I don't have to worry about her sneaking off with random guys. Not that I was worried about it. Anaïs can do whatever she wants—I could not possibly care less how she chooses to spend her time.

I just don't want it to happen in front of me or anybody who knows me.

"She doesn't have any friends here," Kay says haughtily, "and she's engaged to a Young King. If you weren't going to welcome her into Spearcrest, then somebody had to."

"And who put you in charge of that job exactly?" I relax back into my seat, but my voice is cold and cutting. "Nobody asked you to do this. Anaïs isn't your toy, Kay, nor am I—not anymore. If you want some little plaything to amuse yourself with, then find your own. Anaïs is mine."

"You don't own her," Kayana says, crossing her arms.

"I never said I did. But she's engaged to me, not to you."

"If you care so much about her, then you would have brought her here."

"Oh, I never said I care, Kay. In fact, I don't give a single flying fuck about her." I resist the urge to add that I care as little for Anaïs as Kay cared for me when she broke my heart and betrayed my trust. "You coming in here to start a fight over Anaïs is a bore to me. We never let things between us get ugly, so let's not do so now. Anaïs isn't your concern or your business. Stay in your lane, and I'll stay in mine."

"You're so rude," Kay says, shaking her head in disgust.

She's not wrong in this instance. When I need them to be, my manners can be exquisite. I can be the most courteous high-society gentleman. But right now, I'm drunk, bored and in a terrible mood. The last thing I need is Kayana Kilburn, the girl who strung me along and threw me away like so much garbage, giving me shit over my own fiancée.

"Yeah, yeah." I wave a dismissive hand. "You're usually more fun than this, Kay. Are you not getting any action lately?"

She glares at me. "I'm getting more than you."

"I get plenty."

"Not tonight, since Anaïs clearly rejected you."

"Rejected me?" I sit up, shocked by a lightning bolt of anger. "Is that what she said?"

"No." Kayan smirks. "I was guessing. But thanks for confirming it."

"How did I confirm it?"

She shrugs and, with that self-satisfied smirk, turns and leaves the booth.

The rest of the night is a complete failure. I try to make the most of it, but nothing works. I dance with pretty girls—girls my type, in sparkly dresses with beautiful doll faces and sweet, easy temperaments, but nothing happens. It's like I'm dancing with paper dolls. I just end up bored, moving from one to the next.

I even kiss a girl during a slower song, and she receives and returns my kiss, lovely and pliant, her lip gloss tasting of strawberries. But it leaves me completely dead inside. It doesn't give me so much as a goosebump.

In the end, I leave the club with Iakov, and the evening rapidly devolves from here on out. The night flashes past: stumbling alongside the Thames, leaning over a bridge to throw up in the rain, a seedy club with a black door and a sign in flickering red neon that reads *Nosebleed*. Smashed liquor bottles, heavy metal music, Iakov with his shirt off beating someone up—or getting beaten up, or both.

Knowing him... probably both.

The night ends with a blackout, but at least I'm no longer thinking about Anaïs.

Chapter 7

LE ROI SOLEIL

Anaïs

Accepting Kay's invitation to go partying teaches me several crucial things.

One: that London is exactly as dark, crowded and chaotic as it's described in books and poems–like Paris if Paris had been dipped in grey paint and moody cynicism.

Two: that clubs are stressful and pretentious, not at all like the parties I used to go to in Aurigny. They're full of people with expensive clothes, who are wearing too much perfume and dancing to loud, repetitive music. At least in Aurigny, we always had the sun, or at night, the starlight, the beach, the sea.

A good party in Aurigny meant laughter, joy and skinny-dipping in the pink light of dawn. Here, the marker of a good party seems to be how much money you're willing to pay for alcohol.

Three: that people in England drink like absolute crazy. They drink aggressively, recklessly, obsessively. Not for the fun of it, not even for the buzz. They drink out of habit, joylessly, to obliteration.

Four: that the world of rich people is small, and that when I'm spending time in a place frequented by the wealthy, I should be careful who I make out with. It's why I was always so careful to only make friends from Aurigny, not from the Côte d'Azur. Just because I've left France doesn't mean the rules are different here.

Finally: that Séverin Montcroix is much more handsome in real life than in photographs.

That's saying a lot because his social media posts and professional portraits are so impeccably curated they feel more like fiction than reality, a modern take on Rococo portraits. But his good looks are real—they defy any camera lens that might ever have tried to capture them.

His beauty is for fairy tales: raven's-wing-black hair, eyes green like moss or the underside of birch leaves. His skin has that olive richness to it he's probably inherited from his mother's Moroccan royalty heritage, his features graceful and handsome. The dusting of freckles on his nose gives him a sort of whimsical youthfulness, and there's a slight curl to his lip that gives his mouth a sort of disdainful shape. That, he must get straight from his father.

Only blue-blooded French aristocracy could manage to look so effortlessly displeased and arrogant all the time.

But if photographs concealed Séverin's real beauty, they also concealed his childish impetuousness and ridiculous imperiousness. I expected him to be exactly like all the Côte d'Azur old money kids I've been forced to meet over the years, but I've never before met anyone who exudes quite this much delusion and self-importance.

I'm pretty sure that when he pictures himself, Séverin Montcroix sees a crown on his head and an ermine-trimmed fur around his neck.

When I finally get back to Spearcrest after my unfortunate encounter with him, I go straight to sleep and spend the next day cleansing myself of everything that happened at the club.

I wash the smell of expensive alcohol and designer perfume off my skin; I drink litres of water to flush out the alcohol still coursing through my veins. I eat a healthy breakfast and try to think only positive thoughts.

Cleansing my body is the easy part. Cleansing my mind, not so much.

I would love to be the kind of girl who could sit in a square of sunlight and meditate her troubles away. But the only way I can ever process anything is by sketching the thoughts right out of my skull and onto paper.

So I grab my sketchbook and tin of pencils, wrap myself in a thick jumper and pull a woolly hat over my damp hair, and head out into the Spearcrest grounds.

Spearcrest is beautiful. I could even imagine myself loving it if it wasn't so full of archaic rules and rich kids with arrogant sneers. Luckily for me, most students seem to either still be in bed or nursing their hangovers because the grounds are mostly empty when I stroll out of the sixth form girls' dormitory.

I cross the manicured lawns with their emerald-green grass, the rows of aspens and benches lining the paths. There is a patch of trees north of the campus that's calling to me, big ancient oaks with gnarly trunks and towering firs that spike the horizon with velvet green.

Instead, I end up settling in the Peace Garden. It's a square of beauty; it stands out like a window to another world, with its colourful flowers and marble statues, all arranged with mirror-like symmetry around an ornate fountain.

Hoisting myself up on the rim of the fountain, I settle myself: legs crossed, sketchbook balanced on my knees.

When I left Aurigny, the sketchbook was perfectly empty, blank pages awaiting my thoughts and feelings, but it's filling up fast. There are scribbled sketches from my first quick tour around the school, dreamy doodles from my first sleepless nights. Illustrations of the details of Spearcrest, the little features which caught my eye.

Like the geometrical pattern of the cupola crowning the library, or the intricate curlicues of the wrought-iron gates, or the thorny skyline formed by the turrets and finials of the Old Manor, and beyond that, the pines and firs.

Today, though, I'm not in the mood for sketching the school. But the flowers of the Peace Garden, with their moist petals and lush softness, are exactly the kind of gentle shapes I want my pencil to follow. My mind curves to the petals, softens with them, becoming elastic and alive.

As I draw, the spell of my pencil gliding across the paper takes shape. It wraps around me, around my blossoming mind, reshaping my thoughts around the shape of flower stems, flower petals, the powdery anthers. I lose myself in the images, in the mesmerising glide of the pencil.

My pocket vibrates, startling me and sending a pencilled line across one flower. I pull my phone from my back pocket and glance at the screen. My favourite name in the world appears over a picture of a boy holding fistfuls of torn-up grass-like spikes through his fingers.

I accept the call and wedge my phone between my shoulder and my ear, doing my best to incorporate my erroneous line into my drawing.

"Hello, Noël."

"Hello, *ma petite étoile*. How's it going?"

All the tension inside my body disappears, dissipating within me like a cloud of steam released into cold air.

My brother's voice floods me with a warm wave of relief. My entire body melts, releasing tension I didn't even know I was holding.

"It's... well, it's going."

"England not living up to the dream, then?"

His voice is light. When Noël worries, you would never know. When Noël is sad or angry, you would need an eagle's sharp eye to even guess. He's a master at concealing his emotions—I've learned everything from him.

And I've still got a lot to learn.

"What dream?" I ask, keeping my voice as light as his. "Who's dreaming of this?"

"Someone must dream of it somewhere. London, the city that inspired so many writers. The North where the Industrial Revolution started, the savage moors where Cathy and Heathcliff loved each other too fiercely. Right?"

"Maybe." I smile at the phone, even though he can't see me. I smile at the dreams his words weave. "Somebody's dream, maybe, but not mine."

"No, *petite étoile*. I know what your dream is. Soon, I promise." He's silent for a minute. "So... have you met him yet?"

I hesitate. "Met who?" I ask, even though I know who.

"The Montcroix heir." Noël's voice wobbles with a fake flourish. "The aristocrat boy with the divine eyes. The stranger-fiancé."

"Yes." I try to keep my voice calm and neutral so that Noël doesn't guess the exact circumstances of our meeting. "I've met him."

"Oh, you have, have you?" I hear him moving around, the clinking of spoons and ceramic. It must be early morning in Japan. I imagine Noël has just woken up and is pattering around his flat, making coffee and breakfast, his phone on loudspeaker. He doesn't sound remotely sleepy, but Noël's always been a morning person. "Well? What was your impression?"

I tap my chin with a finger, trying to find a good way of putting into words what Séverin feels like as a person.

"You remember Louis XIV?"

Noël bursts out laughing. "*Le Roi Soleil?*"

"Yes." I nod and smile even though he can't see me. "Picture him, and you can essentially picture Séverin Montcroix."

"When I think about him, all I can think of is that picture of him dressed as the sun with feathers in his hair."

"Yes." My chest bounces as I let out a silent laugh. "That's exactly it. You've got it."

"Okay, okay." Noël gets his laugh under control. "Alright. So... the Montcroix heir is, what? Self-obsessed, power-hungry and, presumably, a bit of a fuckboy. Is that about right?"

"Mm-hm."

"You two aren't getting along, then?"

That's a loaded question and immediately sends a reel of images spinning through my mind: laughing and dancing in the kaleidoscopic lights of the club, Séverin's body pressed to mine, his hands sliding under my shirt and his hot lips pressing wetly against the hypersensitive skin of my neck.

Not memories I want unspooling in my head while my older brother is on the phone. I shake my head and answer truthfully.

"No, not really."

The laughter ebbs out of the conversation, dragged out to the distance to be replaced by a darker current. In that current, my sadness and anger swim like dark creatures below the surface.

I've been trying so hard to keep them at bay. They come from a place of inevitability: sadness that Noël had to leave me, that I had to leave my friends, my home. Anger that my parents drove Noël away, then forced me into this impossible situation.

We could be sitting together right now, helping each other through life, through heartache. Having breakfast together the way we used to, every morning, *tartines aux chocolat* dipped into bowls of coffee and talking about difficult things over card games.

But we're not. And it's all because of our parents.

"Everything alright?" Noël asks again. His intonation is different this time, as if he wants the real answer.

"No. Not really."

"I see."

Noël falls silent again. His silence is the space he makes for me to share my feelings, like a blank canvas ready for the painter's brush. Even when we were young, Noël understood how difficult I found it to express myself sometimes. Talking with a brush or a pencil is fine, it comes easily and doesn't feel taxing. But talking with words can sometimes feel like an almost insurmountable task.

"Anaïs." Noël's voice is gentle when he finally speaks. There's no sadness in his tone, but I wouldn't expect it anyway because Noël's emotions are always kept private, even from me, sometimes even from himself. "We've bought the tickets. You only have to wait one year. One year is nothing, and we have a plan. Get your qualifications in the UK, use them for your university applications, then move here and continue your education. If you rush things now, if we change the plan, get you out, then what's going to happen? You come to Japan without your qualifications, and then what? Struggle to catch up? Struggle with university applications?"

A lump rises in my throat. I know Noël is right. The only reason I went through with this whole move to begin with was to secure the English A-Levels. English qualifications will go over better in Japan because I'm applying for English-speaking courses.

The end goal has always been to follow in Noël's footsteps and escape to Japan, where I'll be reunited with him and finally get to live my own life.

A life away from my parents' expectations, from the rich, upper-class people they so desperately want to be part of, from this archaic engagement with a spoilt, vain heir.

"I know," I say finally. "I know, Noël."

"Did something happen?"

Even if I wanted to tell Noël, where would I even begin? How would I begin to tell the story of trying to distract myself with a pretty boy in a club only to end up exchanging insults with my fiancé, like some political puppet in a mediaeval marriage?

Even thinking about these events is surreal, like something I've imagined into my memories.

"Nothing I could possibly describe to you." I let out a breath that's half-laugh, half-sigh. "Honestly, it's all just *Roi Soleil* stuff."

Noël laughs. "Yeah? What does that make you, then? The future queen consort?"

"Mm... more like the court jester. Or at the very least, a low-ranking valet."

Noël's laughter fades, and he sighs.

"You're going to be okay, Anaïs." Noël's voice is low and soft. "Remember the stars. Remember how remote they are, so far from everything that nothing can possibly get to them. The world can admire your light or hide it away, but the Montcroix heir, for all his status and money, can't get to you, no matter what. You'll remember that for me?"

"Yes," I whisper into the phone. "I'll remember."

"Bright and untouchable," Noël reminds me. "Like a star."

"Yes."

"You'll keep texting me often?"

"Of course."

"And you'll remember how much I love you and how much I can't wait to see you?"

"I can't wait to see you either."

"Love you, little sister."

"Love you more."

I hang up first so he doesn't feel bad for hanging up on me. I stare at the phone for a second, his little face in the circle above his name. He looks exactly like me, and we both look like the exact mixture of our parents. We have our mother's colouring and lanky build and our father's straight black hair and eye shape. The same hair and eye shape that made every French person ask us the question, "But where are you *really* from?" from the day we were born, even though we were both born in France.

French people never really see us as truly French, but in Japan, where my brother now lives, people always ask him where *he's* from, so I guess they don't see him as truly Japanese either.

Neither of us truly belong anywhere—but that never mattered when we had each other. And we might be on opposite sides of the world right now, but that doesn't matter. I'll always have Noël, and he'll always have me.

One year. I only have to make it through one year.

One year, and then everything will be okay. I'll be free, with Noël, and my real life can finally begin.

Chapter 8

LE BARONNET

Séverin

"In her essay *In Plato's Cave*, American philosopher and activist Susan Sontag purports that 'All photographs are memento mori. To take a photograph is to participate in another person's mortality, vulnerability, mutability. Precisely by slicing out this moment and freezing it, all photographs testify to time's relentless melt.' Who can tell me what we understand *memento mori* to mean and, more specifically, its meaning in this particular statement?"

Hands fly up around the classroom in my peripheral vision. I'm sitting with my chin in my palm, my eyes glazed over. Our photography teacher, Jacob Weston, loves the sound of his own voice, but his words are little more than white noise, a dull backdrop to my thoughts.

My thoughts about the problem that is Anaïs Nishihara, her blue sequined skirt, her bare feet and the memory of her nipples tightening underneath my fingertips. Anaïs Nishihara calling me a "*gros bourgeois*" and disrespecting me in front of Iakov and having the audacity to still be engaged to me.

Almost two weeks have passed since the incident at the club. After that night, I don't know what I expected. A confrontation, an altercation—something.

But nothing's happened.

"Mr Montcroix—penny for your thoughts. Photography as *memento mori*?"

I look up with a sigh. With his tieless suit and carefully tousled hair, he tries so hard to appear cool—not like the other teachers. He raises his eyebrows at me, fixing me with an insincere smile.

"Sure," I say.

He doesn't seem happy, but he's also not up for dragging something out of me. He knows by now I'm not the kind of student to get involved in classroom discussions. The relationship between me and my camera and whatever's on the other side of my lens is my own business.

He's wrong anyway.

Photographs aren't a reminder that we're going to die. Photography has nothing to do with death. Or even life. Like most things humankind concerns itself with, photography has everything to do with power.

The power to capture something. It's the photograph, not the person being photographed, that will remain. The photographer doesn't *participate* in the other person's mortality, vulnerability, or mutability. They *capture* it. They *control* it. They *own* it.

Weston wants us to believe he loves photography because it's an act of connection, but *I* love photography because it's the contrary.

It's an act of separation, of possession, of conquest.

I remember the sight of Anaïs in the middle of the dancefloor, with the large sequins of her skirt catching the shifting lights. The glitter smeared on her temples and eyelids, that beatific expression, those awkward, gangly arms lifted up like branches shaking in a rough wind. Back then, I'd wished I had my camera with me.

If I had managed to capture that image, would things have been different? Would I have been able to capture something of hers, keep a bit of her for myself? It would have been better than nothing since nothing is all I'm getting from her at the moment.

How can someone who's supposed to be mine be so elusive?

"Now for your assignment."

I shake myself from my thoughts and refocus my attention on Weston's voice. He might come up with a lot of trite rubbish, but I still have every intention of passing his class with flying colours. When it comes to academia, I'm not like Evan, who thinks the bare minimum is good enough, or Iakov, who lives his life as if death is his shadow and nothing matters except outrunning it.

I actually take my studies seriously, and I have no intention of leaving Spearcrest with anything less than straight As.

"I would like you to take a portrait based on the idea of *memento mori*. You can take as many pictures as you'd like, but you'll present only a single portrait, and it should be accompanied by a 3,000-word essay. Your essay should show a thorough exploration of the theme, as well as a clear and developed explanation of your portrait."

Memento mori. How uninspired.

What's worse is that you can tell Weston is really proud of himself for having come up with this. I sweep the classroom with a glance: from the rapturous expressions of the other students, he's not the only one who buys his bullshit. I suppose this sort of influence on others is to be admired.

After all, it's not so different from the influence the rich and wealthy wield in high society, the way they fawn over each other's highbrow sensibilities.

"For this assignment, I have the pleasure of announcing that we will be upholding a great Spearcrest tradition by combining the photography and fine arts classes. Photography and fine art are cousins—their relationship is old, intimate and sometimes fraught with conflict, but it is ultimately a close relationship. Each of you has been paired up with a fine arts student tasked with the very same assignment as you: except that their portrait will be drawn rather than photographed."

The wave of excited murmurs that follows his announcement sends a self-satisfied smile to his face. Weston ushers us out of the photography classroom and to one of the fine arts studios down the corridor. Apparently, we'll be sharing their space while we prepare for our assignment.

This new development doesn't bother me. At least we don't have to listen to Weston's self-aggrandising philosophising for an hour. Besides, the fine arts girls tend to all be cut from the same cloth: airy, flowery girls with names like Felicity or Clementine. Girls who listen to the kind of music their grandfathers listened to and speak in social media poetry and take themselves a little too seriously—but I don't mind that.

Because with those girls, you at least know where you stand.

Unlike that creature of chaos and sequins, Anaïs Nishihara.

Who, of course, is a fine arts student.

I walk into the art studio and spot her immediately. Not because she's the most beautiful girl in this room but because she's the only girl who doesn't look up when the photography students enter the room.

She sits cross-legged even though she's perched on her stool, her long legs folded awkwardly underneath her like those of some ungainly bird. Her shoulder-length black hair falls like a curtain to cover her face, but it's not hard to see what she's looking at because she's hunching over the pages of a sketchbook, scribbling dreamily.

The teachers are talking, and I don't hear them. Anaïs clearly hasn't realised I'm in the room, and I want so badly for her to notice that I have to resist the urge to throw my whole backpack at her just to get her attention. Part of me wants to sneak up on her, glance at the pages of her sketchbook, see what she's drawing with such intent focus.

Another part of me remembers the sensation of her body under my hands and the flowery, sea-salt smell of her hair against my mouth and wants to feel those things again.

Those are the parts of me I ignore, the parts that were placed too far from my brain to deserve any say in my actions.

Weston reads out our pairs, which have been chosen for us by the teachers. That wasn't cute back when they did it in the lower school, but now that we're all old enough to drink, vote and fuck, it's just insulting.

I hold my breath until my name gets read out.

"Mr Montcroix and Miss Wilkins."

I let out a breath of relief but don't move until Weston reads out Anaïs's name.

"Miss Nishihara and Mr Pembroke."

Parker fucking Pembroke. Parker is the son of some insignificant British baronet. He has more confidence than he should, but he's never been on my radar before. I didn't even realise he was in my photography class.

I turn to see him stroll across the room in the direction of Anaïs's desk. She still hasn't looked up, which gives him the perfect opportunity to sweep her with an appraising look. Anaïs isn't much to look at, but Parker is looking anyway. Exactly why he's looking, I would love to know.

Parker pulls up a stool right next to Anaïs and sits down. He leans over her arm to look at her sketchbook, and she looks up.

She looks...

Well, she looks exactly the same way she did in the club, minus the glitter and the outfit. The austere Spearcrest uniform sits a little awkwardly on her gangly frame, and the combination of her white shirt collar, black tie and plain shoulder-length hair makes her look younger than she is. She smiles up at Parker and gives him her hand.

He laughs and takes it. They shake hands. My eyes narrow, and my fingers curl into fists. Why is it taking so long for them to shake hands, and why are Parker's fingers lingering on hers? They're partners for a stupid school assignment, they're not getting married.

I don't even realise I'm still standing near the door until Weston comes to stand right in front of me, blocking my field of vision.

"Everything alright, Mr Montcroix? Miss Wilkins is over there."

Biting back a tart retort, I make my way over to Miss Wilkins. She wears flower clips in her long blonde hair, her ribbon curls bouncing daintily with every movement. Her lips are glossy and pink, a dusting of silver framing her big doe eyes.

"Hi, I'm Sev."

I offer her my best smile when I introduce myself to her, but still make sure to position my body in a way that allows me the perfect vantage of Anaïs and that smarmy idiot, Parker.

Miss Wilkins doesn't seem to notice.

"Hi," she says breathlessly. "I'm Melody."

"It's a beautiful name," I tell her, my eyes flicking up to Parker, who's showing Anaïs something on the screen of his camera. It's still hanging from his neck by its strap, forcing them to stand close together. Why not just take the strap off?

"Thank you. I'm actually named after my grandmother, but she's still alive—she used to be a dancer for the Royal Ballet—so everyone calls me Mellie."

"Mm." I glance from Parker and Anaïs back to Melody—Mellie's—face, her sparkling eyes. I smile tightly. "Well, it's a pleasure to meet you, Mellie."

She beams and plays with the purple tassel dangling from her sketchbook. The cover of it is plastered with flower stickers and painted vines. If I let her, Mellie could be the perfect distraction. She is exactly my type and clearly interested.

"You see that girl over there?" I point to Anaïs with a gesture I hope projects airy nonchalance. "Do you know her?"

Mellie glances over her shoulder. "Not really. She just started at Spearcrest—she's a transfer student."

"Right."

Mellie hesitates. "Her name is Anaïs."

"Yeah, I know." My eyes narrow as Anaïs settles on her stool with her sketchbook on her lap, saying something to Parker that makes them both laugh. "Is she generally a... friendly person?"

Mellie shrugs. "Honestly, she mostly just keeps to herself. She doesn't talk to anyone unless we have group work. She's not mean or anything, she's just... a bit odd, I guess."

"Mm."

I nod slowly, a little pacified by Mellie's information. Then she leans forward, enveloping me in the sugar-sweet cloud of her flowery perfume. "There's a rumour that she's..."

She stops, and I look up at her with a frown. "That she's what?"

"Um... that she's your fiancée."

If Mellie knows this rumour, then surely that means everybody in Spearcrest knows it. I didn't talk about my engagement to anybody apart from my friends—although it wouldn't surprise me one bit if they were the ones who spread the rumour—and I don't know how much Anaïs has been telling others. Of course, the most likely possibility is that someone read it in a gossip column, and that's how the rumour spread.

But if Mellie knows Anaïs is my fiancée, then so does everybody else. That includes Parker Pembroke, that posh English twat.

Mellie starts talking about the assignment and her plans for her portrait. I force myself to calm down, to not overreact. I don't feel possessive over Anaïs—I don't want her, so really, why should I care?

But then again, Anaïs was fully ready to have sex with a random person in London, and Parker is doing what he's doing, *knowing* she's engaged to me. Put like that, it's perfectly rational to be displeased with the situation. This isn't about wanting Anaïs for myself or even about Anaïs at all.

It's about pride and dignity.

I need to handle the situation with maturity and poise—the way a Montcroix ought to. I'm the first person to admit I can be prone to impulsivity, so I need to ensure—

Anaïs raises her arm and gently takes Parker's face in her hand, tilting it to a certain angle. Her touch is delicate, like she's arranging a flower in a vase, and Parker moves easily, guided by her.

I'm on my feet. My legs move of their own accord, carrying me across the classroom.

Anais has already let go of Parker's face when I stand next to them, and they both look up. My entire body is buzzing like a live wire.

"Get up, Pembroke." My voice is low and, luckily, calm. "We're swapping partners."

Chapter 9

Le Prince

Anaïs

Séverin Montcroix looks like some sort of rockstar fairy prince in his school uniform.

His tie is loose, top buttons undone. Fine gold chains glitter around his neck. There are jewelled rings on his fingers, and his eyelashes are so thick and dark that he looks like he's wearing eyeliner.

It wouldn't surprise me if he was.

He stands glaring daggers at Parker and speaks imperiously. "Don't make me repeat myself, Pembroke."

"We can't swap," Parker says. He's clutching his camera, and his left leg bounces up and down. He's either nervous or annoyed—or both. "Mr Weston and Miss Godrick paired us up."

At first, Séverin is perfectly silent. Then his eyes narrow. He leans forward ever so slightly and smiles. It's a curious smile: hollow and glacial. But Séverin isn't cold—there's a dangerous kind of fire burning in his green eyes. His voice is barely above a whisper when he speaks.

"You don't want to do this, Pembroke."

The two of them stare at one another, an unspoken battle taking place between them. I observe them with curiosity, like two animals communicating without words.

Finally, a victor emerges. Parker sighs, stands up and says, "I'll catch you later, Anaïs."

He grabs his things and walks away. Without even looking at him, Séverin takes his seat, swinging his backpack up onto the tabletop.

"That was incredibly rude," I tell him.

His eyes flick up to meet mine. They really are a striking shade of green, the murky green of pale jades, ringed with grey. How many colours would I need to mix on my palette to find this particular hue?

His eyelashes are long as a girl's, lending a delicateness to his face that balances out the strong shape of his nose, cheekbones and jawline.

"You created this situation," he answers. "If you don't like how I deal with these sorts of problems, then don't cause them."

After the night at the club, I was so nervous about seeing him again. Nervous it would bring back memories of our first meeting. Worried it would be difficult to separate the Séverin I'm engaged to from the green-eyed stranger with the sensual mouth.

But I needn't have worried.

Any soft, lustful memory I might have fades in the stark reality of him. Because despite everything that happened between us, Séverin Montcroix is exactly as I expected him to be.

Spoilt, prideful and entitled.

"There was no problem for you to deal with." I look away from him as I speak, flipping my sketchbook to a new page. "I had a partner for my assignment, which our teachers chose for us. We were both following instructions and preparing our portraits. I'm not quite sure how any of that came across as a problem to you."

"Oh really?" he sneers. "You're not sure how flirting openly with some random guy when everybody in Spearcrest knows you're my fiancée might be a problem?"

"*Flirting?*" I laugh, more in surprise than anything else. "Please tell me you're joking."

"Does it look like I'm laughing?"

I glance up at him. With his frown and his furious green eyes and his lush pout, he looks more like a petulant fairy princeling than ever. I cover my mouth, stifling a snort of laughter.

"Ah, no, you're right. You don't look like you're laughing."

He points an accusatory finger at me. "You don't fool me, Anaïs. You know exactly what you're doing."

"Well, I *did*." I point at my sketchbook. "Because I'd decided on a composition and angle for my portrait. But since you've taken my partner away, I'm back to square one. So no, right now, I don't know what I'm doing."

"I'm not talking about the portraits," he hisses, voice tight with barely repressed frustration. "I'm talking about the flirting."

"What flirting? The flirting where I was talking about *memento mori* with Parker?"

"The flirting where you two were holding hands, giggling and gazing into each other's eyes like lovesick schoolchildren!"

I wait, hoping Séverin is about to follow this sentence with a splash of laughter. But the laughter never comes. The eyes are still aflame with righteous anger. The proud chin and strong jaw are set with determination.

It's a shame he's so annoying because he'd probably be quite fun to draw.

"You've really been gone from France too long," I say, shaking my head. "What are you going to say next? That my wrist bones are too exposed? That I need a chaperone to escort me from one classroom to the next?"

He leans so close I can smell his perfume—an unexpectedly warm, woody fragrance, like expensive leather and sandalwood.

"Look," he grits out through clenched teeth. "*You're* the one that's moved over here for me, *you're* the one who needs my name. The least you can do is not embarrass me by openly flirting with any guy who gives you an ounce of attention."

I laugh incredulously. "If by talking you mean flirting, then what shall I do? Lock myself away in a tower until you decide you want me?"

He sneers. "You'd be waiting a long time. I don't want you, and I never will."

The coat room at the club flashes in my mind, soft and dim and full of pleasure. I raise my eyebrows at him and say nothing.

His eyes narrow. "*That's* not going to happen again."

"Finally," I say with a small smile. "Something we agree on."

He glares at me and opens his mouth to say something, but he looks up, and his eyes widen slightly.

"So," he says briskly, "*memento mori*—thoughts?"

I follow his gaze in time to see Miss Godrick approaching us. Her teacher planner is in her arms, and there's a slight frown on her face.

"You two aren't supposed to be working together," she says as she comes to a stop next to us.

Séverin looks up with an expression I've never seen on his face before. A courteous, open smile tilts the corners of his pretty mouth and reveals pearl-white teeth.

"Ah, I'm so sorry, Miss Godrick. Anaïs has just moved here from France—I'm not sure if Mr Ambrose has told you about the… unusual circumstances we both find ourselves in—but in light of everything, I thought it might be a good idea to partner up together on this assignment? Especially since Anaïs and I are both so busy with our studies. We have so few opportunities to spend time together, and I know how much my little Anaïs misses home…"

He turns to me. It's fascinating how beautiful and genuine he can make his smile look even when I know it's false. I roll my pencil in my fingers, itching to sketch his face, to capture this intriguing phenomenon of false loveliness.

"Ah, yes, I understand, Mr Montcroix," Miss Godrick says, smiling warmly at us both. "Thank you for explaining. I think in this case it should be fine for you two to partner up on this task. I'll let Mr Weston know. You two keep up the good work."

Séverin's smile doesn't fade until Miss Godrick's back is turned.

I tilt my head. "Who's the liar now?"

He shrugs. "Guess it's my turn this time. You're still a gold digger, though."

"And you're still a *gros bourgeois*," I reply.

"You're not going to need a *memento mori* because I'm going to end up strangling you with my own bare hands."

"You need a *memento mori* to remind you that you won't be able to dismiss death as easily as you dismissed Parker and Miss Godrick."

"No." He smirks. "I'm too beautiful to die."

"Too vain to live. Narcissus drowned looking at his own reflection."

He takes his camera out of his backpack and pops the cover open. Holding it up to his face, he adjusts the lens and mutters, "Keep talking. My essay will be about how your mouth is a *memento mori* because everything you say brings you one step closer to being murdered at my hands."

"Those frail aristocratic arms couldn't squeeze the juice out of a lemon," I say, smiling sweetly for his camera. "I doubt you could choke me, let alone strangle me."

"Choke you?" he says, peeking up at me above his camera. "I don't want you like that, Anaïs."

"I thought you didn't want me at all."

"Stop talking. I want to take your portrait while your mouth is closed. My essay will be about how only death will be enough to make you stop talking."

I raise my eyebrows. "Those are all different ways of saying you have no idea what *memento mori* means. At least Parker knew what it meant."

His features twist into a grimace. "Your comebacks are worse than your fashion sense."

"At least I have one."

"Barely. You weren't even wearing shoes the last time I saw you. Like a goddamn pauper orphan out of some tragic fairy tale."

"And you look like the evil fairy prince that steals babies from their cradles to replace them with goblins."

He lowers his camera and smirks. "Better a prince than a pauper."

"Ah, yes, the Montcroix motto that inspired this engagement."

He flips me the finger, and I return the gesture. Soon after, Mr Weston takes the students away to develop their photographs, and I sit and use one of my sketches to draw my portrait. When the bell rings at the end of the lesson, Séverin is nowhere to be seen, so I make a quick exit.

I'M BRUSHING MY TEETH and getting ready for bed when my phone vibrates. I open the text sent from an unknown number. There is no message, just a picture of a photograph. I open it.

It's a blurry photograph of me in the art studio. My mouth is open, and my expression is amused. With the white collar of my uniform and my plain black hair, I barely recognise myself. The photograph is far from flattering, and a text pops up underneath it.

Séverin: Best I got. Memento mori: remember you will die, so put in a bit more effort while you're alive.

I rifle through my backpack in search of my sketchbook and pull out the portrait I drew after he left. It's Séverin, a cocky smirk on his face, an extravagant crown on his head. I take a picture of it and send it, followed by a text.

Anaïs: My portrait of you. Memento mori: remember you will die, so don't be afraid to delude yourself to your heart's content.

His reply pops up two seconds later.

Séverin: Fuck off, Pauper.

I leave him on read, only because I guess it will frustrate him far more than any reply could.

Chapter 10

L'Invitation

Séverin

Despite the terrible picture I sent Anaïs, I submit a different one for my assignment.

It's a photo I snapped right in between two insults. In that picture, Anaïs is perfectly centred. She sits in that little cross-legged hunch, her sketchbook on her lap, hiding most of her body. Her head appears above her sketchbook, and her mouth is rounded, pursed around a word—probably an insult. It's not a smile necessarily, but her expression has the mischievous quality of some cartoon woodland creature. Her fey eyes glitter with a sort of wild energy.

After I submit the assignment, I immediately feel as if a weight is lifted from my shoulders. I delete the text chain between Anaïs and me, then solemnly vow to resume ignoring her. Not a message, not a word, not so much as a glance. I want her to believe she means nothing to me and that I don't have a single second to waste on her.

Unfortunately, avoiding Anaïs is easier said than done—especially when pretentious and overzealous teachers are involved.

Every year, the Arts Department runs a residential trip to the Isle of Skye. Its purpose is usually to get us all to experience the beauty of nature and develop our artistic vision and voices with the inspiration of everything nature has to offer.

The real reason everyone goes on the residential, though, is that the accommodation is co-ed, and everybody fucks like crazy.

When Weston announces the trip, I'm immediately cheered up. Time away from Spearcrest will be a welcome distraction. And getting laid will hopefully push the thought of Anaïs out of my head once and for all.

"As you all know, every year, we set a theme for the residential trip. Last year's theme, The Sublime, inspired our students to create pieces that have since been featured in some of the best galleries in the world. We expect this year to be no exception. This year's theme is *Aletheia*, the concept of Truth. The philosopher Heidegger differentiates the idea of *Aletheia* from the idea of Truth as we understand it by translating it as 'disclosure'—the interpretation you make will be left up to you."

Truth and disclosure strike me as two very similar things, but before anybody can raise their hands for questions, Weston continues.

"This year, however, we wish to reflect a unique cohort with a unique approach to the trip theme. This year, we wish to pose the theme as a question: what is more truthful, a painting or a photograph? We wish you to question the concept of truth—or disclosure—and investigate what it means to you and how you perceive and practise that truth. Instead of the photography and fine arts classes working on the same assignment separately, you'll be working in pairs. Between the two of you, you will need to search deep within yourselves and decide which of your art forms is the most *truthful*. You will present your findings in the form of a 3,000-word essay due once you return from the trip, and you will later present your work at the prestigious Spearcrest end-of-year exhibition."

The Spearcrest Exhibition is a big deal—each year, a panel of judges select the most talented artist to receive an award and a cash grant. I don't care about the grant, but I do care about the award and the prestige.

It would give my mother another reason to show off to her friends, and that's the greatest gift I could ever give her.

"Are we going to be in the same pairs as last time, sir?" Parker Pembroke's plummy accent pipes up from somewhere in the classroom.

Weston nods. "Yes, Mr Pembroke. You'll be paired with Miss Wilkins."

I turn to throw a disdainful smirk at Parker. He ignores me but lowers his head, pretending to be taking notes.

What is up with him anyway? Parker is rich and good-looking (by English standards), I can't imagine he must struggle for dates. So why this sudden interest in Anaïs? It's not exactly like she's drop-dead gorgeous. Especially when compared to the other girls in her class.

Of course, the satisfaction of witnessing Parker's disappointment is quickly offset by the realisation that my plan to keep away from Anaïs—or the problem that is Anaïs, as I like to think of her—is going to have to be put on hold.

Unless...

Nothing is forcing me to do the work the way the teachers want us to. This kind of pretentious philosophical assignment is easy to bullshit. If the teachers had tasked us with taking thirty different shots of each other around the Isle of Skye, I'd be forced to see Anaïs. But the way things stand, I can still hold her at arm's length, where she should be—where I should have kept her that stupid, annoying night in the club.

My father must be reading my thoughts, though, because a couple of days before the residential, I get a text from him.

Papa: *Progrès avec la petite Nishihara?*
Any progress with the little Nishihara?

I roll my eyes. This man texts me about once or twice a year when he needs me to do something. I respect the fact he doesn't bother with insincere small talk—it's a habit I've inherited from him—but sometimes I wish he wouldn't be quite so brusque.

I consider leaving him on read for a few hours, but this isn't a conversation he'll drop, and it'll just hang over my head until we've had it.

Might as well get it over and done with.

I text back.

Sev: More or less.

He replies straight away.

Papa: Then do more.

I sigh.

Sev: Like what?

My phone vibrates, startling me. Of course, he's calling me. It's not like I can pretend I don't have my phone on me, so I answer.

"Your school sent me that letter about the residential trip," he says without so much as a hello. "It says you've been paired up with a girl from the art department. The Nishihara girl—she's an artist, no?"

For a man so used to navigating the intricacies of high society, he can be about as subtle as a hammer to the jaw.

"I've already been paired up with her, Papa. I don't see how being paired up with her on a school trip is going to help."

He chuckles drily. "Come on, Sev. This engagement is important, we *need* it. This poor girl has left her entire life behind just so you two could get to know each other. So do that. Get to know each other. Do *something*. What do you want this to be, some mediaeval thing? Two strangers and a bedsheet with blood on it?"

It is *a mediaeval thing*, I want to say. Whether we're strangers or not. I could fuck her, date her, fall in love with her—and it would still be mediaeval.

"What is it you want me to do, exactly?" I ask, not hiding the sullen edge in my voice.

"Whatever it is you do to get girls to fall into bed with you," he snaps. "I'm sure I don't have to tell you how to win a girl, Sev."

"I'm not going to get her to fall into bed with me," I snap, heat suddenly rising in my face.

"Oh, you know what I mean. God, you kids these days. Speak to the damn girl, Sev. It's not complicated."

"Right."

There's a moment of silence. My father doesn't sound stressed or angry at all. As far as he's concerned, he's just pushed two inanimate objects together, expecting them to do the rest. Like a kid squishing two dolls face-to-face and thinking that means they're in love.

"Right," I repeat. "Fine. I'll do what you say. Just stay out of it."

"Right," he says. "If you don't want me to get involved, don't give me a reason to get involved."

He ends the conversation briskly, the same way he finishes a business conversation after he's gotten what he wanted out of it. After he hangs up, I keep glaring at my phone until the screen turns dark, and I'm just glaring at my reflection.

THE NEXT DAY, I have Anaïs brought to me during lunchtime. I'm sitting with the other Young Kings in our usual haunt: the sixth form rec room next to the dining hall. It's meant to be for all sixth formers to spend their free time in, but it became Young King property as soon as we started in the upper school.

Since then, it's been ours. We spend our free periods, breaks and lunchtimes there. The only people who are allowed in the room are either there to amuse or serve us. I include our girlfriends in this, though girlfriends amongst the Young Kings are a rare occurrence.

I've not had a girlfriend since Kayana, and I never will. Evan, the romantic American that he is, is the only one of us who still has real , official girlfriends. Although that barely counts, given his long-running obsession with the stuck-up *casse-couille* Sophie Sutton. Luca dates girls but only if he thinks one of us wants her, just to remind us not to fuck with him. Zachary doesn't even seem to notice the existence of girls outside of Theodora Dorokhova.

And as for Iakov... who knows what Iakov gets up to.

The door opens, and two Year 12s return from the mission I sent them on. Anaïs, the object of said mission, trails behind them in slow, graceless steps. It's clear she doesn't want to be here, but I told the Year 12s that not bringing her wasn't an option.

My eyes stay on her as she approaches.

Her school uniform is tidy but plain, like a kid in the lower school. Her hair is clean and combed but hangs plainly around her face. She wears no make-up, no jewellery, and there are no pins on her blazer. Flecks of paint stain her sleeves, hands and chin.

If I didn't know this girl was the heiress to billions, it would have been the last thing I would ever have guessed about her.

I can't quite put my finger on what it is about her that annoys me so much. But the more I look at her, the more I realise it's not her appearance I dislike. She's pretty enough—if she made an effort, she might even be beautiful.

No, it's not her appearance. It's her... air. There's something about her that just feels otherworldly. Inquisitive yet indifferent. Distant. As if she's not of this earth but some strange celestial being who looks down on the rest of us as if we're all small and insignificant.

Her eyes land on me, and she gazes at me without fear, anger or concern. Just a vaguely questioning look.

If the other Young Kings notice anything off about her, they don't mention it or act like it. Evan, who is copying the answers to his science homework from Zachary's book, looks up and gives a small wave. Iakov is too busy frowning at his phone to even notice I've brought her over. Luca watches with the callous curiosity of a scientist observing the subjects of an experiment.

Zachary, though, sits up as soon as he sees her, smiling broadly.

"*Bonjour, la future Madame Montcroix,*" he says in a perfect French accent.

I suppress a shudder. "Ugh, don't call her that."

"*Bonjour,*" she answers politely, turning to look at Zachary. "Hi. I'm Anaïs."

Zachary, too, ignores me. "*Oh, enchanté, Anaïs. Je m'appelle Zach.*"

I throw him a dirty look. "I've not brought her here for your amusement, Zachary."

"Maybe so," he says with a smirk, "but I'm amused nonetheless."

"Why am I here, then?" Anaïs asks, turning back to me.

"Am I not allowed to see my own fiancée?"

She raises her eyebrows in a dubious expression. "You're allowed everything, from what I understand. Those boys"—she points to the two Year 12s who are, wisely, retreating—"referred to you as a king. Do they not know we guillotined our monarchy in France?"

Zachary laughs delightedly. I glare at her.

"Don't teach me about my own history, Anaïs. I'm as French as it's possible to be—my family name goes back hundreds of years."

"Your name is very old," she says. "Its joints must hurt all the time."

Her tone is so blank it takes me a moment to realise she's being sarcastic.

Before I can make a trenchant reply, Evan looks up from his homework and says, "We don't have a monarchy in America."

For a second, everyone stares at him. He shrugs. "Just saying."

"Thanks for the contribution, Ev." I roll my eyes and turn back to Anaïs. "Has your teacher told you about the trip?"

She nods.

"How are you getting there?" I ask.

She shrugs. "Same as everybody else, I guess? Coach? Do English schools not use coaches?"

"This isn't just any school," I sneer.

"Oh, do students here travel in hot air balloons made of solid gold and pegasi fed on amethysts?"

Her tone is deadly serious. We all stare at her for a second. Then Iakov lets out a single bark of laughter that sounds more like the growl of a wolf than a sound of amusement.

"Obviously not," I snap. "But the coach is uncomfortable, and it takes ages. We have permission to drive there, and since I have a car, I thought you could come with me instead of taking the coach."

She's silent for a second.

"No, thank you," she says eventually.

"It's not a request, Anaïs."

She sighs. "Then why ask?"

"I was trying to be polite."

"Polite enough to ask, but not to respect my answer." She shakes her head. "Typical old money behaviour."

"Ah, of course, I forgot I'm speaking to the revolutionary Anaïs, the billionaire pauper."

"I'm not a billionaire," she says, raising her eyebrows. "My parents are."

I laugh in triumph. "Hah! Only rich kids say that!"

She sighs and links her fingers together in front of her in a prim gesture. "Okay. I'll go with you in your car. What else?"

No comeback. I beam. "Nothing, really. That was all."

"So can I go back to my lunch now?"

"Yes." I wave a hand at her. "I allow it."

She turns around and walks away without another word. I call after her. "And don't wear something stupid!"

She stops for a second. Then she turns, raising both middle fingers at me, and leaves.

"I, for one," Zachary says, nodding solemnly, "rather like the future Madame Montcroix."

Chapter 11

LE TRÉSOR

Anaïs

Séverin waits for me in the student parking area of Spearcrest, leaning against his car with an air of elegant boredom. It's too early for the sun to have started rising, but the car park is lit by two old lamp posts. In that dim lamplight, Séverin is wearing ripped black jeans, an elegant black jumper and his usual array of gold jewellery.

I falter in my steps. Although he did give me clear instructions to "not wear something stupid", his opinion wasn't at the forefront of my mind when I dressed this morning. Instead, I was inspired by the fact we would be driving for over eight hours.

With that knowledge in mind, I opted to wear my comfiest clothes: loose cotton trousers, my oldest trainers, and one of Noël's old gym T-shirts that's gone soft with time and use. On top of that, I've got a big blue sweatshirt with big sleeves for tucking my hands in and a white baseball cap.

When he sees me, Séverin raises a dubious eyebrow.

"Are those pyjamas, and do you still need to get changed?"

I sigh. "I'm sorry, I left my ballgown and diamond shoes in my room. Didn't realise I was going to be travelling with French James Bond."

"James Bond drives an Aston Martin. This is a Porsche."

Drawing closer, I peer at the sleek black car with its tinted windows and shining rims. "It looks like the kind of car rich dads buy when they are having a mid-life crisis and decide to leave their wives for young social media models."

"And yet *you're* here, Anaïs." He smirks. "Remind me to ask for a refund."

Séverin takes my bags from me and places them into the small boot at the front of his car. It's impeccably clean, a stark contrast to the state Noël's car used to be in. Although to be fair to Noël, he used to drive all over—I can't imagine that Séverin, the boarding school princeling, must have many opportunities to use his ridiculous car.

After he puts my stuff away, Séverin walks to the passenger side and opens the door. I tilt my head.

"What a gentleman."

He rolls his eyes. "Just say thank you."

"Oh, thank you." I drop him a mocking curtsey. "Thank you ever so much, milord."

I move to get into the car, but Séverin puts his hand on my shoulder and pushes me away. I look up at him in surprise. Holding my gaze, he slams the passenger door shut.

"Open your own door, then, *Jeanne d'Arc.*" He walks around the car. "My manners are wasted on you."

If it wasn't for the number of times he's thrown insults to my face, I might have felt a little bad. But I know better. Séverin, like any privately educated rich kid, isn't a nice person; he just knows how to appear polite and courteous to disguise his disdain for anybody other than himself.

We both get into the car. The interior is just as sleek and polished as the exterior, and even I have to admit that travelling like this must be much more comfortable than travelling by coach. As soon as I get in, I kick off my shoes and curl up in my seat. Séverin shoots me a look but says nothing.

We set off, the car driving so smoothly the engine is barely more than a soft hum.

I sit with my cheek on my fist, staring out of the window. The sky is still dark, the sun a mist of grey pallor low in the sky. The silhouette of Spearcrest, with its turrets and chimneys and spiky trees, slowly disappears from view, replaced by narrow country roads framed with bushes. Instead of rain, dead leaves flutter sadly from their branches as they tremble in the wind. They gather in piles by the sides of the road and swirl in swathes when we drive past them.

"You can go to sleep if you want," Séverin says after a while. "I don't mind."

"I can't sleep if there's another person there," I mumble against my wrist.

He frowns. "What do you mean? Have you never had a sleepover before? Shared a bed with a boyfriend?"

"I've had sleepovers before. But I don't sleep. Usually, I'll just stay up and doodle or lie there with my eyes wide open."

He glances at me. "That's so weird. What are you afraid of? That someone's going to stab you while you're asleep?"

"I'm not afraid of anything."

Even as I speak, I suddenly remember being very young, asleep on the couch, and waking up to my parents' voices. Nowadays, they don't argue so much—they barely talk—but when I was younger, they argued all the time.

Maybe Séverin is right after all.

"Everybody's afraid of something," he says, oblivious to my inner revelations.

I lift my head from my hand to look at him. "Really? Even you?"

"Of course."

"What are you afraid of, then?"

I wonder what this information might be worth if I sold it to a gossip blog. I half-expect him to come up with a pretentious, secretly self-congratulatory answer. Something like the fear of failure or the fear of fear itself.

But he doesn't.

"Eels," he blurts out.

"Eels?"

He shudders. "*Anguilles.*"

"I know what eels are. Why eels? Did you have an incident with an eel?"

He shakes his head. His handsome face is twisted in a grimace of disgust and dread. "No. I've never even seen an eel. And I'll do everything I can to avoid ever having to see one."

"Should you be telling me this?" I ask, doing my best to suppress a smile.

"Why, what are you going to do? Dump a bucket of eels in my bed?"

I laugh but say nothing. He turns to glare at me. "That's not even funny. You twisted little bitch. You know, my parents described you as this sweet, arty girl. Either they were lying through their teeth or you've got everybody fooled."

I try to think about how my parents described Séverin, but they never did. They just told me I was getting engaged to him and that it was just what I had to do for the family.

Then they made it sound as if it was Noël's fault. If Noël hadn't betrayed the family and left, he could have taken any of the beautiful girls of the French aristocratic elite for a fiancée, and I would have been free to pursue my art and choose who I wanted.

Their attempt at turning me against Noël didn't just fail, though. It backfired.

I sigh. "I'm actually a very sweet person. You know there's a very common Japanese dish called *unadon*?"

He raises one hand and shakes it at me. "I don't want to hear about it."

"It's basically rice and grilled fillets of—"

His hand lands on my face, covering my mouth. His skin is surprisingly soft, and the metal of his rings is warm against my lips. He throws me a dangerous glance. "Just. Stop."

Although it would be funny to lick or bite his hand, my head is suddenly filled with memories I've been doing my best to avoid. Memories of my first time meeting him—memories that heavily feature his hands and the things he did with them.

I push him away.

"Alright. I'll stop."

We're both silent for a moment—I'm sure Séverin is busy gathering himself after the ordeal I've put him through with the mental images I've forced upon him. I'm doing the same, quickly banishing memories that have no business being in my head.

"What are you afraid of, then?" he asks. "I told you my fear. It's only right you tell me yours."

As if I would ever tell him my fears. I don't even want to think of my fears—they all revolve around losing my brother. I pretend to think, tapping a finger on my chin.

"Hmm... I would have to say... the fear of fear itself."

THE SUN HAS JUST appeared over the horizon, a blurry orb of milky light, when we get on the motorway. Above us, the sky is the deep, angry grey of storm clouds, dark but rainless. Séverin drives in silence, one hand on the steering wheel, the other resting casually on the console between us. From the corner of my eyes, I notice that he keeps twirling the rings around his fingers. Maybe he's not as relaxed and careless as his slumped posture would seem to indicate.

I glance away, turning my attention back to my sketchbook, tracing mindless doodles across the pages. Patterns of leaves and vines spread across the page, fuzzy where I've rubbed shadows into them with the pad of my middle finger.

"Why is there so much paint on your clothes?"

Séverin's voice is barely louder than the music quietly playing from his car stereo. When I look up, his eyes are firmly fixed on the road. There's a slight frown on his face, as if the matter of my paint-flecked clothes is of particular annoyance to him.

But his displeasure does nothing to mar the beauty of his silhouette. His profile is proud and princely. I grip my pencil, turning it in my fingers as I repress the urge to capture the graceful shape of his face in my sketchbook.

"Because painting is messy, and acrylic is particularly difficult to get out of clothes."

"I didn't know you painted," he said. "Are you going to paint that portrait you drew of me?"

"My *memento mori* portrait?" I flip through my sketchbook and grin down at my sketch of him. "No. I don't like painting people I know."

It's only half a lie. Séverin doesn't need to know it's *him* I don't want to paint.

"Why not?" he asks, still frowning.

Because to paint a true portrait, you want your subject sitting with you. You need to observe them closely, the way their features are set, the bonework beneath the flesh. You have to observe the way their clothes fold around the shape of their bodies, the way the light hits and traverses their skin, the places where their blood flows and pools.

And more than that, you have to get a sense of them.

Their smiles, their expressions. The movement of their eyes and arms and hands, the way their chest rises and falls. The way their gaze softens or hardens, the way they tug on their lips with their teeth, the tiny subconscious tics they have. That might be the way they bite on the skin around their nails or the way they play with their hair or bounce their leg when they're bored or restless.

When you're painting a portrait, those are the things you want to notice. Those are the things you use to form the image of the person. Paintings aren't photographs: they don't just capture the surface level of what the person looks like at that very moment. Painting someone is like catching the essence of them, cupping it in your hands like a butterfly.

Holding it too tightly will crush it. Hold it too loosely, and it'll fly away from your painting, leaving it empty.

"Because it's harder to paint people you know," I say.

If I sat and stared at Séverin for too long, I have the feeling I'd be the one captured, not him. Beautiful like a fairy prince, he'd cast a spell on me. The kind of spell that makes human maidens starve for the taste of fairy fruit and cut the ruby heart from their chests in exchange for a cruel fairy kiss.

"You can't be a very good painter, then," Séverin says. He turns for a split second, long enough to throw me a smile.

I shrug. "I'm not."

"Does that mean I'm going to win the assignment, then?" he asks.

"What do you mean?"

"It's a competition, isn't it? What is more truthful, art or photography."

"It's not a competition. It's a debate."

He shrugs. "What's the difference?"

"A debate is the exchange of ideas and opinions. There's no winner or loser."

"This is real life, pauper. There's always a winner and a loser."

"I'm not a pauper," I point out.

"No, you're right, you're not. You're the opposite, aren't you? *Le trésor des Nishihara. Mon trésor, maintenant.*"

The Nishihara treasure. My treasure, now. His voice drips with sarcasm when he says it. He watches me with a slight smirk, as if waiting for me to react.

I sigh. "Fine. I'll paint your portrait."

His eyes widen, and his smirk fades. "Really?"

"Mm-hm." I nod and smile sweetly. "I'm going to draw a portrait of you as the *Roi Soleil*."

He turns to frown at me. "Louis XIV?"

"Yes."

"Why?"

"Because you remind me of him."

He rolls his eyes and looks away. "Oh fuck off."

I offer him my sweetest smile. "You don't like Louis XIV?"

"It's not Louis XIV I don't like, *trésor*. It's you."

Chapter 12

Le Bisou

Anaïs

I WAKE UP WITH a start and sit up in surprise. Without realising, and against the odds, I must have fallen asleep. I can't tell how long I've been sleeping—outside the car windows, the sky is just as bleak and grey as it was before I fell asleep.

Next to me, Séverin is pulling free from his seatbelt. Looking around, I realise we've stopped, parked in some corner of a service station.

"I didn't mean to fall asleep," I say, still a little groggy and confused.

Séverin smirks. "You talk in your sleep, you know."

"No, I don't."

"You do. You mutter all sorts of things."

"Like what?"

"Like my name. Over and over again."

I roll my eyes and unbuckle my seatbelt. "I must have been having a nightmare."

We get out of the car, and I wince as I stretch my stiff legs. The air is already colder than it was when we left Spearcrest. Although it's not raining, the presence of rain is all around us: in the puddles mirroring the orange lights of the lamp posts, the tiny pearls of raindrops dangling from the tips of leaves, the smell of damp grass and fresh mud.

We go our own ways, and when I return to the car, Séverin still isn't back. I wander away through the trees to the edge of a little pond. Beyond it, the trees are sparser, opening up to a vista of rolling hills and citadels of grey clouds.

It's a pretty view. Sitting on the stone bench by the pond, I tuck my legs under me and pull out my sketchbook and pencil from my tote bag. The tip of my pencil glides across the page, taking the shape of water, grass, hills and clouds.

Footsteps approach, heralding a dark silhouette. Instead of saying something cutting or insulting, Séverin sits down next to me, sipping on a cup of fragrant black coffee.

"Have you spoken to your parents recently?"

I turn around with a frown. Not the question I expected. "No, why?"

Séverin isn't looking at me. His eyes are pointed to the pond, but they're a little glassy, as if his gaze is turned inwards.

"When was the last time you spoke to them?" he asks thoughtfully.

"Uh... a few days after I arrived at Spearcrest? It's been a while."

I don't have the heart to tell him my parents and I hardly ever speak. It's not something he needs to know. It's not something he'd care about anyway.

"What did they say?" he asks.

"Nothing much." I try to remember the telephone conversation, a brief chat with my mother while she was in between meetings. "They asked me if the flight was alright, if I'm settling into Spearcrest, if I got my timetable... that kind of stuff."

"They didn't ask about me?"

I suppress the urge to laugh. "No. They just told me to try and get to know you."

He finally turns to look at me. The green of his eyes almost looks gold in the desolate daylight. He gives me a searching look, refreshingly free of ire and resentment.

"Why didn't you?" he asks finally. "We wouldn't even have met if it wasn't for that ridiculous night at The Cyprian."

"I thought you didn't want this engagement," I answer truthfully. "I thought it might be better to just leave you alone."

He's quiet for a second, but his eyes remain on mine. His beauty is a strange sort. It has a vulnerable edge to it, something delicate and lovesome. The curling of his eyelashes, the faint dusting of freckles, the rose petal softness of his mouth. But there's cruelty and arrogance there, too. In his aristocratic nose, the tilt of his jetty eyebrows, his sneer.

"It's a little rude, don't you think?" he says in a lofty tone.

I shrug. "You didn't exactly approach me either."

"That's different."

"Why? Why should it be one rule for you and another for me?"

He gestures vaguely. "Because of power."

"Right. I forget. Because you're the prince, and I'm the pauper, right?"

"Non." He grins suddenly. "*Plutôt le roi et le trésor.*"

Is he teasing me or provoking me? It's hard to tell. His emotions are always so naked, but his desires are impossible to fathom.

"Well," I say mildly, "we've met now. So what's the problem?"

"The problem is that a meeting isn't enough." His tone is a little sullen now, and I half-expect him to cross his arms and stomp away like a grumpy toddler, but he doesn't. He continues moodily. "If we don't put on at least a bit of a show, they're going to force our hands."

"Our parents?"

"Yeah."

By this point, it seems pretty clear Séverin's had a conversation with his parents I'm yet to have with mine. They probably haven't gotten to it yet; they're always busy with work and meetings and social engagements.

But I'm also beginning to suspect my parents might trust me a little more than the Montcroixes might trust Séverin.

If they didn't, I wouldn't have been able to plot my escape.

"What kind of show?" I ask slowly.

I'm not opposed to the suggestion, but I'd rather know what Séverin has in mind before I commit to anything. A low growl of distant thunder rumbles through the sky with ominous timing.

He grins, pulling out his phone.

In the next moment, his arm loops around my neck, pulling me to him. I smell his perfume once more, that warm, woody fragrance, like expensive leather and sandalwood.

Holding his phone up, he wraps his fingers around my chin and kisses me on the cheek. His lips are surprisingly warm. There's the tiny artificial shutter sound of a photo being taken on his phone.

Then he releases me. I sit in stunned silence while he taps away at his screen with a satisfied smirk. The shape of his kiss glows hot on my cheek as if his lips were hot metal when he kissed me.

I brush my fingertips against it.

"There," he mutters. "This should shut them up for a bit."

I raise an eyebrow. "I doubt a kiss on the cheek is going to convince them we're falling in love."

"I'm not trying to convince them we're falling in love," Séverin says, not looking up from his phone as he types. "I'm just trying to convince them we one day might." He sends his text and looks up, putting his phone back in his pocket. "Why? Are you sad I didn't kiss you on your mouth, trésor?"

"Don't even think about it," I say with a light laugh.

He stands and stretches, his top lifting slightly to reveal a sliver of smooth flesh and hard muscles. I lift my eyes to his face, where a dangerous smirk curls the corners of his lips. "Is that a dare?"

"It's a warning."

He shakes his head. "Well, you can calm down. I'd rather kiss every ugly toad in this pond than your mouth."

I stand, putting my sketchbook and pencil away. "Good."

"Great," he says, turning to head back to the car. Then he mutters, loud enough for me to hear him quite clearly, "You fucking pain-in-the-ass."

"Moody asshole," I mutter back.

"Gold digger."

"Toad kisser."

Despite our spat, the rest of the journey is pleasantly peaceful. We drive through the day and dusk, the grey clouds growing steadily darker. Séverin bops his head to his music. I alternate between doodling and gazing out of the window at the passing lights. The landscape slides by like a dream: shadowy mountains, velvety pines, dotted lights.

It's deep into the night when we finally arrive.

We're staying in a place called Corrimore, in the middle of the Scottish highlands. Séverin pulls up by a set of rustic wooden cabins on the edge of an enormous lake, trees and mountains lining the distance under a pitch-black sky sown with stars.

The further north we went, the fewer streetlights there were until we were driving in complete darkness. Now we've arrived, the only lights are coming from inside the cabins, the lanterns in the cobblestoned car park, and the stars high above.

I stumble out of the car, groggy and disoriented from sleep. I gaze up at the sky with my mouth half open in awe.

It's breathtaking how different the sky looks when it's not stained purple and brown by photopollution. The true colour of the night finally appears, the deepest shade of blue, like ultramarine mixed with dioxazine purple. The moon is a bright crescent, sharp as a blade, and each star is a tiny knife tip.

I close my eyes and smile, breathing deeply. This is exactly what I needed. The black space opening wide around me, the sky as far as the eye can see and further. The silent yet powerful presence of the lake, the mountains, everything that lives here.

Séverin says my name, bringing me back to reality. He's grabbed our suitcases, and he leads me to one of the cottages. By the looks of the cars and coaches lined up in the car park, most of the others have already arrived. Inside our assigned cottage, we're greeted with a beautiful interior. Wooden beams, cream rugs and cosy sofas, big chimneys and piles of logs next to crackling fires. A staircase leads upstairs to the bedrooms, the upstairs corridor overlooking the living room.

"Ah, Miss Nishihara, Montcroix, you've made it," Miss Godrick says delightedly, standing from the kitchen table where she's been sitting typing on a laptop.

She tells us our assigned rooms. To my immense relief, everyone has their own room. After that, she hands us our itineraries for tomorrow and then leaves since we are the last of our group to arrive and staff have their own cabin.

The moment she closes the cabin door behind her, an explosion of cheers and whoops follows. Students descend from their rooms, carrying bottles, coolers and stacks of plastic cups. Despite the long and tiring coach journey, nobody seems to be in the mood for sleep.

Grabbing my suitcase, I try to make a beeline for my room, but Séverin takes my arm, stopping me.

"Are you coming back down for the party?" he asks with a slight smile. "The residential trip parties are legendary—a true rite of passage."

"Given what happened last time I went partying, I don't think it would be smart to go," I say, tilting an eyebrow. "Don't you agree?"

His eyes fall from mine, lingering over my mouth. Then he moves his gaze back to mine and gives a little half-grin. "Fair enough."

"Alright, then." I walk away with a little wave. "Enjoy yourself."

He opens his mouth as if to say something, but hesitates, then seems to think better of it. With a nonchalant wave of his hand, he turns and walks away. I hurry to my room, closing the door behind me.

A bedside lamp is on, casting warm light over a large bed, wooden furniture and a small, old-fashioned furnace in the corner. A basket of logs and twigs is propped on the floor next to the furnace. The window overlooks the lake, where the mirror-smooth surface reflects the stars in ripples of silver glitter.

After brushing my teeth and washing my face, I throw my clothes off and slide into the bed. My bare legs glide against smooth, cold sheets, and my head sinks into the soft pillow.

The deep thump of loud music and the babble of voices and laughter already fills the cabin. I roll to my side, tucking myself deeper into my blanket. Despite all the napping I did on the journey, I feel worn out, my eyes dewing with sleepy tears.

I wonder if I'm going to struggle to sleep, but the moment I close my eyes, I might as well have plunged into a black abyss. Sleep swallows me into silent darkness.

CHAPTER 13

LA BOUTEILLE

Séverin

I TAKE A SWIG of wine from the bottle in my fist, and two drops roll onto my tongue.

Holding the bottle in front of me, I shake it. My eyes widen. It's empty. Odd—it was full when I picked it up off the kitchen island.

Flopping onto the couch, I let my head roll back into the plush cushions, eyes closed. Fingers tangle in my hair, and a warm mouth moves against my ear, but it barely registers. Even with my eyes closed, my head is spinning. Alcohol burns through me, loud like static.

The last time I was this drunk was that night in London.

The night of blue sequins and small breasts in my hands and the scent of lilacs and sea salt.

I open my eyes, staring up at the darkened corridor overlooking the living room. Behind one of the closed doors, cloaked in shadows, is Anaïs. Is she asleep? I sit up, suddenly annoyed. It doesn't seem fair that Anaïs should be asleep right now.

Why should she be resting, lost in some blissful dream, while I'm sitting here thinking about her?

Teetering to my feet, I stand unsteadily for a second. The girl who was next to me—one of the art girls with pretty hair and a flower name—falls back with a wistful sigh. I make a silent vow to come back for her.

As soon as I've dealt with this Anaïs problem.

I vaguely remember her room number. Even if I didn't, I'd be prepared to knock on every door. Stumbling up the stairs, I make my way to her door and knock. There's no answer.

Is she asleep? Am I going to need to knock harder to wake her up? Why didn't she come to the party, anyway? She said it was because she didn't want to repeat the mistakes we made last time—but we actually know each other now. What does she think is going to happen? That we're going to make out by accident? That I'm going to trip and land with my hands under her clothes and my mouth on hers? That—

The door opens, startling me out of my rhythmic knocking.

"Séverin?" Anaïs's face, pale and soft with sleep, appears behind the door. "What are you doing?"

I sigh. "Just say Sev. Nobody calls me Séverin."

"Why are you trying to break my door down in the middle of the night?" Her voice is rough from sleep. Her confused frown is slowly morphing into a glare. "You scared me."

"I just wanted to see you," I try to explain.

"You've seen me," she says, shaking her head and brushing tousled strands of black hair out of her eyes. "Go to bed."

"Let me in."

"I don't think that's a good idea."

"Come on, Anaïs." I soften my tone, caressing her with my voice. "My little trésor, my little bride. I just want to talk."

She sighs. "You're drunk."

"No, no, look."

I hand her the bottle I'm still holding.

"It's empty," she says.

"Exactly," I answer, waving the bottle in her face. "How could I get drunk from an empty bottle?"

She takes it with an unimpressed look but steps aside. Smiling at my unexpected victory, I stumble past her. Her room is small but cosy. Her bed is a little rumpled. I throw myself onto it, flopping on my stomach. My face lands against her pillows, which smell like lilacs. I breathe in deeply, then turn my head to look at Anaïs as she puts away the empty bottle I've given her.

She's wearing a T-shirt that's about five sizes too big for her. Her black hair is feathery with sleep, her cheeks a little flushed. Fuck. She looks quite cute. She looks cute, softened and sweet in sleep, like whipped butter and honey. Even her long graceless limbs look cute, those awkward elbows and knees. There's a tiny pencil tattooed on her ankle.

She sits on the edge of the bed, grabs a plastic water bottle from the nightstand and hands it to me.

"Drink," she says.

I shake my head. "Don't need it. M'not that drunk."

"Drink it," she repeats. "If you throw up on my bed, I'll take your room and leave you here to sleep in your own sick."

"M'not going to throw up." I wave a hand at her. "I'm a Montcroix. Montcroixes don't throw up."

"Ah, of course. Being a Montcroix makes you closer to a god than a man. I forget."

"I never said that," I mumble sullenly, face still squished into her pillows. "M'not a god."

"No? What are you?"

I rub my face into her pillow and grin. "Your future husband."

She sighs. "Why are you here, Séverin?"

"Because I'm horny."

The truth drops from my lips. A truth I didn't mean to admit. But now I've said it, I'm hornier than I was before. There's a buzzing underneath my skin, like trapped electricity. Excitement—no, not excitement. Lust.

Hot, pounding, simmering lust.

I'm not hard yet, but I'm in that kind of mood where I want to be. The kind of mood when I might normally indulge in a slow wank, without urgency.

But Anaïs's presence, instead of dousing this slow, growing heat inside me, is doing quite the opposite. Her long bare legs, her pretty, unimpressed eyes, the hard points of her nipples underneath her ungainly T-shirt... They're like dry grass, stocking the smouldering heat of my desire into full-blown flames.

She isn't even my type. She never will be. I don't think about her like that, and being engaged to her makes me repulsed by her on principle alone.

Clearly, not repulsed enough.

"So why come here?" is her cool, collected reply.

"You know why."

"I guarantee you I don't."

"Because of you. Because I want—" I try to think of a way to explain exactly what I want. "I want you."

She doesn't flinch. Instead, she tilts her head, fixing me with a thoughtful gaze. A thoughtful, searching gaze.

"You're being flippant," she says slowly. "You're being flippant, or... or this is part of that thing you do where you want us to fight. Or this is one of your *winners and losers* things. But you're definitely not here because you want *me*."

"You don't know what I want."

"I know what you don't want. So do you—you're just too drunk to remember."

"What about you, trésor? What do you want?"

I reach for her arm. She doesn't move away but glances down at my hands with narrowed eyes. Before she can even move, I grab her, dragging her to me and pinning her under me on the bed.

My breath is quick, and my heart is suddenly hammering. Anaïs doesn't seem fazed. Or angry or concerned or... anything. She looks up at me, perfectly calm, distant as always—distant as a celestial being tasked with observing humankind without interfering.

"I don't want anything," she answers. "Just to be left in peace to sleep."

"We could spend the time doing something much nicer than sleeping." Gently cradling her head in one hand, I brush the pad of my thumb from her chin to her jaw. Her throat shudders as she swallows, but her face remains a calm mask. I have no clue what she's feeling, but she's not pulling away. That's something. "Can I kiss you?"

She shakes her head. "No."

"Why not?"

My voice is a hoarse whisper. The smell of her, the warmth of her, envelops me in a cocoon. A cocoon that makes the real world feel very far away, as if our engagement is a universe away. As if this moment exists outside of time and space—in whatever dimension Anaïs exists in.

"Because," she says, "you're trying to make a mistake, and I'm trying to stop you."

I lower my lips to hers, close enough to feel the warmth of her breath. "This isn't a mistake."

She moistens her lips with the tip of her tongue. Is that a nervous gesture or an enticing one? I can't tell with her. Her face gives nothing away. Even her eyes—those pretty doe eyes—give me nothing.

"You don't want to be engaged to me," she says finally. There is no self-pity in her tone, no resentment. She speaks with that dreamy neutrality of hers, like it's impossible to faze her. "You don't want me in Spearcrest. You don't even like me."

Her eyes drop to my lips, and then she looks back up quickly.

"Give me one good reason to let you kiss me," she adds. "And I will."

"Because..."

I stop, staring down at her. My hips are pressed between her legs, and I'm definitely a little hard. But even with her body underneath mine, the evidence of my desire undeniable against her—even now, she manages to keep her cool, to keep me at arm's length. How is that possible?

"Because I want to," I say finally. "I don't need another reason. I want to kiss you, to put my fingers on your tongue and make you suck. I want to lick your nipples until you make those sounds you made that night at the club. I want to make you so wet you're dripping. I want to taste that wetness and pleasure you with my tongue and make you feel so good you come undone."

Her eyes are wide. She blinks slowly. Under my chest, hers rises and falls a little quicker than it did before.

Now I've said all those things, the ghost of what could happen rises between us. It makes it harder to control myself, to resist doing what I want to do. Touch her, kiss her, taste her.

Have her.

I lower my mouth to hers before she can say anything. I half-expect her to shove me off her, but she doesn't. Her mouth opens slowly underneath mine. I kiss her, deep and slow, tasting her, exploring her.

Her tongue meets mine, shy and sweet, sending blood rushing to my cock.

Now I've started kissing her, I can't stop. My hunger, rather than abated, is whetted. I crave more.

My mouth slides from her, and I kiss her jaw, her neck. She pushes her head back, exposing her neck to me. There is a little constellation of beauty spots on her skin—I kiss them all. I find her pulse point and bite down gently on the skin, sucking on it.

A tiny whimper of pleasure breaks the silence.

I look up; our gazes meet. There's shock on her face. Her cheeks are crimson. I let out a low laugh of satisfaction and kiss her greedily. She might not want to admit that she wants me, but she can't hide how much she's enjoying this.

My kisses become deeper, dirtier. My hands roam her body, palming her breasts, tugging on the hem of her T-shirt. She's wearing panties underneath it, and I slide two fingers between her legs to find the fabric warm and wet.

"Fuck," I mutter against her lips. I move my mouth to her cheek, kissing her temple, speaking against her ear. "You're so fucking wet, trésor. I want to taste you. I—"

Anaïs's eyes go wide. She looks at me as if she's just broken out of a trance. Slamming her hands against my chest, she shoves me off her. I move back, and she scrambles away, cheeks ablaze.

"You—you should go," she says. "Please, Séverin."

"What?"

"I already let this get too far. You should go."

I sit up slowly, incredulous. "You're... rejecting me?"

"I'm stopping you from making a mistake," she says, tugging her T-shirt down and tucking her hair behind her ears. "You're drunk, Séverin. If anything happens now, we'll both regret it."

"I never regret anything I do," I tell her with a glare, getting to my feet. "You're just too proud to admit you want me."

She licks her lips nervously. "I didn't say that. If you came to my room sober, then it would be different."

"If you reject me now, do you really think I'll come crawling to your bed like some pathetic loser?"

"You don't have to if you don't want to," she answers calmly.

"Fine, then." I've never felt angrier in my life. My entire body shakes with frustration and fury. I pierce her with a hateful look. "Your loss, trésor. I'll just go find someone else."

"Yes," she says, nodding slowly. "I think that's probably for the best."

She doesn't even have the courtesy of looking jealous. For someone so new to Spearcrest, Anaïs knows how to play games just as well as any Spearcrest girl. Without another word, I turn around and storm out of her room, slamming her door shut behind me.

As soon as I'm back downstairs, girls crowd me. But it quickly becomes obvious that neither I nor my cock are in the mood anymore. Anaïs's rejection and insulting dismissal hit me like a bucket of cold water, extinguishing the flames of desire she'd kindled so high and bright.

Extricating myself from the arms of art girls, I make my way to the kitchen. With any luck, I'll drink myself into a coma and wake up with no memories of this tragic night.

Chapter 14

La Chapelle

Séverin

I wake up with a pounding headache and a sore neck, draped on a couch. A bottle of champagne is still nestled in one arm, and my leg is propped on a girl who looks more passed out than asleep. Bottles and cups litter the floor and furniture, and stark daylight filters in through the shutters, casting bleak light over the mess.

"Fuck." I groan, wiping my hand across my eyes.

The sound of quiet footsteps on creaky wood makes me look up. A tall, willowy figure makes its way down the stairs. My stomach churns.

Anaïs is wearing shapeless faded jeans and a massive blue sweatshirt. Her silky black hair is tucked behind one ear, the rest hanging around her face like a curtain.

She bites her lip in concentration as she makes her way to the door, clearly trying to remain as quiet as possible. Her gaze sweeps through the room, and our eyes meet. The corner of her mouth lifts in a slight smirk.

"Good night?" she whispers.

Despite the truly concerning amount of alcohol I consumed, despite the skull-splitting headache hammering through my entire body—I can still remember last night.

Every single part of it.

Fuck my life.

With great effort, I lift my arm to give her the middle finger. With a quiet laugh, she returns the gesture and walks away, disappearing through the front door.

I DON'T SEE HER the rest of the first day, which suits me fine. She's out, following the itinerary the teachers sent us, probably ambling through nature like she belongs to the highlands and the lochs, probably feeling fresh as a daisy. Fuck her. I have a hangover to nurse, anyway.

But I don't see her that evening or the next morning.

By the evening of the second day, I'm annoyed again. Is *she* avoiding *me*? Hardly seems fair, given what happened between us. I might have been slightly drunk, but *she's* the one who made out with me, got all wet and moany, and then had the audacity to reject me.

I've never in my life been kicked out of a girl's bed. It stings like an open wound. But I still have the courage and dignity to face her.

She's acting like she's not even realised we're paired up for this trip and assignment.

Luckily for me, Melody Wilkins—Mellie to her friends—hasn't been getting on so well with Pembroke. She's also pretty, friendly, and seems only too happy to spend time with me instead. So on the afternoon of the third day, when the teachers force us on a hike to go see some castle ruins, I have Mellie at my side to keep me company.

The afternoon is cold but dry, with low white clouds in a deep-blue sky. The hills here are emerald green, and the trees an explosion of colours: red, orange, yellow. Mellie keeps pausing for pictures, and I watch her as she does. She's very Spearcrest: golden hair shaped into effortless waves, violet manicure—daisies painted on the nails of her ring fingers—and her lips are lush and pink as a rose.

Normally, a girl like her would need to make next to no effort to excite me. A flirty gaze and the light scratch of her nails across my arm would be signal enough that she wants me, and I'm only ever happy to oblige.

Sex, just like drinking, is one of those things I will always indulge in if I can. Unlike Luca, I don't get bored with the things I enjoy. Pleasure is pleasure; if I can have it, I will.

But something is missing with Mellie. I don't know if it's the silly nickname or the affectation with which she says, "Oh my god, how simply *gorgeous*!" every time she stops to take a picture, but it's just not working for me.

By the time we reach the castle ruins, I'm in a thunderous bad mood.

I had every intention of dragging Mellie with me to some shadowy part of the ruins and fucking her into centuries-old walls. But I'm just not in the mood to have sex with her—even though I'm definitely in the mood for sex.

The teachers gather us in front of the castle to give us our instructions. When they've finished, I glimpse movement from the corner of my eye. Anaïs, her hair tied back and her sketchbook hugged to her chest, is already wandering away from the edge of the group, a dreamy look in her eyes.

She doesn't even look around to see if I'm there; she simply disappears into the ruins.

"This fucking girl..." I mutter to myself, stomping off after her.

A hand at my elbow stops me. I turn in surprise to find Mellie gazing up at me with soulful blue eyes.

"Don't you want to join us?" she asks.

Her voice and eyes suggest she's not interested in sharing thoughts about truth in art. Unfortunately, what she's offering is not what I'm in the mood for. I shake my head.

"Maybe later, beautiful," I tell her.

She nods, cheered by this glimpse of hope, and her hand drops from my elbow. I turn around and stifle back a curse. Anaïs is gone.

The ruins are sprawling, but she can't evade me forever. I stride in the direction I saw her walk in and plunge into the maze of collapsed stone.

The castle is much darker inside. Moss and ivy crawl along the surface of the rock, which exudes a profound cold, almost like a breath. Night is already falling, and tendrils of mist crawl like ghosts up the hills we climbed earlier, creeping around the corners of walls and pillars.

Ghost-like of all is Anaïs. Several times, I seem to spot her in the corner of my vision but turn to see the branches of a tree poke in through the empty frames of windows. Other times, I think I've caught a hint of her smell—the delicate perfume of lilacs and a faint chemical smell similar to sesame seeds—and follow the scent down a corridor to find myself at a dead-end.

I'm about to give up when I find a series of stone steps leading away from the castle and down the hill through trees. Following the steps, I descend into a small copse. There, nestled amongst twisted tree trunks and tangles of thorns, is a tiny little chapel. Candles burn on a ledge of stone at the foot of a small statue of Jesus.

I pause, staring at the chapel. It's so small only a child could fit inside, but the statue is painted with bright, fresh paint, and most of the candles are lit. This tiny, isolated place of worship might be in the middle of nowhere, but it's not abandoned or forgotten. Grabbing my camera out of my bag, I snap several shots of the chapel.

Once I'm done, I turn around and almost jump out of my skin.

"*Putain de merde!*"

Balanced on the enormous trunk of a fallen oak, Anaïs sits like a strange, sinister statue in a nest of leaves and shadows. She's wearing blue jeans, a cream jumper and a sky-blue woolly hat. Her sketchbook is propped on her folded legs, and she holds a pencil in her hand.

Although my heart has already leapt out of my chest, she seems perfectly calm.

"I didn't take you for the religious kind," she says.

Her tone isn't mocking. As usual, it's slightly dreamy. But there is a note of amusement in her voice, the slightest twinge. I draw closer to her with a frown.

"I'm not."

She shrugs, as if she doesn't need convincing because she doesn't care, and gets back to her sketching. I step right in front of the tree trunk she's perched on, almost closing the space between us.

"Are you avoiding me?"

She looks up. "No. Why?"

Because you're never anywhere to be found. Because you don't seem to want to spend so much as a second in my company. My thoughts are so loud I'm almost nervous she'll hear them.

Now I think about it, Anaïs doesn't seem to want to spend time with anybody at all. Aside from that night when she came to the club with Kayana Kilburn and the others, I've never seen her spend time with anyone in Spearcrest. I never see her with her classmates or at campus parties.

How could anybody be happy with that kind of life? Does she not get lonely? Being alone when surrounded by people is worse than loneliness—one of the worst things I can imagine. And yet it doesn't seem to bother her at all.

"At what point were you planning to work on this stupid assignment, then?" I ask her.

She shrugs. "Whenever you want."

"Now."

"Alright, why not?" She holds up her sketchbook. "I'm drawing the chapel you just photographed. We can compare work if you like."

"What's there to compare?" I smirk. "The assignment is Truth—a photograph is always going to be more accurate than a drawing. Even if this is a debate and not a competition, photography is still most truthful—it will always be."

"The assignment is *Aletheia*," she says. "Not quite the same as Truth."

So she's been drinking the Weston Kool-Aid? Artists are so pretentious. Although I don't know why this should surprise me: Anaïs is a billionaire heiress in battered trainers and ugly clothes who thinks she's not part of the *bourgeoisie* she so openly despises.

No matter how unearthly she seems, she's just as pretentious as any other girl in her art class.

"Okay," I say, suppressing a sigh. "So *Aletheia*—what is it the German guy said? Disclosure?"

"Heidegger. Yes, disclosure, but also unhiddenness. Unconcealedness."

"Oh, is that it?" I roll my eyes and check through my camera for the shots I just took. Turning the camera around, I show her the monitor. "Go on then, have a look."

She does. Leaning forward, she tucks her hair behind her ear and takes the camera in one hand, pushing the button to cycle through the photos. The camera still hangs around my neck by its strap, and she's so close I can smell her. Lilacs and sun and that chemical sesame seed smell.

I watch her as she looks at the picture. She has pretty eyes and delicate features. I'm struck with the sudden and intrusive thought that if Anaïs had some style—if she wore make-up and dresses and did something nicer with her hair—she might actually be my type. Maybe that's the reason I want so badly to make her come.

Grabbing my camera out of her hand, I recoil from her.

This is why I should never think with my dick.

Because my dick is stupid and, lately, intent on leading me into disaster.

Chapter 15

LA CHASSE

Anaïs

THIS MIGHT BE THE most surprising discovery I've made since leaving France: Séverin Montcroix actually has talent.

My impression of Séverin before I arrived in Spearcrest was that of a rich, vapid playboy. The type of guy to make bottles of Moët and a fat Rolex his personality and use that personality to surround himself with clout-chasers and sycophants.

And he sort of is those things. But his photography is a revelation, like realising a smooth gem has facets to it.

His photographs exhibit a good eye for composition and a preference for crowded, moody shots. His style is very much like him: ostentatious, almost sullen, needlessly emotive. I don't say any of this to him as I peer at his work, but he suddenly snatches his camera out of my hands.

"Well?" He glares at me as if I've just mortally insulted him. "What do you think, then?"

I nod. "They're good shots."

"Enough *disclosure* for you?" His tone drips with mockery.

"Just because you've captured what you can see doesn't mean you've captured what's truly there."

"What does that even mean?" He takes my sketchbook out of my hands to glare at my sketch. "What the hell am I looking at?" He flips my sketchbook around to show me my own sketches, an indignant expression on his face. "You're just drawing made-up shit!"

I resist the urge to roll my eyes at him. For such a talented photographer, he severely lacks imagination.

"It's not made up," I try to explain. "If I was just drawing what I can see, it wouldn't exactly be truthful, it would just be a cheap imitation. I'm trying to capture the essence of the place, what it feels like, what it might mean to me."

"That's the most pretentious shit I've ever heard." He flips through the pages. "Do you really think this is truthful?"

He brandishes a page from my sketchbook. A drawing of a boy with his skin sprouting birds, his eyes wide with horror, his hands clutching branches and twigs.

"It's truthful to me. It's truthful to what I felt when I drew it." I reach for my sketchbook, but he steps slightly back, leafing through the pages. "You don't have to like it," I add. "You don't even have to look at it. Just give it back to me."

"No, no"—he looks at me, a sudden glint of wickedness in his eyes—"isn't that the point of this assignment? To debate the meaning of truth in art and photography?"

"I don't think the teachers set the assignment with the intention of us tearing each other down."

He smirks. "I'm not tearing you down. If I was tearing you down, you'd feel it, trésor."

It sounds like a veiled threat, but since I doubt Séverin is in the business of making idle threats, I don't push it.

"Alright," I say, getting up to my feet. "You win the debate. We'll say photography is the most truthful art form in the assignment."

I reach for my sketchbook, but Séverin hides it behind him with a smirk. Even though I'm not normally violent, I have the sudden urge to slap the smirk off his face. To shove him down, grab my sketchbook and run away. I take a deep breath, reminding myself how far away and cold the stars are.

"Don't patronise me," Séverin says. "You don't have to let me win. I'm willing to debate this with you."

He doesn't sound angry like he normally does, and a wicked glint shines in his green eyes. With the pale daylight reaching him in green dapples through the canopy of the trees, he looks more like a capricious fairy prince than ever, and I'm reminded of the stories of fairy tricks and games.

Séverin is in the mood to play.

But I don't like games.

"Debate requires good listening skills," I say tartly, "which I'm not sure you've developed yet."

Pushing myself off the fallen tree I've been sitting on, I step towards Séverin.

He steps back, just out of reach. He flips through my sketchbook and turns it around to show me a page. "And who's this, trésor? Tell me. I'll use my listening skills while you answer."

I tear my eyes from the green spell of his to look at the page he's showing me. A sketch of Noël's face. Even though I drew it from memory and imagination, it captures his likeness almost perfectly. That's how deeply his face is imprinted into my subconscious.

I ignore Séverin's question and step towards him. "Give me my sketchbook."

"No, I want to look. Who is he?" He flicks through the pages to another sketch of Noël. "Is he your *boyfriend*?"

"Give it back."

"Or what, trésor?" He tilts his head, flashing his teeth in a grin. "What are you going to do?"

I cross my arms and fix him with a firm look, hoping my calm will dispel his strange bout of mischievousness. Somehow—I can't quite fathom how—this is about yesterday. This is about Séverin on my bed, pinning me underneath his body and asking me, in a low, husky voice, for a kiss. This is about all the things we did, all the things he wanted to do.

All the things we *didn't* do.

"I'm not going to let you kiss me again, if that's what you're trying to achieve."

His playful grin flickers but doesn't disappear. "I wouldn't be so sure if I were you."

"No. I'm sure."

This time, he's the one who steps closer. He closes my sketchbook, holding it behind him. His eyes glower, and his voice becomes imperious.

"I think," he bites out, "I can get a kiss from my own fucking wife."

My heart seizes in my chest, like a struck animal curling in on itself. "I'm not your wife."

"But you're going to be." His grin grows more dangerous, more satisfied. Whatever attack he thinks I levelled against him last night—this is his retaliation. "Unless you break off the engagement."

"You're the one who's so desperate to get laid," I point out. "*You* break the engagement."

His eyes narrow. "Let me make something clear. I can get laid anytime I want, regardless of this engagement. As for you, I can—"

I lunge into him, sidestepping him swiftly. I grab my sketchbook from behind him and yank it out of his hands. Dashing away from him, I make a run for the hill, hoping I can lose him in the castle ruins.

"You little fucking shit!"

His angry yell is right behind me. The stamping of his footsteps sounds far too close for comfort as I scramble up the rough stone steps up the hill. I've almost reached the shadowy walls of the castle ruins when his hand fists into my jumper.

He yanks me back, dragging me off my feet. My heels dig into wet grass and soft earth, finding no purchase. I fall hard on my ass. He laughs out loud, a wild sound of triumph, but before he can reach for me, I roll out of his way.

Hauling myself up, I dart into the trees.

I run away from him, adrenaline pumping through my body. I know I'm being reckless and irrational. There are going to be consequences for this, but it's too late to stop.

My shoulder smashes into the low branch of a pine tree, and I stop to catch a sharp breath.

A weight slams into my back. My sketchbook flies out of my hands, and my body crashes to the ground. Mushy grass and spongy moss cushion most of the impact, but my thigh collides with the root of a tree protruding from the ground. An explosion of pain bursts in my leg. My chin and cheek scrape against the ground as I drag myself away from the weight on my back—the weight of Séverin.

I'm almost out from under him when he grabs me and flips me around. I kick out without even looking or aiming. My heart is one erratic drumbeat; adrenaline is a deafening rush in my ears. Séverin dodges my first kick, but the second catches his shoulder.

"Fuck!" he bites out.

He throws himself down on me, straddling my hips so I can no longer kick him. I try to push him off, but he grabs hold of my wrists, pushing them down into the cold forest floor. I squirm and buck, but his weight settles on me, pinning me down so that I'm all but powerless.

And that's when something hard presses against my belly, and I freeze.

I find myself in the same situation as that night he came to my room—and yet, somehow, completely different.

Above me, Séverin's face is flushed. His hair is a sweaty mess of fallen strands, half-covering one eye. Whatever emotion is on his face, it's not anger. I'm not even sure what it is—a feral mixture of triumph and amusement, hunger and excitement.

He looks like the wolf that's about to eat the lamb.

"Don't stop fighting me," he says when I grow still. His voice is low and silken. "Go on, trésor. You got this far—why stop now?"

This is far more frightening than any of his anger, any of his insults. He's not asking this to scare me off—he's asking me because he wants me to fight him. And a part of me wants to do just that. A wild, repressed part of me wants to lash out at him, to hit him so hard it hurts my own hands, to scratch and claw at him until I draw blood.

I've never felt this way before about anyone.

But this isn't me, I remind myself. And whatever path Séverin is trying to drag us both down isn't a path we could come back from.

It's a dark, dangerous path. The kind of path I try to avoid.

"I'm done fighting." I pant, trying desperately to squeeze air into my constricted lungs. "You win."

A shadow crosses his face. Then his eyes narrow, and a deadly smile curls the corners of his aristocratic mouth.

"No," he says. "You're not done."

And then he grabs the collar of my jumper in his fist, pulling me up to him, and crushes his mouth to mine.

Chapter 16

LA POMME

Séverin

Anaïs's mouth opens in a gasp of surprise, and I slip my tongue inside. Her lips are soft, so soft I want to bite into them. She tastes like peppermint. She tastes like wilderness and desire.

She tastes like my newest addiction.

She pulls away from me with a strangled whimper. Her hand, which I released when I grabbed her collar, collides with my face in a hard slap. My cock hardens against her, and I grind down so she has no choice but to feel it. She doesn't get to ignore my want, not this time.

She slaps me again, the same place she slapped me the first time. I laugh and kiss her cheek. It's hot and smells of French summers. She tries to slap me a third time.

"See?" I catch her wrist and kiss it. "You're not done fighting, trésor. Not one bit."

"*You're* the one who wants to fight," she snaps. This is the most anger I've ever heard in her voice. The most emotion. "Not me."

Her hair is tangled with blades of grass and fragments of fallen leaves and mud smears her cheeks and clothes. She looks like an angel that's just been dragged down from the stars and through the mud.

And I can think of so many ways to send her back to heaven.

"I don't want to fight," I tell her truthfully, lowering my mouth to speak against her ear. "I want to fuck." Pulling away, I gaze down at her. Her eyes are wide, her lips are pink and shiny. I let out a low, dirty laugh. "And I think you do too."

Her cheeks are the bright red of fairy tale apples. Cupping her face in my hand, I reach down and bite her cheek. Maybe I'll fall into a hundred-year-long sleep.

I already feel like I'm under some sort of spell.

"*Salaud!*" she yells. Her hand flies up to cover her cheek once I pull away. She looks angry and irritated. She looks a mess. It's the most satisfying feeling I swear I've ever felt. I could come just from the trembling of her voice, the tears of annoyance and pain glimmering prettily in her eyes. "*T'es un salaud!*"

"*Oui.*" I rub my thumb over the two red marks on her cheek. "*Je suis un salaud, et t'es une menteuse.*"

"I never lied to you," she says, her voice quivering in anger. "I'm not lying to you now, and I won't ever lie to you. Unlike you, I'm not ashamed of my own desires. If I want something from you, I'll ask you for it. I won't wait until I'm drunk in the middle of the night, and I won't steal it from you after chasing you around like a bloodthirsty animal."

She's breathing hard, and all I can think about is crushing the breath from her lungs with another kiss. We stare at each other and, for the first time, it feels like we're truly looking at each other. Not at the façade we present to the world but at the exposed souls within.

Words battle on my tongue. I want to tell her she's not as brave as she thinks she is. I want to apologise for stealing a kiss from her. I want to test her bravery and dare her to hit me again, to bite me, to hurt me. None of these things feels like the right thing to say.

Or maybe they're all the right thing to say.

The shrill sound of a whistle pierces the air. We both freeze, our bodies stiffening. Around us, everything is plunged into shadows. When did that happen? I didn't even notice the night falling.

I get to my feet and pull Anaïs up by her arm. She glares at me but lets me help her up.

"Come on, trésor." I sigh, suddenly tired. "We don't want to end up spending the night stranded here, do we?"

Even in the purple light of dusk, she looks like an absolute fucking mess. Mud stains her skin and clothes. Her hair looks like she's been living in the forest all her life. A crimson bite mark glows on her already-red cheek.

She looks torn up and damaged and dirtied.

She looks like I had my way with her right there on the forest floor. I wish I had.

I pick up her sketchbook from where it landed at the foot of a tree, wipe the cover with my sleeve and hand it to her. She snatches it from my hands, clutches it to her chest and stomps away. I follow her, brushing my hand through my sweat-dampened hair. It's a good thing the whistle just blew because who knows what might have happened otherwise.

I can't remember the last time I was this turned on. Or worked up. Or conflicted.

This is definitely something I should never do again. It was uncharacteristic, unwise, and, let's be honest, utterly uncivilised.

And I can't stop thinking about doing it again.

As soon as I get back to the cottage, I head straight for my bedroom and run the shower as hot as it will go. I peel off my dirty clothes and throw them into the hamper. I tragically disrespected Yves Saint Laurent today.

I'm about to step into the shower when I spot my reflection in the bathroom. My eyes widen.

If Anaïs looked a fucking state, then she at least got her revenge. My hair is a tangled, sweaty mess, my skin is covered in mud and scratches. There's a bright red handprint on my face, finger-shaped welts splayed across my cheek.

So the rotten little Nishihara treasure isn't at all as quiet and composed as she would have me believe. The revelation tastes like victory. Even the welts on my face—this raw, painful evidence that she's just as capable of emotions as I am—feel like a win, a shining trophy.

I capture a few snapshots of my post-Anaïs face, wishing I had managed to take some shots of her post-Séverin face. Then I step into the shower, letting the hot water run over me. I close my eyes with a blissful sigh.

Memories from earlier run through the darkness behind my eyelids. Anaïs snatching her sketchbook from my hands. Anaïs running from me and the pounding blood in my veins as I gave pursuit. The exhilaration of tackling her to the ground, wrestling her down, pinning her under me. Her body under mine, the warmth of her, my hips pressed against hers. Her flushed cheeks, those bright, shining eyes, her blows and insults.

Wrapping my hand around my cock, I stroke myself slowly. I'm already hard, and touching myself is the relief I need but not the relief I want.

What do I want?

I don't like Anaïs. She's plain, boring, pretentious. I don't want her. She's mine, all but gifted to me, but I want nothing to do with her. I don't want her company; I don't want to get to know her; I don't want to spend time with her.

What I want is to get under her skin. She acts so superior, so unbothered—but I want to bother her. Make her squirm. I want to kiss her again, taste her mouth. Pin her down and reach underneath those unflattering baggy clothes of hers and touch her all over. I want to fuck a spectrum of emotions across that impassive face of hers.

Anger, hatred, excitement, resentment, desire, regret.

Pleasure.

My hand moves faster, pumping my cock. I'd give anything to see what she looks like when she comes, what she looks like when I'm the one making her come. Would she arch her back or would her thighs tremble uncontrollably? Would her eyes squeeze shut or open wide? Would she let out a whimpering sigh or a broken cry?

I want to make her do all those things. Kiss her moans and suck on her nipples. Grip her trembling thighs and let her chase her own pleasure on my tongue.

My cock twitches as my orgasm crashes into me, tearing a groan of surprise from my mouth. My entire body tenses as I come hard. When I'm done, I feel empty and exhausted.

A few minutes later, I crawl into my bed and shove my face into my pillow with a sigh.

I don't know what I'm doing right now, but if I hoped a good wank was going to be enough to calm me down, I was deluding myself. I'm Séverin Montcroix, for fuck's sake. Since when have I been the kind of guy to sit and wallow and feel sorry for myself with my cock in my hand? I've never been a one-girl type of guy, so this little fixation needs to stop.

Before I fall asleep, I make myself a solemn promise: tomorrow night, I'm going to make my way to a girl's room—Mellie, her friend, any girl that wants me—and drive every thought of Anaïs out of my system once and for all.

BOTTLE OF WINE IN hand, I leave my room. Mellie's room is down the corridor—having to go past Anaïs's room on my way there feels satisfyingly symbolic—and she already knows I'm coming. I'm going to get us both tipsy and have slow, lazy sex all over her bedroom.

After that, I'll be back to my old self. I'll finally be able to think more clearly.

I'm creeping down the corridor when a cold draft slithers past me. I shiver and peer through the gloom. The window at the end of the corridor is cracked open. Is someone on the balcony? Maybe some students have snuck out for a cheeky joint or cig?

Tiptoeing down the corridor, I peer through the glass. There's someone sitting on the balcony. Even though she's wearing a big baggy hoodie and has her back to me, I recognise her immediately. How could I not?

I stand at the window and watch for a bit.

Anaïs is sitting cross-legged, as usual. Her canvas is propped against the wooden pillars of the balustrade. She's painting, her paintbrush gliding smoothly across the surface of her canvas. Now and again, she pauses. Her head tilts up, facing away from me and towards the mountains and the stars.

She seems so... serene. Almost absent. Like she's only half-here.

Pushing the sliding door as quietly as I can, I step onto the balcony. She mustn't have heard me because she carries on painting. The process is strangely fascinating. The way she dips the paintbrush in her little plastic cup of murky water, swirls it, then squishes the wet end on her thigh to let the excess water run free. Underneath her big hoodie, she's wearing a pair of plain grey shorts. The water from her paintbrush slides down her bare leg, leaving a trail that glimmers in the starlight.

She pushes the wet brush into the squirts of paint, mixing her colours on the surface of her palette. It's a wonder she can see any colours in this darkness. I doubt starlight is enough for her to differentiate the shades and hues she's using. But maybe that's the appeal.

Once she's happy with the colour on her brush, she paints. In long, gliding strokes, then in short, feathery flicks. Sometimes she pauses and wipes something with a little finger or scratches at something with the pointy end of her paintbrush.

The longer I watch her, the more I envy her.

It's never something I expected to feel towards her. But she seems so at peace, so lost in her work, so... content. She's completely alone, sitting in the dark on a cold balcony, but she doesn't seem lonely or sad. Somehow, Anaïs has this ability to transport herself to a place that's just her own. Even though she's so far away from home, even though she has neither friends nor allies here.

I'm beginning to suspect she's happy despite being alone, but also *because* of it.

And that's something I can't help but envy.

Chapter 17

La Vengeance

Séverin

As if sensing my presence, Anaïs turns, peering at me from the shadowy alcove of her hood. If she's still angry about what happened between us near the ruins, she hides it. When she sees me, a slight frown draws her eyebrows, more surprise than anything.

"Oh," she says. "It's you. How long have you been here?"

"I just came out," I lie.

She watches me for a second. Her body language remains unchanged, but there's an edge to her now. An invisible tension, a taut rope of unspoken things binding us. I sense her caution, too. Is she wondering if I'm going to attack her again? Does she suspect me of wanting to steal another kiss from her?

I do want that. I want a lot of things.

But this time, I'm coming in peace.

I hold my bottle of wine up. "Drink?"

Her eyes narrow. Now my gaze has adjusted to the darkness of the night, I can make out her face more clearly. Her cheeks and nose are flushed from the cold. There are little flecks and smears of paint on her chin, her cheeks. A white speck adorns the left corner of her lips like a beauty spot.

Anaïs seems to debate my offer for a second; I don't blame her for not trusting me. Finally, she nods. Maybe she's trying to pick her battles.

Lowering myself down onto the balcony, I take a seat next to her canvas, my back to the mountains and loch. I pop the bottle cork in my fist, stifling the sound. I'm not in the mood to disturb the stillness of this moment. Right now, I feel like an explorer who's stumbled into a dream-like fairyland. Any sudden motion or noise might send the world and its creature fading into golden vapour.

I take a sip straight from the bottle and hand it to Anaïs. I half-expect her to wipe the sleeve of her ridiculous hoodie on the neck rim, but she doesn't. She places her mouth right where mine just was—an indirect kiss—and drinks unceremoniously.

She licks her lips and passes me the bottle back with a nod. "It's good wine."

"Would you expect anything less?"

She looks away, a hint of a sneer on her lips. "Knowing you, I'd expect your family to own the vineyard that produced this wine."

A low laugh slips from me. "We do."

"Of course."

"I think you'd like Château Montcroix. I'll take you there sometime."

"I wouldn't dream of such an honour. Like a modern Cinderella."

"You're not Cinderella, trésor. You're the rich forest witch who lives with the bears and the birds."

"If only."

Rolling her eyes, Anaïs leans into her canvas and resumes painting. Watching her is quite fascinating. Her face, which is normally like the smooth, unmoved surface of a lake, comes alive when she's painting.

She widens her eyes, tilts her head. She purses her lips, bites them, chews on the insides of her mouth.

Glimpses of emotions appear and fade on her features. Surprise, affection, annoyance, sudden realisation, satisfaction, confusion. I wish I had my camera to capture and immortalise each expression, collect them like trophies.

"What are you painting?" I ask, genuinely curious.

Her eyes don't move away from her canvas, but she sits back and purses her lips in thought. She taps the handle of her paintbrush against the little cushion of her mouth. "I'm... not sure yet."

"Hm." I take another sip of wine. "Another reason photography should win the debate, then."

"Oh, really?"

I nod, even though she's still not looking at me. "Whatever you're painting can't be completely truthful if most of it is straight out of your head."

"Because thoughts are lies? Imagination is deception?"

"I'm not saying that."

She finally looks up. "What are you saying, then?" She takes the bottle from my hand. "Go on, I want to know. If you're going to win the debate fair and square, then you're going to have to work harder."

She takes another swig of the wine. Her head tilts back as she drinks, exposing the graceful line of her neck before it disappears inside her hoodie. When she's done, she wipes her mouth with her sleeve but keeps the bottle in her hand. "Well?"

I lean towards her. "Are you really picking a fight with me? On the one time I'm being nice?"

"I'm not picking a fight." She gives me a nice, false smile. "You might not know this, but I'm not the kind of person to pick fights."

I ignore the obvious reference to our little scuffle on the forest floor—it's not somewhere I want my mind to go right now.

"I did not know this, no," I say instead in my sweetest voice. "I don't know much about the kind of person you are. We might be strangers for all I know about you. It's a wonder we're even engaged at all, isn't it?"

She chuckles, a surprisingly girlish sound, almost coquettish. "You make it sound like you're engaged to a stranger. That sounds very old-fashioned—practically mediaeval."

"I even hear there's going to be a display of a bloody bedsheet in the grand hall of the Montcroix family home."

She takes another sip of the wine and hands me the bottle back, shaking her head as she swallows. "Don't joke about that. I actually wouldn't put it past your crazy family. Aristocrats are unhinged."

"Hey, now, come on." I smirk. "We're the modern *bourgeoisie*, a true feminist institution, don't you know."

"There's not a feminist bone in your body."

I shrug. "You might think I'm the devil in disguise, but even Satan would admit all genders deserve equal political and social rights."

Plopping her brush into its plastic cup of milky water, she rests her hands on the balcony floor between us. She leans her weight on her arms as she leans closer, peering into my face.

"Is that the line that gets all the girls into your bed?" she asks in a low, mocking voice.

I can't draw away from her because my head is already resting against the wooden posts of the balustrade, but I have no desire to. Her proximity isn't unpleasant; I can smell that delicate French summer scent of hers, the fragrance of wine on her breath, the chemical smells of her paints and varnish.

"I don't need lines to get all the girls into my bed," I assure her. "I have my face for that."

"I'm not sure your face is that reliable," she points out. Her tone is quite serious, but there's a glint in her eyes that isn't just starlight.

I raise my eyebrows and give her a look. "Oh, it's reliable."

She gives me a grin. It's a little crooked, a little fey.

"If it was," she says, "you wouldn't have to steal kisses, would you?"

Is she being serious or not? She's looking straight into my eyes, and her face is inches from mine, but it's too dark to read her properly. Not that I've ever been able to read her in broad daylight, anyway.

If she hated being kissed so much, she wouldn't get so close now, would she? Someone that's been burned isn't likely to put their hand anywhere near a flame.

"I would hardly call that a kiss," I say with a shrug, looking her right in the eyes to gauge her reaction. "More of a peck, really."

"A peck is something you'd give to a sister or cousin, not a fiancée."

I grin. "Exactly."

Her eyes narrow. "I suppose this doesn't surprise me. Inbreeding is a defining feature of French aristocracy."

"Oh, ouch," I say blankly. "*Toutou* is scratching at me with her little claws."

"You bite, I scratch. Fair, no?"

"Maybe." Grabbing her chin, I push her face to the side. Two red half-moons are still imprinted on her cheek. "Looks like I left a mark."

She pulls away and points at the three slight finger-shaped bruises on my cheek and temple. "So did I."

"Does that mean we've evened the scores?" I ask.

I don't resent her for slapping me any more than I regret kissing and biting her. In Spearcrest, there's nobody to challenge me, deny me. I thought I loved that, but this is far more interesting and fun. I don't want Anaïs to stop fighting me any more than I want to stop fighting her.

She shakes her head. "Not quite. I still owe you one for that stolen kiss."

"Fine, you can steal it back." I give a dramatic sigh and tilt my face towards hers. "Go on, then. I'll pretend I don't even know you're here. I'll act ever so shocked and scandalised."

"Alright," she says.

I close my eyes and purse my lips, amused by the idea of Anaïs stealing a kiss from me. It's cute that she thinks of it as stealing kisses. It's cute that she thinks she could ever steal a kiss from me. Does she not realise that if she asked, I'd go down on her right here on this balcony?

Something cold and wet swipes across my lips. My eyes fly open. For a moment, I wonder if she's just licked me. She's staring at me with wide eyes, biting her lip as she holds back a laugh. In her hand is her largest paintbrush, shaking from the force of her suppressed laughter.

I touch my lips and look down at my fingers. They're covered in paint.

"You sneaky little shit!"

I swipe my fingers at her face, but she scoots back. She catches my wrist in her free hand.

"*Now* we're even," she says, her voice squeaky with amusement, trembling with laughter. She extends her hand out to me. "Deal?"

"Sure." I take her proffered hand and yank, pulling her to me as I tilt my head. I press my lips to hers, smearing paint all over her mouth. I move back with a grin. "*Now* we are."

She doesn't bother to wipe the paint from her mouth. She swipes her fingers across her palette. I try to jerk back, but not in time. She runs her wet fingers over my face, forehead to chin. She glances down at my torso—my black designer jumper.

"Don't you *fucking* dare," I snarl.

With a high, wild laugh, she presses her palm into my chest. I look down at the three lines of paint she's left behind. Then I look back up, fixing her with a deadly glare.

"That's Dior! Now you've really fucked up."

She scrambles back, still laughing, out of my reach. She tries to stand up, but I'm quicker than her. Grabbing her plastic cup of mucky water, I toss it at her, paintbrushes and all. She throws her arms up with a cry, but it hits her square on the chest.

I climb to my feet, and we stand on opposite sides of the balcony. She drops her arms and looks down at her drenched hoodie. Then she looks back up at me. We stare at each other.

And then she shatters into laughter.

"Worth it," she has the audacity to say.

Her laughter is contagious. I try to resist it, but she looks ridiculous in her shorts and drenched hoodie, paint all over her laughing mouth. My face cracks into a smile.

"Fucking nutcase," I say, shaking my head. "Come on, trésor. Let's get you cleaned up before you catch pneumonia. I don't want a dead wife on my hands."

"I'm not your wife," she mutters, but she follows me away from the balcony. Her voice is still full of mirth.

"Not yet."

The words ring true when I say them, which takes me by surprise.

We close the balcony door and sneak down the corridor. It's not until we get to my door that I realise I completely forgot about my plans to visit Mellie.

Chapter 18

L'Orgueil

Anaïs

Séverin's hand is warm around mine as he leads me into his bathroom. It's strange to see him in this sort of mood. Laughter makes him seem more youthful, more alive. It makes his green eyes sparkle like multi-faceted gems.

In his bathroom, he runs a towel under hot water and washes the paint off my face. He's surprisingly gentle, and I can't help but hold my breath while he rubs the towel over my lips. They tingle when he's done. I lick them quickly, just to moisten them. His eyes follow the movement.

With the messy lines of paint down his face, he looks a little feral. He steps into me, his throat shuddering as he swallows.

"Trésor." His voice is a sigh.

"Stop calling me that," I whisper.

"Make me."

My breath is short. I shouldn't have come back to his room with him. I take the towel from his hand and rub it across his mouth, wiping away the paint smeared there. Desire unfurls inside me like vines, growing leaves and flowers.

I glance up. Séverin's eyes are fixed on mine. Green like pale moss, like Japanese jadeite, green like evil spells in fairy tales.

"Don't make me beg you," he says suddenly, his voice a rasp.

"I don't want you to beg me," I reply.

"What do you want?" he asks, drawing me to him by my waist.

I don't like lying, but I don't think I dare tell the truth. So I don't do either. I throw my arms around his neck, and I kiss him.

He gasps against my mouth. His mouth is soft as a blooming rose under mine. He parts his lips and sweeps his tongue against mine, pouring liquid flames into me, trickling through my stomach and between my legs.

He moves back, dragging me with him. We half-kiss, half-stumble into his bedroom until we almost reach his bed. I place my hands on his chest and push him away. He looks at me with hooded eyes, kiss-drunk and sensual.

"I'm drenched," I say haltingly. "I should go change."

"Take it off," he replies, pressing his lips to my cheek and tugging on the hem of my hoodie.

"I'll be cold," I tell him. He catches my earlobe between his teeth and bites down lightly. I close my eyes with a shudder. "I should go."

"I'll keep you warm," he rasps against my ear. "Stay."

I sigh as he kisses down my neck, sucking on the sensitive skin. There are so many reasons I shouldn't stay, but I can't think of one. He tugs on my hoodie, pulling it over my head. Underneath it, my thin bralette is wet too, my nipples hard from the cold. Sev's eyes darken as he gazes at them.

Instead of taking my bra off, he pushes me down into a sitting position at the edge of his bed and kneels between my legs. He takes my waist in his hands, pulls me towards him, and presses his mouth to the hollow place between my collarbones. He kisses a wet, warm line down my chest, between my breasts, until I can't help but arch into him, every nerve alive with sensation. My entire body is a taut violin string, singing with want.

He finally pulls down my bra straps, exposing my breasts. They're cold and sodden, and I suppress a shiver. Sev looks up with a lazy grin.

"Don't worry, trésor." He palms my breasts, rubbing his thumbs over the nipples. "I'll warm you right up." He kisses each breast tenderly. "I'll get you nice and hot and *wet*."

"Stop," I gasp, my face burning with embarrassment.

"Stop what?" His tone is arrogant. He sucks one of my nipples into his mouth, and I let out a whimper. "Stop this?" His mouth moves to my other nipple. He licks it, his tongue soft and hot. I'm so turned on I ache. "Or this?"

"Stop talking," I hiss. I unhook my bra and throw it aside. Grabbing his paint-smeared jumper, I pull it over his head. He lets me, laughing as I pull on his T-shirt. Underneath it, his skin is smooth and constellated with dark beauty spots. I grab his shoulders. "Come on."

I try to pull him up, but he resists, kissing me instead.

"No, trésor," he murmurs against my mouth. "Not yet." He pushes me onto my back with a firm hand and drags my shorts down my hips. "I want to taste you." He kisses my lower stomach, my hips, my inner thighs. "I want to taste how wet you are."

"Please," I choke out, covering my eyes with my hands, my hips squirming in his grip. I'm so turned on I feel like I could come just from his words. "Stop talking."

"No." He bites lightly on my inner thigh and laughs, low and devious. "I want to fuck you with my tongue and make you come so hard I send you back to the stars."

And then he does exactly that.

In a few short and exquisite minutes, I learn exactly why Séverin Montcroix walks the world with such self-assurance. He's not just beautiful and charismatic or talented at photography. He's also incredibly skilled with his mouth.

He feasts on me with eagerness and abandon, like he's starving and I'm the only thing that can keep him alive. He licks and sucks and responds to every noise of pleasure I make like it's a holy commandment.

When I'm so close to orgasm that my hips grow still and my back arches off the bed, he lets out a low, humming laugh and works me with his fingers until I'm whimpering, every muscle tensed.

Then he licks me, deep and slow and rhythmical, and I come so hard my entire body shakes. My hips buck, but Séverin keeps me firmly pinned with one hand, working me with his fingers and tongue until I slump against him, a wet, shuddering mess.

He looks up at me. His lips and chin are wet, the lines of paint still crossing his forehead and cheeks. His eyes are bright and wild, his feral grin dripping with arrogance and danger.

"*Tu aimes ça?*" he asks roughly.

Do you like that?

"*Qu—quoi?*" I ask, dazed with pleasure, still trembling all over.

"*My langue, my bouche. Ma tête entre tes cuisses?*" His grin widens. "*Tu aimes ça?*"

My tongue, my mouth. My head between your thighs.

"*Oui,*" I whisper.

"You should never have rejected me, then," he says, wiping his hand across his mouth and rocking up to his feet.

"I didn't reject you." I prop myself up on my elbows with a frown. "You were drunk."

"We're drunk now," he points out.

I frown. "No, we're not." I sit up. "Why are you starting a fight?"

"I'm not starting a fight." He shrugs. "I just want you to admit you were wrong for rejecting me."

"Are you serious?" I get to my feet, my shaking legs almost buckling under me. "I can't believe you're doing this right now. You're really choosing your pride over sex?"

"I'm not choosing anything," he says with a hateful little smirk. "Admit you were wrong, and then we can fuck."

"I don't *want* to fuck you." I throw him a glare and angrily grab the nearest piece of clothing, one of his stupid black designer jumpers.

"Oh, yes you do," he replies. "*Petite menteuse*—little liar. Who's being proud now?"

I pull his jumper on and storm to his door. "You really are the worst."

"Still made you come, though." He rakes me with a look, naked lust in his eyes. "And now you won't be able to get the thought of me out of your head."

I wrench his door open and give him the middle finger. "Arrogant asshole!"

"Prideful little witch." He answers my gesture by blowing me a kiss. "*Pense à moi la prochaine fois que tu te touches, mon trésor.*"

Think of me next time you touch yourself.

"Fuck you!" I slam the door on him.

He laughs from behind the door. "Fuck me yourself."

ON THE LAST DAY of the residential, I ask Miss Godrick if I can take the coach back, and she informs me that there are more than enough spaces. The trip back to Spearcrest is long and uncomfortable, but it's better than sharing a car with Séverin after everything that happened between us.

As much as I loved the Isle of Skye, with its craggy mountains, misty lakes and windswept moors, I firmly decide to forget all about it. I made mistakes there, which I intend to keep there. Once I return to Spearcrest, I need to focus on my plan and avoid any further mistakes.

I can imagine that's easier said than done, but I'm determined.

Life at Spearcrest resumes, cold and grey and bleak but familiar now. I resume my lessons, my quiet afternoons hidden away in the little art studio. Aside from the occasional encounter with Kayana Kilburn, who checks on me and invites me out now and again, I keep myself to myself.

Kay's kindness is not lost on me, nor does it go unappreciated. I know she's trying to be nice, trying to make me feel like I belong in Spearcrest. I politely decline all her invitations. Parties and drunk indiscretions are not part of my plan.

I manage to stick to the plan and stay out of trouble for almost two weeks.

Then a voice calls out to me on my way out of art class one afternoon. I'm so startled I almost drop my armful of school books. I spin around.

Séverin is leaning in the doorway of the photography classroom. His shirt sleeves are folded back, his arms crossed, and there's a dangerous grin on his face.

I turn away quickly.

"Trésor." There's a dark warning in his voice. "Don't make me chase you; you know I will."

I pause, considering my options. Would Séverin chase me through the corridors of Spearcrest and tackle me to the marble floors in front of everyone?

Probably.

I turn back to him with a sigh.

"Good girl," he says. "Now come here."

Although he doesn't raise his voice, it carries clearly over the bustle of the corridor. A few students look up, wide-eyed, glancing between us. He pierces them with a glare, and they hurry away, a silent reminder of the power he holds in this place.

I obey him reluctantly, approaching him in slow, cautious steps.

"What do you want?"

He gestures impatiently. "Just come."

I follow him into the classroom, where he leads me to a computer. Rolling the seat towards me, he points to it. "Sit down."

I drop my pile of schoolbooks and my bag on a desk and do what he says. There's no point in starting a fight with him, especially now we're back in his territory. And especially not after what happened last time.

When I'm in the desk chair, he rolls it towards the desk and says, "Right. What do you think?"

I look at the computer screen. A gallery of black and white images awaits my attention. Clicking through them, I immediately recognise the mountains, the lake, the castle ruins, the trees. I look back up at him.

"Are those the pictures you took for the assignment?"

He nods, and I turn back to the screen. The collection is strong: all the shots are moody, murky, misty—full of character. Naked tree branches like black skeletons against a backdrop of bruised clouds; a close-up of the lake, where the water is obsidian, and spiky sedges pierce the surface like needles; a wide shot of the mountain, wreathed in mist and blurred by a veil of rain.

"Well?" Séverin prompts. He turns the chair so I'm facing him. He leans on the armrests, trapping me between him and the chair, and peers into my face. "What do you think?"

"They're great shots," I tell him.

He narrows his eyes. His eyelashes are so thick it almost looks like he's wearing eyeliner. I can smell his perfume, feel the warmth exuding from his skin. "Are you just saying that because you can't be bothered debating for the assignment?"

I shake my head. "No. Your pictures are excellent. I thought the same thing when you showed me your camera roll that time. You're very talented. You have a brilliant eye for composition."

For a second, he just stares at me, eyes narrowed in mistrust.

He clearly doesn't believe what I'm telling him, but all I can think about is how close he is. The warmth of him, the intensity of him. His intoxicating smell: expensive leather and comforting sandalwood. By now, I should be able to recognise all those things as signs of danger.

Because physical proximity to Séverin Montcroix never ends well.

"Look," I say firmly. I plaster myself back in my chair, creating as much distance as possible between us. "If I didn't like your photography, I'd just say it."

He nods slowly but finally pulls away. I almost breathe a sigh of relief, but then he continues. "Alright. So when are we going to work on the assignment, then?"

Did I just mishear him? Or have I stepped through some inter-dimensional crack and into a parallel universe?

Because out of all the things I expected the least from Séverin, it would be him caring about schoolwork or that he would bother taking the time to work on an assignment together.

Unlike Séverin, I actually need to do well in this assignment. I need a strong essay, and most importantly, I need some amazing paintings. Miss Godrick told us about the end-of-year exhibition award and the grant that comes with it.

I didn't lie when I told Séverin I'm not a billionaire—my parents are. Because the moment Noël moved away, they cut him off, and I'm pretty sure the same fate awaits me. If I win the exhibition award, it would mean a lot more to me than an ego boost from governors. It would mean the grant—enough money to start afresh in Japan without being a burden to Noël.

My art means everything to me. One day, it will pay for my way in the world. If I won this award, I'd be earning this money with my art. It would be a dream come true.

I have every intention of making that dream a reality. And Séverin, with his caprices and his games, would only get in the way of that.

"Look, we don't have to work on this together," I say cautiously. "You've got your photographs, and I've got my sketches. We can both do our work separately and just pretend we've done it together."

He shakes his head. "No, let's do it properly. Photography is the only thing I'm actually good at. I want a good grade on this. Even if the assignment is stupid."

"It's not stupid."

He rolls his eyes. "If you won't admit it's stupid, then you have to at least admit this whole *Aletheia* thing is incredibly pretentious."

"Why, because it's a Latin word?"

"Because it's pointless. Do you think successful photographers care about the philosophical meaning of truth?"

"I don't think you can fairly accuse every successful photographer of not questioning their art form and its meaning. Just because you're repulsed by the idea of introspection doesn't mean everybody is."

He glares at me. "Introspection isn't what we were talking about."

I shrug and try to get out of my chair. He's still standing too close for me to get up without having to push past him.

"I'm pretty sure the whole point of the assignment is introspection," I point out.

"Ugh, you artists and your delusions of grandeur." He gives an exaggerated sigh. "Fine. We'll introspect on it later. Meet at the library tomorrow after class?"

I nod, suppressing a sigh. "Fine."

He flaps a hand at me, dismissing me with all the authority of a beautiful, tragic king. "See you there."

"Sure." I scramble off my chair, grab my things and make my escape before he can say anything else.

As relieved as I am that he seems to be completely ignoring what happened the last time we saw each other, I don't quite trust it.

Because everything with him feels like some twisted, perverse game. Because Séverin is someone who's proven himself to be just as prone to violence as he is to courtesy, aggression as he is to sweetness. Even when he went down on me on his bed, it seemed to be an act of mixed desire and defiance, domination and tenderness.

Being around him throws me off-balance, like walking in quicksand. I don't trust him but, more than that, I don't trust myself when I'm around him.

Hopefully, he'll stand me up at the library tomorrow, and I'll be free to work on the assignment on my own, at a safe distance from him. If we keep each other at arm's length, I might actually stand a chance at making it through the year with minimal damage.

That night, I get a text from Noël.

Noël: How are things going with the *Roi Soleil*?

I bite the inside of my cheeks, debating what to answer. I decide to go for the truth, though not in its complete form.

Anaïs: Surprisingly well.

He sends a shocked emoji, then a text.

Noël: You're not falling in love, are you?

My heart skips a beat. For a second, I feel almost disoriented. I'm not falling for Sev, but I also don't completely hate him. Even after everything that's happened. I send Noël the green-faced emoji.

Anaïs: Obviously not."

Noël: Just checking. Remember the plan, *ma p'tite étoile*.

Anaïs: I remember.

Chapter 19

LA PIÈCE DE RÉSISTANCE

Séverin

The Spearcrest library is the most renowned part of campus. It's over a hundred years old, enormous and ornate. Inside, everything gleams and glows like warm gold.

It's not a place I spend a lot of time in. Being surrounded by self-satisfied try-hards isn't exactly my idea of a good time. This is the kind of place where people like Sophie Sutton, the prefect Evan's obsessed with, spend all their time. People like Zach and his Theodora, who probably have all sorts of arguments in hushed tones amongst old tomes.

I can't think of anything worse than bumping into any of them.

Still, when I reach the top floor where I told Anaïs to meet me, I can't help the surge of pleasure warming my chest. After what happened on the trip, I half-expected her to find an excuse to avoid meeting me, but there she is, sitting cross-legged on her chair like a little goblin, her sketchbook propped on the desk, her laptop open. She's wearing a baggy hoodie over her uniform.

It reminds me of the hoodie I peeled off her that night when I finally got to see the colour of her nipples and taste her pussy. I still have that hoodie—her shorts, too. I keep them in my drawer like a prize, a trophy.

Part of me hopes she'll come and claim them.

Any excuse to lure her back into my room.

I draw a deep breath to calm myself down and tiptoe across the wooden floor. Anaïs always puts me in the mood for mischief, for playing games. For other things, too... Sneaking up behind her, I wrap my hands around her neck and whisper in her ear. "Boo."

"Oh no," she sing-songs, "a sadomasochist ghost!"

I give her neck a little squeeze and let go with some reluctance. "There's not a sadomasochist bone in my body, trésor."

She looks up as I pull up the seat next to hers. She points at the faint bite mark on her cheek. "This feels pretty sadomasochistic."

"It was self-defence. You hit me first."

"You wanted me to hit you. Sadomasochist."

"And you liked hitting me." I smirk, plonking my backpack down on the desk, and sitting down. "I think you might be the sadomasochist, trésor."

"I don't like pain," she says levelly. "I'm a normal person. I like feeling good."

"If you did"—I smirk—"you wouldn't have run away from my bedroom that night."

She glares at me, colour rising to her cheeks. "I didn't run away."

"Sure you did," I say sweetly. "You still need to give me back my jumper, by the way."

"And you've still got my hoodie," she retorts.

"Your shorts, too," I add. "You're not getting either back."

"Then you're not getting your jumper back either," she says with a shrug. "I'm going to wear it to keep me warm while I paint."

"Give me my jumper back and paint naked." I smirk. "I'll keep you warm instead."

"Only if you do so by setting yourself on fire."

Her words are harsh, but she's not angry. My chair is close enough to hers that our shoulders are almost brushing. She could pull away if she wanted, put distance between us, but she doesn't.

Maybe it's because she doesn't dare or because she doesn't want me to think I intimidate her. Being with Anaïs is like playing a fucked-up game of chicken. We're both daring each other to be the first one to pull away, but we're also daring each other to get closer.

"If I set myself on fire," I say, leaning into her, "then who would lick your cute pussy and make you come the way I did?"

"Shut up!" She pushes me away, staring around frantically. "Lower your voice! You have such a dirty mouth."

I let her push me away, my grin widening. "You didn't mind my dirty mouth last time."

"I'm not here to talk about it," she hisses. Then she narrows her eyes and leans forward, lowering her voice to an angry whisper. "You're not about to get laid in the library, so don't even think about it."

It's not what I had in mind—I was genuinely just trying to wind her up. But now she's mentioned it, I doubt I'll be able to think of anything else for the rest of the evening.

"You're far too loud for the library, though I suppose I'd enjoy the challenge." I pull my laptop out of my bag and set it next to hers. I throw her a sidelong glance. "Are you sure I can't tempt you? Quickie in the Ancient Philosophy section?"

She rolls her eyes. "I'm sure."

I give a tragic sigh. "Shame. I've always fantasised about sneaky library sex."

"I'm sure you'll have no problem finding someone else to tempt."

I turn back to her, startled. She's resumed typing on her laptop, her expression a blank mask. Was she being sarcastic or sincere—or both?

"You want me to sleep with other girls?"

"I don't really care what you do."

"But *if* I slept with other girls," I insist, "you wouldn't care?"

She frowns and looks up. She seems surprised by my serious tone. "No. Why should I?"

"Because we're engaged?"

"It's not a real engagement, though, is it?" Her tone is bone-chillingly calm, her body language unbothered. "You might be my fiancé, but you're not my *boyfriend*."

I stare at her for a second. That delicate face, those pretty eyes. The smooth façade of her, unruffled by emotions. That baggy hoodie and the body I know is underneath it. I understand the logic of what she's saying.

But I'm not happy about it.

Because if I can do what I want, then she, too, can do whatever she wants. Or whoever she wants.

And I realise with stone-cold certainty that I will break someone's hand from their body before I ever let them touch her.

Anaïs brings our focus back to the assignment after that, and I let her. Now is not the time or the place for me to process the painful realisation that I want to keep Anaïs to myself when she doesn't feel the same way about me. I'm going to need to wrestle with that particular problem later.

Anaïs turns her laptop to me and shows me her gallery of work. I scroll through it, scrutinising her sketches and paintings in the hope of distracting myself.

Her art is the opposite of her: bursting with life, with emotion, with creativity. Her outward appearance, that plain shoulder-length hairstyle, her neutral features, bare of make-up—they're all in stark contrast to the complex, ornate quality of her work.

I stop on one of her paintings.

It's a huge, complex image. Mountains and a sky swirling madly with stars and a lake, all merging one into the other in rich shades of blue, purple and indigo. In the centre of the painting is the silhouette of a face, almost ghostly. Dreamy eyes in a bed of thick eyelashes and a mouth fallen half open and smeared with stars.

"What's this one?" I ask Anaïs, unable to tear my eyes from the image.

She leans a little closer to look over my shoulder. A strand of her hair brushes against me.

"Oh," she says. "That's the painting I did on the balcony."

"The one you were working on when I was there?"

"Mm-hm."

"You went back for it?" I ask, remembering how we left it behind when I took her to my room.

"Of course."

I finally tear my gaze from the image and turn to look at her. "Is this... is that supposed to be me?"

She lets out a low laugh. "Yes. I suppose you could say that's *Aletheia* you."

I look back at *Aletheia* me. The dreamy eyes, the sensual mouth, the smear of stars on the lips and chin. There's even a faint outline of bruising on the cheek—the marks her fingers had left on my cheek that day. Her brushstrokes are so expressive, and the beauty in the image is breathtaking.

My chest constricts; my heartbeat quickens.

"It looks nothing like me," I say, clicking away from the image.

"It's not meant to look like you," she says serenely. "It's meant to look the way you felt to me that night."

I click back to the image. "What, like some sort of feral fairy prince?"

She bursts out laughing. A real, genuine laugh, where she covers her mouth and her eyes crease.

"That's—" She interrupts herself with another peal. "That's exactly it, yes."

"You're just trying to mock me." I glare at her. "Is this payback for... for what we did? Or for the thing in the forest? The stupid stolen fucking kiss?"

She shakes her head, and her laughter fades from her face. "No, don't worry. I still owe you for that."

I pull a face at her. "I'm shaking in my boots."

"You *should* be shaking in your boots." She smirks. "Your pointy boots."

I shake my head in disbelief. "Your sense of humour is fucking trash."

"At least I have one."

I give her the middle finger. She returns the favour.

"Are we going to do some work?" she asks. "Or shall we keep trading insults?"

"The assignment is due next week, so we should probably get some work done," I say. "You couldn't keep up with me, anyway."

She gives me a look.

"I was talking about trading insults. Get your mind out of the gutter, trésor."

An annoyed expression flashes across her face, but she purses her lips shut, as if she's holding back the words she wants to say. I glance at her pursed mouth. Her pout is perfectly kiss-shaped.

I glance away. Not the train of thought I need to be following right now.

With great reluctance, I get to work.

In the end, we settle on the idea that there are different interpretations of truth and that fine art expresses a wider array of those interpretations.

It's a pretentious idea and absolute bullshit, of course. I don't believe for one second that a fairy prince painting of me is more truthful than any given photograph I have of Anaïs. But there's a sort of moving conviction to Anaïs's ideas that's weirdly compelling. Most importantly, I'm confident Weston will eat this shit right up.

I don't even mind losing the debate to Anaïs, and to her credit, she's graceful in her victory. She doesn't gloat the way I would have. Once we've exchanged notes, she closes her laptop and stands up.

"Where are you going?" I ask, looking up in surprise.

"I've got everything I need now. Until the exhibit, all we need to do is write up our essays, but we can do that on our own, right?"

"Don't you want to discuss the exhibit?"

"No, students are doing separate displays." She frowns. "Did your teacher not tell you?"

"He told us, yeah. Something about some stupid prize."

"Stupid or not"—she grins—"I intend to win that prize. So I'm not going to give you a chance at sabotaging my display, thank you very much."

I lean back in my chair to get a proper look at her as she packs her stuff away. A strand of hair is tucked behind her ear. Her lips gleam slightly from the Carmex she's just put on.

"Since when do you care about prizes?" I ask.

"I don't. I care about that lovely grant that comes along with it."

"What do you need that grant for? You're rich."

"I'm not rich," she says. "My parents are rich."

"Only rich kids say that," I sneer.

"You don't say that," she points out, slinging her backpack on her shoulder.

She gives me a little wave and starts walking away, but I grab her elbow. "You better not use that stupid painting of me for your display!"

"Oh no?" She leans over me so quickly my heart leaps in my chest. She speaks into my ear. "Too bad. It's going to be my pièce de résistance."

I turn my head, hoping to catch her cheek with a kiss, but she's already pulled away, yanking her arm out of my grip.

"You better not!" I call after her in a whisper-shout. "You better throw it away!"

She turns back, a wicked grin on her lips.

"Make me," she mouths.

And then she runs off.

Chapter 20

La Cigarette

Séverin

I'm smiling to myself on my way back from the library when a voice speaks up from the darkness.

"Having fun?"

I turn around. Iakov lurks in the shadows like an expressionless statue, his shoulder propped against a cedar trunk. A cigarette dangles between his lips, and he's in a T-shirt and jeans despite the icy cold. A flurry of new scratches and bruises mark his face, neck and arms.

"What do you mean?" I ask, veering off the path to the sixth form boys' building to join Iakov under the tree.

He hands me a cigarette and shrugs. "With your girl."

"She's not my girl." I take the cigarette and light it. I can already tell I'm going to need a cigarette for this conversation. "What kind of fun are you talking about?"

"Any kind." His expression is so neutral that I can't tell what his end goal is. To tease me? Mock me? Lead me into a trap?

"No fun. We've just been paired up for an assignment, that's it."

"The assignment from your trip?"

I shrug. "Yeah, that one."

"The trip you drove her to?"

"Yeah, that one." I cast him a glare. What is he trying to get at?

"What happened on that trip?"

"Nothing."

"Right."

Iakov nods slowly, his gaze resting on my face. What's with the interrogation? I would honestly rather deal with Evan's dumb questions or Zachary's dry, devastating remarks over this stone-faced questioning. It's like having a conversation with Anaïs, minus the unbearable sexual tension.

I narrow my eyes at him. "What is it? Spit it out."

"What's going on between you two?"

"What's going on between us two? Nothing, absolutely nothing. What could happen? She's pretentious and annoying—and she's, she's not my type, anyway. I didn't choose this engagement—you know I didn't—we've just been paired up for this stupid assignment, but it's done now, so things are back to normal."

"Right," Iakov says again. "Pembroke told everyone he was her original partner, and you made him swap."

That prick. Although it doesn't surprise me that he's running his mouth, it still pisses me off. I make a mental note to give him a little reminder to stay out of Young King business.

"Who cares what Parker fucking Pembroke is saying?" I ask, hoping my tone carries nothing but disdain.

"He wants your little fiancée," Iakov points out. "I can tell."

"He'll have to kill me to get her," I snap.

Iakov lifts a black eyebrow. His grey eyes are piercing. "Right..."

The silence stretches and lingers like cigarette smoke. It becomes heavy and stifling. I flick the ashes off the tip of my cigarette and let out a sigh of irritation.

"Look. Just because I don't want her doesn't mean I want anybody else to have her. Nobody gets to have what's mine. Especially not some limp-wristed loser like Parker."

He nods and says nothing. He doesn't look convinced—he doesn't look much like anything. The more I think about it, the more I realise Iakov is exactly like Anaïs. They are both inscrutable, mysterious assholes who constantly mess with my head with their complete lack of emotion or expression.

Why should I have to feel every emotion so strongly when they get to feel none at all? Hardly seems fair.

"Say what you want to say," I spit, "and be done with it."

"If you love her," Iakov says, "you love her. So what?"

"So—does it look like I love her? Why would I love her?" I glare at him. "Love is a poison—I've been there before, why would I go there again?"

"Kayana wasn't the beginning and end of your world," Iakov grunts. "So she cheated on you. So what?"

Iakov is the only person who could bring this up without risking my fist crashing into their face.

"It's not about the cheating."

"Yes. Alright, so she turned down your proposal and refused to get engaged to you when you two were sixteen. It was a stupid idea anyway. And so, alright, it broke your heart. *So what?*" Iakov finishes his cigarette and throws the butt at the ground, stuffing his hands in his pockets. "You're going to let some stupid teenage relationship get in the way of this?"

"What's this?"

"This thing you have with your girl."

"She's not my girl."

"Your fiancée. Same thing."

I sigh and rub my hand across my face. I was in a great mood when I left the library, but my good cheer has been shot between the eyes and lies stone-cold dead at Iakov's feet. "You know I don't want this engagement."

"Break it, then."

"I can't. You of all people know it's not that easy going against your family."

He nods. "I'd still do it. For—" He interrupts himself and shakes his head slightly. "For the right person. I'd do it."

"Well—trust me when I say I can't break this engagement. I'm stuck with it and—"

"Then make her break it."

"No, I—" I stop in my tracks.

Make her break the engagement.

Could I do such a thing? She doesn't want it any more than I do, and she hates being in Spearcrest. She's never said so, but it couldn't be more obvious. If I had to guess where Anaïs would rather be, it would be somewhere vibrant or close to the sea. Anaïs would probably live a completely different life if she could. She would choose independence and freedom and art over the cushy, glittering life of the billionaire fiancée to the Montcroix heir.

Even if I convinced Anaïs to break the engagement or forced her hand to do so—then what?

My parents wouldn't just take their failed enterprise in their stride and move on. They'd be furious at me, to begin with, for costing them their businesses, their future alliance, their future billions. For letting the Nishihara heiress slip through my fingers.

But then they'd do damage control, shop around and find someone else. Use our name to lure in another billionaire heiress to keep us rich for generations to come.

Then I would find myself in the same situation, just with a different bride.

And as far as brides go, Anaïs isn't the worst I could do. She certainly won't look good photographed on my arm, and the gossip blogs will have endless fun cruelly criticising her style. I imagine her, bare-footed in some crazy outfit, dancing all by herself at one of my parents' galas. I imagine the horror on their faces, my mother's mouth dropping open at Anaïs's eccentric antics. That prospect doesn't displease me.

The prospect of a future with Anaïs doesn't displease me.

"I'll think about it," I say eventually, looking away from Iakov.

"Look, do what you want, man." Iakov's deep voice has an edge to it, an emotion I can't quite work out. "If you don't want her, get rid of her. If you want her, have her. Fuck Kayana, fuck your heartbreak, fuck pain. Life is for fucking and hurting. If you want to do that with your weird little bride, then do it. Fuck everything else."

I stare at him, surprised by this sudden outburst. For a man of few words, Iakov sure has no trouble making his opinions known when he wants to. I toss my cigarette into a bed of wet mud and mushy grass, and we head to the sixth form boys' building together.

We walk in silence the entire way, but his words weigh heavy on my mind for a long time after that.

Chapter 21

LE PORTRAIT

Anaïs

My first term at Spearcrest ends with a flurry of assignment deadlines, exams, and new snow. I wait for winter break with bated breath, half-hoping my parents will call me home to Aurigny, half-hoping they won't.

On the one hand, I'm dying to return home. Dying to see the white house in the hills, the sapphire sea, my friends. On the other hand, holidays have been particularly bleak in the Nishihara household since Noël left. It's always the same dilemma lately: I want to be home, but I dread seeing my parents.

In the end, my worries turn out to be a waste of time. On the first day of winter break, I get a curt text from my mum confirming I'll be staying at Spearcrest over the holidays.

It hurts, but there's no point in wallowing. I grab my sketchbook and pencils and head through the delicate snowfall to the Peace Garden. Sitting in the middle of the marble gazebo, I prop my sketchbook on my lap and start drawing, losing myself in the pencil strokes.

I start by drawing the outlines of dark trees against the moth-grey sky, but I end up doodling a face instead. Gorgeous features, sultry eyes, thick eyelashes. A lush mouth with a disdainful curling of the lip. Thick black hair falling romantically over one eye.

"What are you drawing?"

I look up with a start. Kayana Kilburn is strolling up the gazebo steps, a vision in the hazy winter daylight. She's wearing a cream sweater dress and thigh-high boots under a long camel coat. There are gold rings on her fingers, her nose, lining her ears, adorning her long braids.

She looks good enough to belong on the pages of a magazine, but the sparkle of glee is missing from her hazel eyes.

"Nothing," I say. "Are you alright? Not going home for the holidays?"

She shrugs and ambles closer. "Spearcrest might be depressing over the holidays, but trust me, my family would be more depressing."

I understand more than she thinks.

"I trust you," I tell her.

Scooting over to one side of my bench, I let her take a seat next to me. She glances at my sketchbook and looks back up at my face.

"Things going well with Sev?" she asks.

Her tone is light, but I sense something hidden beneath it.

"They could be worse," I answer.

She glances at me. Her make-up is a work of art: her eyelids shimmer, her eyeliner is symmetrical and perfectly tapered, her mouth is the colour of burnt caramel. But her eyes are a little red, as if she's been crying. She seems to want to say something but hesitates.

"Do you... like him?" I ask cautiously. "We're not together. In case you're wondering."

A laugh of surprise bursts from her. "Oh god, no!" She sighs. "We used to go out, but it didn't work out."

"Oh, I'm sorry to hear that."

"Don't be. We weren't compatible, and it didn't end well."

I say nothing. It's an odd feeling listening to this. Kay looks sad, and I have the impression she wants to talk. I didn't expect her confession, but it doesn't completely surprise me either. Séverin's reputation as a playboy is well-earned, and Spearcrest is full of beautiful girls, so of course he has a past here. And although I don't feel any dislike towards Kay—she was the first one to befriend me, and she seems so sad it hurts my heart—I still can't help the uncomfortable twisting sensation in my chest. It would seem I'm just not as indifferent as I wish I was hearing about this.

I've always known I wasn't Séverin's type, but Kay is a painful reminder of how different I am to the girls Séverin likes.

I know I shouldn't care. Comparing yourself to others is a quick poison, and I try not to drink it if I can help it.

"He wanted us to get engaged," Kay says. The words fall out of her mouth like she couldn't even help them. "He thought we were in love, and he wanted us to get engaged after we left Spearcrest. He thought we were the perfect couple, that we looked good together. I'm not sure he ever really saw the true me." She shakes her head. "I don't know why I'm telling you all this. I think you're perfect for him. It makes me feel better to know that I hurt him back then so that he could be happy now. With you."

"We're not together," I say quickly.

"You're engaged," she points out.

"It's an arranged engagement, it's not... it's not a real relationship. We barely get along." I gesture to her with a little smile. "Not sure if you can tell, but I'm not exactly his type."

She laughs. "You're not, but I think that's why he likes you." She takes my sketchbook and peers at the page. "This is amazing. You've really captured him, somehow." She returns the sketchbook, the sadness creeping back into her face. "You're very talented. Sev is a lucky guy. I hope that when I get engaged, I end up with someone like you."

Her sadness is disconcerting and a little heartbreaking. I point at my sketchbook.

"I can sketch you if you like," I tell her.

Her expression brightens. "Really?"

I nod and turn to a fresh page. Opening my pencil box, I select my 6B for thick, creamy lines. I sketch her messy and lush and full of life. Brilliant eyes, smooth, glowing skin, glossy lips. I draw her hair in a cascade of braids around her shoulders. Her expression is confident and fearless, but I leave the rue in her eyes.

When I'm done, I hand her my sketchbook. Her eyes widen.

"Oh!" she exclaims. "I look—I look beautiful."

I laugh. "You *are* beautiful."

She tilts her head, her eyes glued to the sketch. "I look kind of sad."

"Are you?"

She lets out a breath that's half-sigh, half-laugh. "I suppose I am, a little bit. I'm always sad during the holidays. It's so lonely here."

I speak before I can think. "Well, if you get lonely, you can come sit with me while I draw. I'll paint your portrait if you like."

Her eyes light up, and she suddenly crosses the space between us to kiss me on the cheek. "You're a star, Anaïs. I would love that."

A FEW DAYS LATER, I'm on my way to the library to work on some essays when a figure in black appears as if by magic in my path.

Séverin is wearing an oversized black turtleneck sweater and black slacks under a long black coat, looking like a gothic detective. There's a cigarette between his lips, and he's holding an elegant leather duffel bag.

"Trésor!" he calls, approaching me in a few quick strides. "I didn't know you were still here."

I shrug. "You should've asked."

He frowns. "You should've said."

"I didn't know you smoked." I point at his cigarette. "That's a disgusting habit."

"I know." He rolls his eyes but immediately tosses his cigarette to the floor and stomps on it. "I'm quitting."

I nod. "You should."

"Shit, I will, alright?" He licks his lips and gestures at me. "You're staying here over the holiday? Not going back to France?"

"I'm staying here," I say, keeping my voice neutral.

My family's state of affairs is none of his business, and this is not the time or place to be spilling my little mess of complicated feelings about going home.

But Séverin's eyes soften as if I've just told him I'm to be abandoned for the rest of my life. He steps closer.

"I'm spending Christmas with my family. Would you like to come? I'm flying by private jet. If you pack now, you could leave with me." He lets out a sheepish laugh. "It might be less peaceful than staying here, but it might be fun. Christmas with the Montcroixes. *Ça te dis?*"

I can't help but smile at him—a real smile. "Sounds like a very fancy affair. I'd take you up on your offer, but I have to stay. I've made plans."

He steps closer still. I can smell him, cigarettes and that warm, woody perfume of his. "Who with?"

"Nobody who's going to chase me through trees and steal kisses from me, if that's what you're worried about."

"As if I would ever worry about that," he says, but it sounds like a lie, and his eyes drop to my mouth like he can't even help it. "You don't need someone else to do that anyway, not when I'm doing such a fine job of it already."

"True." I chuckle and wave my hand. "No, I'm going to be working on a portrait of Kayana Kilburn."

"Oh." He frowns but doesn't step away. "You're hanging out with Kay?"

"Is that too weird?"

"Why would it be weird?"

I raise my eyebrows. "You know why."

We stare at each other in silence. He sighs.

"My relationship with Kay is long dead," he says. "I've moved on, as has she. Anyway"—he catches my chin on his fingers—"I spend too much time worrying about your irritating little ass to worry about the past. You better stay out of trouble while I'm gone."

"Nothing to worry about," I tell him, but I don't pull away. "I'll be resting, doing homework and painting. Not exactly high-octane stuff."

"Fine." His fingers trickle down my chin, caressing my neck with a featherlight touch. He rests his hand on my throat. "You'd better paint my portrait when I get back, though."

"I've already painted you."

"But that's not *my* painting." He pouts. "And I didn't get to sit for it."

"You just want a reason to force me to stare at you for ages."

He grins. "You already do that, it's totally embarrassing. Anyway, I want a portrait to hang in Château Montcroix."

"Fine." I smile up at him. "I'm not working for free, though."

"I'll think of a way to reward you," he says with a suggestive smirk. "I can think of many ways to reward you."

His phone rings, startling us both. We jump apart like we've been caught in a scandalous embrace. He grabs his phone from his pocket and glances at the screen. "Fuck. I have to go."

His cheeks are flushed—as flushed as mine feel.

"Well, see you soon," I say, making my retreat up the library stairs.

"Wait." He chases me and catches me by my hand, stopping me at the top of the stairs. Leaning down, he presses a light kiss to my cheek. " *Joyeux Noël*, trésor."

I turn my head and return the cheek kiss. "*Joyeux Noël*."

HIVER

"Si tu ne m'aimais pas, dis-moi, fille insensée,
Que balbutiais-tu dans ces fatales nuits ?
Exerçais-tu ta langue à railler ta pensée ?
Que voulaient donc ces pleurs, cette gorge oppressée,
Ces sanglots et ces cris ?"

Alfred de Musset

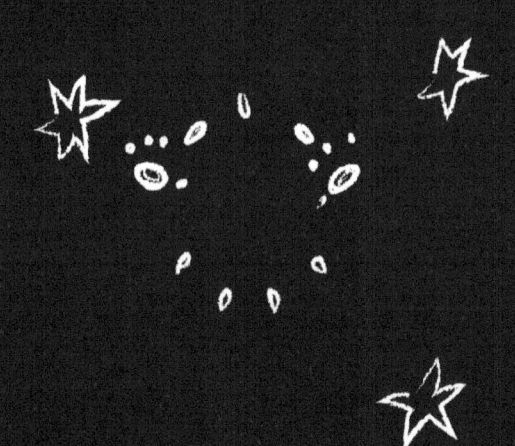

Chapter 22

Le Crapaud

Anaïs

Between homework, coursework and painting Kay's portrait, the holiday flies by in a flash. I spend Christmas day with Kay, who dances around the sixth form girls' common room with her completed portrait like she's in love with it.

Later, Noël calls me for a bit, and I'm eventually forced to hang up on him when he tries to sing Christmas carols at me. In the background, Kay cackles at his singing. We spend the rest of the evening cuddled up on the couch, watching movies.

The holidays end as swiftly as they begin. Classes resume, and with them, a fresh wave of assignments, deadlines and exams.

I retreat into my own company, hiding away in the little art studio or remote corners of the library. My hours sink into my work: my paintings for the exhibition, which I need to win, and my essays and coursework for my A-levels, which I need to pass with flying colours. The only reason to stay here in Spearcrest is to secure the top grades I'll need for my Japanese university applications, so leaving Spearcrest without them is just not an option.

Although I trust in both the quality of my art and my rudimentary Japanese (our father, having been born in France, never spoke it with us, but Noël and I both took lessons as kids), I'm not as confident with my academic abilities. Essays take me ages to write and even longer to write well. I find research a little bit boring, and my third A-Level option is maths: a versatile subject, but something that definitely doesn't come easily to me. So I have no choice but to spend time studying when I'd rather be drawing. For a while, the library becomes my second home at Spearcrest.

I'm on my way there one Friday afternoon when I get a strange notification on my phone.

"*Dinner at The Fable booked for 19:00.*"

I stop in my tracks. Around me, snowflakes flutter past the poplars lining the path to the library. They land on my eyelashes and cheeks, refusing to melt as I frown at my phone. I click on the notification, but no information turns up.

"What?" I mutter to myself.

"Everything alright?"

I turn around with a start. Why do people never announce themselves in Spearcrest?

Sitting on the edge of a statue half hidden underneath tangles of creeping ivy and thorns, a young man is smoking a cigarette. The white smoke curls in the icy air, a stark contrast to his dark eyes and the black fuzz of his buzz cut.

Although I don't know his name, I recognise him from the time Séverin unceremoniously had me brought to him in the rec room. He's one of the other filthy-rich, unreasonably good-looking in Séverin's gang of so-called Young Kings.

"What are you doing?" I ask, walking over to him. "It's freezing out here."

"Thinking," he says with a shrug. "I like the cold. What's up with you?"

"I just got a weird notification on my phone." I drop my phone into the corner of my tote and shake my head. "It's nothing, probably."

"Is it the dinner thing?" he asks.

Narrowing my eyes at him, I draw closer. "Do you know something I don't?"

"Sev got a text from his dad yesterday. Some dinner date thing. I don't know."

"Oh."

"He's full of secrets when it comes to you."

"There's really nothing to say," I assure him.

"Sure."

We stare at each other in silence for a moment. I stick my hand out.

"I'm Anaïs, by the way," I say.

I'm pretty confident he knows who I am. He nods and takes my hand in a bear-like grip. "Iakov."

"Well, Iakov, did Séverin tell you what he's going to do to get out of this weird dinner thing?"

Iakov lets out a low, deep laugh that sounds more like a growl than a sound of amusement. "Ha, no. He's going."

"Really?"

"Yea—why not, huh?" Iakov raises an eyebrow.

"I'm sure he has better things to do."

"He doesn't." Iakov's deep voice is tinged with amusement. "Maybe he thinks it'll be fun."

"Maybe." I'm unconvinced. Séverin doesn't strike me as a dinner date sort of guy. "He's probably just trying to get his parents off his back."

"Maybe." Iakov pulls a box of cigarettes from his pocket and hands it to me. I shake my head, and he shrugs and starts on a second cigarette. "Maybe it won't be so bad."

"The engagement?"

"The dinner." Iakov's mouth stretches in a grin—more a grimace than a smile. "Sev can be great company when he wants to be."

He pulls his phone from his pocket and glances down at the screen. The grin vanishes from his lips. He stands. "I'm off."

"Well... bye, I guess."

"See ya."

I follow Iakov with my eyes as he trudges away, disappearing amongst the trees. I like him. He's the opposite of Séverin: calm and cold and unconcerned. Distant and untouchable—like Noël.

I'M IN THE LIBRARY typing an essay for my English class when I'm startled for the second time today by a figure swooping into my field of vision. I turn to see Séverin, still in his uniform, his collar open to reveal the necklaces sparkling on his chest. His cheeks are flushed from the cold, and a jet-black strand of hair falls over his eye.

He pulls out the seat next to mine and collapses into it with a sigh.

"What should we do, then?" he asks, as if we've just been in the middle of a conversation.

It's a good thing I bumped into his friend earlier. "About the dinner?"

"Yeah."

I sigh and push my laptop away. "You know my parents didn't even tell me about it?"

He frowns. "What do you mean?"

I pull my phone out and show him the notification. "They just added it to my calendar via my email. That's it."

"Wow." For a moment, he just stares at my phone. Then he sits back and laughs out loud. His green eyes crinkle, and he throws his head back. Of course, he has to laugh in the most handsome way possible, as if he's posing for a photoshoot. "Your parents are ice cold, trésor."

I sigh. "You have no idea."

"Well, you can tell me all about it over dinner."

"We don't have to go," I say quickly. "We can ignore it if you want."

"We could," he says, "but I doubt that would get them off our case. Maybe we should go just to appease them. My parents got off my back for a few weeks after I sent them that picture."

"What picture?"

"The one I took on the trip." He raises his hand and pokes my cheek with his index finger. "*Le p'tit bisou.*"

"Really? That worked?"

"Yea. My mum was all moony-eyed about it at Christmas. She got it framed, look."

He pulls his phone from his pocket and shows me a picture on his camera roll. A woman in an emerald-green velvet gown holding a picture frame next to his cheek and grinning from ear to ear. Inside the picture frame is the selfie Séverin took of us on our way to the Isle of Skye.

I take his phone in my hand to take a closer look at the woman in the picture. Her olive skin, the long, glossy length of her jet-black hair.

"Your mother might be the most beautiful woman in the world," I tell Sev, handing him his phone back.

He takes it with a grin. "Yeah. Lucky I inherited her good looks, huh?"

I look at him. When he smiles, his beauty comes to life like the blossoming of flowers. It's breathtaking and surreal. It makes me feel suddenly odd, as though a strange chemical reaction is happening in my chest, making my ribs feel tight. I look away.

"If you say so."

"Look," he says in a serious voice, sitting up suddenly. "Let's just go to this stupid dinner thing. We'll get a night out, their treat, eat great food, get pissed, and have a good time. It's not like we have anything to lose by going, right?"

I can't help it. I smile. "Fine. I'm going to order one of each dessert."

"That's the spirit, trésor." His grin returns to his face. "I'm going to get the most expensive bottles. Pass out in the limousine on the way back."

I nod. "I'll ask the driver to carry you to your bed."

He laughs. "Don't be a dick. *You* carry me to my bed."

"Like a fairy tale princess."

"Yeah?" He leans into me. His face inches from mine, he pouts. "Will you kiss me awake, then?"

I put my palm on his mouth, creating a safe barrier between his pouting lips and me, and push him away.

"No. You might turn back into a toad." He licks my palm, and I snatch my hand away. "Ugh! Maybe you already *are* a toad. You're as slimy as one."

He stands up. "You're mixing up your fairy tales, trésor."

"Didn't know you were such an expert, *crapaud*."

"Don't call me that," he says with a wince. Then he points an accusing finger down at me. "And don't you dare try to draw me as a toad."

"Now I want to do nothing else. Maybe I'll use it for the exhibition."

"I warn you. Don't do it."

"Or what?"

"Or I'll kiss you and turn *you* into a toad, too."

I shudder. "Disgusting."

He flips me the finger. "See you later, toad kisser."

I return the gesture. "Dress to impress, pretty princess!"

Later, I stand in front of the narrow mirror next to my bedroom door, putting the finishing touches on my look.

The fact Séverin is always so fussy about clothes—and his blatant disdain for my style—has the opposite effect than what he wants. Instead of wanting to impress him with a sleek, stylish outfit to complement his own moody rich-kid aesthetic, it makes me want to displease him even more.

If I get him to physically wince at my outfit, then I'll consider this evening a victory.

To that purpose, I'm wearing my brightest clothes—the clothes I would've worn for a beach party.

A mesh top embroidered with big silver stars, a velvet dungaree dress, ochre socks and my battered white Converses for comfort. I wear my hair the way I always do since it's too straight and thick for anything else, but I put extra effort into my face.

Blue lipstick, thick silver glitter lines under my eyes and on my eyelids, thick yellow sun rays.

Before I set off, I glance at myself in the mirror. My heart tightens.

I like how I look. I like who I am.

But I can't help, for a second, wondering what I would look like if I was wearing a pretty sparkling dress, high heels, lipstick. If I looked sophisticated and sexy, like Kay.

I shake my head at my reflection. I like who I am, and I have nothing to prove to anyone, especially not Séverin Montcroix.

Chapter 23

Le Poison

Séverin

I almost laugh out loud when Anaïs emerges from the girls' building.

She's wearing a purple dress and yellow socks and those stupid goddamn shoes she always wears. Enormous silver stars cover her arms and throat, and there are suns drawn on her eyelids.

She looks like a rainbow explosion, and I want to drink in the sight of her.

I give her my arm.

"Looking splendid tonight, wifey."

"Don't call me that." She turns and sweeps her eyes pointedly up and down my body. "You could have made an effort."

"I'm sorry I don't look like a literal clown."

She gives an airy shrug but still takes my arm. "Clowns make people happy."

"Clowns make people scared. Depressed and scared."

She leans into me to murmur in my ear. "Is that why you're dressed like you're going to your own funeral?"

"It's going to be *your* funeral if you keep trying to insult my fashion sense."

"What fashion sense?" she says.

I open the limousine door and help her in.

"This is going to be a long fucking night," I say to no one in particular.

But even as I say it, I'm struggling to keep the grin off my face.

***

INSIDE THE LIMOUSINE, THE polished upholstery and low light make for a cosy, intimate atmosphere. Possibly too cosy and intimate, especially when the tension that's been building between Anaïs and me since that first meeting at the club.

If we'd been smart, we would have fucked right then, just to get it out of the way.

If I'd been smart, I would have fucked her that night at the club, against the door in the coat room. And I would have fucked her on the forest floor instead of biting her, and I would have fucked her in my room when she was still wet and shivering from her orgasm.

If I had, then maybe I wouldn't feel the way I do now. Constantly on edge, constantly frustrated, the thought of her reigning like a tyrant over my mind. Even during the holidays, when I was away from her, I found myself thinking about her all the time, talking about her non-stop.

Even my parents have noticed the mess she's made of me. I'm pretty certain that's the reason they talked the Nishiharas into setting this little evening up.

I pour us both glasses of champagne but make a silent promise to myself to avoid drinking too much tonight. Even though I made some grand promises to order the most expensive bottles at the restaurant, I also have to learn from my mistakes at some point.

And if there's one thing I've learned, it's that being drunk around Anaïs can only end in disaster.

Sweet, wet, hot disaster.

"What have I done now?" Anaïs says suddenly.

I frown. "What do you mean?"

"You've been glaring at me ever since we got in the limo. Are you that angry with my outfit? It's the ochre socks, isn't it?"

She sticks one leg up, pointing her foot at the ceiling. I laugh and push her leg down.

"No, trésor. I don't care about your yellow socks."

"My *ochre* socks."

"Just say yellow."

"But they're not yellow."

I roll my eyes. "You artists are so goddamn pretentious."

"Is that why you're glaring tiny daggers at me?"

"I'm not glaring anything at you." I glare at her. "And if I was, it wouldn't be tiny daggers. It would be sledgehammers."

She laughs. "Big, thick, veiny sledgehammers."

I stare at her over my glass of champagne, trying to resist her contagious laughter.

How can I reconcile the versions of Anaïs that exist in my mind?

Anaïs, the faceless fiancée. The daughter of billionaires, the fridge I was chained to when I was thrown into the ocean of this engagement. Anaïs as I pictured her before I ever met her, as some desperate social climber.

Then there's the real Anaïs. Her ridiculous clothing and plain black hair. Anaïs, whose oddness keeps her at a distance from everybody.

Anaïs, who refuses to let me gain the upper hand or have the last word, ever.

And finally, there's the Anaïs that lives in my mind and refuses to be evicted.

She's the girl in the club, dressed in sequins and dancing gracelessly in shifting colours. The girl who pulled me boldly away from the dancefloor and begged me so prettily in the coat room. The girl I pinned to the forest floor and stole a kiss from. The girl who squirmed and whimpered when I made her come on my tongue.

They're all the same girl, and it would seem I'm obsessed with her.

"Why did you go to the club that night in London?" I ask suddenly.

If she's surprised by the question, she doesn't show it. She shrugs. "Kay invited me. I thought it might be a good idea to be nice."

"Is that why you danced with me that night? To be nice?"

She raises her eyebrows. "You approached me, remember?"

"But I didn't know who you were."

"Neither did I."

I stare at her. Part of me wants to tell her the truth. That I wish I hadn't found out who she was, that I wish I'd still fucked her even after finding out. That I regret how I behaved that night, that I regret every chance I had at having her, being with her.

That I wanted her then and still want her now.

"If you hadn't found out who I was," I say, "if we didn't know—would you...?"

My voice falters. The question hangs in the air, unfinished. Anaïs gazes at me. Like I always do, I wish I could read her expression.

"Would I what?" she says.

"You know what I'm trying to ask."

"Are you really asking me if we would have had sex that night?"

I glare at her. "Yes, trésor. That's obviously what I'm asking."

She sighs. "*Obviously* we would have."

My chest tightens at her words. I don't know what answer I expected from her, but this was certainly not it. Her lack of expression combined with her disturbing honesty is a weapon that somehow strikes true every time.

"How is that obvious?" I ask. "How are you this sure?"

"Because." She flaps a hand. "Because no matter all your talk about hating what I wear and about me being a gold digger, you didn't care about any of those things before you found out my name. You saw me, and you liked—well, you liked *something* about me. Whatever you liked then, I'm pretty sure you like now. And if I hadn't known it was you, I would have had no reason to back away, either. So, of course, we would have had sex."

"I don't like you, I just—" I lean forward. "What did *you* like, then?"

"What do you mean?"

"You said I danced with you because there was something about you I liked. But you're the one who led me away from the dancefloor—you wanted me too. So what part of me is it *you* liked before you found out who I was?"

She laughs, a soft sound, surprisingly sweet. "Isn't it obvious?"

"My idea of what's obvious seems very different from yours."

"Well, it's not like I was attracted to your good humour and sweet disposition," she says, lips quivering in a repressed smile.

"What were you attracted to?"

"Why are you fishing?" she asks, sitting up to lean forward in perfect imitation of my gesture earlier. "You know how pretty you are. You don't need me to tell you."

"You think I'm pretty?" I ask, voice low.

It's not the word I would have chosen for myself, and it's not like I give much of a shit what Anaïs thinks about my appearance. But those lovely words in her mouth feel unexpectedly, delightfully good. They feel like silk against me, and I can't help but want to arch into them, to savour them.

She nods. "Yes, Séverin. I do."

"How about that night on the trip?"

"What night?"

"That night I came into your room and got on your bed? Was I not pretty then?"

She sits back with a sigh. "You were drunk."

"So?"

"So, don't be stupid." She narrows her eyes at me. "You know you were making a mistake. You would have regretted it the moment you woke up."

"I didn't regret what happened in my room, though."

Her laugh, this time, is edged with sarcasm. "You should. You ruined a perfectly good moment with your pride."

"It was a little more than good."

"Fine. It was wonderful. It was breathtaking. And then you ruined it."

"I just wanted you to admit you shouldn't have rejected me," I point out sullenly.

"I didn't reject you. If I'd rejected you, I wouldn't have made out with you in your bedroom, would I?"

We stare at each other across the dim light of the limo. The air is too hot, the silence too heavy, suffocated by white leather and polished glass.

"Anyway, it's happened, and now it's in the past," she says. "Why fixate on it?"

It's a good question.

Why can't I stop thinking about everything that's happened between us? The coat room, the forest floor, the balcony, my bedroom?

Because no matter how much I hate the engagement we're trapped in, no matter how much I resent our parents for forcing us into it, I just can't find it in my heart to hate Anaïs.

It doesn't matter that she isn't my type, that I didn't choose her. I still want her. And more than that, I'm starting to fear that I might like her. More than like her. But love is a poison, a poison I've tasted before.

And I'm wiser now, smarter. I can recognise the warning signs. The way I think about Anaïs even when she's not around, the way I want her—all the time. How I feel when I'm around her, simultaneously on edge and relaxed, annoyed and amused, frustrated and satisfied.

Love is poison, and Anaïs is handing me the cup.

I can't take it. I refuse to take it.

"I'm not fixated on anything," I say finally. "I was just making conversation. Don't look too much into it."

The shadow of a smile appears on her lips. Whether it's feigned or genuine, whether it's amused or bittersweet, I can't tell. I can never tell with Anaïs. Does she think of our kisses, of what could have been? Does she think about me at all when I'm not around? Does she struggle to sleep at night? Does she touch herself, thinking of my mouth?

"Don't worry," she replies. "I won't. You know why?"

"I don't know, but I'm sure you'll waste no time telling me."

"Because if I wanted to kiss you, Séverin Montcroix, I wouldn't need to be stupid drunk to gather the courage to ask. And if I wanted to sleep with you, I wouldn't make you earn it—I'd just do it. And if I liked you, I wouldn't run away from it and play games. No matter how scary it might feel, I'd face my fears, and I'd like you, no matter what."

Chapter 24

La Pratique

Anaïs

Despite the awkwardness we spend the rest of the journey in, Séverin is a perfect gentleman when we get out of the limo. He offers me his arm and leads me into the restaurant, walking me to our table by the arch of a great window. Outside, an extravagant garden glows with the light of hundreds of lanterns and candles.

The Montcroixes definitely were the ones who selected this restaurant.

It exudes luxury, from the entrance of gleaming glass to the white upholstery. The ceiling drips with teardrops of crystal that refract the golden lights into a thousand shifting fragments. Shimmering piano music ripples through the air, mingling with the murmur of conversation and the discreet tinkling of cutlery.

Once we've ordered, Séverin props his elbows on the table and rests his chin on his linked fingers.

"This is very romantic," he says, looking around us with a grimace. "Do you think our parents are hoping we'll fall in love?"

My mind flashes back to my parents, the glacial distance between them. I shake my head.

"No. They probably just think they could eventually sell our engagement off as a love match. I'm sure they think it would play well in the tabloids. They would get to take credit for bringing us together. But whether we adored each other or hated each other every day of our lives, I don't think it would ultimately matter to them."

His eyes search my face, though I'm not sure what he's looking for. He looks thoughtfully away, his eyes reflecting the glitter of the garden lights. "I don't know. I think my parents might care a little. You don't think your parents want you to be happy?"

I shrug. "I think they expect me to be like them."

"In what sense?"

"In the sense that their marriage is for business and not pleasure. They both accept it. They might not like each other, but they still make it work because they have to, because it's the..." I gesture vaguely. "Financially smart thing to do, I suppose."

"Oh." His gaze returns to my face. "Your parents don't get on?"

I let out a low laugh. "That's one way of putting it. But then, they didn't get married with that in mind."

He grimaces. "That's bleak."

"Are you telling me your parents actually like each other?" I ask, more to tease him than anything else.

But to my surprise, he doesn't respond with a dry or angry comment. He answers with complete sincerity. "Yeah. They might be assholes, but they love each other."

I stare at him. How unexpectedly sweet. Looks like Séverin Montcroix, for all his blustering and insults and womanising, is a romantic at heart.

"I think that's why they're doing all this," he continues, gesturing at us, at the restaurant, the magnificent view of the garden. "I think they would feel better if they believed we were in love."

"Well, how hard can it be?"

His eyes widen. "What, to be in love?"

I laugh. "No. I don't believe in all that. I mean, to make them believe we're in love."

"What do you mean you don't believe in all that?"

We get interrupted by the arrival of food. The waiters arrange the plates beautifully in front of us and pour wine into our glasses. But Séverin's eyes remain on me, the weight of his gaze resting on me even when I look away. The waiters withdraw discreetly, and I immediately tuck into my food.

"Well?" Séverin says, frowning imperiously at me. "What do you mean, you don't believe in all that? You don't believe in what—*love*?"

"I don't know what you want me to tell you. I believe people want to be together, sure. They want security, or affection, or even sex. But love, like the concept of a utopia, is just that. A concept invented by artists and poets and writers to give them something to write about."

"Wow," Séverin says drily. "An artist who doesn't believe in love? How edgy."

"I don't think you can make fun of me for being edgy when you dress like you're allergic to colours and call yourself a Young King at school."

"It's not edgy to dress cool. It's edgy to pretend not to believe in emotions."

"You surprise me, Séverin," I say sweetly, biting into a succulent forkful of fish. "I would never have pegged you for such a bleeding-heart romantic."

"I'm not a romantic," he says, glaring at me.

"Is that why you were trying to kiss me that night on the trip?" I ask, grinning at him, unable to resist the urge to tease him. "So that we can fall in love and live happily ever after?"

"Don't be a little shit," he says. "I wouldn't waste love on you."

"Smart. Save it for someone better."

"I'm not saving it for anyone. I've sworn off love, actually, but that's none of your business."

I raise an eyebrow and speak in an awed tone. "Sworn off love? But Séverin, what else will break the curse and free your heart from its cage of ice?"

He throws me a glare. "Don't mock me."

"Don't make it so easy for me to mock you."

"Anyway," he hurries to add, "I wasn't even speaking about actually falling in love. I was just trying to make you realise how stupid you sounded."

"Well, it might be love that keeps your parents together," I say with a shrug, "but they can't believe in love all that much if they forced you to get engaged to me."

"I think that's why we're here, though. Because they want us to fall in love."

"Well, fine then." I set down my cutlery and lean forward. "Let's give them what they want."

His green eyes narrow. He looks at me with mistrust, which is ironic given I've never been anything but honest with him.

"You're saying let's fake being in love?" he says.

"How hard can it be?"

He cocks an eyebrow. "You're going to fake a fake emotion?"

I reach one hand down the side of the table, lifting my fingers. "Give me your hand."

Still frowning, he mimics my gesture, reaching his hand across the table. I tangle my finger with his and let our hands rest on the snow-white tablecloth.

"There. It's not that complex, is it?"

He pulls away with a grimace. "It's not complex, but it feels weird as hell."

This time, it's my turn to cock an eyebrow. "Oh. Weirder than chasing me through the woods and kissing me and getting slapped?"

"Definitely. But for what it's worth, trésor..." He tips his glass of wine towards me. "I actually think you might be onto something."

"Really?"

"Mm-hm. I like your idea, and I'm willing to give it a try. We're already here anyway. Might as well make the most of it."

I take my glass and lift it to his. "Let's. *À ta santé.*"

He smirks, and there's a dangerous edge to his smirk. A sort of dark delight, almost predatory. He touches the rim of his glass to mine. "*À la tienne.*"

KEEPING TRUE TO HIS promise, Séverin orders the most expensive bottles on the menu. True to mine, I order one of every dessert. The combination of wine and sugar is a heady elixir. My cheeks feel warm, and my skin buzzes. I wiggle my feet under the table and stretch back against my chair, wishing I could curl up and go to sleep.

"How are the profiteroles?" Séverin asks.

His cheeks look as warm as mine feel. He's taken his jumper off, revealing a loose black T-shirt in a fabric that looks impossibly soft.

I don't even hide it when I shamelessly look at his chest, his neck, his collarbones, with the fine golden chains pooling in the dips. His arms are quite nice for someone who looks like he spends all his spare time writing bad poetry in moonlight.

"They are to die for," I say.

Stabbing one through with a fork, I stretch my arm across the table. Séverin leans forward, taking the proffered dessert in his mouth. His lips wrap around my fork, leaving it clean when he pulls away. I feel a flutter where I definitely shouldn't.

I watch the shudder of his throat as he swallows. His tongue slips between his lips, licking them clean. I take a quick sip of wine.

"Better than I expected," he says with an appreciative nod. "Do you miss France?"

I answer without hesitation. "Yes. You?"

"Sometimes. What do you miss the most?"

"The sea. The smell of the sea, the parties on the beach, skinny-dipping, the shock of the water, then the pull of it. And I miss the flowers. Our house was near fields of lilacs and mustard flowers, and we had herb gardens and oleander trees all over the property. I miss those. What do you miss?"

He thinks for a moment, sipping his drink. Alcohol suits him. It makes his eyes hooded and sensual, his handsome features relaxed.

Sober, he is the taught string of a bow, full of unreleased tension and powerful emotions.

Tipsy, he is a ribbon of silk, malleable and soft.

"Don't make fun of me," he warns in a low voice.

"I would never," I lie.

"I miss my parents, honestly. Ever since I started at Spearcrest, I barely see them. They might be stuck-up, uptight assholes who only care about status and money, but honestly, none of that matters to me. They've always given me everything I wanted. I miss them."

"Was it nice seeing them during the holidays?"

"Yes, although they kept asking me about you. They want you to come stay with us sometime."

I've spent enough time around the rich French elite to know that staying with the Montcroixes would probably not be my idea of fun, but I don't want to offend Séverin. And I certainly don't intend to tell him about my plan to run away to Japan.

Not now, not when things between us are this strange and soft.

"Well, how bad could that be?" I say finally. "I'm sure we could put on a show."

He shakes his head. "You could never fool my parents into thinking you love me. Not in person. They'll see right through you."

"I bet I could. We just need to practise."

He lets out a cackle—a genuine noise of amusement. "Practise how?"

"However you want, Séverin. *Sevvie?* Shall I give you a nickname? *Mon choux? Nounours?*"

"Don't you dare."

"Well, what do your girlfriends call you?"

He smirks and tilts his head. "I don't do girlfriends, trésor."

"Ah, of course. You're a real Lothario, a Casanova of the modern age."

"Well"—he suddenly leans across the table, resting his face in his cupped palms and smiling—"what do *your* boyfriends call you?"

"You don't need a nickname for me," I say airily. "You already have one, remember?"

"You know I say trésor in the most sarcastic and insincere way possible, right?"

"Then say it like you mean it."

He raises his eyebrows and is silent for one minute. Then he gets up, startling me. He walks around the table to stand behind my chair. His hands rest gently on my shoulders, slide up to my neck. I suppress a shudder, but my nipples stiffen at his touch.

He rests his thumbs delicately along my jaw, tilting my head back so I'm looking up at him. Then he leans down until his lips are so close to mine I can feel his breath on my mouth. I close my eyes.

He doesn't have to steal this kiss.

This kiss, I'll give him for free.

"Trésor..." he murmurs against my mouth.

"*Oui... ?*" I murmur in reply.

He releases me suddenly. My eyes fly open. I sit up, watching him as he returns to his seat and picks up his glass of wine. My breath is still trapped in my throat.

"How was that, then?" he asks. "Convincing enough for you?"

I clear my throat and force myself to breathe. "Yes. Very convincing."

He smirks. "I thought so."

It *was* convincing.

Too convincing.

Chapter 25

La Limousine

Séverin

We're both a little giggly and tipsy when we leave the restaurant, but I've successfully avoided getting drunk. I'm in full possession of my functions. And I've decided I'm going to kiss Anaïs.

And I don't mean a peck on the lips.

I'm going to kiss the breath from her lungs. I'm going to kiss her until she can taste my fucking *soul*. I have a feeling she won't fight me on that. Her desire is palpable, brushing against me in invisible tendrils.

Anaïs's face, as always, is an emotionless mask. Even when she's a little tipsy, her cheeks are bright pink and her eyes glassy. But for all the emotions she keeps hidden, her desire glows like a light from within, tantalising, irresistible.

I see it in the way her eyes linger without shame or embarrassment on my mouth, my neck, my arms. I feel it in the way she leans into me when I give her my arm, her body heat reaching me through our clothes.

Outside the restaurant, I stop and face her, taking her face in my hands. Her cheeks burn against my palms.

"Do you think our parents would want us to kiss now?"

"Why?" she breathes, and then, in the same breath, "Yes."

"Because that's what people do when they're in love," I say, even though she's already said yes. I brush a thumb over her lips. They part wetly. "They kiss each other like they'll die if they don't."

"I'm not sure what you mean," Anaïs mumbles, closing her eyes. "You better show me."

I laugh, but the sound comes out broken and hoarse. My throat is tight, my heart is beating too fast. I'm not nervous about kissing—I've kissed more girls than I can count—but I'm nervous about kissing *her*.

I hesitate. Her eyes fly open. She smirks. "Why so shy?"

"I'm not shy."

Taking my wrists in her hands, she frees her head from my hold and moves to press her mouth to mine. I move back, letting her lips brush against mine but evading the kiss. She looks up. I tilt my head.

"Do you remember when I asked to kiss you, that time in your room?"

"I remember." She pulls a face. "How could I not? You keep bringing it up."

"Well, it's your turn, trésor. Ask me."

"Why?" she asks, frowning. "I know you want to kiss me."

"Because." I take her waist, pulling her closer. "I'm always the one to beg. I want to hear you ask this time. Come on, trésor, ask me. Make it pretty."

She says nothing for a second, and I wonder if I've perhaps gone too far. But then a slow smile blossoms on her pretty lips. Standing on the tips of her toes, she wraps her arms around my neck. She presses her cheek to mine and speaks against my ear.

"Please, Sev. Kiss me. Touch me. Please me. Make me feel so good I come undone."

I laugh. "Very pretty."

"I should think so." She moves away and smiles at me wickedly. "I'm stealing your lines, after all, and you're an expert."

I kiss her before she can say anything else because I want to kiss her, and touch her, and please her, and make her feel so good she comes undone. Her mouth falls open under mine, warm and pliant. Our tongues meet, wet and lingering.

I kiss her slow and deep, and my entire body aches with desire. Pulling her closer, I press her body to mine. Her arms wrap around my neck, her fingers burying themselves in my hair. She arches and a sound of pleasure rises from her throat, low and keening.

A discreet cough startles us. We move apart with sharp gasps.

The limo driver gestures politely to the open door. "Excuse me, Mr Montcroix, Miss Nishihara. We should be on our way."

Anaïs and I exchange a glance. She lets out a sudden burst of laughter and gets inside the limo. I follow her in, and the driver shuts the door behind us.

For a moment, we just sit side by side. A dull rumble and passing lights behind the tinted windows tell us that the limo is in motion. I glance at Anaïs.

She sits with her hands resting at her sides, looking ahead with glazed-over eyes. Her fingers tap the leather seats, and her right leg bounces up and down. She's not as relaxed as she's trying to make it look.

She licks her lips nervously and glances at me.

"Do you think the driver is going to report back to our parents?" she asks.

"Oh, yes." I cast a glance at the closed partition. "I'd bet my life on it. He's probably been asked to report every detail."

"Alright." She hesitates. "So, everything according to plan, right?"

"What do you mean?"

Her brows furrow slightly. It's not a full-blown frown, but it's more emotion than I'm used to from her. "Don't be an idiot. I mean the kiss."

Heat rushes through me. Why is she talking about the kiss as if it's a memory, as if it's already behind us? It's far from a memory—it's very much in the present.

My mouth is still wet from that kiss, my heart still racing, my cock still straining against my trousers.

"So that's the story you're going for?" I ask in my most casual tone.

"What do you mean?"

"That we only kissed because of our plan to make our parents think we like each other. That's the story you want to go for, right?"

She turns slightly and narrows her eyes. "We *both* decided on this story. There's no reason for you to keep whatever you're thinking to yourself, so if you want to say something, say it."

"Fine, I'll say it." My words burst out of me, partly fuelled by annoyance, partly by the flames of arousal still leaping through me. I feel as though my skin is about to ignite right off my body, and I want Anaïs to burn with me. "You're trying to pretend that there was nothing else to that kiss, but that's a lie. You wanted it—you wanted *me*."

"I never said I didn't."

I open my mouth to accuse her of being a liar, but her reply stops me in my tracks.

"You're admitting it?"

"Admitting that I wanted you to kiss me?" She raises her eyebrows and then laughs out loud, throwing her head back against the pale leather of the seat. "It's not a crime, Sev. *Of course* I wanted you to kiss me. How could I not?" She gestures at my face, the silver stars on her sleeves catching the light in blurry glitters. "You've seen your face in the mirror. You know it's a very kissable face."

The satisfaction that courses through me at her words feels better than anything I've ever experienced. Better than alcohol, better than sex. It sends shivers through my skin. I smile before I even realise I'm smiling.

"You *fancy* me," I say, leaning to her and narrowing my eyes. "How embarrassing for you."

"Yes," she says, rolling her eyes and dismissively pushing my face away from her. "How very embarrassing for me to be a horny eighteen-year-old."

My heart skips a beat and throws itself against my ribs like it's trying to break out. "Horny, you say?"

"What do you expect?" she says with a sigh. "I've been here for several months, and you ruined my only chance at getting laid. And ever since you were mean to Parker, none of the boys at Spearcrest want to speak to me. So thanks for that too."

I glare at her. "If you're horny, you don't need a Spearcrest boy to sort that out for you. You have a perfectly good fiancé who's more than capable of doing the job."

She tilts her head. "When he's not kicking me out of his bed out of pride."

"I never kicked you out of my bed. You ran off."

"You chased me away."

"When I chase you, trésor"—I smirk—"it's never away."

She bites the insides of her cheeks, trying to hold back a smile, but her face finally cracks.

"Alright, that's fair," she admits. "I'll give you that."

"Well?" I prompt her. "So what do you think, then?"

"About what? About your *fiancés-with-benefits* idea?"

I shrug and lean forward. "What's the worst that can happen?"

"I'll tell you what I think." She rests her hands on the edge of her seat and leans forward. The limousine is full of her perfume, her warmth. "I think you're still turned on from before, and you're trying to make decisions with the wrong part of your body."

She's probably not wrong, and I can't blame her for pointing it out.

"If you refuse," I warn her, crossing my arms, "I can tell you right now you don't stand a chance of sleeping with anybody else. I'll beat anyone who touches you to a pulp. I wouldn't even get Iakov to do it—I'd do it myself. In front of you, if I can help it."

"Ah, so this is how you get all the girls?" she asks with a sardonic grin. "You make yourself the only option so they have no choice but to get into bed with you?"

I shrug. "If you weren't too proud to admit you want me, you'd actually find out how I get all the girls."

"I'm not proud. I want you. See how easy that was to admit? I didn't even need to threaten to beat up a single person."

"At this point, trésor, I'd fuck you just to shut you up."

"I dare you," she says with a laugh.

Gripping the back of her seat with one hand, I wrap the other around the back of her neck, drawing her to me.

"Open your mouth," I command in a low growl.

She does, and I kiss her open lips.

Not the hungry, desperate kind of kiss we exchanged earlier, but a slow, lingering kiss. I move my lips slowly against hers, luxuriating in their silken softness.

She pulls away to breathe, and I follow her, tugging on her bottom lip with my teeth. She smiles—I kiss her smile.

I push her back against her seat, sliding my mouth from her lips to her jaw, kissing right below it. My mouth finds the flutter of her pulse, and I kiss that too, sucking on the skin lightly. Her breath becomes an erratic hiss.

"Do you like how that feels?" I ask against her pulse.

"Mm-yeah," she mutters.

A hum of satisfaction and anticipation vibrates in my throat. I'm about to make her feel so much better. I'm about to make her feel things no man will ever make her feel.

Taking the straps of her hideous dungaree dress, I push them down, bunching her dress around her waist. The top she's wearing underneath it is sheer except for the big silver stars, and my breath catches.

She's not wearing a bra.

Her small tits are exposed by the sheer fabric, her nipples half hidden by the points of nearby stars.

Without meaning to, I let out a low laugh. My voice is rough and breathy. I'm nervous.

It's the last thing I expected from myself. Pleasuring girls is my greatest skill, my one true talent. But this isn't any girl. This is Anaïs Nishihara. Anaïs, the girl who might as well have fallen right out of the sky. Anaïs the little weirdo, my unwanted bride, my twisted trésor.

Chapter 26

La Bague

Anaïs

Séverin kisses me through the sheer fabric of my top, the heat of his mouth imprinting itself onto my chest. His tongue pushes against the fabric, hot and wet and insistent, finding my nipple. His mouth closes over it, and he sucks.

A bolt of red-hot pleasure crosses through me from head to toe.

I arch my back, pushing into his mouth. My hands grip the leather seat on both sides of my legs so tight my knuckles have gone white. I have the mad urge to run my hands through Séverin's raven-black hair and pull, but I resist it.

All I can think about is him and his mouth.

It moves from one nipple to the other, leaving the fabric of my top wet where his mouth just was. Underneath it, my nipples are tight and so sensitive I have to clamp my teeth tight over the whimper, trying desperately to escape my mouth.

Séverin's confidence in his skill isn't misplaced. It's both devastating and elating at once. Devastating because now I know his confidence isn't just bluster. Elating because his hands are reaching for the hem of my skirt, gripping it, pushing it up.

When it's bunched around my waist, his mouth moves away from my breasts. He sits up, and his eyes meet mine. I can barely hold his gaze. Everything about him suggests sensuality and pleasure: the decadent green of his eyes, those thick black eyelashes, that soft, wet mouth. His lips curl into a crooked grin.

"Does that feel good, mon trésor?"

I open my mouth to tell him I'm not his trésor, that I'm not his. But the words refuse to come out. I lick my lips and nod. "Mm-hm."

"Ah, good. Now..." He lowers his head and kisses my thigh right above my knee, his eyes still on mine. "Spread your legs for me."

His hands are on my thighs—he could spread my legs with the slightest push. But his request, in his low, husky voice, makes me tighten with pleasure.

I obey him, spreading my legs open.

"Mm," he murmurs against my thigh. "Good girl."

He kisses a slow, wet path up my thigh. His kisses are unhurried, torturous. By the time he reaches the top of my thigh, I have to stop myself from grinding against the seat. My core is an aching pulse, desperate for friction.

It's not just his mouth or his touch that's making me like this.

Anyone could have kissed my nipples, kissed my thighs. But there's something about Séverin I can't explain. All the things I despise about him—his arrogance, the heat of his emotions, his imperiousness—all those things become tantalising now he's on his knees in front of me.

His mouth finally reaches the apex of my legs, and he kisses me through the fabric of my panties. Soft, sweet kisses, closed lips.

He takes my hips in his hands and pulls me towards him, making me slump back into the couch. I reach out and slide my fingers into his hair, holding his head for balance.

He looks up and murmurs, "You're so fucking wet for me."

The shameless pride with which he says this sends heat flooding into my face. Then, as if to reward me, he kisses me, deeply and wetly, through my panties. If the fabric wasn't sodden before, it soon is.

I wriggle my hips, struggling against his grip, arching desperately against his mouth, craving more. More of his mouth, more wetness, more friction.

More everything.

Moving one hand away from my hips, he touches me through the wet fabric. He rubs his thumb up and down the line of my pussy, repeatedly brushing over my clit. A whimper of pleasure finally breaks through my barrier of silence. He looks up once more.

"Ah," he says, low and husky, "you like that, too."

Of course, I like that, I want to say. I'd have to be a robot not to. But I can't speak. His touch is casting a spell on me, a spell that's turning my bones into brittle sugar and my blood into warm honey.

He hooks my panties with his thumb, gathering them aside. Cold air touches my wet pussy, then the hot ghost of his breath. His thumb resumes the same motion as before, brushing lightly up and down, gliding through hot wetness.

"Oh fuck," I whimper. "Sev, please—"

He doesn't stop. My hips writhe uncontrollably against him as he continues his slow, steady rhythm. He watches me with a solemn expression. I stare at him in shock, realising I'm about to come.

Then he stops. He glances up at me and shakes his head slowly.

"No," he says. "Not yet, mon trésor."

He kisses my inner thighs. I fist my fingers in his hair, pulling.

"Please, Sev."

"Yes, trésor," he murmurs. "I'm going to give you exactly what you want, I promise." He sits up suddenly, pushing my hands away. He kisses me on my mouth. "But not like this. I want you to come on my tongue. I want you to fuck yourself on my mouth. Use my face for your own pleasure. Can you do that for me?"

I stare at him half in disbelief, my face burning at his words.

He leans into me and speaks against my ear. "Answer me, Anaïs. My little treasure, my pretty slut. Will you come on my tongue?"

"Yes," I whisper, as if it's a secret between us.

He nods. "Good girl."

And then he bends down in front of me and kisses my pussy like it's a mouth. Sweet kisses at first, then deep kisses, tongue flicking out, delving inside.

He kisses me until his tongue finds my clit, and my hips buck against his hands. I grip the seat, my eyes squeezed shut, my body trembling with gathering tension.

Séverin builds a slow rhythm, his tongue moving up and down, lightly at first, then in slow, insistent licks. His fingers dig into me, pushing me closer. Every noise and motion from me is like a signal straight to his brain, telling him what to do.

My orgasm, already so close, looms above me like the black clouds before the summer thunderstorms.

A polite knock at the limo window makes us both freeze.

"Mr Montcroix, Miss Nishihara. We've arrived."

Seized with panic, I try to sit up, but Séverin's hands pin me in place. He looks up from between my thighs and slowly shakes his head, as if to say no.

And then, slowly, deliberately, he slides his tongue against me. He doesn't change what he's doing, keeping the same torturous rhythm, slow and inexorable. My hips grow still as my pleasure gathers.

And then it slams into me.

The black cloud of tension released into a deluge of impossible pleasure. I slap my hand over my mouth to stifle my cries. My orgasm slams into me in waves, almost painful. I grind against Sev's mouth, riding each pulse, craving more even as I come.

Before I can even recover, Sev rises against me. Lifting me against him, he sits back, dragging me over his lap. Catching my mouth in tiny kisses, he quickly loosens his belt. His cock springs free, hard and gleaming with pre-cum. He pulls a condom from his pocket and bites the cover off, then rolls it on with expert speed.

I glance nervously towards the door. "Sev, we're here, we should—"

A kiss stifles the rest of my sentence. He catches my bottom lip between his lips and sucks on it. The arm around my waist pulls me closer, the blunt head of his cock sliding against my drenched pussy.

"Trésor," he growls in my ear. "The world could be ending, and I still wouldn't care. We're not getting out of this limo until you come all over my cock. Do you understand?"

He doesn't even wait for a reply. He thrusts himself inside me in one stroke, drawing a rasping cry from me. I clutch his shoulders for purchase and arch at the sensation of his cock sliding in and out of me in hard, deep strokes.

I should've known Sev would fuck hard.

He holds my hips firmly in his hands, controlling their movement. Making sure I can't escape him as he pounds relentlessly inside me.

"You feel so fucking good," he groans against my neck. "You take my cock so well, my gorgeous trésor. I should've done this sooner. Fuck."

His breath hitches. His eyes are wild, glazed over with pure lust. I can tell he's close, but instead of chasing his orgasm, he wets his fingers to work my clit.

"Come for me," he hisses in my ear. "Come on my cock, trésor. I want to feel your pussy clench around me, I want to feel your sweet juices dripping down my cock, fuck—"

Our gasps mingle as he strokes the tiny bundle of nerves, and he doesn't relent when I squirm and whimper. My second orgasm crashes into me before I even know it's coming. I cry out and writhe on top of Sev, my pussy clenching around his cock.

He lets out a rasping sigh. Burying his face in my neck and gathering me close to him, he fucks himself inside me, his thrusts growing erratic. He comes with a deep groan, his fingers digging into my hips as his hips buck against mine.

For a moment, we just stay exactly as we are. His hands on my hips, my arms around his shoulder, his head buried in the crook of my neck. Our panting breaths grow quieter as our heartbeats go back to a normal pace. He looks at me and grins.

"That," he says in a lazy drawl, "was fucking exquisite."

I laugh and slowly lift myself off him. "It was pretty good."

"It was more than good, trésor." He smirks. "You're just trying to provoke me. You want me to fuck you again."

He's not wrong, but I'm painfully aware of the driver waiting outside the limo. There's no point in trying to think of some excuse or alibi for why it took us so long to get out. The driver isn't stupid—he knows.

Sev fixes himself up and then helps me re-adjust my clothing. He even brushes his fingers through my hair and tucks the strands behind my ears before pressing a kiss to my cheek.

"Come on," he says with a sheepish grin. "We've made poor Fabien wait long enough."

When we get out of the limo, I don't even dare look at the driver. I mumble a thank you and hurry away. Séverin tips Fabien and then hurries after me.

The night is dark and icy and hazy with frost. The glacial wind raises goosebumps all over my skin, sending me crashing back to reality.

Have I just messed up? I don't regret what I did—I'd do it again if I could. But I've definitely messed up. Getting on with Sev is one thing. It doesn't interfere with the plan.

Sleeping with him, on the other hand... how does that fit into the plan?

"Hey." Sev catches up with me and turns me around to face him. His eyes search my face, and he gives me a small smile. "Don't overthink this, okay?"

"Why would I?"

"Because you look worried. I've never seen you look worried before."

I hesitate. Sev is normally so emotional that talking to him feels like defusing a deadly bomb. But right now, he's calm, relaxed, completely at ease.

"I don't want things between us to get... confusing," I say finally.

"There's no confusion," he says. He looks completely serious. He sighs, and his breath curls like white smoke in the icy air. "We're already engaged. We've agreed we'll put on an act to keep our parents off our backs. Sex is a separate issue. It's our business. We get to decide who we fuck—right?"

Is he talking about us or in general? I'm not naïve. Sex with Sev doesn't mean he's now going to devote his entire life to me and never touch another girl.

"Alright." I nod. "We'll put on the fiancés act and keep the sex thing separate from the engagement thing. We'll be... allies. Right?"

He frowns, running his hand distractedly through his hair. "Allies who fuck?"

"Allies who... do whatever they want," I say cautiously. "That's what you want, right? To keep your freedom?"

He's silent for a long time, his eyes on mine. We stare at one another. For the first time, I can't tell what he's thinking. I never expected it would make me feel so lost.

He bites his lip and lets out another deep sigh.

"Yes," he says. "You're right. It is what I want."

"Alright. So..." I extend my hand out to him. "Allies?"

He takes my hand. "Allies."

We stand hand in hand for a moment. My heart is beating fast, and I can't help a heavy sense of regret settling over my chest, as if I've just made a mistake.

Séverin lets go of my hand and pulls something out of his pocket.

"You should have this," he says.

I open my hand, and he drops an object in my palm. My heart catches.

A ring.

A beautiful antique thing crowned with opals and diamonds that glimmer dimly in the orange light of the Spearcrest lamp posts.

"What's this?" I ask in a half-whisper.

"It's the engagement ring my parents wanted me to give you," he says with a shrug. "It's stupid, but since we're playing along, you might as well have it."

There's a sudden lump in my throat that's come out of nowhere. I don't even feel sad. We are playing along, he's right. I look from the ring back up to Sev.

"I can't wear it on my finger."

He shrugs and shoves his hands in his pocket. "Don't wear it. It's fine. I don't care."

"No, I mean, I can't wear it on my finger because I'm always getting paint on my hands. This ring is clearly valuable. But I want to wear it—I'm going to wear it."

He watches me for a second. There's a softness in his face that wasn't there before. I have the sudden urge to kiss him full on his handsome mouth.

He pulls his hands out of his pockets and, for a split second, I'm terrified he's going to take the ring back. I step away, but he doesn't reach for me. Instead, he unclasps one of the gold chains from around his neck and holds it in his hands.

"Give me the ring back."

I hand it to him, and he threads the chain through it.

"Turn around."

I turn and let him fasten the necklace with the ring around my neck. His fingers brush against my skin as he secures the clasp, sending little shivers through me.

Shivers that have nothing to do with the cold and everything to do with Sev's touch.

"There," he says, turning me back around by my shoulders. "All done."

"Thank you."

We look at one another. His mouth moves as if he wants to say something else, and my eyes linger on his lips, the shape of them. I want to press my mouth against his, kiss him one more time. His eyes mirror mine, dropping to my mouth. I wonder if he feels the same.

"We should go back to our rooms," he says in a husky voice.

I shudder, and the muscles in my belly twitch.

"Yes," I say reluctantly. "It's very cold."

"Alright."

We both stand there without moving. I normally love an excuse to run away after sex and avoid the awkwardness of pillow talk.

But being away from Sev is the last thing I want to do right now.

Oh, I've *definitely* messed up.

"Goodnight, Sev," I blurt out.

I give him a quick kiss on the cheek and hurry away.

"Goodnight, trésor," he says and watches me leave.

Chapter 27

Le Choix

Séverin

When I get back to my room, I strip off all my clothes, step into the shower and run the water as hot as I can.

I close my eyes, letting the hot water beat down on the back of my head, my neck. In my mind, I replay the electrifying memory of Anaïs coming on my tongue, grinding herself against my mouth, and then on my cock, her pussy clenching around me.

I've never come harder in my life than I did in that limousine, my mouth tasting her pulse, my senses filled with the scents of lilacs, sweat and sex.

What if I never come this hard with anybody else ever again?

With a sigh, I rest my forehead against the tiles.

And I replay the end of our conversation. Our alliance. Giving her the ring.

Agreeing that we would play along with the engagement.

Agreeing that what I wanted was my freedom.

When all I really want is to have Anaïs in my arms, in my bed. To have her naked and soft and vulnerable underneath me, to touch her all over and to make her come over and over again, with my mouth, my fingers, my cock.

I don't even want to sleep with her and send her away—I want to sleep with her and lie in bed with our bodies tangled together. Talk, laugh, argue, fight, and play with her.

What I want isn't a fake fiancée, or an ally, or a fuck buddy.

It's a relationship.

"*Putain de fucking merde*," I bite out.

I'm sitting in the centre of the sixth form boys' common room. The other Young Kings are all here too. And given we represent the elite of Spearcrest, we form a sad lot.

Evan is half-collapsed on one couch, frowning at the inside of a Shakespeare play.

Zachary sits with his legs crossed elegantly at the ankles, his fingers steepled together, his eyes glazed over in sinister thought. He looks like a movie villain plotting some terrible scheme.

Iakov, reeking of cigarettes and looking like he's not had a good night's sleep in weeks, is lying down flat on the floor, eyes closed.

I'm glaring at my empty notifications and brooding over a cup of black coffee.

Luca, who has training on weekend mornings, is last to stride into the common room. A stark contrast to the rest of us, he seems refreshed and in high cheer. His cold grey eyes rake over us, and he lets out a sneer.

"What a pathetic sight."

"What's your problem?" Evan asks, glaring up at him.

"I don't have one," Luca says. "I'm in rather a good mood today, actually. Archery went exceptionally well. Maybe it's because, unlike the rest of you, no girl has me by the balls."

"That's because no girl wants to be near your angry dick," Zach drawls without opening his eyes. "They're probably scared acid might come out of it when you come."

"I assure you, girls don't have a problem with me and my angry dick." Luca sits down and raises an eyebrow. "Some girls even prefer an angry dick."

"Who knows what girls even want," Evan mutters from behind his book.

"Probably the same thing we want," Zachary says drily. "You know, a modicum of respect and honesty?"

"Some girls crave chaos," Luca says.

"Girls want safety," Iakov snaps from the floor. "Not chaos."

"You're an expert on girls now?" Luca sneers.

But Zachary sits up and glances down at Iakov with an expression of concern.

"Everything alright, Kavinski?" he asks.

Iakov grunts a vaguely affirmative response. Zachary, still frowning, relaxes slightly in his seat.

Evan suddenly looks up from his book. "I don't get it. What does Laertes mean when he says: 'the canker galls the infants of the spring, too oft before their buttons be disclosed'? What does he mean by infants? He doesn't want Ophelia to get pregnant?"

We all turn to look at him. Even Iakov cracks one eye open to ask, "What the fuck are you talking about?"

"He's not talking about infants. He's talking about flowers." Zachary sighs.

Evan pulls a face of complete incredulity. "He's talking about flowers?" He glares back down at his book. "That makes even less sense!"

Zachary rolls his eyes. "He's telling Ophelia not to sleep with Hamlet because he'll take her virginity and ruin her."

"That's fucked up," Evan mutters.

"Is that why you're having no luck with Theodora, Zach?" Luca asks lightly. "Because her dad's angry about your *canker*?"

A dull silence falls in the room. Theodora is a no-go topic amongst Young Kings—we all know that. Luca must really be feeling bold today.

Zachary drags his gaze away from Evan and to Luca. There's so much icy hatred in his eyes, it's a miracle Luca doesn't drop dead.

"Did you think that barb was particularly trenchant?" he asks, voice dripping with disdain. "Because it did little to impress me." He stands, and his lips twist in a cold, insincere smile. "Why don't you try harder, Luca? You're starting to bore me—actually, that's a lie. You've always bored me."

He leaves.

In the silence he leaves behind, Luca cackles. "You guys are wound up too tight. All of you. What's it going to take to get those sticks out of your assholes? Shall we head into London tonight? You all look like you could do with letting out some steam."

Evan sighs and sets his book aside. "My head's a mess. Might as well. I'm in."

"Me too," Iakov grunts from the floor.

Going out clubbing is only going to make me think of Anaïs in a sequined skirt, dancing in changing lights, but what's the alternative? Staying in Spearcrest and thinking of Anaïs in silver stars writhing on my cock?

"Fuck it. Count me in too."

Music pounds, vibrating through my bones, my veins.

In the crowd of bodies, in the pulsing of lights and shadows, it's easier to get out of my head. Loud music drowns out my thoughts. Tonight, I'm on the dancefloor. Tonight, I'm losing myself.

Girls press themselves against me, dazzling me with their shine. Shiny eyes, shiny lips, shiny dresses. They glitter like statues of gold and silver, waiting for me to collect them, to place them high on the shelf of my esteem.

I wrap my arm around a slim waist, and my cheek brushes against perfumed hair. Isn't this what Anaïs wanted? For both of us to be free and do what we want?

Isn't this what I wanted? To ignore my fiancée and take any girl I want to my bed? I don't even know what I want anymore. To be free? For my parents to leave me alone? To do what I want, when I want? To fuck my way through life without consequence?

Anaïs?

Maybe it would be simpler to figure out what I don't want. To be engaged to someone who doesn't want me. For my parents to manipulate my life like it's a puppet, and they hold the strings.

And I definitely don't want the freedom of fucking whoever I want if it means Anaïs gets to do the same thing.

Pulling myself out of the tangle of shiny girls, I leave the dancefloor.

My eyes glide over the crowd, searching faces. What if she's here too? What if she's looking for someone to drag away from the dancefloor? Someone to touch her and make her feel so good they'll erase the memory of me from between her legs?

My eyes catch on a familiar face, and I make a beeline through the crowd.

Kay looks stunning as usual in a tiny dress of cream silk, her hair down to her waist, her skin sparkling with gold. Gold shoes, gold jewellery, gold rings in her braids. She sits at a table with three young men courting her, her dark-brown eyes assessing them, measuring them.

I drop myself down next to her on the leather couch, to the men's surprise and annoyance. I shrug and turn to talk to Kay, ignoring them.

"Where's your new protégée, Kay?"

"My new protégée?" She leans back against her seat and takes a sip from her glass of champagne. "Who would that be?"

"Don't play games."

"I'm not. I'm a very open-hearted person, as you know. I have many protégées in Spearcrest."

"But there's only one of them who's engaged to me."

Kay's glossy lips stretch in a little smug smile. "Oh. Is it my sweet bestie Anaïs you're asking about?"

"She's not that sweet."

"You're wrong. Do you know she painted my portrait?"

"I heard."

She waggles her eyebrows. "Jealous?"

"Why should I be?"

"Because she only paints portraits of people she likes. Did she not tell you?"

I roll my eyes. "If you two love each other so much, then why is she not here with you?"

Kay laughs and then sets her glass down, turning to face me properly. Her men await without speaking, perfect puppies desperate for her attention. "She's like a bird, your fiancée. Very pretty but elusive. I've tried many times now to get her to come out with us, but she always turns me down."

I steel my features so that she doesn't realise how glad that makes me.

"Maybe she's not the partying kind."

"No, I think Anaïs is exactly the partying kind." Kay's eyes narrow. "I think Anaïs would be an absolute blast on nights out. But I think her first time out in London spooked her, and now she doesn't dare try again. Maybe you know what put her off so much?"

"I wouldn't say put off," I say, suppressing the urge to glare at her. "Maybe she's just being cautious. She is engaged, after all."

"So are you." Kay's smile is mocking. "And yet here you are."

This time, I glare at her. Kay accusing me of straying is ironic, but that's not why I'm angry at her. I realise I no longer care about any of that. Our relationship, asking her to get engaged after Spearcrest, finding out she was sleeping around the whole time.

I'm angry because I don't want to be here, dancing with other girls. I want to be here, dancing with Anaïs. But I don't think Anaïs wants to be here with me, and Kay seems to know that.

"I don't think Anaïs cares about me being here," I reply, bitterness seeping into my voice.

"Hah, for once, I think you're absolutely right." She lets out an airy laugh. "Such a cruel twist of fate. You could fuck every girl in this club, and Anaïs wouldn't care at all. Ironic, isn't it?"

"How is that ironic?"

"Ironic because if Anaïs so much as kissed someone other than you, I think you would lose your shit."

Kay isn't wrong, but I'd rather die than admit it. "Anaïs can do whatever she likes."

"Oh, good." Kay gives a melodramatic sigh of relief. "Because I'm throwing a little get-together after the exams, and I invited Anaïs."

"Great."

"You don't mind, do you?"

I wave my hand in dismissal. "Why should I?"

"You're right, you shouldn't. I'm glad we've cleared that up. I was a bit worried when Parker told me he was going to ask Anaïs to go with him."

My gut churns. For a second, I'm scared I'm about to throw up across the table.

But I swallow and bite down hard. Kay is watching me with that cocky little smirk, looking like the cat that got the cream.

"Some shit party you're throwing," I say finally, forcing my voice to remain low and calm. "If you're inviting the likes of Parker."

"I didn't invite him," she says, "but Anaïs gets to bring whoever she wants. Including Parker."

"As if she'd go with him."

"Why wouldn't she?"

"Parker's a loser."

Kay shrugs. "That's what you think, not what Anaïs thinks. Luckily for Parker, it's her he's asking to the party, not you." We stare at each other for a second. Kay gestures to the men facing her. "Do you mind, Sev? Unlike you, I intend to end the night in somebody's bed."

"Fine." I stand. "I presume I'm invited to your little get-together?"

She grins. "Of course. Bring a plus one if you wish."

"Fine."

"Great," she says. As I walk away, she adds, "Oh, and Sev?"

I turn back to look at her.

"Choose your plus one carefully, will you?"

I glare at her and walk away without a word.

Chapter 28

L'Ordre

Anaïs

Séverin must have been right about the limousine driver spying for our parents because a week after the date, I get a text from my mother.

Maman: Hope you're well, Anaïs. Your father and I are glad to hear things are going well with Séverin. x

I lock my phone and throw it in the bottom of my bag. I'm sitting in a corner of my usual art studio, working on a painting. With a sigh, I resume my work. These days, painting is the only thing that feels familiar and safe.

The only aspect of my life where I'm completely in control.

With my painting knife, I crush and mix my colours: burnt sienna and silver imit and pearl white to complement the sage greens and misty blues on my palette.

I'm working on one of my exhibition pieces, a painting based on the Isle of Skye mountains. The outlines are done, and I'm in the middle of painting the backdrop of moody clouds when the door to the studio slams open.

Startled, I turn, my brush jerking across the canvas.

"Shit! Oh—Séverin."

He stands in the doorway. His uniform is perfect and crisp, the necklaces and rings glittering at his hands and throat.

But his hair is in disarray, strands falling across his forehead. A deep flush is in his cheeks. He's breathing hard like he's been running.

He stares at me from across the room, his chest rising and falling.

"Um, are you alright?" I ask.

He nods, slowly crossing the room. I'm sitting in front of my canvas, which is propped against a drying rack next to the window. Outside, the sky is gunmetal grey, the sun already a long-forgotten blur low in the sky.

"I've been looking for you," he says finally.

I frown. "If I'm not in lessons, I'm usually here, painting."

"Why here?"

I gesture with my brush at the window. "Good view."

"There are better views in Spearcrest," he says haughtily.

"Right...?"

"I'll show you," he says. "If you want."

"I'd like that."

Silence falls once more. The studio is completely silent. There are no classes on the corridor; the teachers are all in their offices. Outside, everything is deadly still, branches and leaves suspended in the windless air.

"Did you... um, did you want something?" I ask finally.

We've not talked since the night of the date; we've not so much as texted. But the tension of that night, instead of dissipating in the time we were apart, seems only to have grown.

Sev stands right next to me, looking down at me with a slight frown. In a sudden movement, he crouches next to me and takes my chin in his hand.

"You've got paint all over your face," he says in a thoughtful tone.

"Yea. That happens a lot. I told you."

His eyes fall from mine, dropping to my mouth, then my throat. His hand follows his gaze. He tugs on my shirt collar with his thumb.

"You're wearing the ring," he says.

"Yes. Why wouldn't I?"

His lips move in the ghost of a smile. "It looks nice. Gold suits you."

I lick my lips. I'm nervous now.

Nervous because of his soft, thoughtful voice, the needless intensity of this moment. His presence is like a pool of gasoline, the iridescent gleam screaming danger. One spark, and we'll both go up in flames.

"Are you going to Kay's party after the exams?" he asks suddenly, his words rushing out of his mouth.

I nod. "Yes. I thought it might be nice. And I'm always saying no to her. I felt bad."

"I didn't think you liked parties."

I let out a soft laugh. "No, I like them. But the parties I'm used to aren't like the parties here."

"What parties are you used to?"

"The beach, cheap drinks, bonfires, night swimming."

He bites down on his lips. I have the feeling there's something he wants to get off his chest or something he wants but doesn't know how to ask for. Emotions pour off him like a tangible heat, searing my skin.

"Who are you going to the party with?"

I frown. "Uh... myself?"

"Nobody asked you?"

My heart stops, caught in a vice of hope.

"No," I answer softly. "Why?"

He stares at me, his green-gold eyes searching mine. Is this why he's come here? Does he want to ask me to go with him?

"I was just asking," he says.

"Well... okay." My voice is low, the heat emanating from him melting my vocal cords. I lean into him without even realising. "Is there anything else you want to ask?"

He licks his lips slowly. I hold my breath, wondering if he's tasting the ghost of the kiss that hangs between our mouths. But then he shakes his head and stands. "No. Nothing. If somebody asks you, just say no."

"Pardon?"

He pushes his hair away from his forehead. "If somebody asks you to go to the party, just say no, alright?"

His audacity almost makes my heart stop. My voice shakes when I speak. "I'll say no if I want to say no."

"And if you want to say yes?"

"Then I'll say yes."

Ask me, I want to shout at him, *just ask me*.

He glares at me, takes a deep breath. The flush in his cheeks darkens. His eyes glitter with a dangerous spark. "The party is in Spearcrest. If you go with someone else, it'll look bad on me."

"Who cares?" I get to my feet, sick of him looking down on me, sick of this uneven power balance he seems hellbent on establishing between us. "We both agreed this engagement is a fake thing, an act. We shook hands as allies, remember? You do what you want, I do what I want. Who cares what other people think?"

"This isn't *your* school!" he exclaims, a strange emotion tightening his voice. "You don't have a reputation to uphold. You don't have to deal with the repercussions of your actions."

"We're in college," I say coldly, "not a mediaeval royal court. Why are you taking this so seriously?"

"Just because you're too high and mighty to care about the world around you doesn't mean it doesn't matter." He suddenly straightens himself up. "I know we made a deal, and I'm not going back on it. You can do what you like in private. But if somebody asks you to this stupid party, say no. I'm not asking you—I'm *telling* you."

"You don't get to tell me what to do," I say. To my embarrassment, I feel a lump in my throat. "I'll say yes to whoever I want, and I'll do whatever I want. In fact, I'm going to say yes to the first person who asks me to that party, even if it's the devil himself."

"The devil himself is exactly who you'll be dealing with if you do this," Séverin bites out.

"I'm not scared of him," I say. "Or you."

"You should be."

Séverin storms out, slamming the door shut. Behind him, a complete vacuum of emotion remains.

I glare after him, trembling from head to foot, adrenaline coursing through me. Does he really think I would fear him when he's too much of a coward to ask me to some party?

Séverin didn't come here because he doesn't want me to go to the party with somebody else. He came here because he wants to go to the party with me. He just didn't have the guts to do it.

Part of me wants to follow him and tell him I see right through his fiery exterior and into the soft glowing ember of tenderness within.

But it's not my job to force this immature idiot to grow up and face his own feelings. It's not my job to make him realise that the hierarchy he's created for himself in this school has become a self-made prison.

Once my heartbeat stills, I try to get back to my work, but I'm too restless to paint.

I set my canvas aside. The accidental line made by my brush when Séverin burst into the room is a dreary reminder of what happened. I wash my brushes, my knives and my palette, dry them, pack them away and leave the art studio.

THE NEXT DAY, I'M sitting on a bench outside the main campus, sipping tea from a paper cup and chewing absent-mindedly on a sandwich. It's bitingly cold outside, so the grounds are pretty empty. But I like the dust-grey sky, the trees surrendering the last of their leaves to the sharp wind, the frosty grass glittering in dulled sunlight.

I sit with my phone in my lap, staring at Noël's face in its little circle.

Should I ask him for advice? He's always been my first choice whenever I've needed counsel in the past. His advice is measured and calm.

It's rarely what I want to hear, but it's always wise.

I type some words in the new text bubble but delete them straight away. How would I even phrase this? How would I begin to explain this stupid, petty argument to begin with?

As open-minded, emotionless and non-judgemental as Noël is, there's no chance I can tell him about the things Sev and I have done. Not when I'm still planning to abandon him and our engagement at the end of the school year.

This thought rears itself, small at first and then monstrous and dark.

I'm leaving at the end of the year.

The more time I've spent with Séverin, the more it's obvious he doesn't suspect my plan. When I was first working out a way of escaping the engagement, I always assumed Séverin was doing the same.

The womanising socialite, the high-society playboy—why would he settle with a bride he didn't choose? An arranged marriage? A future trapped in married life?

Now, I'm not so sure. If I had to put money on it, I would guess that Séverin has no plan at all. Séverin, the incurable playboy, seems ready to go through with this engagement.

And that hurts like a knife to the chest.

"Hey, Anaïs."

I look up with a start, almost dropping my phone.

Parker, the boy from the photography class, is approaching me across the lawn.

He's a handsome boy—though his beauty fades to ashes when compared to Séverin's—but who's comparing?

There's nothing to compare.

Séverin is sullen and mercurial and doesn't know what he wants. Parker is walking towards me with a bright smile and determined steps, looking like he knows exactly what he wants.

"Remember me?" he asks, stopping in front of me.

"Of course. Parker, right?"

"Right." He stands with his hands in his pockets, kicking the frost off the grass with boyish hesitation. "Are you going to Kayana's party?"

My heart twists in my chest. "I think so, yes."

"Well, I was wondering if... well." He smiles. "Do you want to go with me?"

The two paths branch out in front of me.

Say yes and teach Séverin he can't tell me what to do. He might be a king here at Spearcrest, but I don't answer to any monarch. Say yes—and risk Séverin's fury.

Say no and pacify Séverin with obedience. Make what remains of my life here easier for the time I've got left. Séverin would love this: my pride sacrificed so that his may be spared.

I don't want to go to the party with Parker. I don't even want to go to the party at all.

But I can't bring myself to give Séverin the satisfaction.

"I'd love to go with you, Parker."

Chapter 29

LE POING

Séverin

THE COLD AIR WHIPS against my face as I run through the trees.

A little ahead of me, Iakov and Evan half-race each other. This is supposed to be a casual run, but Evan's an athlete at heart. He can't help but be competitive.

As for Iakov, he's running like a man being chased by his demons.

I roll my eyes and keep pace behind them. Unlike them, I'm not running to compete or to escape demons. I'm running to clear my head.

Before Anaïs arrived, life used to be simple. Especially when I replaced love and relationships with fleeting pleasure.

I had everything I wanted; I did whatever I wanted. Parties, power, drinking, flirting, fucking. Girls fell into my bed at the snap of a finger and left just as quickly. Life was a rigged game: designed for me to win.

Anaïs ruined everything.

Like wild weeds in a flowerbed, she invaded my life, my mind. Thoughts of her wrap around me like vines until I can't think of anything but her.

If I could tear her out of my head and burn her away, roots and all, I would. I would rip her out of my life and go back to tending pretty blooms.

Evan and Iakov run to the lake at the edge of campus.

Students aren't allowed there, but it's the perfect spot if you're looking for some quiet space to think. Iakov strides to the end of the wooden jetty and, without ceremony, strips. He tosses his T-shirt, sweatpants, shoes and socks aside, careless about where they land.

Then he jumps into the lake.

"What's his problem?" I mutter to Evan.

"Who knows," Evan says.

Iakov emerges from the water and wades closer to us, brushing a hand through his short hair.

"Come on," he says. "Good water. Clears the head."

Evan and I exchange a glance. Evan shrugs, and I sigh. We imitate Iakov, taking off our clothes and jumping in the water.

The shock of the cold takes my breath away, but as soon as my body adjusts to the temperature, I understand why Iakov is doing this. He's not wrong about it clearing the head.

I swim through the icy water, and my head feels clearer than it has in a long time.

Clear enough for me to realise how truly fucked I am.

Once every thought and pretence and lie and question is stripped from my mind, only one thing remains.

I want Anaïs.

I crave her like sugar, like something I know is bad for me but tastes too good to give up. I want her like a tyrant because she doesn't seem to want me, doesn't listen to me, fights me at every turn.

Do I want her because she doesn't want me?

But I'm not sure she doesn't. I'm not sure of anything with her. She would tell me if I asked, I'm sure of it. I'm just too scared to ask.

Heaving myself up on the jetty, I let the cold air hit my wet limbs. It's painful and bracing, but it feels good at the same time. Evan is swimming in strong laps around the lake, his blond hair darkened by the water.

Evan has always struck me as a complete fool. He's a star athlete, one of the most popular boys in Spearcrest. Unlike me, Evan craves love, and girls would throw themselves at his feet to give him what he wants.

And yet he still wants Sophie Sutton. A girl who hates his guts, who puts him down at every turn, who would die before she ever gave him a kind word.

To me, that was always the most embarrassing part of Evan. How could he want someone who so blatantly disliked him? When he could have anyone else he wanted?

But now, I'm starting to understand.

I'll never understand what Evan sees in Sutton, but I understand his pain. Nobody would choose to want someone they can't have. Sophie's made Evan miserable for years—they've made each other miserable for years—but Evan doesn't have a choice but to suffer.

And now, I'm in the same position as him.

What a tragic state of affairs.

Later, when we're heading back to the dorms after our swim, I walk alongside Evan.

"Are you going to Kay's party?"

He shakes his head. "No. What's the point? Sophie's not invited."

"Fuck Sophie—right?" I hold his gaze. If Evan can break away from Sophie, then I can break away from Anaïs. Right?

"Sophie is a nightmare I can't wake up from," Evan says loudly, glaring at me as if I'm Sophie. "You can slap me all you like, Sev. I'm never gonna wake up from this."

I have no reply, so I look away. I suspect he's right, anyway.

But fuck *this*. If I ever end up sounding like him, I think I'd rather jump from the top of the clock tower.

So as soon as I get back to the dorms, I make sure I don't end up like him. I grab my phone, scrolling through the pretty names in my contact list.

My eyes fall on a familiar name. Melody—Mellie. The art student with the flower clips. Perfectly my type, perfectly willing.

I type out a text and press send without hesitation.

"*Salut, mon ange*. Would you like to be my date for a party this Friday?"

She replies straight away.

"Oh my god, I would love to be!"

"Perfect. See you Friday."

She sends me back a heart emoji. Locking my phone, I toss it on my bed. I won't let Anaïs Nishihara become the nightmare I can't wake up from.

I'll be her nightmare instead.

My good mood buoys me until Friday, and then it's pierced by a bullet which sends it crashing and burning.

The bullet is that piece of shit, Parker Pembroke. The gun firing the bullet is Zachary. He waltzes into the rec room at lunchtime with a pile of books under his arm and a bar of black chocolate between his teeth.

He takes a bite, snapping the thin bar, and then points it at me in accusation.

"How come you're not taking the future Mrs Montcroix to Kayana's party?" He shakes his head and drops onto a couch. "I was looking forward to seeing her again."

I look up from my phone, where trite social media posts scroll past my thumb. "What?"

"You're not going to the party tonight?" Zachary asks, raising an eyebrow.

His unshakeable calm grates against my impatience like nails on a blackboard. I glare at him. "Of course I'm going."

"Without Anaïs?"

"I'm going with someone else."

Evan and Iakov both look up at me as though they seem surprised.

"You're not taking her?" Evan asks in a surprised tone.

"Why would I?"

"Perhaps because she is your future wife?" Zach says with false courtesy. "You'd think one would rather have one's fiancée on one's arm rather than let someone else bring her on his."

"What are you talking about? Speak like a normal person."

"I'm talking about young Master Pembroke—you know he's technically a baronet?—crowing to all who would listen that he is bringing your fiancée to Kayana's party."

Kay warned me he would ask, and Anaïs told me to my face she would say yes to whoever asked. But I never believed for even one moment this might happen.

My entire body shakes. I can barely control my voice.

"He's doing *what*?"

Zach shrugs. "He's in the dining hall right now, holding court to a whole host of Spearcrest king aspirants."

I'm on my feet before Zachary's even finished his sentence. Evan exclaims, "Sev—wait!" but I'm already bolting out of the rec room.

Underneath the bright chandeliers of the dining hall, sixth formers sit at the trestle tables or queue for their food. I don't even need to search the crowd before I spot Parker Pembroke. The smugness radiates from him like a pungent stench.

I head straight for him. He looks up when I approach and beams.

"Everything alright, Montcroix?"

"Not really," I bite out. "I hear you've been running your mouth and spreading rumours you shouldn't."

"I'm not sure what you mean, mate," he says glibly.

"*I'm not your mate.*"

He shrugs.

"We're not mates," I repeat, "and we're never going to be. Pitiful little baronets don't belong amongst kings. So, is there a reason you should have my fiancée's name in your mouth?"

Pembroke's smile falters, but his eyes brighten. This, I'm guessing, is what he wanted.

"She doesn't belong to you," he says, trying to sound casual. "Neither does her name."

For a moment, I'm more shocked than anything else. Shocked at his audacity, his recklessness.

"You must be truly fucking stupid to say something like this."

Everyone at his table is watching us. Silence has fallen in the dining hall, thick and stifling. Students gather closer, watching the scene unfold.

"I'm not stupid," Pembroke sneers. "And I'm not scared of you."

I keep my voice low, hoping he'll hear the warning in my tone. "Oh, you should be."

"Why should I? Everybody knows your engagement means nothing. If you wanted to go with her, you would have asked her. If she wanted to go with you, she wouldn't have agreed to come with me. So what's the problem?"

"The problem, you clueless little rat, is that she is *my* fiancée. My future wife. She's not yours to claim."

Pembroke lets out a high, fake laugh.

"Do you think I'm scared of you? What are you going to do, get your mates Kavinski and Knight to beat me up? Without them, what are you? Nothing. Just some French fuckboy." He stands and leans against the table, an ugly smile on his face. "So if I want to talk to your fiancée, I can. If I want to take her to the party, drag her to a dark corner and bend her over to fuck her until she doesn't even remember the name of Montcroix, I c—"

Pembroke doesn't get to finish his sentence before I'm on him.

Chairs and tables go flying back, plates and cutlery shattering as they hit the floor. Everyone jumps back, the crowd forming a circle around Pembroke and me.

I crash my fist into his face. He moves his head, and I miss, punching the table behind him. The pain doesn't even register. I punch him again, hitting him square in the face.

He scrambles back with a yell, and we both slide off the table as it tips and falls.

The rage coursing through me is maddening fuel, lending strength to each blow I rain on Pembroke. He flails, trying desperately to hit me back. His fist connects with my skull right over my eye, and I reel back.

My hand is around his collar, strangling him. He tries to hit me again, but I grab one of his flailing arms and twist it back. He lets out a high, wild cry of pain. I keep pulling on his arm, forcing him to twist his body until he's on his stomach.

Then I ram my knees between his shoulder blades, pinning him down. His arm is still in my grip, wrenched all the way back. The rage is still burning red inside me, urging me to keep pulling until I hear a crack or a crunch until he's screaming and bleeding and—

"Sev." A hand lands on my shoulder. "Let him go."

I look up. Through the crimson mist of violence and adrenaline, I see Iakov's face, his almond-shaped eyes narrowed, fixed on me.

"Come on," he says slowly. "Let go, man."

I look down at Pembroke's face. It's pressed into the floor, pale and gleaming with sweat. His eyes are wide with fear, wet with tears of pain. He looks... pathetic.

I let go of his arm but don't get off him straight away. Instead, I move my knee to the back of his neck and press down hard, drawing a strangled whimper from him.

"Remember this, you stupid piece of shit. I don't need to get my friends to beat you up. And if you ever so much as go near Anaïs, I'll break every part of you. I'll destroy you and your pathetic life. Do you understand? She's mine, *enculé*! *My* fucking fiancée, *my* fucking wife—*mine*!"

My voice has risen to a roar. Iakov grabs my arm, pulling me away.

I stand and straighten my clothes. My hair is wet when I brush it back. I look down at my hand, assuming it's sweat, but I see blood.

The crowd of students parts, and Mr Ambrose strides calmly towards me. He stands for a moment in complete silence, looking from me to Pembroke.

"Everyone, please exit the dining hall so that our kind staff may clean it." His voice is cold and hard as marble. "Mr Pembroke, Mr Montcroix. My office. Now."

Chapter 30

PUTAIN D'IDIOT

Séverin

After Mr Ambrose is done with me and Pembroke, he sends us both to the infirmary. The two school nurses take us to opposite ends of the room, but I don't bother to look at Pembroke.

He's a worm, a nothing. He tried coming for a Young King but couldn't put his money where his mouth is. I doubt he'll trouble me again.

The nurse cleans my face. My left eye is bruised and swollen, and I have a cut above my eye where Pembroke's face broke the skin. The nurse makes me sit in silence while she cleans the wound, then seals it shut with surgical glue.

Once she's done, she dresses the wound, hands me an ice pack and tells me to stay and rest for a bit.

I lie back on the bed with a groan, my face throbbing against the ice pack. Shit. I'm going to look a mess at the party, but I'd rather die than not go. A point needs to be made, and I'm going to make it even if I do so looking like this.

At least Parker looks worse.

I've half-slipped into an uneasy sleep when voices pull me back to consciousness. I open my eyes and see Evan and Iakov making their way to me through the quiet room.

"You alright, man?" Evan asks, sitting on the edge of my bed. "You look rough as shit."

"Pembroke looks worse," Iakov points out, grabbing a chair and pulling it closer.

"I'm sure he does." Evan nods. "But what's the point? Now you're both going to miss that stupid party."

"I'm still going," I grunt.

Evan's eyes go wide. "You are?"

"What did Ambrose say?" Iakov asks, sitting heavily down. He plucks the cigarette sitting on his ear and rolls it between his fingers.

"He said our parents have to come for a meeting first thing next term. Big meeting, and then probably suspension for three days."

"Oh shit," Evan says. "Are your parents going to be pissed?"

"They forced me to get engaged to Anaïs so that our family wouldn't get bought out by hers. I doubt my dad will be angry at me for beating up the guy who was trying to fuck her."

"Did Pembroke say that?"

My stomach churns, and my fists clench. "He said he can do whatever he likes, including taking her to the party, dragging her to a dark corner, bending her over and fucking her until she forgets my name."

"That's very bold," Evan says.

"That's very *stupid*." Iakov snickers. "What was he thinking?"

"He wasn't." I shake my head and swallow hard. "I wanted to kill him, Iakov. I wanted to rip his arm from its socket and beat him to death with it."

"I know," Iakov says.

"Look, I don't get it," Evan says, leaning closer to me. "What's happening with you and Anaïs? I thought you wanted to get rid of her. You'd think... Do you like her or something?"

"Obviously not," I snap.

"Are you sure?" Iakov says, raising an eyebrow.

"I'm sure."

"You still want to get rid of her?" Evan asks, sounding dubious.

"I want—look, get off my case. I don't have to like Anaïs to not want someone else to fuck her. She's *my* fiancée, for god's sake. Whether I fuck her or not is my business. Whether I like her or not is also my business."

"Right," Iakov says, not even pretending to sound convinced.

"Look, I'm just going to say what I think," Evan says, raising his hands. "If you want her, don't ruin everything with her—just tell her. Trust me. And you're going to have to marry her anyway, so if you want her, then really, what's the problem? So what if your parents made this match? If it works, then it works. You could be happy. You could both be happy. Just be honest with what you feel."

"That's rich coming from you," I sneer, slumping back into my pillow.

"My situation isn't like yours," Evan says with a glare. "If S—if the person I want was already mine, if she was engaged to me, do you know how happy that would make me?"

"I don't want Anaïs." I sigh. "Go away, Evan."

"I'm just saying, man," he says, shaking his head. "Ruining your own chance at being with the person you want hurts like shit. Take it from me." He stands. "I would be a shit friend if I didn't tell you the truth. Anyway, get well soon."

"I will," I say sullenly.

He rolls his eyes. "You coming, Iakov?"

Iakov looks at me. I hold his gaze, even though it's unnecessarily intense. He raises an eyebrow.

"*Kto ne riskuyet, tot ne p'yot shampanskogo,*" he says.

"I don't speak Spanish," I say, just to annoy him.

He lets out a snort of laughter. "Stupid fuck."

I give him the finger. He shrugs and walks away.

When I meet Mellie outside the sixth form girls' building, she doesn't look surprised.

I'm guessing she must have heard about the fight—I wonder if she knows what it was about, if she minds. If she does, she doesn't show it. She greets me with a kiss on my cheek.

"Aw, that looks so painful," she says in a baby voice. "I'm so sorry."

I shrug. "It looks worse than it feels."

She's wearing a tiny pink dress and strappy silver heels. Pink eyeshadow and glossy lipstick adorn her face, and her hair bounces in loose curls around her shoulders.

She is the picture-perfect representation of everything I want. When we arrive at the party, me in black trousers and a loose silk shirt unbuttoned halfway down my waist and her in pink with all that golden hair down her back, we're going to catch everyone's eyes.

This is what I want.

This is what I want, right?

I try not to think about Anaïs. It would do me no good. I need to be calm, collected, careless. Besides, it would be rude to Mellie to have her on my arm while I'm thinking of another girl—even if that girl is my pain-in-the-ass fiancée.

As soon as I arrive at the party in the old building behind the arboretum, I realise coming here was a mistake. I'm too tired, too on edge. My nerves are shot, my skin is electric.

To dull the edge, I grab two glasses of champagne and give Mellie one. We tap our glasses together. She takes a sip of her drink; I down mine.

I head over to where Zachary is standing, shoulder against a pillar, with Iakov. Although they're talking, Zachary's eyes are searching the crowd.

I follow his gaze and am completely unsurprised when it ends on Theodora, looking breathtaking in sage-green silk, surrounded by hopeless admirers. I'm sure this must be torture for Zach; I'm almost cheered up by his pain.

It's proof Evan and I aren't the only ones suffering. It's proof that even someone as smart and self-possessed as Zachary isn't above heartache.

Both Zach and Iakov give me unconvinced looks when I introduce them to Mellie, but they greet her politely. I'm glad Luca isn't here because I'm certain he wouldn't miss an opportunity to make a cutting comment, or worse yet, make a move on Mellie.

We stand for a while, just talking and drinking. The music becomes louder, faster. Mellie tugs on my hand with growing insistence. Suppressing a sigh, I follow her to the dancefloor where couples are already writhing.

And that's when I spot her.

Kayana Kilburn is standing between two old stone pillars, flushed from alcohol. She's in caramel silk and diamonds, and her mouth is open in a wide smile. She's holding another girl's hand, and they're dancing together.

The other girl, of course—inevitably—is Anaïs.

Tonight, she's in gigantic flowy trousers in ochre silk. Instead of a top, she just wears a Calvin Klein bralette in royal blue. Her plain hair hangs down the same way it always does, tucked behind her ears, unadorned.

She's wearing dramatic flicks of blue eyeliner but no other make-up. Her only jewellery is the slim gold chain around her neck, the antique Montcroix ring hanging against her sternum.

Where it belongs.

Now that I've seen her, I can't look away. I don't want to look away.

But I force myself to, turning Mellie in my arms so my back is to Anaïs. Her presence burns against my back like warm rays of sunlight. I place my arms around Mellie's waist, pulling her closer, hoping—wishing—that her proximity, her sweet perfume, her soft curves will elicit a reaction from me.

Even a flutter in my stomach—even a semi—would be a godsend at this point. A rope for me to hold on to, a hint that I'm not completely lost.

Then the song changes, the music shifts, and the crowd moves. Mellie moulds closer to me, arching into me. I look down to smile encouragingly at her.

When I look up, I see Kay moving in the crowd, caught in some boy's arm. My gaze searches the room against my will and finds what it's looking for: Anaïs.

She's standing against a pillar, a bottle of beer in her hand. She sips slowly, her gaze moving lazily over the crowd. Her eyes brush over mine, at first not seeing. Then the full force of her gaze settles on mine.

My heart catches in my throat. She raises her bottle at me, saluting me over the crowd with a slight smirk.

Holding her gaze, I pull Mellie closer to me. I let my hands curve over her ass, her waist. I pull her flush against me and cup her cheek. Anaïs raises an eyebrow and takes a sip of her beer.

She doesn't think I'm going to do this. And because she's looking at me, I can't *not* do this.

I tilt Mellie's face and kiss her full on the mouth. She lets out a little moan, and her mouth falls open under mine. My eyes still on Anaïs, I deepen the kiss, sliding my tongue into Mellie's mouth.

Anaïs never breaks the gaze.

I'm so hard my legs feel unsteady for a second. I grip Mellie closer, but I'm not stupid. My cock isn't hard because I'm holding her, kissing her. My cock is hard because of the way Anaïs is watching me, because of the way I can see the dull flush in her cheeks even from here.

Mellie pulls away to breathe. I glance down to smile at her. Her eyes are bright and glittery, and I'm struck with sudden guilt.

She doesn't even realise she's being used. How could she know this kiss had nothing to do with her? My dick is pressed against her—how could she guess I'm only hard because a girl is looking at me across the room?

A girl I want, a girl who's already mine—a girl I can't have.

I look up. The pillar is vacant, Anaïs's bottle of beer abandoned on the floor. I scan the crowd for the curtain of silky black hair, the blue bra, the ochre trousers.

Then I spot her, sidling down the wall, making a beeline to the door leading out to the arboretum.

I push Mellie away from me, muttering apologies. She looks at me with confusion.

What am I doing? The girl in my arms wants me, and I don't want her. Now I'm abandoning her in the middle of the dancefloor—probably hurting her. The girl I want is gone because I was so desperate for her to know I don't want her.

When, in fact, I want nothing else.

Iakov was right.

I really *am* a stupid fuck.

Chapter 31

La Menteuse

Anaïs

As soon as I walk out of the building, emerging from the cloud of music and heat, I feel calmer.

It was too warm inside, too loud—too full of Séverin's presence.

Outside, the air is icy and still. The frosty wind flutters the evergreens of the arboretum in a dull whisper.

I take a deep, calming breath. A voice startles me.

"Trésor—wait."

I don't even turn around. Heart in my mouth, I dive off the path and into the darkness of the arboretum.

My steps are long and quiet. I dash through the trees, hoping he won't see me, hoping the shadows swallow me whole.

Quick footsteps reach my ear, drawing closer. I hesitate, debating whether I should break into a run.

The last time I tried running from him, I failed and was caught and punished—with Séverin's particular brand of punishment.

On the other hand, I really don't want to speak to him right now. In fact, I would rather jump off a cliff to my death than look him in the face.

I jerk into motion, but before I can even make the first step, a hand closes on my arm, stopping me in my tracks. I close my eyes and swallow hard, hoping the lump in my throat will miraculously disappear before I'm forced to speak.

"Anaïs."

Séverin tugs on my arm. Not a hard tug, but insistent, impossible for me to ignore. I turn and offer him my sweetest smile.

"Yes, Séverin."

I pull my arm away from him; he lets go. I shiver in the cold air, wishing I'd brought a sweatshirt with me.

"Just say Sev," he says with a frown. "Nobody calls me Séverin."

My smile remains firmly in place. If I keep it pinned to my face, maybe I'll keep all my emotions pinned inside my chest. "Of course, Sev."

The less I fight, the quicker I can get this over with.

"Why are you leaving so early?" he asks. His tone is light, but the fire inside his eyes belies that lightness. It tells me Sev isn't as calm and casual as he's trying to sound.

That makes two of us, I suppose.

"Because I'm not having fun," I say, sticking safely close to the truth.

He steps towards me, so close the heat emanating from his body brushes against mine. So close I can make out his face in the shadows. His eyes, with their thick eyelashes, his dark hair.

How wet and soft his lips are—wet and soft from kissing the girl from my art class.

Something he has every right to do. So why should I be so upset? I have no reason to be upset.

"Come on," he says, reaching for my hand almost impulsively, as if he hadn't realised he was going to. "Stay. Please."

I pull my wrist free from his grip and step back.

"I don't want to," I say, low but firm.

He steps forward once more, closing the distance I've just created.

The night darkens his eyes; the shadows carve his features. He's only a head taller than me, but he feels disproportionately powerful right now. He feels inescapable and unavoidable.

Like the cruel fairy princes he reminds me so much of, he feels wild and fey. I sense the danger of his caprice like dark threads unfurling from him.

"Why not?" he asks, his voice as low as mine, trembling with quiet intensity.

"I don't have to explain myself to you," I say coldly, stepping back.

He steps forward. "No, you don't, trésor. But I would like you to. I'm ready to ask you nicely."

I step back. He follows.

"You can be as nice as you like," I tell him, "or you can be a complete and utter bastard—I don't care. It makes no difference to me."

"You're all thorny and wild tonight," he drawls. "How come?"

With each step I take back, he pursues me. He steps forward, refusing to allow space between us, refusing to give me room to breathe, to think, to evade him.

"Maybe I'm just in a bad mood because someone beat my date up?" I say finally, giving him a mirthless smile.

"Don't lie to me," he says. His smile is genuine, a caress of a smile, tender and sensual. "Tell me the truth. Why are you really leaving?"

"You're hunting for an answer you're just not going to get," I snap.

I take a step back, but this time, my back bumps into the rough trunk of a tree. The icy bark digs into my exposed skin, scraping against my shoulder blades. Relentless and without mercy, Sev steps forward, right against me, so close his breath is warm against my face.

"I want to hear you say it," he says, his eyes boring into mine. "Come on, trésor, *dis-moi. Dis-moi la vérité. La jolie vérité, la sale vérité—j'm'en fous. Mais dis-moi. Murmure, si tu veux.*"

Tell me the truth. The pretty truth, the dirty truth—I don't care. But tell me. Whisper it, if you like.

"There's nothing to say."

He leans forward to hiss against my ear. "*Menteuse.*"

Liar.

I lay my hand on his chest to push him away. "*Salaud.*"

Bastard.

Instead of moving away from me, he sinks his weight against me, making it impossible for me to push him away. Overwhelming my senses with his presence, his heat, the rich smoky fragrance of his expensive perfume.

"We both know you don't think that." His voice is a caress. "You don't think I'm a *salaud* at all."

"You behave like one," I say, squeezing the words out of my tightened throat.

"Is that why you're leaving, trésor?" He brushes his lips against my cheek. "Because of my behaviour? Have I been bad? Are you very angry?"

"Why should I be angry?"

He pulls away, bracing his hands against the tree trunk, keeping me trapped close to him. "You have every right to be angry. You just saw your fiancé—your future husband—kiss a beautiful girl right in front of you."

You're not my future husband, I long to say right to his face. You're not my future husband, and in a few months, you won't even be my fiancé.

But where my heart screams for revenge, my mind whispers caution.

"We have a deal," I say with a shrug. "We agreed to be allies, didn't we? Wasn't that the point? To play along but keep our freedom?"

"That alliance is bullshit," he hisses, his tone suddenly dark and seething. "It's bullshit, and you know it. You knew it even when we made our so-called deal. I'll fight every fucker in this school—every fucker in this world—before I let anybody else have you."

"Oh!" I burst out into a cold, incredulous laugh. "You're jealous, now?"

"No," he sneers. "*You* are. You're just too proud to admit it. Too proud to tell me you don't want me to kiss other girls, too proud to ask me to kiss you instead."

"Hah! You're so deluded you're not even living in the same world as the rest of us!"

"At least I don't act like I'm above the rest of the world!"

"I don't act that way." I glare at him and clench my fists, resisting the urge to punch him. "You're just projecting your childish insecurities onto me."

"My insecurities?" He throws his head back in a laugh. "You must be joking. What insecurities? My life is perfect."

"Your life is only perfect as long as everybody around you believes it's perfect. You're so obsessed with everybody else's perception of you that you barely exist as a real person."

"Is that what you tell yourself to make yourself feel better?" He gives me a cold smirk. "That you don't care what everyone thinks? Is that why you dress like a clown even though you're richer than everyone around you? Mock the upper classes when you only got engaged to gain a three-hundred-year-old name? Is that all because you don't care?"

"I'm not rich." I straighten myself, gathering all my dignity to spit at him, "And I didn't choose to be engaged to you."

"No, and yet you're here. You didn't choose this engagement, but you still moved schools, left your entire life behind to be here. You didn't choose this engagement, but you've not made one attempt at breaking it. You didn't choose me, but you still fucked me."

My face erupts into flames. His cheeks, too, are darkly flushed. His chest is pressed to mine, the hammering of his heart clashing with the hammering of mine.

"So I slept with you," I say coldly. "At least I have the courage to admit why."

"You've never admitted shit," he retorts. "You think you're so brave and honest, but you lie more than anybody I've ever met."

"Oh, *I'm* the liar?" My entire body shakes with anger. "I know why I came here tonight, and I know why I'm leaving. But you? You tried to forbid me from coming with someone else, and you beat up the only person to actually ask me out. You've even made the effort to bring a girl from my class and kiss her in front of me. And yet you're *still* lying to yourself about why you've done all these things."

This time, it's his eyes which widen in shock. This time, it's him dropping his arms from around my head, stepping away from me, putting distance between us.

"I'm not," he says thickly.

"Go on then, Séverin Montcroix—prince of truth. Why don't you tell me why you did all these things?"

"Because—because you're my fiancée, and—"

"You don't care that I'm your fiancée, remember?" I step into him, invading his space. My chest brushes against his, and an involuntary shiver claws through me, stiffening my nipples and sending goosebumps rippling over my arms. "You didn't choose me either. You didn't want me either. Right?"

"Right."

"So then—why? Why not let me come to the party with someone else? Go on. Say it."

"Pembroke didn't want to bring you to this party because he wanted the pleasure of your company, Anaïs, he—"

"You asked me to say no to anybody who asked," I point out, tilting my head. "So that's another lie."

"If you're so certain you know the truth," he snaps, "then why don't you tell me?"

"I *do* know the truth." I take a deep breath, steeling my voice to make sure it doesn't break. "And the truth is this: if you wanted to come to this party with me, then you should have asked me."

For a moment, there is nothing but silence and the melancholy sigh of the wind in the trees.

"You're ridiculous," Sev finally says in a puff of fake laughter.

"If I'm lying, then why did you follow me out here? Why not just let me leave this party?"

"Because..." He swallows hard, his throat shuddering, the gold chains glittering around his neck. "Because I want..."

It's my turn to let out a mocking laugh. "You don't know what you want, Sev. You want everyone to love you, but you don't want to love anyone. You want me to go to the party alone, but you want to go to the party with Mellie. You want to be free, but you don't want to break this engagement. You want to sleep with me, but you don't want me to think you like me."

"I know what I want," he says in a low voice. "I fucked you because I *wanted* to fuck you. You only fucked me to secure the Montcroix name."

Chapter 32

La Méprise

Séverin

When I followed Anaïs into the arboretum, I didn't even know what I intended to do.

I followed her on impulse, like being blown somewhere by an explosion. Not a thought went into the process, and the closer I got to her, the less sense everything made in my head.

Touching Anaïs causes a short circuit in my head.

It makes my thoughts sizzle and fray, leaving only raw emotions behind. When I'm around Anaïs is when I need to be the most in control, but that never happens.

Anaïs always sends me spinning out of control.

Why else would I say something like that to her? Accuse her of fucking me only to secure the Montcroix name?

I didn't say it because I believe it—I only half-believe it. Her family might be desperate for my name, but I know Anaïs now. She probably hardly cares. She probably doesn't care at all.

So why did I say this?

Because I'm fed up with always being the one spinning out of control. Because I've fallen—I'm still falling—and I want to drag her down with me into whatever abyss I'm sinking in.

"You only fucked me to secure the Montcroix name."

As soon as I say it, I wish I had the power to take it back, to burn the words out of existence.

But it's too late; there's nothing I can do. Anaïs's eyes—that pretty shape I like so much—go wide for a moment. Then her features still, as if she's suddenly turned to ice.

She goes cold all over.

"If that's what you're so worried about, Séverin," she says quietly, dangerous ice in her voice, "then let me put your mind at ease once and for all. I don't want your name. I don't care about it at all. Here is the truth you've been so desperate to find out: I agreed to the engagement because I didn't have a choice, but I came here because it was part of my plan to be free of it. If I liked you, it's because I liked you, and if I wanted to sleep with you, it's because I wanted to sleep with you. You don't have a single thing in your possession—not your status, not your fortune, not your name—I either want or need. I have no intention of staying engaged to you. I have no intention of marrying you. I never had."

My stomach drops. I have the sickening falling sensation of stepping into nothing. A horrible unsettling feeling, a pitting of the gut. I blink, and my mouth moves, wanting to form words, my voice a raw rasp.

"What do you mean?"

"Just because I didn't rage and rail like you did doesn't mean I was any more ready to accept this ridiculous engagement, Sev." Her words slice into me, so cold they burn. "But unlike you, I made a plan. I've come to Spearcrest because I need to—I'm leaving as soon as the school year is over, and I'm not coming back. So you don't need to worry about the engagement, and you don't need to worry about your precious name being stolen from you. You can return to your picture-perfect life, to your parties and your champagne and all your beautiful girls. You have my blessing. I'll be living my life freely—I hope you do the same."

I want to shout, to grab her, to force her to explain herself. Is she lying? She has got to be lying. She's always been so calm, so unemotional—this whole time, I believed it was because she was just willing to accept her parents' decision in a way that I couldn't.

How could she have a plan? How could she just leave and not come back? Does she not care about the repercussions of her actions?

Anaïs reaches around her neck, and my heart lurches. My stomach clenches.

"*Don't.*" My voice is low and dull.

There's a pain in my chest like I've been stabbed. My throat is tight, and my eyes burn.

She unclasps the necklace I gave her—the necklace with the Montcroix ring on it—and hands it to me. I step back, hands behind my back.

"I never intended to remain your fiancée," she says quietly, "but I did hope we might become allies. I think maybe we could even have been friends."

"I don't fuck my friends," I bite out.

She tilts her head to give me a sad smile.

"No. You don't fuck people you like, do you? Well, I don't know a word for that, not in English, French or Japanese." She holds the necklace up. The ring dangles from it, the diamonds catching the dim moonlight and reflecting it in brilliant sparkles. "Take it."

"I don't want it."

"Neither do I."

She opens her hand. The necklace drops, falling between us and disappearing in the tangle of frosty grass, moss and roots beneath our feet.

Without another word, Anaïs turns and walks away. This time, I don't give chase.

This time, I let her go.

THE REST OF THE evening is a blur.

I leave the arboretum with a lump in my throat and bump into Iakov, smoking outside. There's no way of telling how far away from the building Anaïs and I strayed during our confrontation; if Iakov heard anything, he keeps it to himself.

He hands me the bottle of whisky he's holding, and I take big gulps, smoothing away the lump in my throat.

He offers me a cigarette, but I decline with a wave of my hand.

I can't even talk.

I stumble into the red-brick building, music and heat swallowing me up like the wet throat of some colossal monster. Mellie runs up to me and tries to say something, but I jerk away from her, mumbling garbled apologies before I lurch through the packed dancefloor.

Kay catches my eye, and I push through the crowd towards her.

She smiles brightly and extricates herself from the grip of some boy to dance towards me.

"Having fun?" she asks through the music.

"Your party blows!" I yell back.

She waves her hand dismissively in my face. "I'm not taking responsibility for your fuck-ups!"

"What fuck-ups!" I shout, outraged, thinking about the ring hanging against Anaïs's chest, warm from her skin, now lying in hard mud and icy grass, the metal cold, the jewels dull. "I never fuck up."

"You never *had* anything to fuck up," she says, a hint of sadness in her voice. "But now you do. It's so easy, isn't it? Fucking up something good out of fear?"

We stare at each other.

"I'm not like you," I snarl. "This isn't the same."

She shakes her head. "If you say so, Sev."

With a wave of her hand, she disappears back into the crowd.

I HEAD FOR THE drinks table and almost bumping into Luca. He loops his arm around my neck and hands me a bottle of liquor.

By the smell of him and the glazed-over look in his eyes, he is about as obliterated as I'm looking to be. I take the proffered bottle, take a deep gulp, and give it back.

"How's married life?" he asks in a loud slur over the music.

"I'm not married."

He waves his bottle, brown liquor splashing over his fist. "I mean—engaged. How's engaged life?"

"Shit."

"You fucked her yet?"

"No," I lie.

If Luca thinks for a second I've slept with Anaïs, he'll have his hands around her neck and his dick inside her before I can even blink.

"You should fuck her," Luca advises.

"No. I hate her."

"I thought you liked her." Luca laughs, a cold and hollow sound. "I thought you *loved* her."

"I don't do love," I remind him. "It's poison."

"But you'd drink that poison," Luca points out, a sadistic gleam of delight in his eyes, "for her."

"I despise her," I tell him. "I wish I'd never met her."

Luca nods and tries to give me a sympathetic look. But sympathy makes him look completely demented. I burst out laughing.

The rest of the night devolves into flashes.

Iakov comes back from outside, his hands in his pockets, looking concerned.

Luca and I with our arms on each other's shoulders, yelling about how loving women is about as fun as pissing acid out of our dicks.

Iakov, Luca and I doing shots, dancing in flashing lights, laughing like maniacs. Luca extolling vengeance, and Iakov telling us a weird and disturbing story about his dad punishing his sisters instead of him when he misbehaved as a kid.

Leaving the party and howling like wolves in the arboretum. Me on my knees in the grass and mud, searching for something, my fingers numb with cold as they rip through hard moss and sharp grass. Being pulled away by Iakov and Luca and screaming something about not letting Anaïs get away with her crimes.

Things get increasingly murky after that.

Sneaking around the school corridors, cackling. Showing Iakov the gallery, where students have started putting displays together for the end-of-year exhibition. Running down the long marble chamber, past the fluted pillars. Luca staring for ages at a picture that's just a canvas painted completely black. Iakov and I laughing hysterically at his expression of grim fascination.

Memories of laughter and shouting. Tearing and ripping and kicking. Luca grabbing the black painting away from its display. Running away from the gallery.

Taking a sharp and impulsive turn to the art corridor, Iakov and Luca shouting my name. Rummaging like a lunatic through the art studios, sending stacks of canvases flying until I find a painting, which I grab under my arm.

More running, cold air, trees. A wooden jetty, the shock of plunging into icy water. A sodden, shivering walk in the dark. More darkness.

Complete darkness.

PRINTEMPS

"Donne-moi l'espérance ;
Je te l'offre en retour.
Apprends-moi la constance ;
Je t'apprendrai l'amour.
Comme je t'aime en mes beaux jours,
Je veux t'aimer toujours.."

Marceline Desbordes-Valmore

Chapter 33

LA PEINTURE

Anaïs

The first Monday back after the break, we're brought into the assembly hall for the final assembly of the year.

If there's one thing they seem to love in British schools, it's gathering students for assemblies—solemn affairs delivered by the headmaster himself, entailing long speeches about the importance of acknowledging the privileges we've been given here at Spearcrest. Making the most of the world-class education we've been provided, remembering to give back to the community and never forgetting those who are not as lucky as us.

It's a nice sentiment when you ignore the sea of Chanel purses propped on the girls' laps and the heavy Rolex watches glimmering on the boys' wrists.

The assemblies are mandatory, so I sidle in with the rest of the Spearcrest students. My heart catches when Mr Ambrose announces this is our final assembly as a year group.

When I first arrived at Spearcrest, I imagined the year was going to stretch out interminably. I imagined the time between arriving here and getting on the plane to Japan would drag endlessly.

But it hasn't. A couple of months, a flurry of exams, and then I'll be gone from here.

I'll never see any of these eerily beautiful Spearcrest kids again. I'll never see their so-called kings, the audacious, arrogant, pretty boys who have taken it upon themselves to impose their self-titled monarchy upon others.

I'll never see Séverin Montcroix, the green-eyed prince, the gilded heir.

And maybe that's for the best.

I had a lot of time to think over the week-long break. Telling Sev about my plan, about the end of the engagement, was like letting go of a burden I didn't know I was carrying. After I told him, after I gave him his ring back, I felt different.

Light, peaceful. Like myself again.

Then the sadness set in. But sadness is a part of life. I worked sadness into my sketchbooks, and I let it flow through me at night, crying in the darkness of my bedroom. That week, I spoke to Noël almost every day, though I never told him what happened.

He told me about Japan, about the local convenience store, the stray cat that sits under the fruit stalls. His studies, his job at his university. The little crushes he has on all the pretty boys and girls in his classes. Noël could hear the sadness in my voice, and instead of dragging the pain out of me, he soothed it with his calm voice, his stories—promises of our future together.

It's a beautiful future. Far from the red-brick walls and rigidity of Spearcrest. Far from the galas and glitter of French high society, far from my parents' demands and choices.

Far from Séverin and his green eyes and his laughing mouth and his kisses.

Polite applause brings me back to reality. The assembly is over, but we're not being dismissed.

Instead, a woman steps up to the lectern next to Mr Ambrose. He raises a hand to silence the murmuring students.

"Can I please ask all students taking fine arts or photography this year to remain seated. The rest of you are dismissed and may leave promptly and quietly."

Students glance at each other but obey, some sidling out silently, the rest looking restlessly around in their seats. A dull sense of doom settles over me. I don't even need to look at the teachers' grim faces to guess this is going to be bad news.

The woman next to Mr Ambrose steps forward. She's wearing a pine-green pantsuit over a blouse of pearl-white silk and black pointy heels. Her hands are in her pockets, and her dark hair is in long twists. Her mouth is set in a severe line.

"Good morning, students. I'm Miss Izem. Some of you already know me, and for those who do not, I am the Director of Faculty for the Arts Department here at Spearcrest Academy."

The two girls closest to me swap a puzzled look. I keep my eyes fixed on Miss Izem, avoiding the temptation to search the room for a glimpse of Séverin.

He's definitely here—he walked in late with the rest of his royal friends to Mr Ambrose's ire earlier.

But I don't need to look at his face to know this is about him. He's probably sitting there looking perfectly happy with himself. Whatever Miss Izem is going to tell us, I doubt he's going to display remorse.

"It gives me no pleasure to make this announcement," Miss Izem says sternly, "but you are all young adults, and I'm sure you'll deal with this with maturity and poise. At the end of the last term, before the gallery was locked up for the half-term break, it would seem a student took it upon themselves to break into the gallery and destroy some displays.

"This will affect some of you more than others since not every display was equally affected. Your teachers and I know how hard you have worked on this project and how important the exhibition is to some of you, especially those of you wishing to pursue a career in the arts. Unfortunately, we have no way of finding out who created this damage. It's most likely that the culprit for this heinous act of destruction and disruption is sitting here among us right now."

She pauses and looks around the room.

"Here at Spearcrest, we pride ourselves on having taught you to a high academic level but also to a high moral standard too. We would like to believe that the person responsible for this will do the right thing and come talk to myself or Mr Ambrose. In the meantime, the department and staff will support you all in repairing damages and ensuring the exhibition still goes ahead. The annual exhibition is an important and beloved Spearcrest tradition. It shall remain so."

With a final stern address from Mr Ambrose, who expresses his disappointment and sympathy, we are dismissed from the assembly hall.

I avoid the main doors—I have no wish to bump into Sev either intentionally or by accident—and head straight for the emergency exit leading to the other side of the building.

Once I'm standing outside, I glance around. Students are trickling out of the building, scattering off in various directions. I have a free period and every intention of heading straight to the arts building, but I wait for a few minutes, leaning back against the wall with a sigh.

The brisk wind brushes through my hair, dragging goosebumps across my skin.

I'm tempted to go check out the gallery, but I can already guess my display was affected by the mysterious assault. For all his over-emotional antics, Séverin isn't stupid. He wanted to hit me where he thought it might hurt—so he chose my display.

My display and my chance at winning the award.

Winning that grant would have made life in Japan easier, but Sev is wrong if he thinks money matters to me. If it did, I wouldn't be running away from my parents. I wouldn't be pursuing art. If I need money, I'll do what normal people do and work for it.

Destroying my display means nothing. I'll start again. There was only one important piece in that display: my painting from the balcony. I love that painting with all my heart. The dreamy colours, Sev's beauty captured through the lens of my emotions that night.

This painting doesn't feel like just a painting. It feels like the last remnant of what I had with Sev. A reminder of what could have been between us.

But that painting is safely tucked away in a corner of the art studio I work in. I'd wanted to put some finishing touches on it, so I'd left it there to dry.

That painting is the heart of my display. So long as I have it, I can rebuild everything else around it. So long as I have it, everything will be alright.

I believe that all the way to the art building. Then I enter the smallest of the art studios to find Séverin waiting there. He's pacing up and down the room, glancing distractedly out of the window.

I freeze in the doorway and take an involuntary step away.

Even though I haven't made a sound, Séverin turns. He raises a hand as I back away.

"Don't."

I hesitate. The wild urge to flee courses through me, the way it always does when I'm around him. But running from him has never solved problems—it's only ever created them.

So I take a deep breath and walk into the studio, closing the door behind me.

Chapter 34

La Clémence

Anaïs

Séverin and I face each other across the room.

The smell of paint and varnish and linseed oil mingle in the air. That strong, heady smell I love so much. It's strange being face-to-face with him here, in my territory, the place I feel safest in. I stare at him, waiting for him to speak, already half-knowing what he's going to say.

He looks beautiful and tragic and tormented. Purple shadows gather under his eyes. Loose strands of his dark hair keep falling on his forehead, no matter how many times he keeps pushing it back. His uniform is a little rumpled, the chains around his neck tangled.

"Anaïs." My entire body stiffens. He's calling me by name. That can't be a good sign. "I have to tell you something."

I raise a hand. "No, you don't. I don't—" I catch my voice. Saying this feels like a lie, even though it's not. "I don't care about the exhibit."

His mouth closes, and his jaw tightens, muscles jumping there. "You don't?"

I shake my head. He came here clearly expecting me to be hurt, to be angry. But I feel none of these things. I just want this conversation to be over. "It's only worth forty per cent of our final mark. It's fine. I'll make up for it."

He shakes his head slowly. His eyes are wide and anguished and glittering like jewels. "What about the award? The grant?"

"It's only money." I try to smile, but it feels forced, almost painful. "I'm rich, remember?"

"Oh."

The sheer strength of the emotions pouring from him fills the room with invisible heat. It wraps around me, suffocating me. How can I remain cool and composed when his emotions burn like red-hot flames whenever he's near me?

"Look, Séverin."

"*Just. Say. Sev.*"

"Alright. *Sev*. Look. I can imagine what happened with the exhibit. But I won't tell on you, so you don't need to worry. And I don't expect an apology. I know that—" I interrupt myself, hesitating, wondering if he's going to be offended. "I know that we probably hurt one another last time. But I…"

I sigh and hesitate once more.

Why is he not interrupting me? Why is he not trying to argue and fight the way he always does? What happened to the boy who chased me through the woods, who forced me to slap him just because it amused him?

And where is the girl I used to be? The girl who could lock herself away and keep herself safe and live in her bubble far away from the world and its messy emotions?

I want her back. But I suspect I won't get her back until I'm halfway across the world from Sev.

So, for the first time in my life, I open my mouth and say exactly what I'm feeling. I let the emotions spill out like green sea water and algae from a gutted mermaid.

"I don't hate you, Séverin Montcroix."

My voice trembles as I speak. Sev doesn't even try to control his reactions to my words. His eyes soften in an unbearable expression. He bites his bottom lip and steps forward. I continue before I can no longer speak.

"I don't hate you. I never have. You're too emotional, too impulsive, too impetuous. But I don't hate you, not even a little. I think, for a while, I even liked you. If things had been different, I think you and I could have been something different altogether. Something splendid and interesting and exhilarating. But things happened the way they did. I don't blame you for not wanting this engagement, for not wanting your hand forced and your fate chosen for you. But you can't blame me for not wanting that either. You can't blame me for leaving."

He opens his mouth, but I continue while I still have the courage to do so.

"I know it hurt you to hear that, and you probably wanted to hurt me back. But I don't blame you. I don't blame you for anything. Honestly, I—" The lump in my throat is making it hard to speak—hard to breathe. "If I look inside myself, I can't find even a morsel of hatred for you. So whatever you've done, I forgive you. I don't care. I don't care at all."

Séverin swallows hard, his throat shuddering. He brushes his hand through his hair, but the strands fall back on his forehead, covering one eye. I hadn't realised how long his hair has grown. His mouth moves, but he doesn't speak straight away.

Then he turns, grabs a canvas propped against the window and turns to show it to me.

"What about this?"

He's holding our painting—well, my painting, his image. Our moment, with the mountains and the stars and the lake in Scotland and all the laughter and pleasure we shared.

It's wrecked beyond belief. The paint is smudged; the canvas is scratched and sodden. Sev's dreamy face is an unrecognisable blur. My most recent changes have disappeared.

How did he even manage to do this much damage?

I let out a sigh that almost sounds like a laugh. *Of course* Sev tried to destroy my painting. He knows me more than I give him credit for. The irony is bittersweet.

"It doesn't matter." I take the canvas from his hand. My eyes sting. "I still forgive you. It's fine. I'll, um... I'll paint over it."

"You said it was *Aletheia*—remember?" His voice trembles. "You said you painted the truth of what you felt that night."

"I did."

"How are you going to paint over it?"

"I'll paint something different."

"And what about that night? That moment? The truth of it, of what you felt then?"

"What about it?"

His eyes become pitiful, almost pleading.

"Is it gone, then?" His voice is wretched. "Completely destroyed? Like the painting?"

I shake my head. "Of course not, you idiot. That painting took me hours. I put so much work and care into it. If you feel bad about that, then good. You should." His features melt with sadness, and I almost have to repress the urge to laugh. "You've wasted time and paint, Sev. You owe me a new box of acrylics. But whatever happened that night happened and nothing can take it away. I don't regret it. I don't regret anything."

I take the ruined painting from his hands and set it gently aside. For a moment, we just stare at one another. I've told him everything I feel, and I feel oddly... light. Free. Like I can breathe again.

He just looks more anguished than ever.

"I came here to apologise to you," he tells me.

"And I've forgiven you."

"Alright," he says.

He waits. We're only a few steps from each other, but the space between us stretches, wide enough to engulf planets, stars, galaxies.

"I thought you'd be angry at me," he says finally.

"Well, I'm not."

"Then why don't I feel better?" His voice breaks.

"Because forgiveness isn't redemption, Sev."

"I don't know how I can even begin to redeem myself, but I'll do everything I can, I..." He sighs and gazes deep into my eyes. His voice comes out in an anguished murmur. "I'd do anything for you, Anaïs."

My chest tightens, and the feeling of lightness suddenly evaporates.

"Even if it's something you don't want to do?" I ask him, throat tight.

"Like what?"

"Like letting me go."

He steps towards me. "Anaïs. Trésor, I..."

He opens his mouth, and a loud buzzing sound emerges from his blazer pocket, startling us both.

"Fuck!" he exclaims, his voice rough. He pulls the phone from his pocket. "Ah, *putain*, shit—I have to go, Anaïs, my parents are here for the meeting with—Shit, I'm late, as well. I'm sorry, Anaïs, I'm so sorry. But I'll—I'll be back!"

He runs to the door, wrenches it open, stops.

Then, with his habitual impulsiveness, he runs back to me. He grabs my head in both hands and kisses me full on the mouth. He releases me and runs out, leaving nothing but silence and confusion and my madly beating heart in his wake.

Chapter 35

LA CONFESSION

Séverin

When I reach the little atrium outside Mr Ambrose's office, my parents look incandescent with barely repressed fury.

My father, Conte Sylvain de Montcroix, is wearing an impeccable suit, his silver hair slicked back. At his side, my mother, Princesse Laila Nassiri, is dressed head to toe in Alexander McQueen. They're both wearing black like they're going to a funeral.

My funeral.

"Button up your shirt and fix your blazer," my father says as soon as I stop in front of them.

I do what he says, speaking as I try to catch my breath. "Sorry, I didn't keep track of the time. There was something I had to do."

"A man's reputation is only as good as his manners," my father says sternly, raking his eyes over me. "When was the last time you got a haircut?"

I push my hair back and throw him a look. "*Ça va, ça va. Arrête, Papa.*"

My mother takes my hand and squeezes it. "*Je suis contente de te voir, mais très déçue aussi.*"

I'm happy to see you, but so disappointed too.

"Je sais, je sais, mais—"

Mr Ambrose opens the door to his office, and my parents turn to face him. He welcomes us inside, and I take a deep breath as I follow my parents in.

If I could, I would rather wait outside. It's not like my parents are interested in my reasons and excuses. But I don't want my father to think I'm incapable of facing this head-on.

Maybe it's time to face *all* my mistakes head-on.

Mr Ambrose shakes their hands, and we all sit. His office is bleak and austere, just like him. Dark leather and sleek surfaces, a wall of pictures of alumni and a bookshelf full of old volumes. I sit between my parents and face him across his broad desk.

He sits back and begins.

"First of all, thank you, Mr and Mrs Montcroix, for taking time out of your busy schedules to be here. I was hoping our next meeting would be at the end-of-year exhibition. It saddens me that we should meet under such solemn circumstances."

My parents nod. Although both of them show no sign of impatience, both sitting elegantly in their chairs, I can tell that they just want to know what I've done.

Mr Ambrose begins with an earnest reiteration of Spearcrest's reputation, history and ethos. Then he continues by reminding my parents of the school's zero-tolerance policy towards misconduct and violence.

My father stiffens ever so slightly in his seat. My mother throws me a glance from the corner of her eyes. Neither of them says anything, but I can tell they've figured out I've been in a fight. I can tell they're shocked—I don't blame them.

I've not been in a fight since my first year at Spearcrest, almost seven years ago.

To Mr Ambrose's credit, he tells the full story very calmly, without any accusation or blame-slinging. When he's done, Mr Ambrose asks me if there is any additional information I wish to add to his statement of events. I shake my head.

To my parents' credit, they handle themselves with the utmost dignity. They don't question Mr Ambrose like everything is his fault. They accept responsibility on my behalf and apologise to Mr Ambrose and ask him to extend their apologies to the Pembroke family.

Mr Ambrose tells them the standard punishment is three days of exclusion, which Parker and I will both serve this week. My parents accept this without protest. They don't complain about the negative impact on my studies or exams. They simply tell Mr Ambrose that I will work extremely hard to keep up while I'm gone.

I offer little contribution aside from formal apologies and agreeing with everything I'm being told. I've had a week to prepare for this, and I'm already braced for the grilling I'm going to face once my parents and I are alone on the way home.

But for now, I'm too busy mentally bracing myself for what I'm about to do.

"Mr Ambrose," I say when silence finally falls. "There's something else."

He raises an eyebrow. He doesn't seem surprised.

My parents do.

"Go ahead, Séverin," Mr Ambrose says calmly, sitting back in his chair and steepling his fingers.

"The exhibition." I brush my hair back and swallow. "It was me, Mr Ambrose. I was the one who snuck into the gallery and wrecked everything. I'm so sorry, sir."

"Right," Mr Ambrose says. "Thank you for telling me, Séverin."

"What's this?" my mother asks, leaning forward and frowning at me. "What did you do, Sev?"

"I, um... the arts and photography students have started putting their work together for the end-of-year exhibition—the one you've been invited to—and I... I wrecked it."

My mom's eyes, so much darker than mine, dark and soulful and framed with thick black eyelashes, widen in her surprise. "Oh, Sev!"

My father offers more apologies and asks Mr Ambrose about the sanction. Mr Ambrose sinks into thoughtful silence before finally speaking.

"In this instance, I think Séverin's actions will not result in additional days of exclusion. Instead, Séverin will serve his sanction in person upon his return. It would be fair for him to serve his sanction by helping the Arts Department and make amends."

Mr Ambrose thanks my parents for coming to meet him. He stands and shakes hands with them and accompanies us to the door. I shake his hand before walking out, but he doesn't let me go straight away. He tightens his grip around my hand.

"You're not a bad person, Séverin," he says quietly. "You're better than the behaviour you've displayed this term. Whatever is causing your actions, I suggest you find a more mature and elegant way of dealing with it."

He's not wrong. "I know, Mr Ambrose. I will, I promise."

***

THE LIMO DRIVE TO the closest private airport is tense and quiet. My father spends it on phone calls, making arrangements with staff and employees, my mother looking mournfully out of the window.

It's only when we're on the jet and mother's had a sip of her white wine that she finally explodes.

"How could you, Sev?" she says in a tragic tone. "During your final year? With exams coming up? And that exhibition? Why on earth would you do something like that?"

My father reaches across the space between him and my mother and takes her hand, lacing his fingers through hers. His eyes, green as serpents and peridots, remain fixed on me.

"*Alors, vas-y*," he says curtly. "*Explique.*"

I take a deep breath and hold his gaze when I speak. "I want to break the engagement with Anaïs."

My father's eyes widen almost imperceptibly, but my mother splutters, almost choking on her wine.

"*Quoi*?" she exclaims. "But I thought it was going well between you two!"

"That's the problem," I say. I try to keep my tone light—I don't want my parents to see me emotional, I don't want them to realise how important this is to me—but it's hard to do when my throat tightens at the mere thought of Anaïs. "It was going well, but the engagement thing? It's ruining everything."

"How?" my father asks quietly.

To be fair to him, I expected a stronger response, an instant "no" or a stern bollocking, at least.

"Because." I gesture. "It's fuc—it's strangling us. Like... it's like trying to grow a flower, but instead of watering it, you've thrown it into the ocean. It's too much."

"You young people are so melodramatic." My father sighs, relaxing into his seat. "Love isn't a little flower drowning in the ocean, you young fool. Love is an inferno. It'll burn wherever it's growing."

"I don't love her," I snap.

Don't I?

Of course not.

How could I love her? I'm like fire, like a trembling volcano simmering with emotions. She's like ice, like a glacier, like a star, remote and cold and untouchable. How could I love her? I want her too much to love her.

"If you don't love her, then what's the problem?" Father asks with a shrug.

"*Je la veux,*" I choke out. "*Je veux qu'elle soit à moi. Je ne veux pas l'avoir parce que tu me l'as donné. Je veux pas qu'elle soit enchaînée à moi. Je veux l'avoir, de son gré.*"

I want her. I don't want her because you've given her to me. I don't want her chained to me. I want her to be mine of her own free will. Saying this out loud, in my own tongue, to my own parents, is the strangest sensation.

Like having wings that were tied down and have finally been freed. It's like pure freedom, sweet and elating.

For a moment, my parents stare at me in complete shock. Then my father shakes his head slightly. "And what does that have to do with the fighting and the defacing and the anti-social behaviour, then?"

"I fought the Pembroke boy because he said he would f—" I interrupt myself and cast a glance at my mother, who's listening with raised eyebrows. "He said he would have sex with Anaïs and make her forget the Montcroix name."

"*Non,*" my mother whispers against the rim of her glass.

"*Si.*" I straighten myself in my seat. "I told him that if he ever touches her, I'll kill him with my own hands. And I meant it."

My parents exchange a glance. The way they look at each other is both sickening and heart-warming. They have this way of looking at each other as if their gazes are reaching deep into the other person's heart.

"And the exhibition?"

I sigh and sit back. I didn't even realise how tense I was when talking about Pembroke until my fists unclenched.

"That was... I was drunk. I had an argument with Anaïs, and I got really drunk, and I wanted her to... I wanted to get back at her, or to... I don't know what I wanted. Honestly, I barely remember that night. I regret it."

I look out of the window, watching the clouds below, the distant earth, and the sky above, getting bluer and bluer the longer I look. Is this how Anaïs feels all the time? Distant and safe? How do I feel like that when I crave the heat and terror of being near her?

"*Tu a l'air complètement perdu, fils,*" my mother says softly.

"I *am* lost." I let my head fall back against my headrest. "I'm lost, and I have no idea what I'm doing."

"You should have told us," my father says quietly. "You should have told us what was happening."

"What would you have done?" I ask, bitterness rising in my voice. "You wouldn't have ended the engagement."

"Certainly not. If I based all my decisions about this family on the hormones of an eighteen-year-old boy, then I would be just as lost and foolish as you, my son." My father shrugs and takes the glass of whisky he's poured for himself but hasn't touched yet. "But I could have given you advice."

"I don't need advice."

My mother laughs softly. "No, you're doing well on your own. So well that you're falling in love with your fiancée and don't know it. You want her, but you don't want to be engaged to her. You told a boy in your school you were going to kill him and got yourself excluded. *C'est pas très joli, tout ça.*"

"Aah," I groan, buried by the stark reality of her words. "*Je suis foutu.*"

I'm fucked.

My father looks at my mum. "*Tu penses qu'il est foutu, notre fils? Hein, ma fleur de nuit?*"

Do you think our son is fucked? Huh, my night flower?

My mother sighs and nods. "*Malheureusement oui.*"

Sadly, yes.

Chapter 36

La Daurade

Anaïs

I sit on the floor in the art studio, forehead resting against the cold glass of the window. Outside, the winter is slowly melting into spring. Long hours of rain follow long hours of dreary sunshine. Everything is grey and sad.

In front of me, the damaged painting sits, waiting patiently for me to bring it back to life. The image that once existed there is gone—it'll never reappear. To repair this, I can't retread where I've already been.

I have to forge a new path.

Earlier in the week, Miss Godrick pulled me aside. She explained to me that Séverin Montcroix confessed to damaging the exhibits. I didn't bother feigning surprise. I just waited for her to carry on.

She explained that Séverin was going to be away for a few days to serve his sanction for the fight with Parker Pembroke. But after he returned, he would be expected to make up for what he'd done.

"It's fine, Miss Godrick," I said to her. "I'm sure he'll do his best to help."

She tells me how sorry she is about my ruined painting and then gives me a comforting squeeze of the shoulder.

But I'm not upset. I don't have anybody coming to the end-of-year exhibition—my parents are busy with work, and Noël is too far away. So the exhibition itself doesn't mean much to me. The grant is as good as gone, and there's no point crying over it.

The only thing that's truly important to me is the grade I get. So long as I secure the grades I need for my Japanese university applications, then I'll be alright.

When I arrived in Spearcrest, the thought of moving to Japan—of being far away from my parents and reunited with Noël at last—was the only thought keeping me going. My motivation for getting through the year, through the mess of Spearcrest and Séverin.

But now, the thought of moving is bittersweet. I think about my life with Noël in Japan, and I can't help the strange, unsettling feeling that something is missing. That when I leave, I'll be leaving a part of myself behind.

I glance down at my sketchbook. It's open on a page that's blank apart from the word *Aletheia* scribbled in the middle. I've been trying to think of something for my display for hours on end. But nothing comes to mind.

When Séverin and I had argued—or debated—the assignment topic, we'd agreed that art was more truthful than photography. My essay was well-written and eloquent. I'd been inspired and had a clear idea about what I wanted my display to look like.

But now that I have to start from scratch, surrounded by my pens and colours and paintbrushes, I don't even know what the truth is anymore.

Normally, my mind is crystal clear. Visions appear, and I'm able to focus on them while I draw or paint, translating the images in my mind on paper or canvas.

But lately, my mind isn't crystal. Emotions swirl and mingle in a chaotic mess. Like a messy palette, I can see glimpses of an image in there, but I can't quite decipher, can't quite organise it into shapes and features.

Because whenever I close my eyes, all I see is Séverin.

Séverin, wild-eyed and feral, pinning me down in that forest. Séverin, lustful and languid, his head between my legs. Séverin, furious and anguished, saying "Don't" when I removed his necklace and ring from around my neck.

I sigh and lie back on the cold tiles with a groan of frustration. This idiot. This stupid, impulsive idiot. If only he'd chosen to be honest—with me and with himself. Things could have been so different.

But while I was busy planning my escape from this disaster of an engagement, Séverin was so focused on his emotions that he never realised he was the one making it into a disaster.

Opening my sketchbook, I hold it up over my head, flipping through the pages. Studies and doodles flutter past, glimpses of Spearcrest, Noël. I pause on a page and lower the sketchbook to peer at the drawing there. Séverin, drawn with a crown and an ermine fur.

Séverin, who calls himself a Young King but can't so much as control his emotions.

Séverin, prince of beauty and pleasure and delusional.

Séverin, the boy who won't get out of my head.

I SPEND THE WEEK in limbo, not knowing what to draw, not knowing what to paint.

Since there's no progress to be made with my art, I give my attention to my other courses, English language and maths. I spend my time in the library, revising or walking through the expansive grounds, hoping something will catch my attention, hoping something will inspire me.

Inspiration doesn't come.

On Sunday morning, I don't bother getting out of bed. I lie on my stomach, the blanket over my head, eyes closed, feeling sorry for myself. It's not something I normally do, but I'm in the mood for angst. I think about the lilacs and mustard fields, the sea, my friends.

My phone rings, startling me. I grope around under my pillow for my phone. My brother's face appears in its little circle. I swipe my finger across the screen.

My voice comes out as a grunt, muffled by my blankets. "Allo."

Noël's laughing voice answers. "Oh, wow, are you sick?"

"I'm sick of this place," I say sullenly.

"Has something happened?" In the background, I heard the jingling of keys, footsteps, movement. "Are you alright, *p'tite étoile*?"

"*Non*. What are you doing?"

"I just got home. I was out eating with friends. Thought I'd check up on you, it's been a while since we talked." I hear him put things down, move around. "Why so unhappy? Did something happen?"

Although I desperately want to tell him about it, I realise I have no idea what to say.

"I wouldn't even know where to start," I say finally, pushing the blankets off me so my voice is less muffled. "I can't paint."

"What are you talking about? Of course you can. Do you remember when you were seven and you painted the goldfish, all warped? I still have that painting."

"You do?"

"Yea, it's on my fridge. I'll send you a picture."

"That's cute."

"*I'm* cute." Noël's voice softens. "So what do you mean, you can't paint?"

"I mean I can't paint right now. My head is a mess."

There's a minute of silence.

"Is it the *Roi Soleil*?" Noël asks finally.

"*Oui.*"

"What's he done?"

What hasn't he done? "It's a long story."

"Well, how about you?"

"What do you mean, 'how about me'?"

"It's not like you to let a boy bring you down. I'm guessing if you didn't care about him, you'd be okay. I'm guessing even if you hated him, you'd still be okay. So what I'm guessing is that you like him."

There's a long moment of silence. Things have gone quiet on Noël's side now. He must be sitting down, focusing on me and my problem. He's normally so supportive and helpful. Calm and mature and always truthful.

But why would he try calling me out like this?

When I don't say anything, he continues. "Okay, so you like him. Does he like you?"

I hesitate. "I think so."

"Has he said so?"

"No. He's an idiot and a coward and incredibly delusional."

"But you still like him." There's amusement in Noël's voice.

"It's like he's not a real person. Bigger than life. Colourful. Grandiose. Like a fairy tale character."

"Right... ?"

"And I want to paint him and humble him and amuse him and argue with him."

Noël's voice shimmers with amusement. "And hold him and kiss him and write him poems and braid flowers into his hair."

I glare at my phone even though this is only a normal phone call, and he can't see me. I'm sure he'll be able to sense my glare—I hope he can.

"Don't make fun of me."

"I'm not—I think it's cute that you have a crush. You deserve to be happy, little sister. I'm glad you like him. It's kind of ideal, no?"

"Ideal?" I sit bolt upright in my bed, completely baffled. "How could it possibly be ideal? It's the complete opposite of ideal!"

"How?" Now it's Noël's turn to sound baffled. "In general, it's good news if you like the person you're engaged to."

"But, Noël." My voice sounds small, even to my ears. "You know I'm moving to Japan soon."

"So?"

"So. The engagement will obviously be over."

"Does it have to be?"

I blink. "Yes... ?"

"Look." Noël takes a deep breath that almost sounds like a sigh. "You're not coming here so that you can give up the things you want as well as the things you don't. If you want to get away from Maman and Papa, you can—if you want to keep in touch with them, you can. If you want to break the engagement, do so. But if you want to stay engaged, then stay engaged. And if you want the *Roi Soleil* but don't want to be engaged to him, then do that. Do what you want. Isn't that the point of freedom? To do what you want?"

My heart beats fast at his words. I hold my breath then finally speak. "What if I don't know what I want?"

"Figure it out." Noël's voice is firm. "You're not a child, *petite étoile*. You're a young woman. Figure out what you want. Then do what you want and do what's right. It's as simple as that."

I let out a weak laugh. "Is it really?"

"*Et ben oui.*" Noël echoes my laugh, a soft, comforting sound. "You know, I learned a Japanese saying tonight."

"You did? What is it?"

"*Tai mo hitori wa umakarazu.* It means that even sea bream tastes less delicious when you eat it alone."

I laugh out loud this time, warm and truthful. "What does that have to do with anything? Sea bream? I can't even remember the last time I had sea bream. They don't serve Japanese food here at Spearcrest."

"You know it's not about the sea bream. It's about who you eat the sea bream with. That's all I'm saying."

"I'll be eating the sea bream with you."

"But it might taste more delicious if you eat sea bream with the *Roi Soleil*," Noël says in a tone of wisdom and affability.

"Don't try to sound like you've just come up with something profound," I say, shaking my head. "You've made me more confused than I was when you first called."

"Liar," he says. "I'm going to bed now, *petite menteuse. On se parle bientôt?*"

"*Oui.*"

"Alright, then. *A très bientôt, mon étoile.*"

"Two months."

"Two months." There's a smile in his voice. "Two months and who knows… you and I might be eating sea bream with the *Roi Soleil* in Japan."

"You can dream."

"I never stop dreaming. You shouldn't either. Bye-bye, *petite étoile. Je t'aime.*"

"*Moi aussi.*"

We hang up, and I drop my phone into the nest of bunched-up blankets. I grab my sketchbook from the floor, where it's lying in a pile with my pencil boxes and tangled-up earphones.

I spend the rest of the morning doodling fish and boys with sun-shaped crowns.

Chapter 37

LA SANCTION

Séverin

THE FIRST THING I do when I return to Spearcrest is hand out the letters of apology my father made me write at his desk.

"When you act disgracefully, your actions don't just disgrace you," he explained with a stern frown, standing at his office window with his hands folded behind his back. "They disgrace the Montcroix name. A legacy that precedes your existence by hundreds of years, a legacy that shall continue hundreds of years after you die."

It was quite dramatic, but if there's one thing my parents have always shown great capacity for, it's drama.

So I sat at my father's desk and penned letter after letter, by hand, with drafts and re-drafts, until they showed the perfect mixture of dignity and contrition. Finally, I wrote them on paper bearing the Montcroix family crest: a shield with a black helmet on a field of white fleur-de-lis.

He made me write one for Mr Ambrose, one for Mr Weston, one for Miss Imez and the Arts Department, and one for Anaïs. I return to Spearcrest with all of them in envelopes in my bag. But only Mr Ambrose, Mr Weston and Miss Imez receive their letters.

On my last night at home, my mother and father summoned me to the small lounge where they spend their rare free time.

Mother was in a robe of green silk, and Father in slacks and a white shirt, the top two buttons undone. At first, I thought I was going to receive a final lecture about my conduct and the importance of holding myself to the highest standards. But that wasn't the case.

My father opened the discussion with his customary directness, handing me a glass of whisky and sitting down with one for himself.

"We've given some thought to your request to break the engagement with Anaïs Nishihara."

I couldn't even help widening my eyes. It was the last thing I'd expected him to say.

"Ending the engagement because you like this girl is about as foolish as ending the engagement for not liking her." Father's eyes fixed on mine, making it impossible for me to look away. "Understand, Séverin, that neither your mother nor I wish to compromise your happiness for the sake of this alliance. However, neither are we willing to ruin a mutually beneficial arrangement based on the whims and emotions of young people. So what we ask of you is this: finish the school year, and remain engaged for what's left of it. Whatever is happening between you and Anaïs, sort it out. Resolve it. Not like a hormonal, impetuous teenager, but like the adult you are now. Then, in the summer, if you still wish to break the engagement, approach us about it again. Not with half-explanations and vague statements of emotions but with clear facts, arguments and reasons. Your mother and I will consider your request and discuss it with the Nishiharas. If you make a compelling enough case, then you may break the engagement."

There was nothing to argue with, and I returned to my room in a pensive mood. In the morning, my father shook my hand, and my mother hugged me and kissed my cheek. They both wished me luck with my assignments and exams.

But the entire journey back, in the limo and the plane and on the way to Spearcrest, my heart was heavy as a rock in my chest.

I ARRIVE IN THE afternoon and immediately sort out the letters. My father will definitely be checking to make sure I did, and I don't want to get into any more trouble this year. When I'm done, I return to the sixth form boys' building to unpack my things. As for my apology letter to Anaïs, I tear it into pieces and throw it away. I won't need it. What I want to say to Anaïs can only be said out loud, in person—no matter how terrifying the prospect is.

There was talk in the group chat of a welcome back party: drinks to celebrate the end of my exclusion. But now I'm here, I'm not in the mood to celebrate. I'm in the mood to see one person and one person only, but I'm going to have to gather my courage before approaching her.

Slumping back onto my bed, I open my phone and pull up my text chain with Anaïs.

Her face in the tiny circle is the photograph I took on the way to Scotland, the time I curled my arm around her neck and kissed her cheek.

I love looking at her face in that photo. Her slight expression of surprise, her pretty mouth rounded in a little silent gasp, her wide, dark eyes. There's the merest hint of a blush on her face, and seeing my lips pressed against her cheek makes me feel jealous of my past self.

But then I guess I'm jealous of every version of me that ever got to touch her, kiss her, pleasure her.

There's a knock on my door, and for a wild second, I imagine it's her. Dropping my phone, I roll off my bed and yank the door open. Dark eyes and a bleak expression greet me.

"Hey," Iakov says. "Smoke?"

He offers me his pack of cigarettes. One is already dangling between his lips.

I grimace at him. "Don't smoke in my room, man."

"Fine." He shrugs and jerks his thumb in the direction of the fire exit door. "Come out, then."

He turns without waiting for me to agree. I follow him down the corridor and through the fire exit door. It leads to the back of the building, where ivy covers the wall and where a narrow alley leads through a copse of trees and to the library.

Iakov stops outside the door, standing in the pool of light cast by a Victorian lamppost. He places his cigarette between his lips and hands me one. I shake my head.

"I'm alright, thanks."

"You quit?"

"It's a disgusting habit."

Iakov grins like a wolf. "So's love."

I tilt my head and watch as he lights his cigarette, the sudden bright glow lighting his face in a sinister flash.

"You're a romantic now, Kav?"

He shrugs and takes a deep drag. "I have eyes."

"And what is it you think your eyes are seeing since you're so smart all of a sudden?"

"I knew you liked that girl the moment I saw you two at that club in London," Iakov says.

I roll my eyes. "Joke's on you. That was my first time meeting her."

"Yeah."

I glare at him, crossing my arms. "So you not only believe in love but love at first sight now?"

"You liked the girl then, and you like her now." Iakov flicks ashes into the growing darkness of dusk. "Even a fool could see it."

"So—what are you saying? I can't see it, so I'm worse than a fool?"

"No." Iakov's lips curl around his cigarette. "You're not a fool. You know it."

I want to lie to him, and if it was any of the others—Evan, Zachary, or Luca—I would deny it till I was blue in the face. But there's something about Iakov's sinister black eyes, his stony expression and the strange little smirk on his face that makes me feel like he knows the truth, regardless of what I say.

And besides… I'm getting sick of denying it.

"Okay. So I like her. Now what?"

"Don't ask me." Iakov waves a hand, trailing a ribbon of smoke with him. "I'm not the right person to ask for advice. I'm the biggest of all the fools."

My mouth drops open. "You?"

He nods. "Evan wants a girl who hates him. Zachary wants a girl nobody's allowed to have. I'm worse than both of them. But you? You want the girl who's already yours. So why are you making things difficult? Fuck her, put that ring on her finger, tell her you love her and be done with it."

"What ring?" I mutter sullenly.

Even thinking about the ring makes me angry. Because when I think about the ring, I think about the night of that stupid date, the looks and kisses we exchanged. Looping the ring on the necklace and putting it around Anaïs's neck when I'd been so scared she'd turn it down or refuse to wear it.

I should never have let her give me the ring back. I should never have let my pride stop me from stooping to pick it up after she dropped it on the floor in the arboretum. If I could go back, I would crawl on my hands and knees to find that ring.

But that's just the effect Anaïs has on me. She makes me want to get on my hands and knees and crawl for her.

"This ring, moron," Iakov grunts.

He reaches into his pocket with his free hand and tosses something at me. It glints in the light; I catch it mid-air. I open my fist.

A ring on a chain, opals and diamonds catching the light. I look back up at Iakov.

"How the fuck do you have this?"

He shrugs. "Heard your stupid argument in the arboretum. You're both stubborn idiots." He gestures at the ring and chain. "Thought you might regret leaving this behind."

I nod slowly and pocket the ring. My chest is full of a feeling I can barely name. Something light and overwhelming that makes my ribs and lungs feel too tight. I sniff, look away and throw Iakov a sidelong glance.

"It's not like you to meddle, Iakov."

Iakov gives a half-smile that's completely Iakov: sharp and toothy and a little feral. "Would you rather Zach get involved?"

I shudder. "Oh god, no. He'd just make me feel like a complete moron."

Iakov raises an eyebrow. "You *are* a complete moron."

"Shut up, Kavinski."

"Fuck off, Montcroix."

When I arrive at my meeting to discuss my sanction for wrecking the exhibit, Miss Imez and Mr Weston greet me at the door of his office. Mr Weston is solemn but warm. Miss Imez is detached and austere.

They're going for the good cop/bad cop approach.

"We've given a lot of thought to what your sanction ought to be," Mr Weston says gravely.

"Since the other students have already fixed most of the damage while you were away serving your exclusion," Miss Imez says pointedly, "we have to think of another way for you to make up for what you've done."

"With this sanction, we do not wish to give you a punishment just for punishment's sake," Mr Weston continues. "We wish this sanction to be formative and productive."

My eyes flick from one to the other. They're clearly ramping up to something, and it's going to be bad news. But then, I suppose there's no point in a sanction if it doesn't make the perpetrator feel like shit.

"As you know, the end-of-year exhibition is the culmination of all the hard work the fine art and photography classes have produced over their final year here at Spearcrest Academy. Over the years, our exhibition has grown in reputation. These days, the exhibition is not only attended by parents, governors and notable alumni, but by respected members of some of the most important art communities in the world."

Miss Imez pauses for effect. She's trying to make me nervous—and it's working.

"For the last five years, I've had the honour of opening the exhibition. However, this year, we want to try something different. We chose the theme of *Aletheia* to encourage our students to explore and investigate the concept of truth. With that purpose in mind, I wish you, Séverin, to open the exhibition."

The silence is deafening.

"Pardon?" I say finally, my voice dull.

"You will be opening the exhibition with a speech, welcoming the guests and introducing the exhibition."

"That's—I can't do that."

"This is both a sanction and a great opportunity," Mr Weston says, raising a hand. "What better way to take responsibility and atone for the damage you've caused than by introducing the exhibition yourself?"

"Won't everyone wonder why a student is doing this, though? And I've never given a speech like that—not in front of—"

My mind races. It's just going to be parents and alumni there. There are going to be other students—my peers. Artists and photographers from the actual business. And press. Definitely press. It's not like I've not done press before, but never like this.

"I'd rather be excluded again," I finish.

"We've made our decision," Miss Imez says with the smile of a benevolent dictator. "I'd like the draft of your speech on my desk by the end of next week."

They dismiss me without further ado. I leave their office like a condemned man walking to the gallows.

And when the door falls closed behind me, I swear I can hear stifled laughter.

Chapter 38

LE JOLI GARÇON

Séverin

The following week is split between worrying about writing the speech and worrying about Anaïs's display. The painting I destroyed haunts me. Has she replaced it yet?

I want to help her, but I don't know if she wants my help. I don't even know if she wants to see me. She's not texted me or come to see me in the photography studio. And I don't blame her.

Why would she want to see me?

She gave me her forgiveness so easily the last time I saw her, and that just makes things harder. Part of me wanted her to shout at me, to insult me, even strike me. Her teary eyes and quiet dignity were so much more painful than any reaction she might have had.

I keep typing messages to send her and deleting them. I want to go to the gallery, to the studio where she spends all her time, to the library. If I could see her, everything would be okay.

But if she doesn't want to see me, then I don't know how I would handle it. The pain would be too much. The pain is already too much—it would finish me off.

So instead of facing her head-on, like I faced Mr Ambrose and my parents, I take the coward's approach.

I creep into a corner of the gallery for a stakeout. She's bound to turn up eventually. I'll be able to watch her from my corner and see how she's getting on with her display. See how she's doing.

See *her*.

Of course, stakeouts are never as quick and straightforward in real life as they are in movies. I wait almost two days for her to make an appearance, spending far too much time lurking in a dark corner of the gallery in the shadow of some discarded dividers. It's not my most elegant or glorious moment, but I almost feel as if I have no choice.

She finally turns up on a Thursday afternoon after everyone else has left.

When she steps in through the double doors, my heart leaps in my chest.

She walks in with that odd gait of hers, long slow steps like a ballerina through water. I devour her with my eyes. She looks as dreamy as ever, a content, faraway look in her eyes. Her black hair is tied back in a messy knot low at the back of her head, loose strands framing her face.

Even from my creepy corner, I can see the smears of paint on her drawn-up sleeves, her hands, her forearms, her cheeks and her chin.

She's dressed as only Anaïs could be, in a baggy navy-blue smock that makes her look like an old-timey factory worker. Underneath it, she's wearing her school skirt and tall white socks and, of course, no shoes. Her socks are flecked with paint and mud.

She looks like a character straight out of her own cartoon world.

I adore her.

With two canvases in hand, she heads for a corner of the gallery between two pillars. A divider stands between us, momentarily blocking her from view.

She moves around behind it, then reappears without the two canvases, backing away slowly from her display and stroking her chin like an old man deep in thought. She tilts her head, narrows her eyes.

Then she whips around and strides out of the gallery.

I slump back against the wall with a sigh, my heart hammering. This girl has really made me into someone I don't recognise because I don't remember ever feeling this disconcerted and anxious at the sight of a girl before.

Let alone a girl with no shoes and paint all over her face.

I wait a minute, then creep out of my hiding spot, tiptoeing towards Anaïs's display as if she might hear me. When it comes into view, it's not what I expect at all. I can't say what I expected.

Paintings crowd the wall, each more colourful and vibrant than the last. A messy field of lilacs blowing in a wind that's so vividly depicted, I can almost feel it against my skin. Blue waves sparkling with sunlight, blue fish underneath the surface. A small statue of Jesus laced with ivy, candles at its feet. A smiling face, I first guess it's her face.

I look closer and realise it's not her, but the beautiful boy from her sketchbook. The one I asked her about that time in the forest.

"Oh. Have you come to finish the job?"

Anaïs's voice startles me. I whip around to see her coming back through the doors in her weird get-up, a big tin box under one arm, another canvas in her hand. She gives me a look that's unsurprised and unconcerned, like she expected me to come back and finish wrecking her work but doesn't care if I do.

I give her a half-smile. "Can't leave loose ends, can I?"

She raises her eyebrows. "I thought loose ends was your area of expertise."

"No." I shake my head. "Montcroixes never leave business unfinished."

"So that's why you're here? For business?"

She walks up to her display and sets her things down on the floor. As she does, the strands of her hair fall forward, and one of them doesn't fall back into place.

I clench my fists, forcing myself not to reach over and push the strand away, tuck it behind her ear with the others. She's close now. Not close enough to touch, but close enough that I can smell that summer fragrance of hers, lilacs and salt.

"I've been wondering if you managed to replace the painting I damaged." To my surprise, the truth falls easily from my mouth. "Looks like you've done alright."

"It might look that way"—she sighs—"but I'm still missing my pièce de résistance." She points at her display, the paintings all surrounding a large rectangle of empty space. "See? That was supposed to be your portrait. I've still not worked out what to put there instead."

"Everything you paint is beautiful. You could put anything there. Why not your cute little boyfriend over there?" I gesture vaguely towards her painting of the boy with the pretty smile.

"Cute?" Anaïs looks at the painting, nodding appraisingly. "You really think so? I'll tell him you said so. He'll be flattered."

Jealousy flares through me. It makes me want to yell and rage and threaten all sorts of violence on the young man. I push it all deep down inside.

"Does he know you're engaged?" I ask in my most casual tone.

She nods. "Yes, he knows."

I say nothing. I long to ask her who this boy is. This boy who's so important she thought of him when she thought of *Aletheia*. The boy she painted to replace the painting of me she made that night on the balcony, the one I so stupidly destroyed.

"Is he coming to the exhibition?" I ask, trying to keep my voice casual when all I want to do is to grab her and kiss her and beg her to love me.

Love me, I want to tell her. *Choose me. Have me.*

"He would if I asked him to," she answers with a peaceful smile. "Would you like me to ask him?"

Obviously not. "I think you should."

She turns her head suddenly, narrowing her eyes, and steps towards me, pointing an accusatory finger at me. "Hey, you're not planning to beat him up too, are you?"

"Why would I?" I look down at her finger. If I step forward, it'll stab right into my chest. So I step forward.

She jabs her finger right into my chest. "For the same reason you beat up Parker Pembroke? Petty, childish jealousy?"

"Why would I be jealous?" I try to sound calm and collected, but my voice is a little rough, my throat full of all the things I want to say but don't dare to.

"Exactly," she says with a smile. "You have no reason to be jealous."

"No reason except the fact he's all over your sketchbooks? What happened to the Anaïs Nishihara who doesn't believe in love?"

She gives an exaggerated sigh. "Fine, you win. I do love him." My heart sinks at her words. "I might as well tell you all about him since you've discovered my terrible secret." I don't even dare breathe as she speaks. "He's twenty-two years old and lives in Japan. He likes books about characters who go on long journeys and books about places near the sea. He loves everything to do with the sea and, when he was a kid, he used to dream of learning how to sail, but honestly, he's far too lazy for that kind of work. He wants to meet you, by the way, and when we talk about you, he calls you the *Roi Soleil*."

"Like Louis XIV?"

"Yes."

"You two talk about me?"

She shrugs airily. "Why shouldn't I? You're my fiancé."

"He's not... jealous?"

Somehow, that's more hurtful than anything else.

"You didn't let me finish, though," Anaïs says with a raised eyebrow.

"Alright, go on."

"He wants to meet you and thinks we should go eat sea bream together because of a Japanese saying he learned recently. He thinks you should come to Japan when I move. Oh, and his name is Noël Nishihara."

There's a moment of dull silence. Her lips curl at the corners. She's such a cocky little shit.

"That boy's your brother?" I look away from her because my face feels hot, and I step closer to the painting. The eyes have a similar shape and colour, the hair is dark and silky, but he doesn't have the same ethereal airiness I associate with Anaïs. Instead, his smile is charming but a little wild. If anything, it reminds me more of Iakov than anybody else. "I didn't know you had a brother."

Anaïs nods. "Yes. It's because he sort of ran away a few years ago, and my parents sort of disowned him."

"Sort of?"

"They'll come around... maybe. One day."

"Where does he live?"

"Japan."

Things finally start to make sense. "Oh! Is that... is that why you're moving there?"

"Yes."

I hesitate. "Why did he run away?"

"Because he didn't want my parents to use him to further our social standing in France." Anaïs's voice is quiet, but there's an invisible edge of sadness there.

"So they used you instead?"

She gives me a little cynical look but says nothing.

"I asked my parents to end the engagement," I tell her suddenly. I want to tell her I'm sorry, that she's a person and not a pawn, that I want her no matter what our parents want. "They said they'll genuinely consider it in the summer."

She shrugs. "Well, it doesn't matter, does it? I'm leaving anyway."

"Do you have to?"

"Yes." She shoves her hands in the big front pocket of her blue smock and suddenly adds, "Do you want to help me?"

"With what?"

"My display."

"Of course I want to help you."

I'd do anything for you.

She smiles. "Do you remember that portrait you wanted me to paint of you?"

I look up in excitement. "Yeah?"

"Do you still want to sit for it?"

"Of course!"

"I don't have much time left, so you'll need to sit still for ages."

"Who cares? Of course I'll do it."

She nods, then adds, "And you can't have it for Château Montcroix. Unless you buy it."

I roll my eyes at her. "You're probably going to paint me as an eighteenth-century monarch or some fairy tale goblin, anyway."

She smirks. "I'm going to paint you as an eel."

"You're disgusting!" I glare at her, suppressing a shudder. "You're the absolute worst."

"That'll teach you to mess with my paintings."

With her sweetest smile, she raises both middle fingers at me.

I return the gesture.

Chapter 39

LE PORTRAIT

Séverin

Spring has finally come, warm and bright and full of colours. Spring has come just like Anaïs into my life, flooding everything with new life.

Spearcrest, now the final exams are upon us, takes on a new atmosphere. Everyone in our year is revising, finishing coursework, getting ready to move back home.

In that final week, I barely see the people that filled my life during my time at Spearcrest. The people whose opinions were so important, the people who took such great care to maintain their reputation. The real world looms closer, and everything is changing.

Seraphina Rosenthal, who was always so desperate to date someone who would match her status, is now apparently happily dating some guy from the local town. A boy with no money, no name, no status. But she seems happy—happier than I've ever seen her.

Kay, who was always so careful to be seen partying and having fun, has been spending almost every day in the library. I hear she's received acceptance letters to Oxford and Cambridge.

Evan, too, is studying almost all the time. He never cared about results before—he's always known he'd end up working with his parents. But now, the former star athlete is never seen without a book in his hands. He follows Sophie Sutton around like a lovesick puppy, and the tension between them is frankly just getting embarrassing.

I can't blame them for changing. I've changed too. The things I thought I wanted never made me happy. Partying, drinking, casual sex… it was fun, but it was never anything more than that.

As for love, I'm not so sure it's a poison anymore.

I'm not even sure I was ever in love before now.

Because this feeling is different from anything I've ever felt before.

I sit completely still in a pool of sunshine, and Anaïs sits across from me. We're both on the floor, like weirdos. Anaïs is wearing baggy white overalls almost completely smeared with paint. Her feet and arms are bare, the sunlight caressing her skin.

My books on my lap, I alternate between revising for my upcoming exams and sneaking glances at her. I try to angle myself a little away so I won't be distracted, but she tuts loudly.

"Don't move," she snaps.

"I didn't!" I protest.

She narrows her eyes at me. "You were looking shifty."

"Shifty as in suspicious or shifty as in about to shift?"

"You're an idiot." She laughs. "Your sense of humour is actually getting worse with time."

"At least I have one." I shake my head slightly. "Not my fault you can't take a joke."

"The only joke here is how bad you are at staying still," she mutters, leaning so close to her canvas that her face disappears behind it.

"You know what's perfect for that?" I ask her. "A photograph."

"A photograph wouldn't capture what I'm trying to capture," she replies. "We've gone over this before."

"What are you trying to capture?" I move my shoulder with a wince. "Cramps and discomfort?"

"What a spoilt, pampered little prince you are," she says, peeking at me over the top of her canvas.

"Sure." It's my turn to mutter. "You keep pretending you're not just trying to punish me."

"You deserve to be punished."

"Punish me another way."

She laughs. "You wish."

"I do."

WE'RE SITTING IN THE gallery one night. I'm working through some practice exam questions on my phone while Anaïs paints. Now and again, I sneak discrete pictures of her, her little thoughtful expressions and pouts of concentration. Then Anaïs suddenly speaks.

"You should have texted me while you were excluded."

I look up, taken by surprise. "Why?"

"Because you were going to say something before you had your meeting, but you never did."

"I wanted to text you," I admit.

"Why didn't you?"

She's not looking at me. Instead, she's mixing colours on her palette, her eyes focused on the tip of her painting knife.

"Because," I answer truthfully, "I was afraid, and I was nervous. I wasn't sure what to say. And I wasn't sure you wanted me to text you."

"You can always text me," she says, looking up. Her gaze is direct and honest. "I want you to. So you never need to worry about that."

Silence falls once more. Outside the floor-to-ceiling windows of the gallery, night has fully fallen. The windows have become a black mirror, reflecting the long room. The lights near the doors are on, but not the rest of the gallery. Everything is dim and peaceful.

"You should have told me the boy in your sketchbook was your brother," I say after a while. "That time in the forest."

"You didn't ask."

"I did."

"You asked, but you didn't want to know. You wanted to fight—remember?"

"I wanted to play."

"You wanted to kiss me, but you were too much of a coward to just ask."

"You might have said no again."

"That's not a good reason not to ask."

I turn to throw her a glare, but she's concentrating on her painting. She refuses to let me see it—for all I know, she could be painting me as an eel. But I don't care.

All I want to do is trace the streak of violet paint that stretches from her jaw to her chin. To thread my fingers through her silky black hair and breathe in the scent of her. To take her in my arms and to my bed.

The silence doesn't last long. Anaïs is the one to break it this time.

"You should've asked me to come to that stupid party with you."

"I wish I had. I wanted to."

"Then why didn't you?"

Because I didn't want to look like a fool.

Because you told me you didn't believe in love.

Because you're the first person I've ever felt this way about, and because you're intimidating and self-assured and unapproachable.

"Because I was afraid you'd reject me again."

"I've never rejected you."

"You told me you wanted to just be allies."

"How is that a rejection?"

I give her a sardonic smile. "Because, trésor, I don't want to kiss and hold and fuck my allies."

Her cheeks redden, but she says nothing.

This time, the silence stretches between us for longer, heavy and warm and full of palpable tension. She watches me as she paints, her eyes lingering on my face, my mouth. I lick my lips, and she follows the movement.

I'm the one who breaks the silence this time.

"You should have told me about your plan."

"I didn't trust you."

"Nobody understands how this engagement feels more than I do, trésor. I would have understood."

"But you didn't understand. That night when I told you. You didn't understand."

"I was hurt."

"Why? We both wanted to break the engagement."

"I don't care about the engagement, Anaïs." I finally give in to the urge to touch her. Moving away from my position, I scoot towards her until I'm sitting right in front of her. "The engagement isn't what's torturing me. Don't you know that?"

She slowly lowers her paintbrush and turns towards me. Blue paint is smeared on her arms, and her face is constellated with tiny blue splashes. That violet streak still taunts me, tempting me to trace it with my fingers.

"You're so dramatic," she says. She tries to keep her voice light, but she can't quite look me in the eyes. "You're not tortured at all."

I wrap my fingers around her chin, forcing her to raise her gaze to mine.

"Anaïs Nishihara." My voice is low and rough. "Your presence in my life is a constant torture. Your existence causes me nothing but pain and suffering. You're slowly driving me mad, and I don't know how to stop it."

Her cheeks burn against my fingertips. Her lips tremble as she tries to form words. I brush my thumb underneath her lower lip, tracing the soft curve of it.

She suddenly pulls away, glaring at me.

"You should have played nice—that night in the club. It would have changed everything."

I laugh softly. "Are you really trying to blame me for the mess we've made of this whole thing?"

"You are to blame."

"Alright. If it's my fault for ruining things when we first started, then let me start again."

She licks her lips and lets out a startled laugh. "How?"

I hold out my hand between us. "Nice to meet you. I'm Sev."

"Oh, don't make us do this," she pleads, covering her face with her hands. "It's too embarrassing."

I smack her arm and then hold out my hand again. "Come on."

She rolls her eyes. "You've been in England too long, I can tell. Ugh."

I wave my hand in front of her. "Don't be rude."

"Fine." She pulls a face but takes my hand in hers and crowds her words out, as if trying to get the sentence out quickly. "Nicetomeetyou. I'm Anaïs."

We shake hands, but I don't let go of her. Instead, I pull her closer, resting my forehead against hers.

"Anaïs. I really like you. I like your pretty eyes and all that paint on your face and the fact you're not wearing shoes. I think I might like everything about you, even the things that make you so different from everybody else. I probably like you *because* you're different from everybody else. I like you, and I want to kiss you and touch you and strip you bare and fuck you slowly." Her eyes widen, and the flush in her cheeks darkens, but I continue boldly. "Wanna come back to my room?"

She laughs and glances at her painting, biting her lip. "I've not finished."

"You can finish it another day."

She gestures at her things. "I need to clean up the mess."

"Or we could come back and do it later." I tilt my head and grin. "What would you rather be doing right now? Cleaning brushes or lying in my bed with my head between your legs?"

"Sev!" she exclaims.

"What?"

"... the second one."

"I thought so."

Chapter 40

Le Lit

Anaïs

Sneaking through the sixth form boys' building and into Sev's room is a breathless, giggly ordeal, but the moment his door closes behind us, he's on me.

He pins me to the door and kisses me with a hunger and desperation that takes my breath away. I grab his head and tilt my face against his, letting him deepen the kiss. I take his desire on his tongue, the metallic heat of it seeping into me.

His mouth moves hungrily from my mouth to my cheek, my jaw, my neck. His kisses are wet and hot and sensual, trailing heat and pleasure wherever they touch. He grips my waist, my hips, dragging me closer. My breath burns in my lungs.

I place both hands on his chest and shove him off me. He moves away with a ragged gasp.

His green eyes are dark with lust, shadowed by his ridiculous eyelashes. His hair's a tousled mess, strands half-covering one eye. He looks feral and beautiful.

Being with him like this, in his room—on purpose, with the full knowledge of who we are, not in some mad, stolen moment, is more frightening and intense than anything we've ever done before.

It's more frightening and intense than anything I've ever done.

For a second, we look at one another, our chests heaving, our eyes wide.

Then Sev hooks his hand into the front pocket of my painting overalls. He backs away slowly through his room, pulling me with him. The back of his knees hits the edge of his bed, and he drops back on the mattress, looking up at me from where he's seated.

He drags me closer until I'm standing between his long legs, bathed by the burning heat of his presence.

With gentle movements, he unhooks the straps of my overalls. Underneath it, I'm wearing an old T-shirt over a triangle bra. Sev doesn't take them off me. Instead, he pushes my overalls down, past my hips and down my legs. I step out of them, and he kicks the garment away.

He pulls me closer so that I'm standing right against the bed. I lay my hands on his shoulders, using him to balance.

With slow, deliberate movements, he lifts my T-shirt. He tilts his head, watching me. His expression is something I can't describe: hunger and triumph and something bold, as if he's daring me to stop him.

He reaches forward and presses his lips right underneath the band of my bra. I bite down on my lips, stopping the gasp that escapes when his warm mouth moves against the sensitive skin.

He trails a path of kisses down my belly, leaving a trail of burning warmth behind until he gets to the waistband of my skirt. The muscles of my stomach flutter underneath his lips, and he lets out a low hum of satisfaction.

Moving back, he runs his hands up my legs and waist, grabbing the hem of my T-shirt. He pulls it off me and tosses it away.

When I'm standing in nothing but my plain white underwear, he looks up at me.

"You have no idea how often I've thought about taking your clothes off," he says hoarsely.

"Because you hate all my clothes so much?" I ask, trying to suppress a smirk.

"Because I want to look at your body—every part of it. Because I want to touch you and kiss you all over." The usual dark humour and acerbic sarcasm are gone from his voice. He speaks earnestly, his words sounding like solemn vows. "I want to look at you, all of you, and make you shiver and squirm. I want to taste your skin and lick your pussy and feel the trembling of your thighs."

"Sev," I say, my breath short, my face full of flames.

He laughs and suddenly rises against me, enveloping me in his arms. He lowers me onto his bed, and I lie back, his blanket cold underneath my skin.

"*Quoi, trésor?*" he says, lowering his voice as he leans down to catch my lips in a soft kiss. "*T'aimes pas ce que je dis? T'aimes pas mes mots cochons?*"

Do you dislike what I'm telling you? Do you dislike my dirty words?

I cover his mouth with my hands. "*Stop.*"

He moves my hands away. His gestures are lazy and gentle. This isn't Sev fighting me in the forest, or Sev rushed and desperate in the limousine. This is Sev, the prince, ruling his world of pleasure and flesh.

"*Non.*" His voice is clear and triumphant. He sounds more impetuous than ever. "Why should I stop? I know you like it. You like hearing the things I want to do to you. And I want you to tell me the things you want."

As he speaks, he settles himself between my legs, tilting my head back with one hand to kiss my neck.

"I want you to be quiet and make me come." I gasp, my voice hitching as he sucks gently on the skin of my neck.

"*Oh, mon trésor,*" he says against my throat. "I'm going to make you come, I promise. But I'm not going to be quiet, and neither are you." He moves his mouth to murmur against my ear. "I'm going to make you scream."

He sits up and wraps his fingers around the waistband of my panties. I glare at him. "*T'as aucune raison d'être si sûr de toi.*"

You have no reason to be so self-assured.

He slides my panties down my legs, tossing them aside. Laying his fingers on my hips, he digs them lightly into my skin, clawing lightly down my thighs and sending a shiver through me that almost makes my back arch off the bed.

"*Ah bon?*" he murmurs. "*On verra.*"

We'll see.

Sev's mouth is pleasure and torture.

He is too tender, too slow. His tongue lingers and caresses. He kisses my pussy passionately, teasing me with his lips, his tongue.

Each lick over my clit is slow and sensual, building an inexorable tension until my back is bowed and my hands fist so tightly in the blanket my fingers ache.

When I'm so close to the edge that I don't even dare to move, Sev pulls away, licking his gleaming lips. A string of wetness connects us for a second, breaking with the distance. His eyes are hooded, his mouth is curled in a satisfied smirk. He projects the lazy arrogance of a young tyrant.

I stare up at him, shocked and appalled, my entire body taut as a bowstring. "Don't stop."

"Why?"

"Because. Because I want..."

He lowers his voice. His fingers tap lightly over my entrance. "What do you want? Tell me."

Speaking our language somehow makes this too raw, too close, too intimate. I answer him in English. "I want to come."

"*Supplie-moi.*"

Beg me.

"*Non,*" I gasp out.

His fingers slide inside, teasing me with slow, wet thrusts. I'm paralysed with want—wanting him to let me come, wanting to feel him inside me, wanting his body pressed against mine.

"*Si, trésor.*" He murmurs against my lips. "*Supplie-moi.*"

"Please." I close my eyes and arch into him. "Please."

He slides against me without another word, closing his mouth over me. He licks me in long, deep swipes, working me with his fingers. My mouth falls open, my body and breath suspended as my pleasure gathers under the command of his fingers and lips.

I come in a shudder, a broken cry tearing from my lips. My hips move of their own volition, undulating against Sev's mouth, seeking more pleasure. I writhe against him until I can no longer bear it, until my entire body is pulsing like a heart, and then I fall back.

Sev watches me, unbuckling his belt, but I raise my hand and scramble to prop myself up on my elbows.

"No, wait."

He stops, raising a questioning eyebrow at me.

"Stand up. Take off your clothes."

He smirks. "Yeah?"

"Yes."

"Why?"

"Because I want to look at you."

His lips curl into a wicked smirk. He raises his hands to his shirt and unbuttons it slowly, his eyes on mine. When he's done, he pushes his shirt off his shoulders. I watch him breathlessly.

Every part of him seems carved by an artist. The musculature of his shoulders and arms, the graceful taper of his hips, the V-line disappearing into his waistband. His gold necklaces glitter on his skin, and the muscles in his arms tighten when he reaches for his belt to pull it free. He opens his trousers and lets them fall down, kicking them away with a gesture of cool dismissal.

My chaotic heartbeat stutters when he stands by the bed in his boxers. Even through the black fabric, his arousal is obvious, the shape of him stretching the fabric. But instead of taking it off, Sev brushes his palm over the bulge, his eyes on mine.

"Do you want to see how hard you make me?" he asks roughly. "Do you want to see how much it turned me on when you came on my tongue?"

My face burns as his words send a deep pulse between my legs. How can he be turning me on this much when I've just had an orgasm?

He caresses himself shamelessly, watching me, enjoying my eyes on him. Then he takes off his boxers, kicking them away. His cock is beautiful, like the rest of him. He reaches for a condom, and there's supreme confidence in the way he rips the wrapper off it with his teeth before putting it on.

He drops one knee down to the bed and crawls to me, bracing his arms on both sides of my head and settling his hips between my legs. He leans down to kiss me, deep and hungry and lingering. Taking his cock firmly in his hand, he rubs the tip against me, tracing my wet slit.

It's an electrifying sight, obscene and shameless, but Sev doesn't care. He watches his own actions, unabashed in his own pleasure.

When he pushes himself against my entrance, he pauses for a moment. His eyes flick back up to meet mine, and he tilts his head.

"Alright?" he murmurs.

I nod. "Mm-hm."

He pushes inside me, watching his cock enter me.

"Fuck," he rasps. "Fuck, trésor. You're so fucking wet."

I turn my face away, and he leans down, kissing my exposed neck, my cheek. He presses his lips to my ears, thrusting in and out of me in slow, torturous strokes.

"You feel so good, mon trésor. Aah, open your legs a little wider for me." His fingers tighten around my hip when I obey him. "Fuck, yes, just like that, good girl."

His words slide like silk against me, making me clench around him. I shut my eyes tight, overwhelmed with sensations—overwhelmed with emotions.

The way Sev whispers in my ear, the way he clutches me as he thrusts deep into me—it makes me feel closer to him than I ever have. It makes me feel closer to him than I've ever felt to anyone.

For someone so thorny, so difficult, Sev fucks with the tenderness of a saint. He kisses me like my body is hallowed ground, and he touches me like he worships me.

Then he turns me around and thrusts into me from behind, his hands sliding underneath me to hold my breasts, my nipples caught and pinched between his fingers. He kisses my neck and murmurs dirty things against my ear, thrusting deep and slow into me, taking his time, sending glimmering waves of pleasure with each thrust.

"*J'adore ton corps,*" he sighs into my ear. "*J'adore ta peau. Tes lèvres.*" He hardens inside me, and his entire body trembles. He quickens his pace, his voice hoarse and strangled with emotions. "*J't'adore. J't'adore et je te veux, tout le temps, pour toujours. Je te veux dans mon lit, dans mes bras, dans mon âme. Sois mienne.*"

I adore your body. I adore your skin, your lips. I adore you. I adore you and I want you, all the time, forever. I want you in my bed, in my arms, in my soul. Be mine.

"I already am," I whisper in a half-moan as he rocks into me.

"Ah, fuck." Sev moves against me, bracing himself. The movement of his hips becomes harsher, less controlled. He buries himself inside me and comes with a hoarse cry.

He rides the waves of his orgasm in erratic thrusts and finally grows still, falling on top of me, his burning skin radiating heat into mine.

The sound of our panting fills the room. With our bodies still connected, Sev picks up my hand in his and lifts it to his mouth, kissing my knuckles.

"I think I might be addicted to you," he rasps against my hair.

I let out a silent laugh. "What does that even mean?"

He sighs, burying his head against my neck.

"Every time we have sex, I want to do it again even more than I did before."

Chapter 41

La Vérité

Anaïs

As much as I wish I could spend what's left of my time at Spearcrest in Sev's bed, that doesn't happen. I have my portrait and my display to finish, and Sev has his speech to write. We still see each other enough for some stolen kisses, but we both have too much work to do more than that.

Two days before the exhibition, I text him.

Anaïs: How's the speech coming along?

He texts back straight away.

Séverin: Not well. Redrafting is worse than drafting.

Anaïs: Can I help?

Séverin: How are you with public speaking?

I wriggle in my bed, repulsed at the mere thought of it.

Anaïs: Not great.

He sends me a stressed emoji, then a text.

Séverin: Then you can't help.

I laugh and lock my phone, but it lights up a few minutes later.

Séverin: You can help me after the exhibition when I'm tense and traumatised from the whole thing, and I need something to help me relax.

I bite my lip, trying not to laugh.

Anaïs: Something like a soothing cup of camomile tea?

His reply pops up.

Séverin: I was thinking something more along the lines of me on my knees in front of you.

This time, it takes me a minute to respond. I lie back, letting my heartbeat still. Then I respond.

Anaïs: Or maybe the other way around…

Séverin: Thanks for the mental image. How am I going to write that cursed speech now?

Anaïs: Just concentrate.

Séverin: The only thing I can concentrate on is picturing your pretty mouth on my cock.

My stomach clenches, and I squeeze my thighs around the throbbing between my legs. If only we didn't have the stupid exhibition to worry about. If only Sev were here in my room, in my bed. If only we'd been doing this all along.

We wasted so much time. Time we'll never get back.

And we have nobody but ourselves to blame.

THE DAY BEFORE THE exhibition, I go to the gallery to check my display for the last time.

It's a bittersweet feeling: I'm proud of my work—it's a beautiful display, full of colour, and it reflects the truth of my world. The new painting, though it was rushed and more conventional than my usual work, fits perfectly with the colours and mood of the display. That painting will never truly replace the one that was destroyed, but it is something I'm proud of.

But my parents aren't coming, and Noël is so far away... I didn't have the heart to ask him to come.

I'm proud of my display—but only strangers will see it.

The gallery is crowded with fine arts and photography students putting the finishing touches to their displays. Everyone looks nervous.

I search the room with a glance but can see no sign of Sev. I'm tempted to go have a look at his display, which he put together at the last minute, but he made me promise to wait for the night of the exhibition to see it.

"I'm not writing that speech for nothing," he said to me when he made me promise. "So you better wait to hear it before you see my display. Then it'll at least be worth it."

"It's not me you need to impress, though," I told him.

He'd rolled his eyes. "Don't be ridiculous, trésor. You're the only person at that exhibition I would actually care about impressing."

It's probably a lie—but a beautiful lie. Still, I can't deny how much I want to see his display, his interpretation of *Aletheia*.

I suspect Sev finds it much easier to lie to himself with his mind and mouth than with his camera.

Later that evening, I return to my room to find a box waiting for me on my bed. A large, slim box in white cardboard, tied shut with a thick ribbon of blue satin.

I pull the ribbon open to find a card of cream paper. I pick it up.

There's a handwritten note there in elegant cursive: *To wear tomorrow night. If you wish, of course. Yours, S.*

I open the lid to find a delicate bed of white tissue paper and, folded within it, a dress in deep, royal blue. Picking it up, I unfold it.

It's an exquisite garment: a full skirt and a stiff bodice embroidered with gold birds, moons and stars.

We were told by our teachers that the exhibition would be a formal event, but I didn't give much thought to what I would wear. Trust Sev to think about it. Trust him to be this extravagant.

Trust him to choose something so beautiful. Not something I would have expected him to choose—but something I might have chosen myself.

On the night of the exhibition, Miss Imez gathers all the students in the atrium of the arts building for a final briefing. I walk in a little unsteadily, my stomach in knots. I don't know why I feel so nervous: we've already been awarded our final marks, and I won't know anybody at the exhibition.

So why are my legs wobbly and my hands sweaty?

I walk into the atrium to find most of the other students already gathered. Everyone is in beautiful gowns and suits, including the staff. Everyone looks polished and professional.

For the first time, I realise this isn't just a school project. This is a real exhibition.

My first one. Maybe that's why I'm so nervous.

A hand settles on my waist. A magical touch because the nerves seep out of me before I can even turn to look at the owner of the hand.

Sev, of course, looks amazing. This should not be of any surprise to me at this point. His black tuxedo is perfectly tailored to his tall, slim body. The lapels of his jacket are embroidered with gold patterns. His shirt is unbuttoned as it always is—a little further than necessary.

I lift my eyes, and my mouth rounds in a silent gasp. His hair is combed back, his face is beautiful as ever. But two lines of vivid royal blue are painted below his eyes, sweeping from the inner corner of his eyes and up towards his temples.

He looks like a living work of art.

"I like the look you've gone for tonight," I say finally, incapable of suppressing my smile.

He returns my smile. "Thank you. You inspired it."

"Your eyes match my dress," I point out. "Thank you, by the way."

"You're welcome. I'm glad you're wearing it." He points to his face. "I would look very silly if you weren't."

"You wouldn't look silly. You would look beautiful, just as you do right now."

He tilts his head. "Ah, careful. You can't say things like that. I might think you're catching feelings."

"You're the one matching your make-up to my dress."

He leans to speak against my ear. "You're the one giving me bedroom eyes."

I laugh and push him away. "I wasn't!"

"Well, you're giving me eyes like you want me to kiss you."

"Am I?"

He nods. His hand still around my waist, he pulls me into him. My fingers curl in his sleeve as I grip him for balance. His lips ghost over mine. Around us, students murmur and turn to watch. I find it impossible to care. We kiss.

"Mr Montcroix!" Miss Imez's voice booms, making the students around her jump. "You should be in the gallery with Mr Ambrose, not seducing art students!"

"Sorry, Miss Imez," Sev says. "I just came to wish my fiancée good luck."

Then he gives me one more kiss, winks, and runs off.

When we finally enter the exhibition, the gallery looks completely different from the last time I saw it.

The paint buckets and paintbrushes are gone, the spare screens dismissed. Dusk is already falling outside the tall windows, and the long hall of marble is lit by the spotlights set into the ceiling.

A crowd gathers at the entrance, the kind of crowd that reminds me of the parties my parents forced me to attend all my life: women in expensive couture, men in tuxedos. The easy sparkle of wealth lights them up, glittering on their throats, their wrists, in their eyes.

I follow the rest of the students into the gallery, and we stand behind Miss Imez and Mr Ambrose, who flank Sev. Mr Ambrose greets the waiting audience and introduces Sev, who turns quickly and scans the crowd of students.

Then his eyes meet mine, and his gaze softens. I shape my fingers into a heart. He flashes me a smile and turns back to the crowd.

Despite all his talk about being nervous, his voice is clear and confident when he speaks.

"Welcome, ladies and gentlemen, parents, alumni and guests, and thank you for coming from all corners of the world to attend this year's annual Arts Department Exhibition. My name is Séverin Montcroix, and the honour has befallen me to introduce this year's exhibition—an honour I never dreamt of or felt prepared for. One might even say an honour that was bestowed upon me unwillingly." He pauses to a murmur of laughter and glances at Mr Ambrose. "I'm sorry, Mr Ambrose—an unnecessary aside, I know. Well, regardless of how this opportunity came about, I am honoured. I've seen firsthand how hard everybody's worked to put this exhibition together, and I hope I do it justice.

"The theme of this year's exhibition is *Aletheia*. This is a philosophical concept of truth—or disclosure. Our displays seek to explore our very own definition of truth. When I first learned of this theme, I must admit I didn't quite understand it. As a student of photography, it seemed to me as though the very act of photographing something—of capturing an image on film—is as truthful as it's possible to get. I didn't bother asking myself what the truth actually is, how it can actually be disclosed because I believed truth to simply mean reality. Whatever I could see, whatever was there in front of me, had to be the truth.

"I didn't choose to challenge my own ideas. I didn't feel it was necessary. In a way, I had chosen reality to be my truth and made my truth to be reality. Whatever I believe had to be right—no?"

Sev pauses and swallows.

"I didn't choose to challenge my own ideas, but I was lucky enough to have my ideas challenged. By an artist, of all people. Artists, who paint what they feel instead of what they see. Artists, who, unlike photographers, take so many liberties with their representation of the truth. Well, it was an artist who challenged my perception. An artist who showed me that truth is more than what's there, what we can see, what's real. Truth, as I've had to learn, is in the eye of the beholder. It's not what's there—it's how we perceive what's there, how we experience it, how it feels.

"I didn't just realise my interpretation of truth—of *Aletheia*—was incorrect. I realised, to my complete and utter surprise, that I had been lying to myself. Everything around me had always *felt* truthful because I'd always been, to an extent, in control of it. I could choose what the truth was. But that's not reality, that's not life, and that's certainly not *Aletheia*.

"So, for my exhibition, I've chosen to show the truth by shedding my lies. Every lie I held on to and disguised as truth, I've tried to let go of. Letting go of lies was harder than it should be because so much of who I knew myself to be was rooted in those lies. And so I learned that the truth isn't simple and easy. The truth is complex, beautiful and, sometimes, difficult.

"My truth is that I'm not in control the way I always thought I was. My truth is that my place in this world isn't defined by the power I might believe I hold. My truth is that I've been naïve, arrogant and cowardly, that I've placed too much value on what others thought of me and not enough value on knowing myself. Most importantly of all, my truth is that I'm hopelessly, devotedly, embarrassingly in love."

He turns slightly, opening his arm to gesture to me. His eyes meet mine, and my heart seizes as he continues to speak.

"Over there, in the blue dress, is Anaïs Nishihara—the artist from my story. *Aletheia*—the truth—is what I see when I look into her eyes. *Aletheia* is the feeling in my chest when I see her, when I'm around her, when I think about her. *Aletheia* is my love for her."

The gaze of the crowd prods me like a hundred arrows, but my eyes are fixed on Sev. He gives me a cheeky grin and turns away, facing the crowd once more.

"So that was my journey with the theme of *Aletheia*—my disclosure to you. I suspect most of my peers will have come to their own conclusions more easily than me. I suspect not everybody lies to themselves the way I've done for a long time. So without further ado, I would like to invite you all to shed your lies, open your minds to the truth, and, of course, enjoy the exhibition."

Applause greets him and keeps going. Then the lights brighten, and the crowd slowly disperses, students breaking off to greet their parents before leading them off to the displays.

Keeping to the edges of the gallery, I try to make a beeline for my display, but a voice stops me in my tracks.

"He's pretty cute after all, your *Roi Soleil*."

Chapter 42

L'EXHIBITION

Séverin

Watching the expression on Anaïs's face when she turns around to see her brother is like an explosion of warmth in my chest. Her eyes go wide, then they fill with tears—tears of joy.

She throws her arms around his neck, and they embrace. When they stand next to each other, they don't even look like siblings—they look like twins.

Noël stands out, just like his sister. For one, he's the only man in the gallery not to be in a tuxedo. Instead, he's in loose trousers and a soft jumper in a bright-green colour. Like his sister, he seems to favour bright colours. Like his sister, he seems authentically, unapologetically himself.

I want to go to them, to soak in the sunshine of Anaïs's joy, but my parents are standing by my display, gesturing me over. Reluctantly, I turn away from Anaïs and go the opposite way to my parents.

My father shakes my hand, dignified as usual, but my mother's eyes are wet and shiny.

"*Mais comme il était beau, ton discours!*" she says in a teary voice. "*Et tes yeux—les lignes bleues—j'adore!*"

They turn to look at my display. Their expressions of surprised admiration would be insulting if they weren't so genuinely sweet. I suppose I can't resent their surprise, anyway. They've never seen much of my photography before.

I'm sure this isn't the first time I've surprised them this evening—or this year.

"What you were saying is actually true," my father says thoughtfully, casting me a glance. "You *are* a liar."

That, I didn't expect. Not when my display is essentially an ode to the girl I love.

"How so?" I ask, glaring at him.

"You gave us the impression the Nishihara girl wasn't to your taste." Heat flushes into my cheeks, but I can't even deny it. "*Mais elle est très belle. Beaucoup trop belle pour toi.*"

I laugh. "*Eh ben merci!*"

He shrugs. My mother flaps her hand at him. "Stop!" She grabs my arm and stares excitedly around. "Can we finally meet her? The Aletheia girl?"

"Let me go find her." I leave my parents standing by my display and almost bump into two people, a man and a woman. Both are in their late fifties and holding on to flutes of champagne. The woman wears bright purple and gold, and the man has long white hair that makes him look like an elegant wizard.

I apologise for almost bumping into them, but the man stops me with a hand on my shoulder.

"No need to be sorry!" He speaks with a heavy New York accent. "We wished to congratulate you on your speech, Mr Montcroix. We were both very moved by your introspection and sincerity."

"Ah—thank you. It was..." I hesitate, then tell the truth. "It was a frightening prospect, but once I started, the truth was much easier to admit than I'd imagined."

The woman laughs. "Yes—lies can be very comforting, but the truth has an addictive quality to it."

"Yes, I think you might be right. If you'll excuse me, I must now find my artist of truth—please, enjoy the exhibition."

They give me warm smiles, and I hurry away, eager to find Anaïs before my parents do.

To my surprise, she's not standing by her display—though a small group of people are observing it with admiration on their faces.

Instead, I find her in a corner of the gallery, near the drinks table, laughing with her brother.

Once I draw closer, it's crazy how accurately Anaïs's drawings captured Noël's likeness. The pretty eyes—which of course, have the same shape as Anaïs's own eyes—the enigmatic smile that seems to both reveal and conceal emotions, the graceful features of someone who seems not quite from this world.

He's the first to look up when I approach, and the enigmatic smile broadens on his face.

"*Ah—le Roi Soleil!*"

Anaïs laughs and pushes his shoulder. "Stop."

"It's rare to meet someone who looks even better in real life than in pictures," Noël says, raising an amused eyebrow at me.

"This must be why art is so much more truthful than photography," I reply, "because you look exactly like Anaïs's drawings of you."

He laughs and extends his hand out to me. "Noël."

I take it and grip it firmly. "Sev."

"So, you love my sister?" he asks.

"Noël!" Anaïs exclaims. But I don't know why she's so surprised; Noël is just as blunt as she is.

I nod. "Yes. How could I not?"

"Good answer. She is easy to love—even though she can be very stubborn sometimes."

Anaïs laughs. "That's rich coming from you!"

She looks radiant. Not just because of the beautiful gown, the flush in her cheeks. She looks happy, joy radiating from her smile, her eyes. She looks like one of her paintings, bursting with life and beauty.

"I love you *because* you're so stubborn, *petite étoile*," Noël says. His expression becomes more earnest as he turns back to me. "So—Sev. Ever thought about visiting Japan?"

I'm surprised, but I answer him truthfully. "I've never been, but I would love to."

"Well, you should come spend the summer. Summers are beautiful in Japan, and there's a lot to see. And Anaïs will be there."

A lump rises in my throat. Anaïs hasn't yet asked me to come with her, and I don't dare ask her. I know she wants to escape; I know she wants her freedom. What if I'm not part of that?

I answer in as light a tone as I can muster. "Maybe."

"Well, do you already have plans for the summer?"

Anaïs glares at Noël. "Maybe he doesn't want to go to Japan, Noël."

"I would love to go to Japan," I say quickly, meeting her eyes.

We stare at one another. My lips tremble, but I don't dare say anything more. I will her to open her mouth, to ask me to come with her. Noël stares between us and sighs.

"If you two like each other so much and want to be together, then why not?"

"Because Japan is far away," Anaïs says, answering his question but looking at me. "Because it might be too far for Sev to follow."

"Because Anaïs might want to go to Japan alone and be free to do what she wants," I say, holding her gaze. "And she might not want her fiancé to follow her like a lovesick puppy."

"I'm starting to understand why you two have taken so long to get anywhere," Noël says, rolling his eyes.

He lays one hand on my shoulder and one hand on Anaïs's shoulder.

"*Petite étoile,* do you want your *Roi Soleil* to come with us?"

"*Oui.*"

Noël grins and turns to me. "*Roi Soleil,* you want to come with your *petite étoile?*"

"*Oui.*"

"*En ben voila.*"

Noël smiles and moves suddenly, kissing Anaïs's cheek, then mine.

"*Allez, les jeunes.* It's sorted, so let's go enjoy the rest of our night."

When I return to my display with Anaïs and Noël in tow, I find a small crowd assembled there. The older couple from before, the man with the long hair and the woman in purple, stand next to my parents, the four of them deep in conversation.

Zach and Iakov, both in tuxes, stand a little further from them, looking at my photographs with cocky smiles. I meet their gaze when I pass them, but they nod and say nothing—no doubt because my parents are there.

I'm sure I'll be hearing their thoughts later.

Once the older couple walk away from my parents, I introduce them officially to Anaïs and Noël. We all exchange small talk for a few minutes. Then Noël, with the grace of an angel, offers to show my parents Anaïs's display.

I give him a nod of thanks as he ushers them away, and he answers with one of his ineffable smiles before disappearing.

Finally alone, Anaïs and I stand shoulder-to-shoulder. My breath is short as her eyes move over my display: the photographs from Scotland, but the others, too. My shot of her that time in the art studio, her sitting cross-legged on her stool. The shot I took of me kissing her cheek—a truthful moment disguised as a fake one. A shot of her, painting me.

"They're in colour," Anaïs finally says. "What happened to your black and white aesthetic?"

"Black and white wouldn't have been truthful," I answer. "Because if the truth is you and how I feel about you, then it *has* to be colourful. My life before you—Spearcrest before you—that was black and white. But you... you're yellow—sorry, ochre—and blue"—I point at the lines I painted around my eyes—"and green and purple and orange. You're light and colours and life."

"You didn't have to do all this, Sev," Anaïs says finally, turning back to me. "I already forgave you, remember?"

"That's not why I did all this, and I didn't tell everyone I loved you for your forgiveness, either. I said it because it is the truth, and it felt good to say it. It feels good every time I say it. I love you, Anaïs Nishihara, *mon artiste, mon trésor*. I don't think I'll ever get sick of loving you."

She laughs and takes my face gently in her hands. "I love you too, Séverin Montcroix, my impetuous fairy prince. You make me feel like I've been cold all my life, but when I'm near you, I feel warm for the first time."

I laugh and brush my lips against hers in the ghost of a kiss. "Because I'm so hot?"

"Because you're so emotional." She laughs and tilts her head. "Your emotions burn like an inferno."

Wrapping my arms around her waist, I pull her closer. "That's because I have to feel emotions for the both of us, you little robot."

She curls her arms around my neck, balancing herself against me. Her skin smells like paint and summer.

"I have emotions," she protests. "You've seen me emotional."

I lean down to speak against her ear. "You're only ever emotional in the bedroom."

She laughs softly. "Then you know what you need to do, don't you?"

"Trust me," I murmur, my voice suddenly hoarse, "I think of little else."

From the corner of my eye, I spot my parents and Noël slowly making their way back to us through the crowd.

My mother's eyes catch mine, and she flashes me a triumphant smile. I glare at her and, with great reluctance, release Anaïs from my embrace.

After that, I barely see Anaïs for the rest of the night. My parents lead her away to look at some of the other displays and discuss her art, leaving me and Noël to talk about Japan, about art and photography, about Anaïs.

"You're good for her," Noël says, out of nowhere, with complete sincerity. "I've never seen my sister so open and expressive before. Even as a little girl, I could only ever really gauge her feelings through her art. She's always shone in my eyes, but she's never shone brighter than I've seen her shine tonight."

My throat tightens at his words. I try to speak lightly. "It's funny you should say that because she always accuses me of being too emotional."

"She might not admit it," Noël says with a smile, "but she admires you for that." He claps my shoulder. "Thank you, by the way. For telling me about the exhibition. I wouldn't have missed it for the world."

I return his smile. "I'm glad you came. I'm glad we finally met."

"Me too."

Noël is eventually called away by Anaïs, and I'm pulled aside by Mr Ambrose to a corner of the gallery. "You've done well tonight, Séverin."

"Thank you, Mr Ambrose."

"I'm proud of you. It takes courage to show honesty, and you've shown much honesty this year."

"Just trying to make amends, sir."

"Be that as it may," Mr Ambrose says, "I thought I would inform you that you've been selected as the winner of this year's exhibition. Mr Drow and Mrs Elmsberg were very impressed by your sincerity, vulnerability, and the quality of your work."

"But I don't deserve it, sir." I gesture out into the gallery. "If you had seen Anaïs's work before I destroyed it, you would know what I mean, sir. I might have shown honesty tonight, but she's shown it all along. She's always been true to herself, to her work. She deserves to win, not me."

"I can't change the board's mind, Séverin," Mr Ambrose says, shaking his head sadly. "I would if I could, but it's not within my power."

"Then I want Anaïs to receive the grant. I don't want it—I don't deserve it. But Anaïs does. Please, Mr Ambrose."

"That is within my power, Séverin." Mr Ambrose fixes me with his dark eyes, a long, searching look that bores right into me. "Are you sure that's what you want to do?"

I hold his gaze and smile. "Trust me, Mr Ambrose. I'm sure."

Chapter 43

LA FIANCÉE

Séverin

Anaïs catches me the following week as I'm packing away my things from the photography studio. She barges into the room, a thunderous frown on her face.

"I don't want your grant."

"What do you mean?" I ask lightly.

I'm kneeling on the floor, placing equipment back into cases, and even though she's towering over me, arms folded, I can't help but be amused.

"The grant from the competition. It's just landed—as if by magic—into my account. I didn't win the award, and I don't want it."

I shrug. "Then do what you want with it."

"I want you to take it back."

"I don't need it."

"I didn't ask if you needed it. You won the competition. It's your grant. You do what you want with it."

"I didn't win the competition fairly. I destroyed your work, which would have won, and I wouldn't have won if I hadn't told every single person at the exhibition that I love you. So I don't give a shit that they chose me as the winner. I don't consider myself the winner, and I don't want the grant."

"Then give it to someone else."

"I asked Mr Ambrose to give it to you because you should have it. Don't you need it for Japan? In case your parents cut you off like they did your brother?"

"So? I'll get a job."

"Alright. Get a job."

I zip the case closed and stand, placing the case on a counter, then turning to face Anaïs. She's breathing hard, like she's in the middle of a fight. Her eyes are burning, but her mouth is trembling.

"You don't have to do this," she says finally, her voice uncharacteristically hoarse and unsteady. "I already forgave you for what you did."

"This has nothing to do with that."

"Why, then? I don't need your money, Sev. I don't need anything from you."

"No, you don't. But I love you—I don't know if you heard my speech the other night. Maybe you missed that part. I love you, and I wronged you, and you forgave me, which is great. But I still love you, and I want you to be rewarded for the incredible work you put into your art, and I want you to be free and not have to worry about money as much when you go to Japan. I would love to go to Japan with you and buy you everything you could ever need or want, but I have the suspicion you'd never let me do that. This is the one thing I get to do, and I've done it. If you don't want to keep the money, then you give it to someone else. Give it to Noël, if you like. But it's yours, not mine."

She looks at me in complete silence for a long moment. She's wearing a bright-blue jumper over her skirt, and for once, she's wearing shoes. There are little smears of white paint on her sleeves. I want to kiss her cheeks and hold her tight.

"This isn't settled," she says finally.

"On my end, it is." I meet her glare with a smile. "Are you coming to the lake on Friday?"

She narrows her eyes and pinches her lips. My smile doesn't falter.

"Fine!" she exclaims, and without another word, she storms out.

"I love you!" I call after her.

Silence answers. Then she pokes her head through the door, still glaring at me.

"I love you too."

ON THE LAST DAY of Year 13, it's a Spearcrest tradition to end the year with a party by the lake past the trees at the north end of the campus.

The weather, having finally softened, seems almost nostalgic, a soft, cool sun falling behind a hazy purple horizon. A bonfire has been built on the sandy bank of the lake. The other Year 13 students sit in pairs and clusters on the grass, the banks, or the wooden jetties scattered around the lake.

Next to me, Evan sits, bouncing his leg nervously, his eyes fixed on a nearby jetty. I follow his gaze and spot Sophie Sutton, his beloved prefect, with her long brown hair, sitting with her legs hanging from the jetty, sharing a bottle of champagne with her friends.

"Just go to her already," I say, shoving Evan's big shoulder.

He shrugs me off with a sigh. "What if she doesn't want to see me?"

"Then she'll let you know. Sutton might be a stone-cold bitch, but at least she's honest."

"Talking of honesty," Evan says, finally tearing his gaze from his darling prefect. "Heard about your little art exhibition speech."

"Don't start," I say, lying back in the grass, propped on my elbows.

"Why wasn't I invited?" he asks, kicking my ankle. "I had to find out about your grand love confession from Zach and Iakov."

"I didn't invite them either," I assure him. "They just crashed the party. I should have known they would make fun of me behind my back."

"Neither of them made fun of you," Evan says. "Not even Zach." His features suddenly soften, and a strange smile plays on his face, a mixture of rue and amusement. "It feels so stupid, looking back. Worrying about... worrying about so much stupid shit. Don't you feel happier now? Now that you've told your girl how you feel? Now that you're no longer hiding?"

"I was never lying," I mumble, disturbed by Evan's uncharacteristic introspection.

Falling in love must really have the power to change someone because Evan would have been the last person I would ever have imagined reflecting on the error of his ways. Him—or Luca, who's sitting gazing out at the lake through a faceful of bruises.

I look around the lake, at the people that have surrounded me for the last seven years of my life. The girls I've slept with and dismissed, the boys I commanded as easily as an army of soldiers. All the students I never deigned to spend time with, never considered worthy of my time.

Why did I care so much about what they would think of me, how they would perceive me?

Evan might be right after all. It does all feel stupid now, looking back. It feels small and pointless and dull.

I open my mouth to admit as much to him, but he springs to his feet, fists clenched, the determination of a warrior about to face a fearsome foe on his face. "Right. I'm going to go talk to her."

I laugh. "You do that, then."

He stomps away, and I continue searching the crowd. Anaïs said she would be here—I'm pretty confident she wouldn't have bothered lying to me about coming.

Watching Evan creeping up to his prefect, Zachary locked in some argument with his ice queen, I no longer feel amusement and disdain.

I just feel jealousy. I just wish I, too, was embarrassing myself over my girl.

Mon trésor. My Anaïs.

I spot Iakov in the crowd and scramble upright. He's standing a little away, one shoulder against the trunk of an old fir, smoking. There's a slight smile on his face as he talks down to someone.

Not someone. Anaïs.

She's wearing a strappy satin jumpsuit in bright green. The trousers are so wide they almost look like a skirt, flowing around her long legs. Her hair is loose—it's grown since I first met her, long past her shoulders now. She looks radiant and earthy, like some elusive forest nymph.

I stand up and stride to the trees. Creeping up behind her, I lean down to kiss her bare shoulder. Without turning around, she reaches up to brush her fingertips through my hair.

"You never told me Iakov speaks Japanese," she says when I stand next to her.

"That's because I didn't know." I wrap my arm around her waist, pulling her to me possessively. "Why? You're not considering bringing him to Japan instead of me, are you?"

"I don't know," she says sweetly. "Iakov, how do you feel about Japan?"

"Kav—don't." I glare at him.

"I've already been," he says.

"You have?" My eyes widen as I look at him. Iakov is someone I would trust with my life—but it looks like I barely know anything about him. "When?"

He shrugs. "I've been multiple times."

"Well, you're always welcome to visit us in Kyoto," Anaïs says.

Iakov laughs a low, sinister laugh, fixing me with a look. "Don't worry, Sev. I won't crash your honeymoon."

Although both Anaïs and I laugh, my heart stumbles at the thought.

When my parents first told me I was officially engaged to Anaïs Nishihara, the heiress to the Nishihara billionaires, I was so busy being angry that I never imagined what that might actually be like.

Not some forced engagement between two pawns in some financial game, but a proper engagement. A ring on her finger, or around her neck. Kisses and sex—not the transactional hotel sex of two people meeting for an exchange of orgasm, but something different. Sex with someone I want in my bed even after we both come.

The future always seemed so vague and far away to me before. I suppose I never planned for it.

But when I picture the future now, it's as clear as a photograph in my mind. It's Anaïs in some outrageous outfit and ochre socks, flecks of paint freckling her cheeks, turning our flat into an art studio. It's tender morning sex on lazy Sundays, followed by croissants and coffee. It's Anaïs and me in Japan, in France—anywhere, just together.

And I can picture so much more.

I can picture her in a wedding dress—no boring bridal white, and she'd probably wear trainers just because it would be more comfortable. A honeymoon spent somewhere full of colour and nature. It's my face between her legs in golden sunlight, her moans drowning out the sound of heavy tropical rain. It's her radiant face and the thousands of kisses I plan to rain on it.

My heart feels full enough to explode, and I suddenly grab Anaïs, holding her tight. Iakov flicks his cigarette butt to the ground and stomps on it.

"For fuck's sake," he grunts. "Get a grip."

But there's affection and amusement in his tone, and he winks at me as he walks away. I take Anaïs's face in my hands. The hazy light of dusk makes her face glow like a star.

"*Petite étoile*," I say, gazing into her eyes.

"That's what Noël calls me," she says with surprise.

"I know. It suits you."

"Does that mean I'm no longer your trésor?"

"No, it doesn't. *Tu seras toujours mon trésor. Le trésor de ma vie, de mon corps, de mon cœur.*"

"How poetic," she murmurs, pouting thoughtfully. "Who would have thought you would be such a hopeless romantic?"

I squeeze her cheeks, mushing her face together. "Don't make fun of me."

She pokes out her tongue. "Don't make it so easy, then."

"I'm allowed to be nice."

She pulls away and gives me a slow, wicked smirk. "But you suit being mean so much better."

I narrow my eyes and tilt my head. "Why are you trying to provoke me, trésor?"

She shrugs. "I would never think of doing such a thing."

But the green satin of her jumpsuit flows like water on her skin, making obvious the rise and fall of her quickening breath, the tightening of her nipples. I clench my jaw and lower my voice.

"Careful, trésor. You don't want to get chased through the woods again."

Her eyes glitter. "As if you could catch me."

Wrapping my hand around the back of her neck, I pull her face to mine. "Who's the sadomasochist now?"

"Still you," she breathes against my mouth.

"No. I don't want to hurt you, *mon trésor*. I want to do many, many things to you but never hurt you."

I capture her mouth in a kiss that steals both our breaths away. She moulds her body into mine, her arms snaking around my shoulders. A tiny moan slips from her lips, and she suddenly pulls away.

"Then give me my ring back."

"What?" I frown down at her.

"My ring. I want it back."

My heart seizes in my chest.

"It's an engagement ring," I say slowly.

She shrugs. "I know."

"I want you to have it," I tell her, voice low. Dusk is falling around us, the creeping darkness wrapping us in a soft cocoon. "But it's an *engagement* ring."

"We're engaged, aren't we?"

I hesitate. "Does that mean we're *staying* engaged?"

"Do you want to stay engaged?" she asks.

"Anaïs. Of course, I want to stay engaged. I want you to be my lover, my girlfriend, my fiancée. One day, I want you to be my wife—if you want. I just want you to be mine, however you want to be mine."

Emotion softens her eyes. She reaches up and kisses me, a delicate touch. "I want to be yours, Séverin Montcroix, however you want me to be yours. So give me the ring."

I unclasp the necklace from around my neck and place it around hers. The ring falls on her throat, and I touch my fingertips to it. It's still warm from my skin. But it's nothing compared to the warmth filling my heart, my chest.

"I fucking love you, Anaïs Nishihara," I whisper.

She laughs. "I know."

"Do you love me too?"

She places her mouth to my ear. Her hair tickles my lips as she does. I breathe in the heady smell of her, lilacs and French summers and linseed oil and desire.

"*Je t'aime. Je t'aime de toute ma vie, de tout mon corps, de toute mon âme.*"

I love you. I love you with all my life, my body, my soul.

I narrow my eyes at her. "Are you making fun of me?"

"I would never dare."

"You mean it?"

The sun catches her eyes, making them sparkle. "With all my heart."

I wrap her in my arms and kiss her, deep and slow.

"Prove it," I command against her lips.

She smirks.

"Make me."

FIN

DEAR READER

Thank you for reading my little tale of stubborn French idiots falling in love.

If you enjoyed this book and wish to support this humble indie author, please consider leaving a review. Without the support of a publishing house behind me, most of my support (okay—all my support!) comes from readers just like you, and the best way you can support me is by posting a review—no matter how short or brutally honest! :')

All my love,

                   x Aurora

Annotation & Study Guide

French References Explained

- **Louis XIV aka le Roi Soleil (Louis the Fourteenth aka the Sun King)** - king of France in the seventeenth and eighteenth century. He is known for becoming king at the age of five, ruling with absolute power and having the Palace of Versailles built. He also made it a rule for everyone in his court to be well-dressed and was called the Sun King because he believed he was the sun around which France revolved like the planets. (Referenced first in Chapter 7)

- **Jeanne d'Arc (Joan of Arc)** - known as the Maid of Orleans, lived in the fifteenth century, claimed to have visions from angels, disguised herself as a male soldier, met the king, and became a military leader. After a series of victories, she was betrayed, captured, tried for cross-dressing and heresy and burned at the stake at the age of 19. Later, she was declared a martyr and claimed a symbol of France by Napoleon Bonaparte. (Referenced in Chapter 11)

Themes to annotate

- The Themes of **Duty** and **Desire**
- The Themes of different types of **Love,** including **Eros** (romantic love), **Ludus** (playful love) **Philia** (love between friends), **Philautia** (self-love), **Storge** (love between parents and children)
- The Themes of **Truth**, **Lies**, **Deception** and **Disclosure**
- The Themes of **Self** and **Society**
- The Themes of **Family** and **Friendship**
- The Themes of **Art** and **Photography**

Critical Thinking Questions

- **Between Sev and Anaïs, who is the more truthful character, and how is this shown?**
- **How are art and photography used to explore the themes of truth and lies?**

- **Compare the way familial love is portrayed in Sev's family and Anaïs's family.**

Acknowledgements

Thank you to my lovely mother, for always being patient, accepting and inspiring. And for being so proud of me you'd think I was a neurosurgeon, not a smutty romance writer. And for proofreading the French in this book and not shaming me for how bad my French grammar has become.

Thank you to the TikTok girlies for supporting me and inspiring me in equal measures. I wish you all knew how much your support means to me.

Thank you Raven, for all your support and help, always.

Thank you M + R, the two loves of my life, for teaching me everything I know about love.

About Aurora

Aurora Reed is a coffee-drinking academic who is fascinated by stories of darkness, death and desire. When she's not reading over a cup of black coffee, she can be found roaming the moors or scribbling stories by candlelight.

Milton Keynes UK
Ingram Content Group UK Ltd.
UKHW011319141223
434366UK00001B/22